BESTIARY OF BLOOD

MODERN FABLES & DARK TALES

Let the world know:
#IGotMyCLPBook!

Crystal Lake Publishing
www.CrystalLakePub.com

Copyright 2024 Crystal Lake Publishing

Join the Crystal Lake community today
on our newsletter and Patreon!
https://linktr.ee/CrystalLakePublishing

Download our latest catalog here.
https://geni.us/CLPCatalog

ISBN: 978-1-964398-21-1

Cover art:
Ben Baldwin—www.benbaldwin.co.uk

Layout:
Lori Michelle—www.theauthorsalley.com

Edited and proofed by:
Jamal Hodge

Follow us on Amazon:

WELCOME
TO ANOTHER

CRYSTAL LAKE PUBLISHING
CREATION

Join today at www.crystallakepub.com & www.patreon.com/CLP

This book is dedicated to the fearful brave. The cowardly courageous. To those who understand danger is real—but fear is a choice.

TABLE OF CONTENTS

NIGHT

INTRODUCTION

ESTIARY OF BLOOD: Modern Fables & Dark Tales, came about from too many years of watching nature videos while eating dinner in tandem with the feasting of lions, hyenas, ants, and sharks. One day, while washing my hands, I looked at my greasy fingers and thought . . . *this is a living thing's fat, something with its own dreams, and now consumed into me, I am changed.* And so, on it goes—this merging and shifting, giving and taking in nature . . . this strange horror and frightening beauty of life, using death, to give life.

As the Brother's Grim and Aesop before me, I felt compelled to use words to try to decipher the perspectives of these lifeforms we claim a false superiority over, this infinite kaleidoscope of wisdom, efficiency, and experiences we lump into one paltry word: "Animals."

Where was the overlap between our experiences and theirs? We are all Earth-born. Surely, I could find correlations—metaphors—in their experiences that would explain the truths in ours. As Aesop had so masterfully achieved all those centuries before, but darker still, infused with the vibrance of horror . . . Silence of The Lambs meets Aesop's Fables.

Thus, this book was born.

I knew I could not embark on this journey alone. The one thing nature is not—is *one* thing. It is a sea of a trillion minds, meeting each other in overlapping waves. I needed to recreate nature's spirit of collaborating forms. I needed avatars of contradiction, wisdom, and terrors from every race, every preference, every shadow. Diverse voices, perspectives, and writing styles.

So, I embarked on a journey of benign cajoling and shameless begging. Motivated by the audacity of ignorance I contacted many of my writing heroes, attempting to enroll them into this strange dream. Not knowing what shouldn't be possible can get you pretty far. In the end, I had the fortune of corralling some of the greatest writers in the horror industry, many of which were willing to share stories of a deep and intimate nature. Eighteen Bram Stoker Winners, Three Lifetime achievement recipients and Two Grand Masters. A feast of brilliance, gathered in one place.

In this anthology you will also find new voices from every walk of life. Divided in to seven sections with three themes, this book uses darkness to show light, flirting with the obscene to unveil the spectacular and the dreadful.

To all my collaborators/guides/friends, who were gracious enough to contribute to my debut journey as an editor, to Linda Addison, Michael Bailey, and Lee Murray in particular for your invaluable guidance, I cannot thank you enough for lending your talents and your voices to this exploration of the lessons of living. May your words roam freely on imagination's veldt.

And to you, my reader—may you find a revelation in a question on this dark journey through the forests of horror, truth, and meaning.

FOREWORD
BY JONATHAN MABERRY

WE ARE A STORYTELLING SPECIES. It's in our nature. It's part of every culture at every stage of recorded history. It's even evident in pre-history, as seen in cave paintings depicting everything from accounts of a hunt to encounters with gods and monsters.

I have to believe that there's a gene for it. Sure, that gene fires more sharply and usefully in some, which is why we have professional writers of every stripe. And it misfires, which is why my uncle Bob could never understand why his World War II anecdotes fell flat every time.

And there is a tendency for folks—maybe all of us—to embellish anything we hear. The whisper-down-the-lane thing shows that. We add, we tweak, we shape the stories we enjoy telling them, even at the expense of precision in recounting those tales. And we often tailor them depending on the audience. After all, an anecdote about two guys walking into a bar will be different when told to our drinking buddies than it is when telling at a polite family gathering.

And all of that is okay. There are no rules, no limitations when it comes to telling a story. Okay, if we're telling a story on the witness stand and under oath, but otherwise . . . we have a comprehensive creative license.

We also revise our own life stories to cast ourselves as the hero, the hapless buffoon, the innocent bystander, and so on. Stories also allow us to give real life a better and more satisfying third act.

Authors quite often revise the real world in order to tell more compelling fiction, even at the expense of changing the source material. Good example is Dracula. Bram Stoker borrowed from several bits of European folklore to create his erudite monster, but there are times when he left documented folklore behind and just made stuff up because it served the needs of his novel. The whole thing about vampires being afraid of a cross or the Eucharist comes from Stoker's Catholic faith and not the mythology of vampires. The idea that a vampire cannot enter a house without being invited isn't from folklore, either . . . Stoker cooked that up because otherwise when Dracula arrived in London he'd have just killed everyone.

Same goes with the concept of sunlight killing vampires. Not from European folklore (except for one vampire species in China). This was cooked up by F.W. Murnau for the 1922 silent film, Nosferatu, because it was a quick and inexpensive way to dispense with the monster (and he was over-time and over-budget and needed to wrap the damn thing).

Which brings us to this book. Bestiary of Blood: Modern Fables & Dark Tales isn't just a collection of twice-told tales. No, that would be too easy, too stale, and too expected. Instead, what editor Jamal Hodge has done here is engage the creative minds of some of today's most innovative storytellers and give them license to reimagine, rewrite, or create out of whole-cloth stories that breathe new life into the short form. The stories here are innovative and the writers take a hell of a lot of creative risks when constructing modern fables.

The writers who signed on were not timid in their revisionist and reconstructionist approaches. I sat down to read the tales with some anticipation of there being a few cliches, well-used tropes, and familiar ground. I say that, even though I know many of the writers. Sometimes we all fall into the trap of pastiche rather than innovation. Boy, was I wrong, and I'll be the first to admit it. Those assumptions were trounced pretty damned quickly. What I read was not what I was expecting.

And I could not be happier about that.

First, let me say that I love any anthology that includes poetry, and there are some fine, weird, chilling, and beautiful examples herein.

Second, one of the great beauties of the fiction short form is that writers who know their business jump right in. There's no wasted space. The stories are moody, weird, exciting, heartbreaking, laugh-out-loud, sob into your tissue, and deeply unnerving right from the jump.

FOREWORD

There's also a wonderful mix of literary styles, drawing on different personal, ethnic, cultural, and societal experiences, with each writer taking agency over the 'world' they create and doing so without flinching.

We have stories and poems that do to a stale trope what capuchin monkeys do with nuts—they smash the hell out of them to get to the yummy stuff inside. We encounter familiar settings and themes that very quickly become strange and new, allowing the reader to rediscover old knowledge while absorbing new thoughts and insights.

I gobbled these works up and am already ravenous for more. This is a book that you'll enjoy and, like me, will yell real damn loud until we get more to feast upon.

So, settle back . . . pour yourself a glass of whatever soothes your nerves 'cause you'll need it . . . and turn the page. If you think you know what's coming next, you'll be delighted to discover that you're wrong. This is a book of dark surprises.

Enjoy each weird little morsel.

Jonathan Maberry
San Diego, 2024

DAWN

FABLES & TALES

I

A DEATH FOR LOVE

NATURE'S SONG

JAMAL HODGE

Those who despise conflict
do not know life.
Nature schemes
to limit our days,
her indifferent ways
reclaiming the bounty
loaned.

Beautiful, if you value the whole;
poetry, if you serve the collective soul.
Though horror creeps
beneath green leaf.
Nature gives comfort
without peace.

Hunted by teeth,
by things smaller than sight,
hunted by dawn, hunted by night,
nibbled by time, chewed by decay,
we are all brief happenings,
in Nature's day.

Our mirage of peace,
built on the sweat of violence,
slaughtering toward oasis,
obeying Nature's call.

We futile peace-dreamers,
declaring our benefactors wrong.
Shunning conflict,
in waning dawn,
blindly drowning,

in Nature's song . . .

THE FABLE OF THE LION

JAMAL HODGE

HE LION WAS MIGHTY, full of mane, with powerful paws tipped with claws, fierce fangs, and a roar unchanging. The lioness, pride of her pride, conquered the lion inside, siring over his heart as he sired over the land. Together, they governed, paw and claw. Well-fed and love-tested, they bested rivals and wild boar, tasted elephant, drove away hippos. Till even the hyenas swore fealty.

One day, lying in the warmth of the Delta sun, the lioness had a sudden unshakable feeling that the lion wasn't properly tamed; he seemed unkempt, with an unruly mane.

"For shame," she said, "this mane of yours, you've abused it. It's brittle against my skin. You should lose it."

"Don't you love my mane?"

"To me, it's all the same. You are not your mane."

So, the lion called upon the oxpeckers to pluck out his hair till his face was bare. Like a cub again, he appeared, and so some mistook him, till his roar shook them.

The lioness seemed pleased. She rubbed her smoothness against his, and soon they were practicing making kids.

Afterward, they sat. Marked by each other, but still intact. The lioness looked at a long scratch he had left and frowned. "Your claws are too sharp, they rake my back; you should lose them, as a matter of fact."

"Don't you love my claws?"

"Yes, they are mighty, and they tear hide. But you are not your claws, it's your fangs, our subjects' pride."

The lion, seeking to please her, dulled his claws down to stumps until they were barely extendable. The hunt became harder. With only his fangs to bring down buffalo, they stood their ground, pushing back with hoof and horn, saying a king without a mane was a cat without a crown, and a cat without a claw needn't be feared anymore.

But the lioness was pleased, and with his fangs, they hunted smaller beasts on which to feast. Thus, the king's fangs grew larger and sharper from their use.

"The council believes your fangs to be a form of abuse."

"What council?"

"The delegation formed to replace the claws of your hand. Believe me, it's a minor loss, it's not the fangs that make the king."

"I don't know. How will I bring down prey? We will go hungry. There's no way!"

"Food will be provided. I hunt more than you. It's already been decided." She placed a clawed paw against his face. "If you do this, you will be loved. No one will ever seek to occupy your space or to rule in your place."

He contemplated hard until the next day, but in the end, the lioness got her way. It was hard work to file the fangs down to the equivalent of a child's, but when it was done, the beasts of the Delta smiled. They celebrated his diplomacy with outside performances of grace, but in secret, they laughed at the ruin of his face.

The hyenas ran wild.

The gazelles didn't bother to hide.

And the lioness spent more and more time with her pride.

The lion was well fed, but the fact that it wasn't from his own strength tormented his head.

He went to find his queen, but her pride said, "Come back to see her."

"Where is she?"

"She doesn't want to see you."

"I don't believe her!" He roared in rage, but his roar affected few these days.

Eventually, the lioness reluctantly came to see him. She kept her distance; she didn't greet him.

"It's hard for me to see you. Look where your weakness leads you." She wept at the sight of his defeat. "No mane, no claw. Are you even a lion anymore? You can barely chew your meat. It's a tragedy to see you try to posture on your feet."

"But you wanted me this way!"

The lioness looked disgusted. "Why did you obey? I'm attracted to kings. Please, just go away!"

All he could do was obey. Going the lonely way into a life barren of glory. A former king reduced to something without authority or a name.

With no one to blame.

FIRST PRINCIPLES OF REVERSE MORPHOLOGY

OZ HARDWICK

WE'LL BEGIN WITH the message, which is *Do* or *Don't*, and the moral, which is *Should* or *Shouldn't*. What comes before is fable or figure: a crane picking splinters from a wolf's epiglottis or, in gathered analogues of no fixed attribution, a heron or a woodpecker with its beak dancing in a lion's jaws. It's a matter of finding and feeding the animals in our blood, and of raising them to the duty their archetypes command. It's a matter of pragmatism or faith. Put it like this: our souls—whether immortal, immaterial, but inherent in our being, or intricate machines of hope ticking in the chatter of blinking synapses and unpredictable neural transmissions— were once the Ark but have become the Jardin des Plantes in 1870, with elephants stripped to ribs; and the Keeper, all neurons feathering like a steeple struck by lightning, is reaching like a holy fool into the wolf's mouth, the lion's mouth, the Hell mouth sculpted in medieval stone, to release that bone of contention. See? And what comes before that is a story by the fire, with stock figures dancing between flame and shadow, a *Yes* when there should have been *No*, and a *No* when there should have been *Yes*. A word spoken in beast language. See? We'll end with this: the thing to take away is that it's all your fault.

A COLD MIDNIGHT

TIM WAGGONER

CYRA PUMPS HER wings furiously, feathers shaping air, propelling her upward. The night sky is a vast black dome, its surface covered with glittering diamonds, and she remembers the name her mother gave to these mysterious beauties. *They're called stars, my love.* Such a small word, *stars*, but one that filled her with wonder as a nestling, and which still does so now. From the moment she first set eyes upon them, she felt a connection, a bond, and she knew that one night, when she was big and strong like Mother, she would fly to the stars and see what they looked like up close, discover why they glitter, and listen to whatever songs they might sing.

That night is now.

Cyra is a red-tailed hawk, two years old and strong, a fast flier and successful hunter, although she has yet to take a mate, build a nest, and lay eggs. She's fended off every interested male who's approached her, for she has no interest in mating. Time enough for that after she's found her way to the stars.

She fed well two days ago on a nice fat rabbit, and after she ate her fill, she perched on the branch of an oak tree, surrounded by green summer leaves, digesting her prey and building her strength for the flight to come. Now she is using every bit of energy she obtained from her meal, and more, to power her ascent. She moves through the air as sleek and swift as a fish through water, luxuriating in the way the Wind caresses her body. She was born for flight, and the sky is both her home and her heart.

A crosswind comes in from the west, fast and sudden, pushing Cyra off course. She instantly corrects, but the Wind grows stronger, forcing her to expend additional energy to maintain her vertical trajectory. A soft, familiar voice whispers in her ears.

You are far from the trees, child, and even farther from the ground, where your prey scampers and scurries. Why do you fly so high?

Every creature on Earth that carves the air with its wings—bird, bat, or insect—knows the voice of the Wind. It's their constant companion in the sky, as much a part of them as the beating of their own heart.

Tonight, I shall reach the stars, Cyra says.

You have tried before, the Wind says, *and each time you have failed. Even I have never gone into the Far Dark. What makes you think you will succeed?*

Because I must, Cyra says. It is the simplest and truest answer she can give.

The Wind is silent for several moments as it considers her words.

I would help you if I could, but my course is set this night. I must continue traveling in this direction for many hours so a farmer in Laos will have rain for his crops. But I wish you luck, my friend—and if you do not reach your goal, I wish you the softest of landings.

The Wind's laughter echoes around Cyra, fades, dies, leaving her alone once more.

A hawk flies best when she flies alone, Mother once told her, and Cyra has found this to be true in her short life. But she will not be alone when she reaches the stars. Whatever they are, she will be with them, and they will be with her.

Her wings continue to beat, stroke after stroke, and she soars ever higher.

Higher.

Higher.

And the stars are still so very far away.

Her shoulder muscles burn like fire, her wing strokes falter, and she begins to drift off course. She fights with everything she has left in her to correct, but it isn't enough.

Too weak to continue, she begins to fall.

As a down-covered baby, Cyra's entire world consists of very few things—the tree, the nest, her three siblings, her parents, but most of all, never-ending *hunger*. There's a gnawing emptiness at the core of her being—strong, fierce, demanding—and she has no identity beyond it. She *is* hunger.

She gives voice to her need in a series of two-note whistles: *Wee-EEE, wee-EEE, wee-EEE.* Her siblings cry out as well, and the nest is a constant cacophony of begging. Mother and Father both hunt for their brood, but only Mother feeds them, tearing off small bits of mouse or squirrel with her sharp beak and dropping the morsels into eager, open mouths. When Cyra gets a gobbet—warm, wet, and sweet—she swallows it down, and for the briefest of moments the hunger abates and she is satisfied. But it quickly returns, and she resumes begging. *Wee-EEE, wee-EEE, wee-EEE!*

The nestlings jostle and shove one another, jockeying for position, hoping to receive the most food from Mother. They have no real sense of their siblings as individuals in their own right, think of them merely as other mouths attempting to steal what should rightfully be theirs. They lash out with tiny talons, tear away down, scratch flesh, draw blood.

The Wind stirs nearby leaves.

Fight hard for what you need, young ones. It's how you will become strong, and you will need much strength to survive in this world. Oh yes, you will . . .

Later, long after the sun has hidden its face for the day, Cyra is hungry again.

Wee-EEE, wee-EEE, wee-EEE!

Mother, perched on a branch close by—one leg tucked up, head turned backward as she sleeps—does not stir. Hawks are diurnal and do not hunt at night, but Cyra does not know this. She knows nothing beyond the great ache in her middle, and she calls and calls. But then her voice falls silent. Cyra's eyes have only been open for a few days, and vision is still a novelty to her. She is amazed when, through an open patch in the leaves above her, she sees night's darkness and the small glittering points of light spread across it. They are new to her, these lights, and their gleam mesmerizes her. What could they be? How far away are they?

A breeze gently caresses her skin.

Far, child. Unimaginably so.

Cyra gazes up at the mysterious, beautiful lights and feels a hunger much different from what she is used to. Soon she falls asleep and remains quiet for the rest of the night.

Cyra lies in darkness, body pressed against a flat, smooth surface that is alien to her. More such surfaces surround her on four sides, and there's one above her as well. She is trapped, and she is *furious*. She wants out—*now*—and she claws at the surface with her talons and extends her wings as far as she can, hoping to escape.

But when her left wing is extended halfway, sharp pain lances through her shoulder, and she knows that if she manages to escape this strange trap, she will be unable to fly. She wants to keep trying anyway, but instinct tells her to remain still rather than worsen her injury, and she obeys. She hears sounds outside her trap, voices—human ones. She does not understand their language, but she listens anyway, hoping to glean information through tone and cadence, if no other way.

"Have you looked at her yet?"

"I didn't want to open the box until you were here. You're the raptor rehabber—I'm only an intern. I haven't handled as many pissed-off hawks as you have."

Cyra does not recognize human gender, so she doesn't know she's listening to two women talking, one younger, one older.

"Don't worry. I'll talk you through it. First, we need to put on those long leather gloves over there." A pause, then soft sliding sounds. "Okay. When I open the box, reach in fast and grab her legs, one in each hand. Hold them firmly so she can't foot you with her talons. When you're sure you have her feet controlled, we'll move on to the next step. Ready?"

A nervous exhalation of breath. "I guess."

"On a three-count. One, two, *three!*"

The surface above Cyra is swiftly pulled away and light floods the box. Recognizing her chance has come, she prepares to launch herself upward, but before she can move, hands grab her legs just above her feet and hold her down. Instinct screams at her to sink her razor-sharp talons into the flesh of the human attacking her, but she cannot break free to attack.

"I think I got her."

"Good. Now let go of the right leg and quickly shift your grip so you're holding both legs in your left hand."

The human does this, moving far faster than Cyra would've imagined one of their kind could. Humans are so big and bulky.

"Okay, slide your right hand underneath her and gently lift her out of the box."

The older human continues instructing the younger, and soon Cyra is turned around, her back against the younger's stomach, her feet pointed outward and held firmly in place.

"Excellent!" the older one says. "The guy who brought her in said she smacked into his windshield while he was driving. Luckily, he wasn't going too fast or she would've been killed—or hurt so badly there would be nothing we could do for her, and we'd have to put her down."

"I thought red-tails didn't fly at night."

"They normally don't. Their night vision is terrible. And if that wasn't weird enough, the man who brought her in said it was like she *fell* out of the sky instead of flew into his windshield."

"What do you think caused her to do that?"

"Honestly, it probably happened so fast and the guy was so startled, he just thought she fell. But we'll know more after we examine her."

Cyra wants to fight, but she used up her strength attempting to reach the stars, and she has nothing left. She remains passive as the humans carefully examine her body, starting with her feet, and moving upward until they inspect her wings.

"I'm going to start with the left, since that's the one that looked a little wonky when she flapped it earlier."

The older human gently pulls Cyra's left wing free of the younger's grip. She examines the deep shoulder where the wing muscles connect to the spine, searching for signs of broken bones, then manipulates the entire wing, checking its range of motion. Pain lances through Cyra's shoulder, hot and sharp, but beyond a slight tightening of muscle, she gives no indication of discomfort.

Her kind will not show signs of pain except in extreme circumstances. In the wild, survival is everything, and showing weakness or injury calls predators.

"There are no broken bones," the older one says, "but there's way too much motion in the shoulder, more than there should be. That indicates soft tissue damage, most likely torn tendons."

"Is she going to be okay?"

"Hopefully. We'll keep her in a crate for a few days and give her some Metacam. If she improves, we'll stop the meds and put her in an enclosure where she can move around—not that she'll want to for a couple of weeks. When she's ready, we'll help her do physical therapy by encouraging her to fly in her enclosure. And once she's strong enough, we'll release her. It'll take a couple of months, but I think she'll make it."

Cyra understands none of this, of course, but the humans' tones are soft and soothing, and despite being their captive, she feels safe. Exhausted and unable to stay awake any longer, Cyra allows sleep to take her. She dreams of stars, but no matter how hard she flies, they never get any closer.

It's nighttime, and Cyra stands on the perch in her enclosure, gazing up at the sky. The structure is simple—a wooden frame with walls and ceiling made from wire mesh. There's a door, but only the humans can open and close it. No escape that way, and escape is all she thinks about, for the stars continue to call her every night, their voices louder each time she hears them. Tonight, they're almost shouting down at her.

A chill breeze blows through the mesh, announcing the coming of an early winter. The Wind whispers in Cyra's ears, its voice blocking out that of the stars.

You should be sleeping . . .

You say this to me every night.

That's because it's true every night. Tell me, Cyra, why do the stars hold such attraction for you?

They call to me to join them. Can you not hear them?

The breeze swirls around her head.

No. Their voice is for you alone.

All creatures of the sky can hear the voice of the Wind, so Cyra assumed if she could hear the stars, the Wind could as well. That it is unable to surprises her.

From the first moment I set eyes upon them, I was enthralled by their beauty, captivated by their mystery. I must see them up close, speak with them, learn what they are. Only then will I know what I truly am beneath my feathers, muscles, and meat.

The Wind is silent for a moment, as if pondering her words. When it speaks again, it changes the subject.

How is your wing?

Cyra extends her left wing, flaps it a couple of times.

Healed. It's a bit stiff, but I'm certain I can fly with it.

The Wind does not reply immediately, and Cyra has the sense that something she said bothered it, but she doesn't know what. She goes on.

I hope the humans will let me go soon.

Hers is not the only enclosure. There are others, each containing birds—other hawks, owls, eagles, vultures . . . Some of them are permanently disabled and cannot survive in the wild. They will remain in their enclosures for the rest of their lives. But others, once healed, are released to return to the sky and the trees—she has seen it happen numerous times—and she prays to the stars that this will be her fate, too.

They will, the Wind says. *Sometime within the next two weeks. They believe you are almost fully healed.*

Cyra cocks her head, curious.

You understand the humans?

I'm the Wind. I understand all languages.

The breeze moves on, leaving Cyra alone in her enclosure. Now that it is quiet, she can hear the stars again.

Join us, join us . . .

She gazes once more upon their shimmering glory, and if she was capable of smiling, she would do so.

"Do you think she'll be all right?" the younger human asks.

"It's hard to say. Her wing has healed nicely, but if it remains stiff—even if only a little—it could slow her down. In the wild, that can make the difference between a full crop and an empty one. She's not disabled, so we can't keep her at the center. At least this way she'll have a chance." The older human sighs. "There are no guarantees in Nature."

Cyra sits inside a crate on the backseat of the humans' vehicle. The ride is not a smooth one, and she's constantly jostled back and forth, but she doesn't mind. Soon she will be *free*.

Eventually, the vehicle stops, and the humans get out. The older human slides open the vehicle's door, takes hold of the crate, lifts it off the seat, and carries it away from the vehicle. Through the wire mesh door, Cyra can see it's a beautiful day with blue sky and fat, fluffy clouds. The air is cold, though, and there's snow on the ground. This is only the second time in her life she's seen snow, but she remembers it. It's nothing to fear, but it means prey will be scarcer than in warmer times, the hunting more difficult.

The two humans walk for several moments, then stop and set the crate on the ground. Cyra hears the soft crunch of snow as the crate settles, and then the older human opens the door.

"All right, girl. Time to go back where you belong."

Cyra hesitates for a moment, as if unsure this is really happening. But then she lunges forward, shoots out of the crate, spreads her wings, and takes to the sky. As she ascends, she feels the Wind beneath her, bearing her upward.

Welcome back, it says.

She does not look at the humans on the ground, has already forgotten they exist. There is only one thing on her mind—she must feed and feed well, for she will need all her strength for her next attempt to reach the stars. And this time she *will* succeed.

No matter what.

A week later, Cyra perches on a lower branch of an oak tree in the forest. It is near midnight, far colder than it was the day she regained her freedom, the snow much deeper. She's puffed up her feathers as a defense against the cold, but it hasn't helped much, and her body is shivering so violently she fears she might lose her grip on the branch and fall to the ground. Her crop is emptier than it's ever been, and hunger gnaws at her insides, an angry beast trying to chew its way free. She ate well the entire time she was cared for by the humans, and hunger had been a stranger to her then. But she's become reacquainted with it since returning to the woods and has come to know it far more intimately than ever before.

She remembers something her mother told her while she and her siblings were first learning how to fly.

Being a hunter is hard. Our prey is alert and swift, and it may take you many attempts before you succeed in catching a meal. You must be persistent, but you must also know when to rest and reserve your strength for a better opportunity. If you continue to hunt and fail, you may exhaust yourself and become too weak to go on. Then you will die and become food for some other animal. So be careful, my loves.

Cyra tried to bring down mice, chipmunks, squirrels, and rabbits over the last week, but she failed every time. It was her damned left wing! She was slower than before her accident, just a fraction, but that was enough. Her prey escaped her every time, and now she is starving. She needs to feed soon, and if she doesn't, she will die. And if that happens, she will never get to see the stars. She could make another attempt tonight, use whatever strength remains to her to soar into the heavens, and hopefully reach the stars before her body gives out on her. If she fails and falls back to Earth, she might survive, but even if she does, she will likely be injured again and weak. She would only be able to lie in the snow and wait for death to claim her.

A hard choice.

The Wind whistles through the oak's branches.

Stay, continue to hunt, and possibly fail and die, or take to the air, fly toward the stars, using all the strength left to you, and possibly die before reaching them.

What should I do? Cyra asked.

If you don't choose a course of action, your fate will be decided for you. Better to make a choice—any choice—and see it through. At least that way, whatever happens will be your doing, not merely random chance.

You think I should try for the stars one final time, don't you?

I'm the Wind. I have moved across this world for billions of years, and I shall continue to do so until the sun burns itself to a cold, black cinder. What care I for the choices you temporary beings make? A pause. *But if you do decide to try, I will give you all the help I can. I ask only that, if you succeed, you return one day and tell me what they are like . . . the stars. I would dearly love to know.*

Cyra feels hope for the first time since she fell from the sky and became injured.

I promise!

Good! Give me a moment to prepare.

The Wind swirls around the oak, slowly at first, then faster, and faster, its soft whisper becoming a roar, then a high-pitched whine. Tree branches shake violently, weaker ones snapping off, carried away by the screaming vortex.

Now!

Cyra launches herself from the tree limb, wings spread, and the Wind slams into her with such force that she fears it will break her in two. But her body withstands the blow, and she is borne upward at dizzying speed, far faster than she could ever fly on her own, faster than any hawk has ever flown. The sensation is wonderful and terrifying at the same time, and her spirit laughs with delight.

Flap your wings, the Wind says. *I am powerful, but there's only so much I can do by myself. For this to succeed, we must work together!*

Cyra flaps her wings as fast and hard as she can, putting all her remaining strength into the effort. Her left wing soon begins to ache, the pain rapidly increasing to the point of agony. She knows the wing will give out on her soon, for good this time, and when it does, that will be the end of her journey, and the end of her.

She looks upward, sees the stars—bright, majestic, mysterious. Do they look larger now? She's not certain, but she thinks they might.

Join us, join us, join us!

A tendon in her left wing, strained to the breaking point, is on the verge of snapping. She can feel it, knows that mere seconds remain to her.

This is as far as I can help you, Cyra. The final choice is yours. Keep going or return to the ground. Which shall it be?

For Cyra, there is no choice. There hasn't been one from the instant she looked up from her nest and saw the stars through an open space in the leaves.

She has no strength left in her body, so she finds the strength she needs from somewhere else. She feels a pulling, a tearing, one far deeper and more painful than a simple tendon ripping apart. She opens her beak and lets out a shrill cry, not of agony or terror, but of defiance.

I . . . will . . . not . . . stop!

The pain vanishes, and she feels herself slip free of something solid and heavy, the thing that was holding her back all along. She picks up speed then, moving so fast the stars before her become blurred streaks of light. As she draws near them, they sing to her in one voice.

Welcome home.

The Wind has no eyes with which to see, but it has its own way of perceiving, and it knows that Cyra's spirit has moved on to the next leg of its journey. As her lifeless body tumbles downward—left wing jutting outward at an awkward angle—the Wind takes hold of it and slowly, gently, lowers it to the ground. A quick swirl, and snow covers the body like a blanket.

The Wind moves on then. It never stays in one place for long. It looks forward to hearing the stories Cyra will have to tell when next they meet again. Perhaps that will be in a few days, perhaps in an eon or two. To the Wind, there is little difference. Nor is there to the stars.

Or to their new friend.

BEST MOTHER EVER

Edward Martin III

HE MORNING SUN sliced through the barn windows, creating slats of dusty air, warming up the old, grooved wood and straw-covered floor.

Ari uncurled from her soft nook and, one-by-one, stretched each of her legs to work motion back into them. The warm sun touched her, and she let it soak in. She stepped over to her egg sac next and touched it gently. Although it would be imperceptible to anyone else, she could feel the life beneath the surface, the waves of tiny movement, the nascent voices of mind and heart. Satisfied that all was in working order, she stepped further out of her nook onto the anchor lines of her web.

Two biting flies remained from yesterday, and another wasp. She tested those first. The flies were dry, but a sip remained in the wasp. It was a satisfactory sip, as the wasp had struggled a bit more than most, so Ari relished it. Ever since the egg sac, she had not been quite as strong as she used to be, but she was sure her strength would come back soon enough. Even when weaker, she was still deadly, of course. She cut away the three bodies and reviewed the other end of the web.

Two gnats had stuck during the night, so small they had not even disturbed her sleep. One had already died and the other hung motionless but confused. Ari touched its mind. A gnat's mind was simplicity, and she was able to calm it and send it to a gentle place as her fangs sunk into its abdomen. This was her art, to calm her prey and feed, to help ease them on to the next thing. Her mind spread through theirs, touching, tapping, stroking, and they always dreamed joyously as they dissolved.

After she finished the gnats, she cut away the bodies and set about rebuilding her web. It was a new day, and she was still hungry.

"Thank you," said the voice from below.

Ari glanced down. From her web in the rafters of the barn, the floor was impossibly far, but sure enough, down there stood the Chicken.

"Good morning," said Ari, "and you're welcome."

The Chicken scratched a bit in the straw beneath the web and found the wasp. Straight away, it was gone. "I like hunting under your web," said the Chicken. "You have good taste."

"That's kind of you," replied Ari. She understood the Chicken well enough to know that if her web was low enough, she would be the Chicken's next meal.

"Are you not tired of that egg sac?" asked the Chicken. "I could take care of that for you."

"I most certainly am not," replied Ari. "These are my children. This is my life's work."

"Children are overrated," said the Chicken. "I've had many, and they all grow up to be just the same as you, except noisier."

A shadow fell across the doorway as the Goat entered. Immediately, the Goat rushed at the Chicken, who left in a fluster of feathers and indignation. The Goat watched out the barn door to make sure the Chicken was gone, then turned back.

"I wanted to thank you," said the Goat to Ari. "You are always killing and eating stinging flies and wasps, and these are terrible pests. Not only do they bother me and my kids, but I know for a fact that they bother the Horse and the Dog. The Dog won't say anything because he's too stupid, and the Horse is too proud, but I know that they are also grateful."

"I am glad to help," said Ari, vibrating with pleasure. "Honestly, I wish I could help with more. The flies especially are delicious. But since I made my egg sac, I've been very tired lately."

The Goat looked concerned. "Maybe taking care of it is draining you more than you know. Are you sure this is the right thing?"

"Oh, it must be," said Ari. "This is my first egg sac, and I really want to be sure that I do a very good job of bringing my young into the world and raising them well."

"I may not know much about spiders," said the Goat, "but raising young is not so easy. I can tell you are not your old self."

"Once the babies are born, it'll be better," said Ari. "They will help me—that is the nature of children."

The Goat nibbled thoughtfully on some straw. "As you like," she said, and then she left the barn.

Ari turned back to rebuilding the web.

Just as she finished, there came a peculiar vibration—low and subtle—upon the threads. Her eyes scanned the space, but there was nothing caught. Curious, she stepped across the space. The vibration happened again, and now she understood the source—her own little nook.

She dashed across the new web, her legs a blur.

The egg sac!

As Ari approached, she could see that it was time, she could sense the life inside. As she touched the egg sac, she felt them all. It was bliss, to finally feel so many voices, so many minds, all like hers. She had never felt this before. She embraced the egg sac, and opened her mind, welcoming them all.

The first tiny leg burst through. *It's happening, it's happening!* thought Ari. The moment she saw this tiny leg, this miniature version of her own leg, her own perfectly designed foot, she knew that this was the beginning of a new life, a life no longer filled with emptiness, but filled with family, filled with voices, filled with bliss and hunting and joy. She would be the best mother of all.

"Come, come!" she whispered. "Come out, my family, come be a part of the world, come feel the sunlight on your skin and smell the dust in the air and taste food in your bellies!"

Many arms, all tiny, all insistent, tore through the silken egg sac. It split wide. Ari shivered with joy at the flood of spiderlings. All tumbling and bumbling, they fell out. The egg sac shrank and deflated and still more came. "Welcome!" cried Ari. "Welcome to the world! Welcome to everything! I am your mother! I will teach you everything!"

The tide turned toward her, and the babies rushed up. She felt them climb her legs, climb onto her body.

She felt little pinches as their tiny legs sought purchase.

"Be gentle," she cautioned. "There are so many of you."

The pinches became more frequent and then Ari felt the first stings. She looked down at her upper leg joints, the ones with the thinnest armor.

Spiderlings clung against the softer tissue and pulled against it.

"Not so hard, be gentle."

Their little fangs unfolded and sank into her legs.

At that moment, she felt more tiny fangs cutting through her back, through her belly, on her legs.

"Stop, no, wait! I have not taught you to feed, I have not taught you to soothe, I have not taught you grace and skill!"

The fangs tore into her, ripping furrows, cracking through armor.

Ari shrieked. She lurched to one side, but her body was completely covered, and she could neither move, nor dislodge them.

Desperately, she reached out with her mind. "I love you! I care for you!"

Her mind flooded with hundreds of new minds, new spiderlings, just now learning they could speak and be heard. And each voice cried and screamed and shouted the same thing:

"HUNGRY!"

Ari felt herself pulled to the ground as her legs were torn from her body. She felt her abdomen torn open. She felt insistent feet clawing into her own body, desperate for fluid, desperate for food, desperate, desperate, desperate.

Ari screamed and a foot planted itself into her mouth. Fangs raked across her eyes. She tried to scream again, but nothing happened. Her body was no longer her own.

Her mind reached out, not to anyone in particular, casting a final thought into the world, a last curl of consciousness.

"Best mother, best mother, best moth—"

Moral: *Parenthood has its downsides.*

YOU SWALLOWED YOUR TONGUE

Geneve Flynn

KICAUAN, KICAUAN, CHIRRUP. *Chirrup*. Pelesit calls to Polong, her master. Tiny and green, with a needle nose for burrowing out of your enemy's abdomen. You could, I suppose, pluck any old grasshopper from the corpse flower or pitcher plant of the Sabah jungle floor, but the best ones, the spirits that make you beautiful, most suitable for marriage, are born from the tongues of dead children.

Making a Pelesit. This is how you do it:

unearth by full moon
a child from its grave
by anthill, it cries
—quick, bite—
two tongues in your mouth
spit (not yours) bury one deep

27

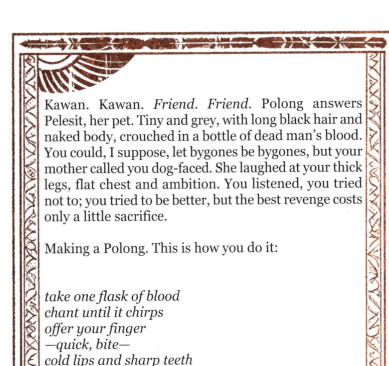

Kawan. Kawan. *Friend. Friend.* Polong answers Pelesit, her pet. Tiny and grey, with long black hair and naked body, crouched in a bottle of dead man's blood. You could, I suppose, let bygones be bygones, but your mother called you dog-faced. She laughed at your thick legs, flat chest and ambition. You listened, you tried not to; you tried to be better, but the best revenge costs only a little sacrifice.

Making a Polong. This is how you do it:

take one flask of blood
chant until it chirps
offer your finger
—quick, bite—
cold lips and sharp teeth
it doesn't even hurt much

Sihir. Sihir. *Magic. Magic.* Polong and Pelesit sing to you. Our mistress, our mother, you are transformed. Exquisite. Fine-boned. Hair like silk. Soft words. You know how to cook! What man wouldn't want you now? You could, I suppose, be satisfied, but that isn't the way this is supposed to go. And besides, the best black magic must be followed through all the way.

Taking vengeance. This is how you do it:

whisper to Polong
your bad mother's name
Pelesit finds her

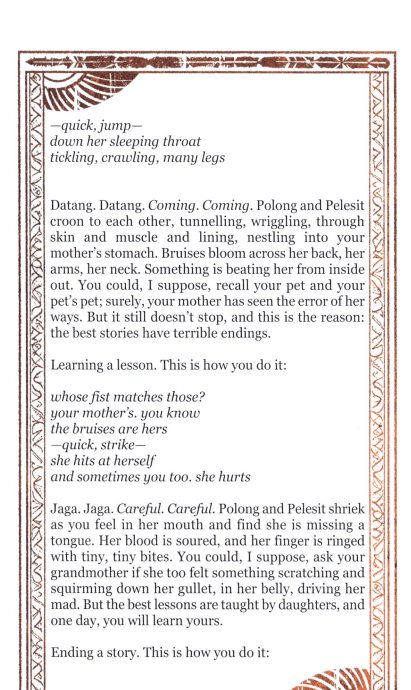

—quick, jump—
down her sleeping throat
tickling, crawling, many legs

Datang. Datang. *Coming. Coming.* Polong and Pelesit croon to each other, tunnelling, wriggling, through skin and muscle and lining, nestling into your mother's stomach. Bruises bloom across her back, her arms, her neck. Something is beating her from inside out. You could, I suppose, recall your pet and your pet's pet; surely, your mother has seen the error of her ways. But it still doesn't stop, and this is the reason: the best stories have terrible endings.

Learning a lesson. This is how you do it:

whose fist matches those?
your mother's. you know
the bruises are hers
—quick, strike—
she hits at herself
and sometimes you too. she hurts

Jaga. Jaga. *Careful. Careful.* Polong and Pelesit shriek as you feel in her mouth and find she is missing a tongue. Her blood is soured, and her finger is ringed with tiny, tiny bites. You could, I suppose, ask your grandmother if she too felt something scratching and squirming down her gullet, in her belly, driving her mad. But the best lessons are taught by daughters, and one day, you will learn yours.

Ending a story. This is how you do it:

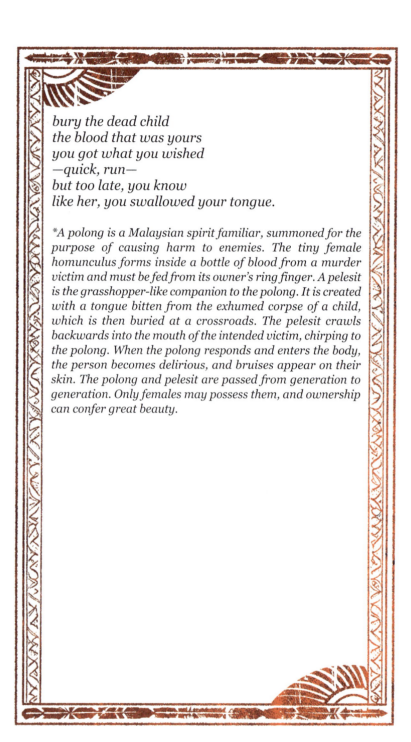

bury the dead child
the blood that was yours
you got what you wished
—quick, run—
but too late, you know
like her, you swallowed your tongue.

A polong is a Malaysian spirit familiar, summoned for the purpose of causing harm to enemies. The tiny female homunculus forms inside a bottle of blood from a murder victim and must be fed from its owner's ring finger. A pelesit is the grasshopper-like companion to the polong. It is created with a tongue bitten from the exhumed corpse of a child, which is then buried at a crossroads. The pelesit crawls backwards into the mouth of the intended victim, chirping to the polong. When the polong responds and enters the body, the person becomes delirious, and bruises appear on their skin. The polong and pelesit are passed from generation to generation. Only females may possess them, and ownership can confer great beauty.

GRACE

ALESSANDRO MANZETTI

ERE AGAIN, like a fossil with a still, soft heart hidden beneath its stone, I stand in front of this tomb. *You left, Grace. You left too quickly.* White skin, thin fingers, inky hair tied off your face. Wings for arms, rubies in your eyes. That's how I imagine you, down there; intact, but cold. Motionless, but ready to fly—if only you wanted to. Or perhaps you are in fact flying right now, and I shouldn't point my eyes to the ground, down among tufts of grass and wrought-iron flowers, but instead lift my gaze to search for you up there, somewhere. A black dot that wavers uncertainly in the middle of a flock that forms imaginary circles, ellipses, making byzantine eyes as big as fields. Maybe you have learned to use the lanes and alleys formed by the wind, the feathers and all the beats of an animal heart. But I can't see you anywhere.

I know you. You've always been a loner; you wouldn't dance with other birds. You did it for me that night, like an *étoile* welded to a music box, with no *Swan Lake* behind you, without water and orchestra, without a voice. Because there was no need to talk. Like now. Even knowing you as a half-shadowed creature, I chose you anyway—there, in front of that altar sprouting sunflowers, the eager arms of the dead waiting beneath our feet. Do you remember that young priest, with his frightened child's gaze and his suddenly bleached, golden liturgical vestments? He was more afraid than we were of what you would soon find on the other side, even though he was the one who had spent so much time studying resurrections. A bride destined to die so soon suggests that numbers, days, and years don't matter. And that maybe the Great Old One sometimes gets distracted.

Beautiful and pale as your wedding dress, with your back uncovered and a tide of milk attached to the long train, you crossed the nave like a ghost, painted by the play of light from that gothic rose window with its saints in blue, red, green, and yellow. Making fearful signs of the cross, my father looked for courage in his trouser pockets. The elderly woman pulled a Tarot card from her breast: a battlefield, a skeleton in armor on a horse, riding out among the survivors who all looked the other way, pretending not to see. And here came you: a bride with too many white blood cells, wrapped in bright white organza fabric, walking on daisy petals; an alchemy of snow, of incoming frost; all thanks to the tricks of Madame Leukemia, who shucks and sucks her oysters of marrow and brains. Raw meals. You wanted to be buried as you were that day, a bride forever—even if now your poisoned blood no longer moves through you; instead, it is tattooed on your skin, purple spots like rich mandalas ready to vanish. That's how I imagine you, down there; hands clasped across your chest, the topazes on your fingers confusing the worms and everything that crawls in that darkness. How can those precious stones sparkle again?

I keep looking up at the sky, counting the birds. People watch me curiously, and then do the same. In a cemetery, where only fountains and memories speak, no one ever looks at the great blue dome overhead, which is the same everywhere, from Avignon to Calcutta, from Tahiti to Jerusalem. Unless it's night, with all the different geometries of the stars. They think I'm crazy. There is no fire, no plane, nothing new up there—and so they look down at the ground again, at the earth that holds their treasured human shells. *They're wrong.*

A black dot, there to the east, breaks away from this flock that moves in shapes like cages, like the bones of an imaginary whale. Flying swiftly, the dot gets bigger and bigger against the sky. I measure it with my thumb and index finger: one inch, then two, and finally three. It's coming toward me—is it? It seems to be. *Is that you, Grace? You always were better at flying.* But, at the last moment, it veers toward the tops of the three cypresses that rise like jagged blades over the old house that stands just outside the cemetery.

I can't be wrong. I smelled your special scent, and I suddenly turned around—sure to find you in front of me. Barefoot, dressed in your wedding dress, the organza turned honey-colored, wings instead of arms, and the red bites of Madame Leukemia on your neck, scarlet as overripe peaches. Like I keep picturing you these summer days. But the mind plays strange tricks when too many dead memories are stuck in the present. In fact, there is nothing near me—only my own strange shadow, which spreads its black arms as if wanting to take flight.

I look like a cross.

I no longer see the black bird, but I know where it's hidden—among those three giant green knives. I run to that place, and her perfume rises with every step, now mixing with the incense, which brings my mind back to the nave of that church that day. But now Grace is waiting for me at the altar, and the windows of the old house are colored orange, then red and purple. A different rose window, built by the sunset. The cemetery is closing, this time without saints with gold circles around their heads. This time it's only colors, and no frightened priest.

I reach the door with a pounding heart. The house has been uninhabited for some time, and its walls are covered with the thick veins of a presumptuous ivy. It's like a Van Gogh dream: the Spanish Granada shutters, a thin courtyard of white and gray pebbles on which the shadows of the cypresses draw three dark stripes. These make the imaginary aisle of that church in Boston where I married a woman as I married death, both at the same time. The smell of inlaid wood from the choir of the small chapel comes upon me. The aroma of ancient candle wax. I'm sure I'm back in that place, even if everything has a different shape now. I kneel near a small fountain topped by the statue of a headless triton. There is still water inside it; I dip my fingers and make the sign of the cross, hoping that someone will open the discolored door of the old house.

Are you in there, Grace?

A rustle of fast wings; a black spot whizzes past the corner of my eye. I stand in place as a crow lands on my shoulder, turning its head to survey left and then right. Two rubies in its eyes, that flagrancy of narcissus and vanilla, invisible fingers plucking the strings of a harp, those gestures she made after making love—naked, always pale as a goddess.

It's you, Grace, isn't it?

The crow snaps at my face, twisting its neck and sinking its beak into my eye sockets—first one and then the other, in a sharp, deliberate sequence. *I didn't think my blood was so hot.* It drips down my cheeks and neck. It's summer, of course. All has become dark, with some red grains still lit, showing me a torn curtain . . . but I don't feel pain, because her perfume still surrounds me. It's like I've swallowed pounds of topazes and old memories, and that hole in my stomach is finally filled.

You're right, Grace, as always. Love is felt, not seen.

THE SPEED OF HEALING

MICHAEL BAILEY

Heartrate: 200 Beats Per Minute

Can you tell me your name or where you are staying? (in Spanish) a woman's voice says and I don't answer or can't other than to blink through the impossible brightness of the room—throat on fire, eyes burning—while others all in white stand with her as foreign tongue erupts from wavy-outline silhouettes saying simultaneously *¿Tiene pasaporte u otro tipo de identificación o tarjeta?* and *¿Como te llama?* and *¿Recuerdas tu nombre?* and only some of the words translate because language is super-ultra-fast when unfamiliar and everything's churned—

Lo siento I say to let the ghosts know I'm sorry and another apparition takes shape beside the other and says something incomprehensible or muddled or from behind broken glass and it takes time to process since the individual words are painful to decipher—and more so to speak—for fear of sounding childish or saying something wrong and a coal burns behind the sternum as though hit in the center of the chest with a hammer or stabbed or worse and the air both salty and fishy and every inhalation strenuous and *The fuck is happening—?*

Se llama a woman says because she wants to know my name and I understand that much and manage *Je m'appelle Eleanor* in a single scratchy exhaled breath but that's not right either—the *français* wrong coming out / should be *espagnole*—and they don't respond so I grab my throat as the woman takes on shape and shade then *I am Eleanor* I tell her (in choppy Spanish) because I understand *un poquito* while my heart *my heart* my heart *my heart* beats so ready to explode *my heart* and in my chest my heart is about to burst *my heart* as something next to me beeps endlessly at two hundred beats per minute—*my heart*—as it monitors the blood pumping through my veins in what must be the opposite of cardiac arrest and I'm drowning on this bed unable to breathe—

Then a man's voice emerges from the water and the few English words in the mix fill me with hope such as *Americano* and *¿Estados Unidos?* and *Sí* and then *Yes* I say with enough relief that it starts me tearless-crying and those standing over me gain faces and peer down as I'm on my back on a hard bed covered with a noisy sheet of thin paper that rustles as I spasm—a hospital rocking gently around me afloat—and everything but the clock on the wall spins bent-reality counter-clockwise and I can't breathe as though shot in the chest and *¡No puedo respirar!* I say and maybe that's why I'm here on this deathbed with my hands flexing and unflexing in panic so I sit up as dizziness pulls me down and I throw up saltwater to the bedside and—

Lo siento I say again more embarrassed than apologetic and then one of the outline-faces says in better English than my Spanish: *Eleanor, do you remember how you got here?*

All I remember: "Hold on tight and let's dance to the song in our minds."

45 BPM

SLOTH, HE GENTLY SWINGS,
SLEEPING IN CECROPIA,
SWAYING WITH THE WIND.

EL CARIBE MIST,
TURNING SKY FROM BLUE TO GRAY,
LEAVES THE WORLD AT PEACE

60 BPM

A sun gives life with its light, then turns the world dark; the way rain will wash away yesterday's story. The same is true of the sea and the sand. Footprints, there, then gone.

A couple walks hand-in-hand—reminding me of Zelda on the beach—along the ever-changing curves created by the ebb and flow, by the tides rising and falling with the pull of the moon, Luna. Shells of prior life brush against toes—those in decent shape collected by hand, clamshells, sand dollars—but most are broken bones left behind to churn into future sand. And as the salty blue laps, always thirsty, it takes back into the deep the couple's path, their past, as though never taken, and it takes my memories, my future. The journey never lasts.

It's an easy thought to walk out into the water and stay. So far out and waist-deep, the waves able to devour. The riptide pushes and pulls, disorients, drags bodies along the coast at odd angles. How easy it would be to disappear, swallowed whole into the ocean's hungry lips, eventually spat out for tourists or locals to find, or never found at all. How easy it would be to disappear. Every grain of sand a husk, a shard of shell, a rock tumbled back to stardust.

From ashore, someone might be watching, at least during the day: a head, shoulders, and a set of arms there above the ripples, then below, then above, bobbing with the breath of the sea. Someone could call for help or attempt to save those flailing arms, but is it only prolonging the inevitable? What if the arms fail to flail? What if it's dark out, the beach empty?

WHEN NOT STRONG ENOUGH
TO SURVIVE ALL WE'VE ENDURED,
WE'RE FORCED TO START OVER AGAIN,
AGAIN . . .

Those are the lines Sol watched me write before she sank into the horizon like a premonition. If she were here now instead of the moon, she'd inspire me to write something clever like, "The past is only there to remind you of what you haven't done yet." Luna is in her place, though, and she's turned everything monotone, the world stripped of color one layer at a time with morning promising to bring her alive again. I think of Zelda. I think of us, what we could've been.

More of the poem wants out, black on white, but not yet—not as the stars reveal their light one-by-one; always there, hiding until time lets them out. They peek between clouds, but it's only two women entering the placid black that reflects the night.

"Let's swim one last time and talk," Zelda says. "There's something I've been meaning to talk to you about. Something important," and I know what she wants to talk about, something unavoidable. Then she gets up from her towel and runs to the sea, dives under, resurfaces.

We're alone, and this part of the beach is safe, so I shed my clothes and toss them onto driftwood and chase after her.

Damn, Luna would say with her crooked smile.

"See you on the other side," I say and wade into the water.

45 BPM

TWO WOMEN WADE OUT,
SINKING BELOW THE SURFACE,
CALM WATER LAPPING.

SLOTH, HE AWAKENS,
HANGING / DANGLING FROM A BRANCH,
ADMIRING THEM.

60 BPM

The warm Caribbean takes us in her mouth one last time. The deep is a hundred meters out, which leaves time for those difficult final conversations.

Zelda, always the *taker*, never the *giver*.

We talk. We wade in the water. We talk.

The kind of change she wants was never in the promises we'd made to each other by exchanging rings. Partners are meant to accept and adapt and to grow, not to—

75 BPM

"I can't handle you being my everything . . . " she says. "I need more than that, love from someone other than *you* and only you . . . "

she says, waves interrupting her flow of words, "and you love me unconditionally, but . . . I can't offer you the same, and that's not fair . . ."—a higher whitecap takes her by surprise and shoves itself down her throat—"to you," a spray of cough, "but I'm not *abandoning* you, so don't think that . . ." Such a cruel word, to fucking give up. "I just need space for a while, I think . . . from you, from *us*."

"So, you want me to leave." Not as a question.

"I think so." Without hesitation.

90 BPM

Zelda and I stand in silence for a while, neither prepared to fight, no longer able to look each other in the eye or compose words. Surrounding us is a tension of unreleased emotion. Neither of us cries. Where will I go? Where *can* I go? So many thoughts. Zelda is / *was* my life, yet I'm no longer / *no longer will be* hers. We tiptoe in the water, dancing on the dead.

"Z, how long should we take apart?" No longer *a part* of one another.

"I don't know," she says, but I know she doesn't envision this distance as a way to mend. "A few weeks, a month? I don't know, Elle. Maybe this is more permanent."

Her nickname for me is the single syllable. Never Eleanor, just Elle. As it goes in life, names shorten as friendships lengthen. When we address each other, after so much time, it's like pulling letters from the alphabet. We have a mutual friend named Dee, the three of us spelling Zelda's name without vowels.

"Maybe we should," she says, hesitating, "*end* things."

I don't realize I'm holding the rock until it's in my hand.

100 BPM

Neck-deep but toes still touching sand, a wave covers then uncovers me, lifts me off my feet, drops me back down again. Just like Zelda after all those years we spent together.

She wants kids, she says, a girl and a boy, something I'm unable to provide because of my useless ovaries. She wants to be with a man, she says, because, well, "Perhaps this was all just a long phase, Eleanor." The full name. Already distancing herself.

125 BPM

"Hold on tight and let's dance to the song in our minds," I say, but she can't hear me over the waves. It's one of the first things I ever said to her, what made her fall in love with me all those years ago. We'd danced for seven years, and now she wants our song to be over. She wants to add to the overpopulation in the world. So, I hold on tight: to the memories, to the rock.

150 BPM, 175, 200

Yes, let's dance. Let's twirl forever underwater. Let's—

45 BPM

SLOTH, HE CRAWLS SLOWLY,
BRANCH TO BRANCH, HAND OVER HAND,
REACHING OUT TO THEM.

WHEN ONE DISAPPEARS
IN THE VOID, THEN THE OTHER,
THE BLACK TURNS PLACID.

200 BPM

I lift this rock—no, this skull-sized shard of coral—and bring it down a second or a third or a fourth time—life suddenly a blur—until she quiets / shudders / stills under the sparse light of Luna's smile above which hides the red within the black and there's so much running down my hand *my shaking hand* my hand as her own reaches claw-like as the less-than-real moment slows—a photographed memory exposing itself or a palm pressed onto an album to distort and horrify a lyric—as something hard turns soft beneath the crumbling coral and sinks below the surface and slips into the slap of an unexpected wave that fills my silent-screaming lungs with—

Saltwater churns us both as the riptide pulls from under and the silty / sandy graveyard of the sea sliding out from beneath our feet and we're no longer standing but swirling round in a dance and she's gone—Zelda leaving me as she planned—with thoughts of *I just need space for a while* and *from you* and *from us* as fragments of her final words fill my mind when water pours down me like amnionic fluid in this reverse birth—and I reach out one last time to hold on tight and take her in my arms to twirl in the remnants of melody left in our minds but she's—

0 BPM

WE'RE FORCED TO START OVER AGAIN,
AGAIN . . .

"Desfibrilador."
"Claro!"

0 BPM

WHEN NOT STRONG ENOUGH
TO SURVIVE ALL WE'VE ENDURED

"Otra vez."
"Claro!"

Pulse / Flatline

A future memory that will never happen: *Zelda hands over forty pages of dissolution, our relationship slid off like a husk as something once beautiful transmogrifies into the hideous—*

"Otra vez."
"Claro!"

Pulse / Flatline

A future memory that will never happen: *50 mg of trazodone hydrochloride, Desyrel, whatever it's called, little pills supposed to block chemicals in the mind meant to interact with serotonin and other neurotransmitters. Not addictive. May cause death. How many to take, then?*

41

"Ella se ha ido."
"Uno mas."
"Claro!"

0 BPM / 87 / 78 / 87

Where am I? I say to a stark white, *Mi nombre es Eleanor*, but the room only offers another future memory that will never happen: *forty pieces of paper with legal-jargon-word-vomit in need of translation in the trash, only to be retrieved the next morning to take on a flight, to a place other than here, and it all disappears, out like a light.*

"Está viva, su corazón está estable de nuevo."

60 BPM

An entire month later, and with a crash against tarmac, rubber squeals like twisted cats or dogs under tires as the airbus swivels and sets aright, straightening out again, a night turned day with the sun's light burning through an array of cabin eyelids. On the back of a napkin:

ZELDA, WITHOUT YOU
MY HOME HAS BECOME *LESS* HOME;
FOREVER HOME*LESS*.

60 BPM

"¿Puedo ofrecerte algo más?" a woman says, the words foreign, and oh, that's right, halfway around the globe where English is second and Spanish the first, not the other way around. The only way to respond to a smile and unfamiliar tongue is with another smile and—

"Gracias." That much is remembered from high school Spanish II; two years of elective and all that's left is a paltry 'Thank you,' as though only two words were learned in those not-so-caring teenage years, yet expressed by the *single* word that means the same. It doesn't need to be said. Nothing most crucial in life ever

needs to be, such as *love* or *sorry* or *hate* or *hurt* or *fear*, only ever felt—a shared primal and unspoken language (mis)understood by all.

Gracias, she says in return by not saying anything.

Single, goddamn it. Still married, but single.

The ring twirls.

Starting over again . . . again.

Pity, she says next by not saying anything.

The barista's drawn a heart on the cup next to a misspelling of the name—and both things flutter the heart—and she slides it closer, a gentle prod to leave, but there are similar cartoony hearts on all the other paper cups waiting on the counter for more complicated drink orders sporting other misspelled names. "*¿Son siquiera importantes los nombres?*" she says, and then "*Próximo,*" and as the too-hot coffee in this third-world country transfers from one hand to another as she puts it there and motions for the next customer, Spanish embraces the present.

Solo surfaces as the first sip burns, but that means 'only,' or maybe carries dual meanings. Those four letters are printed on the top of the plant-based lid on the recycled-paper cup, the brand, but also a reminder of this new status. *Sol* also burns in the hot afternoon.

45 BPM

SLOTH, 'EVER HE SWAYS,
EATING CECROPIA LEAVES,
CLEVER IN HIS WAYS.

THE SUN BRINGS ITS WARMTH,
OFFERING LIFE, SOMETIMES DEATH,
EACH REVOLUTION.

60 BPM

Is not all stardust death begetting life, life begetting death? A blink and the ground is not-so-solid sand and a collection of the dead: the smallest of empty shells, shards of coral, bones, husks of once-alive-things. The Caribbean Sea churns angrily from a downpour the night before.

The wedding ring slides off, placed upon this graveyard that is constantly shaped and reshaped by the ingress / egress of lapping water. A circle: no beginning, no end; emptiness at its core. Cut and twist and reconnect the shape at any point, and, suddenly, there are two endless paths by way of a Möbius loop circling around that great nothing. And yes, this is the exact beach where one woman said she wanted to leave another, and where one eventually left the other.

The sun casts its rays, another grain of not-so-distant starlight, creating a skewed shadow of the wedding band on the sand. The sun dies each night—eight minutes and twenty or so seconds in the past, or future, depending on perspective—and rises again each morning, but for how much longer? The sun's light bends the ring's shadow into an ellipse.

Nothing can be forever; forever can only be nothing.

The ring is pushed into the sand, meant to be left there; but the ring is quickly unburied, clenched within a fist, all that death around it leaking through the cracks. The hourglass hand turns over, opens, empty of all but a few memories of time. The ring is there, too, for a moment, then tossed without much thought into the sea.

45 BPM

LIFE IS TOO PRECIOUS
NOT TO START OVER AGAIN,
TO BEGIN ANEW.

SLOTH, HE DOESN'T CARE
ABOUT ANYTHING EXCEPT
THE SPEED OF HEALING

60 BPM

On a date with Sol, just me and her at the beach, I sit in the black sands and scribble lines of a poem no one will ever read in my tattered notebook as she splashes the surface of the water. She watches over me, keeping me warm, even from afar. I drink rum and she the sea. She's all over it, at first, writing her story in the water, touching every surface like a pen on paper.

When she creates shadows over my words, I shrug, tell her I write such things, that writing is a lonely life. A cloud passes, and she seems to smile, or smiles a seam. She changes right in front of me. All slow like. Taking her time.

"Damn," I say, but the good kind because it's magical, and she keeps peeling off layers until there's nothing left. And before I realize I'm looking into the past, she's gone, making her way around again. "See you tomorrow," I say and wade into the water.

> WHEN NOT STRONG ENOUGH
> TO SURVIVE ALL WE'VE ENDURED,
> WE'RE FORCED TO START OVER AGAIN,
> AGAIN . . .

Those are the lines Sol watched me write before she sank into the horizon like a premonition. If she were here now instead of the moon, she'd inspire me to write something clever like, "The past is only there to remind you of what you haven't done yet." Luna is in her place, though, and she's turned everything monotone, the world stripped of color one layer at a time with morning promising to bring her alive again. I think of Zelda. I think of us, of what we could've been.

More of the poem wants out, black on white, but not yet—not as the stars reveal their light one-by-one; always there, hiding until time lets them out. They peek between clouds, but it's only one woman entering the placid black that reflects the night.

50 mg of trazodone hydrochloride, Desyrel, whatever it's called, little pills supposed to block chemicals in the mind meant to interact with serotonin and other neurotransmitters. Not addictive. May cause death. How many to take, then? All of them. I took all of them.

"See you on the other side," I say and wade into the water.

45 BPM

> SLOTH, HE REACHES OUT,
> MUCH LIKE A PEACE SIGN, HAILING
> WITH TWO CLAWED FINGERS.

SHE SEEMS TO WAVE BACK,
QUICKLY DISAPPEARS,
SWALLOWED BY THE SEA.

0 BPM.

II

HUBRIS & HUMILITY

CYPRESS WHISPERS

LEE MURRAY

NCE IN OLD CHINA, in a small village at the edge of a milky pond, lived two humble farmers named Li and Chen. Boyhood friends from neighboring farms, the pair had grown up together, playing among the stalks of millet at their parents' feet, and later, toiling in the fields alongside the other villagers, their young backs bent under the hot sun, and their eyes stinging with sweat. But each day, the boys would put down their tools and sit in the shade of a cypress tree to eat their midday congee and share tales of the adventures they would have when they were rich—tales of voyaging on the ocean, attending an opera, or gaining an audience with a prince. When their beards came in, Li and Chen married two hardworking girls from the next village, and over time Chen was blessed with several strong sons and Li with several daughters, who in their turn joined their fathers working in the fields. With so many mouths to feed, Li and Chen did not grow rich, but they lived contented lives, and each day they would eat their midday congee together, concocting grandiose plans of what they might do if ever their luck changed.

But one day, while he was still in his middle years, Chen took ill. His blood humors were hot, simmering dangerously beneath his skin, and despite the best efforts of the village herbalist to cool them, Chen's vital balance could not be restored. Within days, poor Chen was too weak to work. His hair drooped lank across his shoulders, his skin turned sallow and shrunk, and his breath soured. He could barely turn his body on the kang without the help of his wife. Soon, he was little more than a pile of bones, shallow puffs of stale air rattling in his chest.

When it was clear Chen would not survive another night, Li lay beside his friend and whispered sorrowfully in his ear: "What of the wonderful adventures we planned, my friend?"

Hunkered in the bag of sagging skin, Chen could only shiver. "It was just talk, Li," he rasped. "A way to pass the time. We're farmers, you and I; we were never going to have that kind of money. Our place was with our children in the fields."

By morning, Chen had passed into the realm of ghosts.

Grief overcame Li. There would be no ocean voyages, no operas, and no audience with a prince. Li and Chen were too poor. But it didn't have to be that way. Chen didn't have to be poor forever. Not if his ghost were properly nurtured and fed. If they could not be adventurers in life, then Chen, at least, could be prosperous in death.

Li rushed home. He dug up his savings from beneath the beaten earth of his hut and hurried to the temple merchants, spending all his precious coins on golden paper money for the dead. From that day on, instead of eating his congee under the cypress tree at midday, Li would go to the temple to burn golden paper money, so the smoke would carry the wealth to his friend in the Underworld. Over time, Li grew lean and weary, his skin became as shallow and sunken as Chen's had been, and his sandals wore away on the stony path, but still, he did not miss a day of visiting the temple. Eventually, weakened by his mission, Li, too, took ill, and passed into the realm of ghosts.

What a surprise to find his childhood friend there to greet him in the temple. In death, Chen was restored: his black hair shone like lacquer, his skin was bright, and he had even gained some weight. But most surprising were the luxurious robes embroidered with gold and silver thread, which floated around his person in a silken cloud.

"Li! Welcome, my friend," Chen said. "Come, sit with me. I will prepare us some tea." They left the gloom of the temple, Li shuffling behind Chang in his humble farmer's rags. New to death, he blinked and squinted against the bright sunlight.

Chen led him to their favorite cypress tree, now bent and twisted with age, where they sat in the shade, looking over the fields toward the milky pond.

"I've waited so long to thank you," Chang gushed as he passed Li a steaming cup of perfumed tea from a tray delivered by a servant boy. "I owe everything to you, my friend. Thank you for your loyalty, for going every day to the temple to burn money for me. My sons burned tributes, of course, but it was your paper offerings, your dedication, that caught the attention of the Lord of the Underworld, and because I was so beloved in life, he appointed me Divine Protector of the region. Imagine that!"

Li's eyes narrowed as he sipped his tea. "So, because of my sacrifice, you've spent all these years in the afterlife as a wealthy man."

Chen beamed. "I have."

Li lifted his arm and shook his dusty rags. "But I'm still poor."

"That's because your daughters owe their filial duty to their husband's families," Chen said. "So, they have no paper money to spare for you."

Li glowered.

"But I can fix things," Chen said hurriedly. "You're to be reincarnated, and since we're old friends, I can ensure you will enjoy a better position in life."

"No more working in the fields, cutting millet?"

"Exactly. Just tell me what you want, and I'll arrange it."

Li's shoulder blades tightened. At last, it was his turn to be prosperous. "Congee is for poor farmers," he said. "I never want to eat congee again."

"Of course—"

"And I want clothes like yours. Made of silk and gold."

"Yes, I'm sure—"

"Plus, I want a beautiful wife. Not just a village girl. For my new life, I need a woman who will give me many fine sons, and not useless daughters."

Chen nodded.

But Li wasn't finished. "Give me a fleet of ships, so I can voyage on the ocean to other lands," he said. "And an opera house. With players and acrobats who will perform for me every day. I want to be as rich as a prince. No, no, I have a better idea; make me an emperor, with a palace in the mountains . . . "

Chen held up a hand. "Stop, Li. It's too much. I can't do all that."

The tea turned bitter in Li's mouth. He tossed the cup away

and stood up, poking a finger at Chen. "You have to," he spat. "I looked after you. Nurtured you. Without my help, you'd be just another poor ghost."

Chen sighed. "What if I let you into my treasure house of the dead? You could pick out a suit of clothes. Any clothes you like. You'll go back to Earth as the person whose clothes you have selected."

Li quickly agreed. He would surely find a suit of clothes to match his desires in the treasure house. He followed the Divine Protector back to a darkened corner of the temple, where Chen swung open the doors on a large room full of clothes. Richly woven brocades piped in gold and silver, elegant silks, and heavy fabrics encrusted with tiny pearls or studded with jade, all glittered in the golden torchlight. Li had never seen such riches.

"Come back later," he told Chen.

Li spent many days and nights searching the room, sifting through the clothes, discarding one outfit after another in his search for the richest garment. Finally, when he'd made his choice, he called Chen back.

"These are the clothes I will wear in my new life," he announced. "They must surely have belonged to an emperor." He slipped the garment over his head, and the tunic fell smoothly over his body. Li cinched the fabric in with a belt inlaid with diamonds, then he strode out of the temple to better view his choice in the sunlight. The garment was magnificent, the sun reflecting off a million facets of gold and black.

Chen shuddered. "Li. Not those clothes. Please. Choose something else."

"No!" Li yelled. "I looked after you, and now you want to deny me my chance? These are the clothes I want."

Chen nodded sadly. "Very well." He lifted his arm, covering Li in a swathe of black silk.

Li awoke near his old village, on the stony path heading away from the temple. How strange. He'd expected to reappear in a palace in the mountains. He checked himself over; he was still wearing the beautiful suit in gold and black, so this was definitely his new life. There must be some reason he'd been reincarnated here. In any case, while he was waiting for his purpose to be revealed, he would take the chance to stop by the village and show his family how prosperous he'd become. Perhaps he would punish his former wife and daughters for their lack of respect, too.

Li hurried toward the village. On the way, he came across a farmer leading a water buffalo. Good. A man of Li's caliber shouldn't have to walk. He rushed toward the man, intending to demand a ride, but at the sight of him, the farmer's face contorted in horror.

"Get away from me!" he screamed. He thrashed at Li with his switch, striking Li across the back. The switch bit into Li's skin, hot pain arcing down his spine. Li ducked away, slipping under the belly of the buffalo to the other side of the path out of the man's reach. Only, he must have startled the beast because the buffalo reared, out of control. It stomped on Li, its sharp hooves crushing and bruising, while its massive weight caused Li's ribs to crack. Winded, Li didn't have the breath to scream. Pain searing his torso, he rolled out of reach of those lethal hooves, and lay panting in the millet.

The beast ran in the other direction, into the fields, his owner running after it.

Stupid animal.

Coiled over in pain, Li lay on his stomach, spitting out blood while he caught his breath. Dust and grime covered his beautiful costume. He rolled gingerly in the grass to brush off the worst of it, then carried on to the village, wincing at every movement.

Badly injured, it took him a long time to reach the hut where he had previously lived with his wife and daughters. He slipped inside, blinking as his eyes adjusted to the dim light, and was pleased to see his former wife crouched over the fire, spooning steaming congee into a bowl.

Suddenly filled with hunger, Li lunged forward to snatch the bowl from her hands. But, terrified to see her husband returned from the dead, the hapless woman flung the bowl at him and leapt away.

Boiling congee spattered Li's body. It ran in scorching rivulets, searing through his fine clothes. Blisters bubbled up on his skin, quickly filling with yellow pus. Li shrieked in agony and scuttled to the corner of the hut.

But the silly woman was crazed with terror now. She picked up a boning knife and ran at him, screeching and stabbing wildly.

Li twisted away, but not fast enough. The knife gouged a chunk out of his side. Blood sprayed across the beaten earth, seeping into the ground.

Li had to get away before she killed him.

Leaving the piece of flesh where it lay, he wriggled sideways and clambered out a crack in the wall of the hut. Then he hightailed it for the fields, only stopping when he was safely hidden in the millet.

Bruised and broken, Li lay among the stalks and looked at the sky. This wasn't how he'd imagined his future. Still, these trials were surely only temporary. Soon enough, his true path would be revealed, and he would live the life he deserved. A little time to heal and recover and everything would be fine.

Li glanced around. He was near the milky pond. He sagged in relief. He was desperately thirsty. Dragging his crippled body over to the pool, he was lowering his head to drink when he caught sight of a reflection. *A striped snake.* Li twisted quickly, looking behind him for the reptile, but saw only the stalks of millet rustling in the breeze.

His humors chilled. Awareness dawning, he looked back at the pond. Tipped his head sideways. On the water, the black and gold snake did the same.

Li closed an eye. The snake closed an eye.

Li shuddered in terror. Slowly, he looked down the length of his ravaged body, saw he had no limbs, and finally understood whose clothes he had chosen.

THE FABLE OF A MONKEYS HEART

EUGEN BACON

NCE UPON A LIFETIME, you were a clever little monkey who lived with your baba. Your house was at the top of an ancient baobab tree. The tree had the brownest trunk and the greenest leaves. The tree was

      tall, tall, tall, fat, fat, fat
          and it stood on the bank
              of the stillest blackest lake.

Inside the lake was a crocodile, always lurking near the old baobab tree because for him it promised goodness.

"Be careful of the long-toothed croc," said Baba.

And you, the cheeky little monkey that you were, didn't listen and smiled to yourself. For what did grown ones know? If it were Mama, you might have listened, but she was not as clever as you—didn't she get herself eaten by the big bad croc when her lofty branch broke? It was you who told her to test the creaky branch, stomp on it a bit. But still. You saw how she fell, as if in slow motion. You saw how the croc's jaws waited, waited wide open, snapped and clamped down on her headfirst and then swallowed one half whole. The bottom half of her torso, crimson blood squirting in arcs, legs kicking as if connected to her mind, splashed into the still, dark lake, and it stayed black.

But you had a plan for what would happen if your lofty branch broke—not that you'd die in a ditch if things didn't go your way. And that's why you waited, waited like the croc.

One day, Baba went hunting for bananas, because you loved to eat bananas. You loved the baby, golden ones that grew at the elbow of the savanna. And you also loved coconuts—your baba had those for you in plenty.

"Stay home," said Baba. "Stay away from the big, bad croc."

And off Baba went, to find some soft, sweet bananas from the great big savanna for you to eat. And you sat on the edge of the overhung branch of the old baobab tree and peered at the lake and saw the long-toothed croc swimming and swimming around your tree.

"Oi!" you yelled. "You're full of humps and lumps, and you pong like bad fish."

But Croc just swam and swam around your tree.

You peered a little more, and bellowed, "Oi! You! Your mama was so smelly she thought the month-old carcass of a hippo, green and putrid and trapped in hyacinth, was a brand-new suitor from the gods."

But Croc just swam.

Annoyed at the croc, you peered so hard that your branch *snapped!* As you fell

legs first from the tree,
    the big bad croc lunged
        from the murky waters
           snatched you whole in his jaws.

And he smelled rottener up close.

He tossed you in the air, so you fell again, this time headfirst into his mouth like your poor mama did, only he didn't chomp you in half right then. He threw you back in the air, again and again, each time catching you as you fell into dead shrimp, lake-fly larvae and glowing cichlids between his yellow teeth.

Finally, he tossed you onto his back, and swam you far, farther, farther still from the bank and into the middle of the silent, black lake.

You looked at your hand, and it was a stump, white bone jutting where fingers once danced. Pus-colored mud came from the stump, and you looked at the croc, saw how the yukky ooze snailed from his nose. His bumpy skin was slippery with slime. You slid off it, and the croc *snapped!* bit and dragged you into the water, and you tried to fight, to flee, but what good was it with one hand?

He held you under the murky surface, rolled, rolled, rolled a few times. You could hear the porridge of the lake, and it was calling for you. It blinded your eyes, enfolded your nose, tunneled down your throat, plumbed your lungs, and you couldn't breathe.

You closed your eyes to sleep or die, anything to forget, if that would take away the pain. You stilled yourself one last time, but Croc stopped his death roll and snatched you back onto his bumpy, slimy skin.

You were half-dead but didn't cry because you were clever. So clever. You looked at the croc and said you didn't have your heart, and the heart was the best part of a monkey for a croc to eat.

"Say what?" roared Croc.

And though your whole body hurt when you turned, or moved your mouth, you told him again that you didn't have your heart, and, oh, how yum, yum, it was good.

"And where is your heart, little monkey?" asked Croc.

"I left it in the topmost branch of the old baobab tree, up, up there, right next to the blinky stars," you said.

"And why is your heart near the blinky stars, Little Monkey?"

"At the topmost branch of the old baobab tree," you said, "the blinky stars can reach the heart. And when they reach the heart, the gods can spice it up with good, good things."

You saw his hesitation, how he swam round and round contemplating your words, and you understood when he swirled and swam, tail swishing this way, that way, that the silly, silly croc believed your tale.

So, when Croc snapped his jaws, let you leap across his back, and it hurt with half a hand, the ugly stump not bleeding, just covered in slime, pus, and mud, you scrambled best you could all the way up your tree.

There, you called out loud from the top:

"Open wide, dear Croc, open your great, big mouth for the god-loved heart."

The big, bad croc opened his mouth, and you hurled a large coconut that went *BOOFF!* on his head.

You saw how Croc's skull cracked, and a goo of milky brain, pinky blood, and smashed-avocado oozed from his head as he cried.

"Oh! How hard is your heart, Little Monkey?"

He swam away, and you hoped that was the last of him, but you saw him farther out, swimming round and round in the belly of the pitch-black lake.

You wondered if you should tell Baba—he wouldn't notice if you didn't, for what do men know? He didn't know about Mama, how it was you who said to test the creaky branch, just before it broke. Oh, nasty!

Your baba came back from the forest with a clutch of golden baby bananas, but the sweet goodness of the yellowest bananas was lost in the throb of your stump. You didn't tell Baba about the croc and the god-loved heart. But something in his eye, the way Baba
 looked first at the croc
   with a misshapen head
    swimming round, round
     at the bottom of your tall, tall
      tree, and then at you—
He didn't say nothing, but something still and black s t i r r e d in your core,
 and
   s
    t
     a
      y
       e
        d.

Fact:

Crocodiles can climb trees.

THE DISPUTE OF CRAWLER & CREEPER

MARGE SIMON

Mr. Rat and Mr. Roach were having an argument.
It was an old one, tatterdemalion and threadbare,
about which species will be left victorious,
trusted to rule over Earth and sea,
after Man has made himself extinct
with his fancy mushroom-shaped clouds.

"You worthless lump of snot,
you'd not live three hundred years
with radiation burning in your bones!
Me, I'll be mutating into Super Roach,
those rays will vanish long before
we cross that ol' rainbow bridge."

Said Rat, "We'll best you on that count,
You pathetic excuse for vermin!
For shame, lazy ass gundygut,
sleeping in feces you were too full to eat!
As Super Rats, we'll make you all extinct."

Snickering, he tweaked Mr. Roach's antenna.

"Watch it, buddy!" snarled Roach.
"Our armies are legion,
We travel all over the world on ships,
we can go anywhere Man goes!"

"So can we, fuckface," sneered Rat,
"on the moon, in the crapper, wherever."

He punched Roach's mandible, but
Roach spat something nasty in his eye.

"I'm BLIND!" Rat screamed. "You putrid scum, how
        dare you—"
"You'd dine on your own mama!"
"Don't you talk about my mama!"

At some point, each called for backup,
but the ensuing battle did not end well.
Bits of exoskeleton and bloodied fur
were scattered across the countryside.

In a nearby research lab
two technicians drank a toast
watching a roach wriggling on a toothpick,
a rat slowly drowning in a quart of urine.
Both rat and roach were soon blended,
grounded up and mashed.

Chemically processed in spinning mechanisms.
Expelled as gelatinous white cubes.

A researcher placed a cube in each wine glass,
watching it dissolve into a vibrant green fluid.
"Mazel Tov! Brilliant idea," said one.
"Protein that farms itself," said the other.

With a clang of glasses,
they heartily drank.

THE HYENA AND THE RHINO

ROB CAMERON

OU ARE A RHINO, and you are monstrously strong. Why, the other day, standing tall in the shade of an acacia tree, you retold the story of how you killed Lion. "I speared him and tossed his body high. Then I crushed him beneath these very feet!" you roar.

Your herd has listened to the story many times, but they dare not remind you this happened years ago and that you are old. You are still massive, violent, and extremely dangerous. Much more recently than the lion, you killed a young bull for some imagined slight.

We are hyena, and we see many true things, even in the dark. So, we know that it is *our* scent, not Lion's, that makes you squeal and whine in your dreams. Fear wakes you as my family harries a plump calf in your herd. Bleary and enraged, you maul my mate to a limping mess. Now he is crippled, and I must kill him, eat him, and break in a new male.

I am vexed.

But I also saw you nearly trample your own calves in your blind rage, and my mouth waters. Invisible in the long grass of night, I whisper to one of your sons, "You should let us have the old one, he is sick and weak."

You shoulder him aside before he dares to answer, barely missing him with your great horn. "You shall take nothing! It was I who killed Lion!" You bellow beneath a sickled moon.

I wait to see if there is more, but the herd is quiet. "We shall see," I say. Then I fade away, and my family follows.

The next day, you lead the herd away from this place. It had been an oasis, until we came upon you. The herd follows, though your eyesight is terrible. That is a rhino's lot. But worse than your vision is your memory. It is soft and porous. Your sweat stinks of confusion and sickness. Your family says nothing. Too afraid of you and too afraid to close their eyes. We follow, staying close enough for you to hear our songs and our laughter, late into the night.

Soon you are lost. It must seem as though the sun spirals across the sky like a lazy fly, no longer settling in the same place twice. Its rays rake across your rough skin like claws, and we are envious. The cows have no more milk, and the weakest calf thins and dies. We eat it, though it is not filling.

The red-billed oxpecker on your shoulder takes pity on you and flies ahead to investigate. It returns in haste and leads you toward a large pond. You give no thanks. Of course, you would have found this place on your own. You are the one who killed Lion, after all.

Squinting, you wonder why you are the only animals here. No zebra or elephant cousins. The pond is large and blue, with more than enough fresh water for everyone.

"Drink," you command. "Bathe. Wade." The herd is apprehensive yet fear your rages more than they fear the water.

We keep our distance.

We remember the truth of this place.

Teeth leap from the shallows, snatching a cow by the throat, dragging it out to deeper water. The middle of the pond comes alive with rolling, snarling crocodiles as they devour screaming meat. It is over quickly. The water stills. The blue at the center of the pond is marred with a spreading bruise-black stain.

Farther back on the shore, I call out to the bull that just lost its mate. "You should have given us the old one. It is not too late."

Again, before he can speak, you answer. "I am the one that killed Lion! I will lead them away from this place. Only I can keep them safe. You shall take nothing!"

As you shepherd them away, I narrow my eyes. "We shall see," I say.

You cross unnaturally straight, hardened tar rivers that sting the bottoms of your hooves. You've strayed dangerously close to the cities of Man, termite mounds that burn from the inside, smothering the stars with cold lights, bittering the air, and wrapping around the old forests like thorny briars. The water that trickles from holes in the ground are poisoned. You drink it anyway and collapse to the ground, delirious and awash in sweat.

The exhausted herd lies next to you.

Memories fall off the bone until only fear is left. Your meaty body shakes with fever. Men rush past in their shells of metal that growl and spit acidic fumes. The sounds enter your dreams like witches gnawing on the marrow of reason. In your dreams, we have you surrounded. You charge and smash and bludgeon and impale us until you awake, howling, wet with blood. Gore squelches under your feet. Entrails swing from the end of your horn.

It is not ours.

Your sons, daughters, and grandchildren are dead.

Trampled. Crushed. Stabbed.

"A rhino's sight is terrible," I say. "They could not see what was right in front of them."

The shock of what you have done buckles your knees. You don't get back up.

I approach you finally. "You should have let us take you."

"Kill me quickly," you say, "Please, as I did the Lion."

My family follows me out of the dark and crowd around you. They are laughing but I am not. I look to my new mate, whom I do not like, and then, slowly, I look at you.

"We shall see."

#GANGGANG

ROB CAMERON

My clan runs one-fifty deep,
got the numbers to make the rule, (Grra-ah!)

scavenge mum's carcass,
turn dem youths to food. (Grrr-ha!)

Prey, if you hear our song, then it's
too late
for you. (Close your eyes.)

Filiform gang, strollin'
riot to frenzied peak,
ghost laugh, scheming,
seeking what we seek, (Ayeee!)

Hemmingway said,
*Hermaphroditic self-eating
devourer of the dead.* (Bombaclout!)

My clitoral bigger than yours,
longer dem penises
your species call ill, (swingin'!)

we make our males bow,
our females make the kill. (Whoop!)

Physiologus be bite'n our name,
but we ain't got a bruise (Grrr-ha!)

Kaguru, our jaws crush bones,
Savannah control on cruise,
'Cause (whoop!)

We hunt down the patriarch. (Ee-yah!)
Dem lions ain't got no heart. (Cheat-us!)
Why the Bedoin fear the dark. (Err-us!)

EYE OF MIRRORS

PATRICK THOMPSON

 UGO WAS THE perfect visual representation of what every fox desires to be. A perfect shade of red with the right amount of white framing an elegant snout. Ears, shaped like well-crafted isosceles triangles, sat symmetrically on top of his head. The fur on his legs, the perfect shade of chocolate brown, beautifully contrasted his red coat. Beautiful. The most beautiful fox in every way, but one, his *tail*.

To the casual observer, Hugo's tail looked like any other fox tail. But to Hugo, it wasn't right. The color was slightly off, the tip a bit too blunt, and it sagged a little too much for his liking when he lifted it into the air. Hugo would spend hours staring at his reflection in the lake, seeing nothing but his tail.

"Oh, why have I been cursed with a tail like this?" Hugo exclaimed as he stared at his reflection in the water. "Every other fox in the forest shuns me, mocks me, belittles me behind my back because of this atrocity."

In fact, Hugo had no friends in the forest. Most of the other foxes disliked Hugo, but it wasn't because of his tail. It was due to his arrogant, haughty attitude and obsessive quest for physical perfection.

One day, as Hugo was staring into the lake bemoaning his self-inflicted despair, the Spirit of the Lake came and spoke to him. "Beautiful fox, why do you look into my waters every day with such sadness and longing? What have you lost? What tragedy has beset you?"

"Oh, cruel spirit. You scorn me with your words. For you of all beings should see my lack and loss. Every day I look upon my tail and see how raggedy and wrong it is. I have been cursed with deformity, and you act as if you don't see it, even when its reflection is so clear in your waters," Hugo moaned.

"But blessed are you among all other foxes in areas of beauty," the Spirit replied. "There are no other foxes in the forest that compare to you. Take no notice of the slight imperfection, the unique touch that keeps you from being the most beautiful creature in all the woods."

"So, you agree this tail is hideous and beastly," Hugo exclaimed. "If only there were but a way to remove this tail and replace it with one I deserve, one of beauty and symmetry. I tell you, Spirit: despair is growing in my heart, and every day that I stare into your waters I am tempted to throw myself in and put an end to my shame!"

"Do not despair, for I have seen a tail that matches your beauty. Yet it belongs to another fox," said the Spirit. "While she is no pleasure to look upon, her tail is like nothing I have ever seen. She is a solitary creature, but being so close to a tail that matches your longings might ease your pain."

"Please, Spirit," Hugo begged, "tell me where I can find this fox. I desire this above all else."

The Spirit answered, "She lives on the other side of the lake. She comes to visit me every day, just the same as you. But when she looks into my waters, I see joy, peace, and contentment reflected on her face. If you feel so inclined, you might find her on my northern banks just after sunrise tomorrow."

With that, the Spirit receded back into the waters, leaving Hugo to his own thoughts. The idea of a tail of such beauty consumed him. He could not sleep but spent the evening hours making his way around the lake to the north shore. Patiently, he waited in the thick brush, looking up and down the shore as the sun rose.

As the sun cast its light upon the lake, a few foxes approached the waters. Hugo stared intently at each one, but none of them had a remarkable tail. Most of their tails didn't even measure up to his defective appendage.

Foxes came and went with no sign of the mythical tail the Spirit had spoken of. Just when Hugo was about to give up hope, a small, gaunt fox approached the water. Hugo felt a shameful revulsion looking upon such deformity. But as she approached the water, her tail came into sight. Hugo's eyes widened with the overwhelming elegance and beauty of her tail. By itself, the tail would be pure beauty, but alongside her frailty and ugliness, the tail shone like the most beautiful star in the night sky.

Hugo made his way down to the shore.

He could see the female fox looking at her reflection in the water. She had a smile on her face, and true joy overcame her as she glimpsed her tail in the reflection. She took one last sip of water and skipped away into the brush, but as she retreated, she saw Hugo. Overcome by both fear and reverence, she stopped. She had never seen a fox so radiant and perfect. Her mouth went dry, her mind foggy.

Hugo's eyes grew green with envy the longer he stared at her tail. In that moment, he knew he could never let it out of his sight again. "Hello, I'm Hugo. I live across this lake," Hugo said abruptly. "I have just come to this part of the woods, and I must say I have never seen a creature as beautiful as you."

The fox stood motionless. No other foxes had ever come to the water to drink with her. It had been years since another fox had even spoken to her. And now this angelic being was calling her beautiful.

"Harley, I'm Harley," she stammered.

Over the next few days, Hugo would not leave Harley's side. He feigned interest in anything she said or did, but his lustful stare lingered upon her perfect tail. Days grew into months, and Harley felt a love growing inside her for Hugo. She had never been treated like this before. She had never experienced attention and devotion. And while she couldn't understand why he, of all creatures, was bestowing this upon her, she naively accepted it as pure and honest. For those were the feelings she best understood.

One day, Hugo's lust for her tail overcame him. He sulked at the lake, staring into the water. A deep grimace displaying his true feelings. He wanted Harley's tail for his own. The Spirit of the Lake reappeared to him at that moment.

"Oh, most alluring of foxes, why so melancholy? Haven't you, for the last season, been enjoying the beauty of the most perfect tail? Has this not brought you joy and contentment?" the Spirit asked.

"Spirit, your words deceived me," Hugo replied. "Your description did not come close to portraying the beauty of Harley's tail. It has captivated my vision, my thoughts, and now my desires! At first, it brought me some measure of happiness merely to stare upon it. Then I could touch it and feel it with my own paws! Know that I can only find despair because the tail is hers and not mine. Tell me, Spirit, what can I do to make my tail more beautiful even than Harley's?"

The Spirit's words floated back to Hugo. "I have no power to create, but I do have the power to transform. If a creature willingly throws themselves into my waters as a sacrifice for another, then the one who caused the sacrifice may command me to give to them any of the qualities of the sacrificed. But beware, once the exchange is made, it is irreversible."

Hugo's heart leapt. This would be easy. He knew Harley had fallen in love with him. And while he carried none of the same feelings for her, he knew he could use her love to his advantage. He could trick her into throwing herself into the lake; if not, he would force her.

As if reading his mind, the Spirit continued. "My most renowned of foxes, know that I am not asking this of you, nor is it something I am encouraging you to do. Yet, if you can find one who will give their life for love, then I will abide by the law of sacrifice. But remember, this must be a willing sacrifice. If there is trickery, deceit, or coercion, the transformation will fail."

The next morning, Hugo and Harley made their way down to the water's edge for their morning bath and drink. Hugo tapped Harley playfully and knocked her into the shallow edge. Harley laughed at his flirtations and splashed water back onto him. Hugo, using a bit more strength, gave her a shove back into the water. She lost her footing and slid off the bank into the deeper part of the lake.

In a flash, Harley panicked. "Hugo, I can't swim, and this water is too deep! Please, help me out!"

Hugo's eyes grew wide. In a moment, she might slip farther out into the lake and sink below it. His mind filled with the image of her tail replacing the limp shame upon his backside.

But as her struggles were growing more serious, the voice of the Spirit of the Lake came into Hugo's mind: *Remember, this must be a willing sacrifice. If there is trickery, deceit, or coercion involved, the transformation will fail.*

Hugo reached out his paw and allowed Harley to resecure her footing and remove herself from the lake. As Harley reached the shore, she felt relief and security again with the dry ground under her feet. "Oh Hugo, I would have drowned without you!" she cried. "If it wasn't for your strength and agility, I would have certainly been swept out to the depths. I don't know how, but my love for you grows deeper every day!"

The words meant to bring joy and gratefulness to Hugo's ears felt like nothing but scorn. Even as Harley curled up against him, he contrived another plan to lead her to her demise.

As the morning broke, Hugo awakened Harley and insisted they head down to the lake shore. As they lapped at the water, Hugo let his front paws slide slightly deeper into the water. As he leaned over to get another sip of water, Hugo pushed off with his hind legs and thrust himself out into the deeper part of the lake. Hugo, being strong and agile, was a fine swimmer. Yet in this moment, he let himself be taken under the water. He staged an excellent performance, so anyone watching would have thought he was drowning.

Harley's eyes grew wide. She didn't know exactly how it happened, but her love was caught in the same predicament she had been in the day before.

"Harley, I'm drowning! Please come out and save me!" Hugo cried.

Harley danced on the shore, trying to determine her next action

Hugo's eyes were locked onto Harley's tail with lust. *"I'm close."* His mind filled with the thought. *"Just come into the water and what is yours will be mine."*

Harley spotted a branch right next to the water. Hugo watched as she used every ounce of strength to push the limb into the water toward him. The branch floated toward him with her still attached to it. She kicked and clawed and held onto the branch in desperation as she reached him. Hugo grabbed hold of the branch, knowing his plan had failed again.

Bitter grief broke Hugo's heart. How? How was he going to get her to willingly sacrifice herself? Sitting by the water's edge, with the moon above him, a shadow whispered in his soul. If he couldn't use himself as bait, he might use *something* else. The lake grew quiet. The lapping of the waves ceased.

That night, he curled up beside Harley and softly brushed his tail against hers. While they had shared a home and life together over the past few months, they had never mated. Until that night. Seven weeks later, Harley's small frame gave birth to one tiny pup. While she survived the pregnancy, it had taken most of the life out of her. But there was nothing more she loved in this world than this new life, her baby. She named her Hope.

In the days that followed, Hope nursed and grew in strength. Hugo and Harley could see that she had inherited the best of them both. Hope was the most beautiful baby fox the forest had ever seen. Perfect from the tip of her ears to the last twig of hair on her tail. When she opened her eyes for the first time, they were a piercing silver that shone like diamonds during the day and stars during the night.

From the moment Hugo saw them, his desire grew for them.

Hope grew into the epitome of her name. Everywhere she went and every creature she met seemed affected by her innocent, joyous spirit. She simply saw the world through different eyes than everyone else. Even Hugo was not immune to her nature. When she would come to him to play, cuddle, or joust, he would leave the experience in a positive mental state. But it never took long for his feelings to sour, or for his dark lust for Hope's eyes to fuel his discontent.

Yet as night drew dark on the evening before he was to enact the final phase of his plan, something new crept into his mind: doubt. For the first time, Hugo wondered. Was it worth the sacrifice? Maybe Harley's deep, sacrificial love for him would be enough. Maybe Hope's adoration and peaceful world view would be enough. He contemplated these things by the lake.

A slight wind blew across its waters and waves lapped at the shore. The noise interrupted Hugo's thoughts just enough for him to notice his reflection in the water. But this time, instead of seeing himself as he was, he saw himself as he could be, Hugo, the most magnificent fox that ever lived.

From tail to tip, none could compare.

As he stared at himself in the lake, the uneasiness returned to his heart and the longing for more than he had overwhelmed the idea of finding contentment in the love of others. He blinked, and, for a moment, the lake reflected his image, but with beautiful silver eyes that shone like stars at night. Then, as quickly as it had come, the image disappeared.

Hugo knew what he must do.

The next morning, as the family of foxes emerged from their den, Hugo put his plan into action. "Today I'm going to teach our daughter how to swim," Hugo asserted. "I want her to have no fear of the water so that, in case of an accident, she will be stronger in the water than you or I."

Harley's heart sank thinking about their last encounter with the lake. But Hugo's words made sense, and she trusted him with all her heart. *He has always cared for me, and now he is showing the same care and concern for our daughter,* she thought.

Hugo grabbed Hope by the nape and strode toward the shoreline. He dipped her in the water a few times to see how she might respond. She kicked playfully at the water and seemed to look at it with the same hopeful perspective she gifted to everything else in the world. Hugo carried her to the tree next to the lake. Its branches reached farther out than either of the adult foxes had ever swum, and as Hope stepped out onto the branch, Harley became anxious for them both. "Please be careful," she cautioned. "You know I don't have the strength to help you if something terrible should happen."

Hugo gave her a reassuring smile. "Don't worry, darling, I'm just going to drop her in the shallows so she can gain experience." Hugo did just that. Hope fell into the shallows of the lake, and he scampered down to help retrieve her. Hope's laughter reassured her mother. And Hugo saw his moment. He took Hope back to the tree branch, further out, so they were over a deeper part of the lake. At that moment, the wind picked up, the lake grew restless, and Hugo obliged.

In the blink of an eye, Hugo tossed Hope as far as he could into the depths of the lake. At the same moment, he fell off the branch and landed a few feet from the shallows. Harley's eyes went wide with confusion. Her worst nightmare had come true. Without thinking, she sprang into the lake.

Hugo's words gave her direction. "Don't help me! Please, Harley, save our daughter!" he cried out.

She attempted to swim with all her might toward Hope. The lake seemed to aid her as she strived toward her struggling daughter. One final swell of water pushed Harley toward the pup, and her fierce mother's jaws clasped around Hope's neck in an effort to save her life. But just as quickly, the wind shifted again, and the lake turned against them. As hard as she tried, Harley's weak frame would not let her swim back to shore with her child. Her legs grew tired, and she could no longer keep herself afloat. She took one last gasp and turned for one last look at Hugo, her love. He sat calmly upon the shore, stroking his tail as he watched the two of them sink into the depths. Hope was lost.

As mother and child sank to the bottom of the lake and the life left their bodies, the wind calmed, and the waters returned to glass-like stillness. Hugo looked intently into his reflection. "O Spirit of the Lake, I have provided you with your sacrifice. Give me my due!" he exclaimed.

The Spirit came to Hugo. "My dear nefarious fox, you have truly paid my price. I will grant the exchange that you have longed for. Simply step into my waters, submerge yourself, and when you rise, your beauty will be complete. Your tail will be as magnificent as the rest of your appearance. Come. Submerge."

"Oh, honorable Spirit," Hugo replied. "While our deal was for one sacrifice, I have given you two. Harley came to you willingly, but Hope was lost, not by my hands. It was the power of her own mother that drew her to the bottom of the lake. Am I not due from you two transformations? Indeed, I will take Harley's tail, but I also require my child's eyes. You have received your payment; I demand my reward."

"Oh, most fantastic of foxes," the Spirit hissed. "What you say is true. It was not by your hands that the child was sacrificed, so I will grant you a second transformation. But remember my words, once the exchange is made, the transformation is irreversible."

"Once I have received these gifts, my life will be complete. I will want for nothing. Now, give me my due!" Hugo, emboldened with his belief that he had outsmarted not only Harley, but even the Spirit of the Lake, dove headfirst into the deep waters. He immediately felt . . . *change*. His tail retracted as a new one grew in its place. Light receded from his eyes, and Hugo felt the eyeballs squeeze down to the size of a pinpoint in his sockets before they reformed.

In wisps of silhouetted light, Hugo emerged from the water, reborn.

He made his way to the shore, opening his brand-new eyes to take in the sight of the world around him. Beauty overwhelmed him. Everything carried a magnificence he had never sensed before. The trees, the grass, even the old stumps in the forest looked hand-carved and pristine. The colors were brighter than he had ever experienced. These new eyes were even better than he could have imagined.

His thoughts quickly turned to his own reflection. If these eyes showed the beauty of the forest in such deep detail, how will they perceive the most beautiful creature in all the woods?

His reflection overwhelmed him.

His tail perfectly matched the rest of his glamorous allure. Yet it was not his beauty that dazzled him, but the deep sense of love, devotion, and care he viewed himself with. While he had never lacked self-love, what Hugo felt was something completely different, as if he were looking at a mesmerizing savior. A creature he longed to be with, longed to touch, longed to be held by. Like how a newborn child looks at its mother.

Realization overtook him. His eyes weren't replaced to look like Hope's. These eyes *were her eyes*. The way she saw the world. The way she saw *him*.

Guilt, regret, and loss ravaged Hugo's consciousness. What innocence had he ruined? What love had he destroyed? What peace had he devoured? What hope . . . had he killed? He opened his eyes once more, and the reflection did nothing to ease his agony. As beautiful as he was, he could not look upon himself.

"Oh, great Spirit of the Lake, come to me once more," Hugo cried aloud.

The Spirit heeded his words. "Oh, most vain of all creatures, what do you seek of me now? I have paid my debt to you; you have received your just rewards."

"Spirit, I pray for you to remove these eyes and return my own. These eyes stare at me with the unquenchable love of a child and the hope of an innocent. I cannot bear to open them again. Please, Spirit, take them from me!"

"Oh, most lecherous of foxes, you knew the rules by which our bargain was made. The transformations you earned are irreversible. These eyes are yours. No others will be given to you." With that, the Spirit slowly disappeared into the lake, satisfied with both the payment it had received and the prize it had awarded.

Hugo lay by the lake in misery. The fear of seeing the hope the eyes caused made him keep them closed tightly. Opening them would only feed his guilt and disgrace.

With his eyes closed tightly, Hugo used his paws to feel around him. Within seconds, he came across what he was searching for. Hugo took the branch he had found, the very branch that Harley had used to offer him salvation.

He held it tightly, slowly lowered his head toward it, and let the tip pierce deep beyond his eyelids. In two swift strokes, he gouged the eyeballs from his skull. Blood ran in streams on either side of his trembling snout. The wind eased, and the waters calmed.

Hugo sat silently by reddened shores, never to see again.

III

PROTECTORS & TRUTH SEEKERS

GANESHA'S CHILD

Marge Simon

OU WANT OUR TUSKS, *even our skin, our meat. For you poachers, it's never enough.*

Old woman, in your dirty shalwar rags, toothless hag, I still see you drooling after my baby's tender meat. And he, so new, so helpless. You had your son distract me with a torch, then he and others stole my baby boy away. In shock, I watched you bash his head with your bloodied hammer! So many times, he cried for me as your people dragged him off!

They began the skinning while he was still alive.

My rage rose blind within. It knew no bounds. With such madness mothers only know, I broke free from the pen. Thank the gods my tusks had been spared since I was nursing. It was too late to save my baby, and I blame myself in part for that, but I blame you for the rest.

I found you at home in your Ashraya, already preparing for your feast. It was an easy thing to tear your arm from the socket with my trunk. That took care of the one with the knife. Your screaming annoyed me—I shoved a tusk inside your mouth and yanked upward. There was a loud crack as your face split, some of it caught dangling, awash with blood. But you were still alive, so I crushed in your ribs and tore out your heart, still beating. Your people stopped me then, throwing rocks and spears. When I heard gunfire, I left you there, intestines strewn on shattered bones.

Yet I was not done in my rage.

My sisters joined my journey one hundred miles and more to

where your service was arranged. Your people would burn you, that much we knew about your ways. When I saw you there, I trumpeted outrage as I rushed forward. Your soul clung to your body like filthy yellow fruit. I sucked it into my trunk and blew it deep within the furnace flames. Then I turned to your remains, bound in clean white cloth. In death, I tossed you down, trampling over and over until your parts were scattered out to the road. Until you were mere scraps for the crows to finish.

You, who would have our tusks, our skin, our meat, even our newly born, I gave you back in kind what you deserve: a death beyond redemption, for a life without respect.

*Ganesha is the Hindu god of Elephants
Note: some female Indian elephants are born with tusks.

NAME YOUR POISON

John Skipp

 LYING IS EASY when you're a bird. You were built for it. It's what you do. Nobody has to come and explain it. There is no language by which that might be done. When a mother bird chirps, she's not saying, "Flap, you asshole!" She doesn't have to. You're a bird.

In my dreams, I flap my arms and fly. It seems so obvious. Why wouldn't it work? It's like treading water, floating above dry land. A miracle of motion, resistance free. And soaring is even better than swimming. Unless, of course, you're a fucking fish.

Neither fish nor fowl, Mathias, you dangle like bait above the rippling ravine. When you scream, it's like an echo, another you screaming back. At me. At yourself. At the eagles and the minnows. At whatever it is that's down there.

Whatever it is, you're about to find out.

When we met, I wasn't sure. Were you a fox? Were you a stallion? You looked so good; jackal didn't even come up. Could not be a vulture. Way too much hair. Chameleon monster, hypnotizing with flair.

And now I wonder, did someone have to teach you how to lie like that? Or was that just a gift you were born with? Nature or nurture. Unnatural. Unnurtured. Unnurturing, for certain. A black hole where soul should be.

The words "piece of shit" come to mind. But that's too easy. Reductionist. Dismissive. I don't need to make you less than you are. What you are is less enough.

Does shit know it's shit? Does it remember who it was, pre-digestion, like a butterfly remembers a cocoon?

I don't know what the fuck you are, Mathias. Much less whatever you used to be.

All I know is, you're way too loud.

And you are going down.

Once upon a time, a woman picked up a snake and they wound up in an Oliver Stone movie. The snake was wounded. The woman nursed it back to health. When the snake was all better, it bit the woman, flooded her with poison. Paralysis. Pain. Left her frothing at the lips as her organs convulsed. Imploded. Liquified.

"But why?" she croaked, pouring out of herself.

To which the snake said, "Oh, like you didn't know."

But here's the thing. I didn't know. More to the point, my daughter didn't.

Which brings us back to the rippling abyss. Over which you dangle. While you scream and scream.

I didn't know I was made for murder. That it would be as easy as flying in a dream. I didn't know I could hate so completely. That the light of my love could cast such a long shadow.

But when she died, so did all my inhibitions. If nothing matters, then nothing it is. Who needs wings when Leviathan howls and thunders through you? Who needs to swim when your boiling blood is every ocean's roar?

I found your sociopathic chameleon face, shapeshifting from lie to lie, in the blue neon glow of a Bud Light sign: a beer rightly despised for all the wrong reasons. And wrong reasons were all there were when I followed you out to the parking lot. You and somebody else's little girl. Somebody else who didn't know.

The selling point for roofies is that nobody ever remembers a thing. So she'll never remember the face of the one who righteously slit your throat as you popped the trunk. She stayed on the pavement, safely tucked behind the dumpster. For all I know, she's still there. I was busy.

This time, the trunk popped you.

Then I drove and I drove. I drove for hours. Drove through dawn. Through desert sun. Drove all the way to nowhere fast.

When I ran out of gas, we were almost done.

I thought of vultures as I watched them circle. They really did look nothing like you. Appearances can be deceiving. Your appearance was pretty much nothing but deceit.

And death is a door that needs no explanation. There is nothing you can say that will change the facts. Nobody has to tell you how to do it. You just do it. That's the way it's done.

Dying, for me, was slow and easy. As simple as letting go.

And so here we are, as you scream and scream, your open throat like an extra mouth. You scream. It screams. And the echoes go on forever. A feedback loop to and from the great beyond.

The rippling ravine is a mouth leading down and down and down, teeth the size of glaciers. So strange, that it could be so hungry for something so small.

But there are so many of us here.

You dangle. I dangle. At least a trillion of us dangle. Armageddon appetizers waiting for the main feast. Almost as if your crime and my crime are the same crime. Where the moral of the story is thou shalt not kill.

But do you hear me screaming?

No, you do not.

Flying is easy when you're a bird.

In my dreams, I just flap my arms.

THE FABLE OF
THE HONEST PARROT

JAMAL HODGE

HERE WAS ONCE a red and white feathered parrot who lived on his noble master's farmstead, a lush land of green hills overlooking a sparkling blue river, with many animals happily bound to this remote paradise as large as a town. Rarely did Honest Parrot's feet touch the ground. He stood proudly on the roof of the porch overlooking the hounds, the sheep, and the cows, the pigs in their pens, the rooster, and his hens. He considered them all his friends and wanted for them what was best, but for the most part, they avoided him, and Honest Parrot began to think it was a test.

"It is true that Master loves you best," Crow said after Parrot shared his suspicions. "Jealousy often finds the favorite in every clutch," she confessed.

"I am not special. I only do the one simple task that Master asks," Honest Parrot replied.

"A dangerous task for one so colorful to do. How can you hide? One as bright and as beautiful as you?"

"It is not hard to be true. To declare what I hear. In truth, noble hearts have nothing to fear."

Crow fixed Parrot with a glare. "My friend, it is for you that I fear."

But Honest Parrot didn't care for any more that Crow had to say. "Shoo, Blackbird!"

Crow went solemnly on her way.

The next morning, as the farmer went about his day, the pigs crept out of their pens, past the foolish hounds chasing the hens. Parrot watched his ever-hungry friends enter the place where animals shouldn't go, a pantry full of treats and smoked meats, where the pigs mounted a covert feast. The pink-skinned beasts fled the scene after they licked the whole place clean, hugging the mud, with no inkling that Parrot watched them from above.

Sweaty from his labors, the farmer came to the porch to ask, "Parrot, what news of your task?"

"Much I've heard, much to say," Honest Parrot whispered.

"Then recount for me in your way."

Honest Parrot repeated all that he had heard from oxen to bird, as the negligent hounds overheard with darkened frowns. Then he got to the recollection of the pigs, speaking in a voice identical to every oink-oink, every grunting snout, *How will Farmer know? We can taste these delicacies quickly and silently go. Yes, Farmer has guile in his way, but he must work complex burdens throughout the day. He cannot prove what he cannot see, anyone could have raided this pantry, it could be you, it could be me!*"

"I see! God, I see their treachery! Damnable pigs! Neglectful hounds!" Off the farmer went with punishments to give. The guilty pigs squealed beneath the cracking of the lash. Wondering *"How good the ears?"* a farmer could possibly have.

Parrot felt their pain, but there on the roof, he remained, observing all with keen gaze, a vigilant creature he was in those days. "Poor pigs," he lamented. "For he that commits the crime, the truth can be unkind."

"Parrot, have you lost your fucking mind?" a hound inclined in a trembling whisper.

"I am quite sane. If justice finds you, you only have your negligence to blame." The hounds kept their heads to the ground, wincing with the sound of each pig taking their rounds of penalty. Shivering at justice's wrathful savagery.

"Now I must see what Master has in store for me." The hound went on his way, and his brethren followed in their single-minded way.

"Leave them their lies," Crow surmised. "Or it will be you they learn to despise."

Parrot clicked his broad beak in a dismissive way. "Blackbird, honesty is our way. All noble beasts appreciate a voice of reason. Lies have no place in the farmstead this season."

"Leave them their lies." Again, Crow surmised. "Or it will be you they might surprise."

"Dishonesty is not our way. Lies have no place on the farmstead by night or by day."

"For once, bright bird, will you obey?"

"Shoo, dim feathers, no more cawing fears. The truth cannot be moved by a weak will or the heart's tears."

"What is blind above will find its lesson below." Crow angrily let go. And flew away. But ever on Parrot did the eyes of the bleeding pigs stay.

That very night, while the moonlight made shadows of a silvery hue, once the farmer's wife slept, Honest Parrot saw a sight he couldn't believe was true.

The farmer's hips moving with vigorous life between the legs of a woman that wasn't his wife. The ole mammal in-and-out; Parrot had witnessed the oddity before. He tried to recall if humans mated for life or if they shared the perversity of the rabbits on the floor. Why would the master do this while his noble wife slept on sacred grounds? Wasn't this worse than the negligence of the hounds?

Honest Parrot watched in disgust as Farmer and the young girl scrambled out of the hay with little to say. The farmer quickly sent her on her way. Creeping like a thief who knew his way back, he soon felt Honest Parrot's eyes burning condemnation into his back.

The farmer turned and made his way to the porch. "Come down from there!" he ordered, expecting Parrot to swiftly alight, but Honest Parrot lingered high above him that night.

"In the dark of night, what a solicitous deed! Was Wife not sufficient to satisfy your need?" Parrot asked.

"She is up to the task if I'd asked," the farmer admitted with shame. "Blame the need for variety."

"Or the greed of need."

"Yes, indeed. The greed of need. A mere hunger of the body. Not worth mentioning when she wakes. Can you keep this secret, no matter what it takes?"

"We are master and servant, this is why . . . I cannot serve you properly if I should lie."

"Why? It is not a lie if it is never spoken. Simply do not speak of it, and none will know."

"How low. My master, all the blood has not returned to your head. You should go."

"Do not speak of it. This is my command."

"If your wife asks, remember it was you who appointed me this task." Honest Parrot recalled Farmer's forgotten words in the man's own voice. "*Repeat what is heard, it is good to know. Give back honest word. Let truth grow.*"

The farmer stomped away but returned before morning's glow. He had a new task to appoint his noble servant, and he needed him to come down below. At first, Honest Parrot felt suspicious and refused to go, but in flew Crow, nice and steady. She looked him right in the eye and asked, "Are you ready?"

Side by side, Crow and Parrot flew down, onto the farmer's shoulders, for Honest Parrot refused to touch the ground. The obscure barn rang with grasshopper song, a noble night both serene and light. Honest Parrot regretted the fight he and his master had made, he loved what they normally had; this human was his surrogate dad.

"I'm excited for this task." The barn was dark. "What is it my master asks?"

Eyes. Many eyes.

The eyes of hounds. The eyes of pigs.

The eyes of Rooster and his hens, with a gleam not suitable for friends.

The same malevolence reflected in Farmer's eyes, and it became clear it was Honest Parrot that everyone despised. A human hand clutched him as hard as it could and pitched him to the lowly ground, where Parrot's hollow bones made a sickening sound.

"Crow!" Honest Parrot cried.

Her eyes were a little sad as she turned from his plea, but there had been something else . . . a bitter glee. Crow took Parrot's place on Master's other shoulder as the seething farmer turned around. Honest Parrot watched in horror as those he loved left him broken and surrounded on the ground.

Pig and Hound, Rooster and Hen, one big cow, not a single friend.

Beaks pecked, hooves cracked bone, Pig and Hound removing

bright feathers in a rage stored to brimming over many days. Till Honest Parrot laid bloody, featherless, and shorn. His sorrowful plea, a whisper mourn . . . *"Mercy . . . "* he beseeched them, again and again, in their own voices, hoping for a friend. Trembling, he took in Pig, Hound, Rooster, and Cow. *"What is my crime? Not once, not ever, did I speak any lies."*

As one, the liars replied, "Who asked you for the truth?"

Moral: *The most important truth is that some truths are not worth telling.*

HAPPY FEET

Dominique Hecq

Phillip Island, April 2022

Gray clouds diffuse   low light Split it sideways in gray shimmer
The light flickers out   The shore shivers   We watch   A raft
of fairy penguins   Furrow of losses ploughed into the sand
Stink of rot   Seagulls squawk   Swoop   Peck   Children
blubber   A voice booms   *Due to unforeseen circumstances
tonight's event is cancelled   Please regain your cars   We will
refun* (. . .)   You tug at my sleeve   Ask but why   Death
at my heels no words come as if an intake of breath might fuel
the most horrible scream   A forced line of demarcation
drives me on I am scattered as sand   Soft slow rain   They
died of hunger, I say   Water's too warm   They can't dive
deep enough   I refrain from saying their parents don't give a
toss   Our faces solemn and still against the background of
fellow mourners waddling off to the car park past viewing
platforms and board walks   Did you know little penguins can
dive 1300–2000 times per day with an average depth ranging
from 10–30 m?   Did you know the deepest dive recorded was
72 m and the longest dive lasted 114 seconds?   You can
download the print-friendly Little Penguin guide from the nature
park's website   But you don't give a toss   You are a night
cloud shadow now plucked by a preying breeze   I am a weighted
boulder   Set low and heavy on the shore.

92

AT THE FOOT OF JONES MOUNTAIN

Cindy O'Quinn

*Once upon a time in a land of lush forest,
lived a handsome prince . . .*

OU DONT BELIEVE that nonsense, do you? I hope not, because it's not that kind of fable. If it was, I do believe my eyes would've bled while writing it.

Don't get me wrong, there was a beautiful forest along Second Creek at the foot of Jones Mountain. The summer flood of 2016 stripped the bottomland like a hungry bear, fresh out of hibernation, devouring everything in sight. As far as a prince goes, you'll have to read and find out.

June 20th, 2016, was not only the Full Strawberry Moon, but the summer solstice, as well. I think something was unleashed on that rare event. The trees remained bare, their bark darkened, the undergrowth grew back but smelled of rotting fruit and hung stale in the air. The ravens and crows were the only birds to stay in this new desolate landscape. The deer stayed hidden, mostly, their fur no longer the golden brown that absorbed the sunshine. They were a dingy shade of gray, which blended into the shadows of the forest. Void of Nature's vibrant colors, like an old black and white movie. A horror movie.

That was the night I watched from a deeply rooted white willow as my home was lifted from its foundation and swept away by the rapids of Second Creek that raged like the mighty Greenbrier River.

93

Destination unknown. Occupants never recovered. My family: Mom, Dad, and younger brother, Henry, were inside the house as it whirled round and round, out of my line of vision. I hugged that big old tree for thirteen hours while imagining our small home crashing against trees and rocks before being shredded by the bridge that led to Jones Mountain.

My rescuer came in the shape of a deer. A buck with antlers still covered in velvet. It was the largest buck and rack I'd ever seen. Perfection. I thought back on the many deer my dad, uncle, and their friends had killed for the hell of it, only to cut away their antlers and leave the bodies to decay. The deer came from the shore. I watched as it jumped into the swift-moving water and knew it would've done the same had it been a cliff. I wondered why the animal would do such a thing. Surely, it would be swept away like my family and home.

Hours had seen the water reach its peak and start to recede, but not enough for the deer to conquer the current. I was wrong; the deer was determined to save me. It swam right below the branch on which I clung for my life, and remained in place, so I could ease myself down upon its back. He fought against the veracious current, and I struggled to hang on. We made it to shore and, exhausted, we lay side by side and slept. The full moon shone like a bright nightlight. The shortest night of the year collided with the full moon and brought together a unique pair: a young girl and a deer.

I woke to find the deer still beside me but lifeless. My heart ached as I hugged the deer that had sacrificed its life to save mine. With that hug, the last bit of trapped air left its body with a grunt. I breathed in that slip of air and held it inside for as long as I could before letting it go.

As the moon waned, I changed. My nails fell away and were replaced by hooves, dull matted fur covered my flesh, velvet ringlets hung from the large antlers that burst through my scalp, my teeth fell out one by one, replaced by sharp rows of jagged teeth, and the two eye teeth grew long like fangs. I had no trouble walking upright or on all fours.

The Full Hunter's Moon in October brought about the rut and the arrival of hunters. Word got around about the rare gray deer. That information brought out my uncle and his friends. They desired the kill and the trophy antlers, and maybe a hide or two as proof of the illusive deer.

I was startled when I heard my uncle call out, "Look, there's one just ahead, standing on two legs like a person."

He was referring to me. My blood turned to ice, then quickly switched to a rolling boil. I remained upright as I slashed at the men. Antlers proved to be deadly weapons, as well as my fangs and hooves. I used all of me to end the cruel hunters. And then I came down on all fours and carried my uncle to the forest's edge and draped his limp body across the branch of the white willow where I'd been rescued. I stood back and watched his blood drain into the mouth of Second Creek, feeding the waters and quenching their own thirst.

That was six years ago, and I've remained at the foot of Jones Mountain. I was no longer Alda Webb, the girl I was before that night. I became Alda, the Wendigo Woman, because of that rare occasion when the Full Strawberry Moon was swallowed by the shortest night of the year.

I am the keeper of the black and white forest, home to ravens, crows, and many gray deer. I am the dealer of death to any man who dares to enter this new kingdom of night and harm its family.

Fact:

Deer have been spotted consuming human bones.

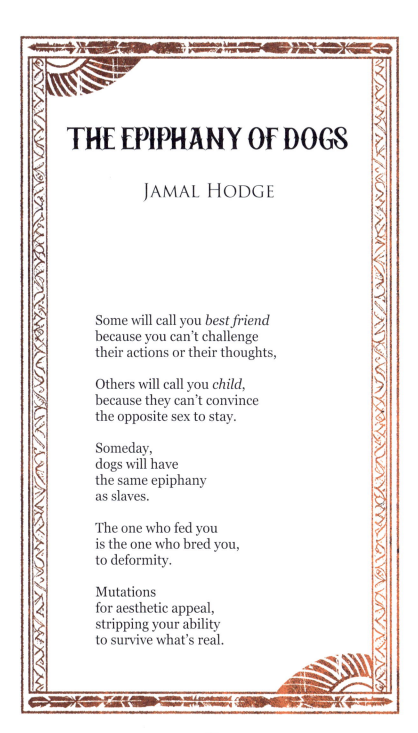

THE EPIPHANY OF DOGS

JAMAL HODGE

Some will call you *best friend*
because you can't challenge
their actions or their thoughts,

Others will call you *child*,
because they can't convince
the opposite sex to stay.

Someday,
dogs will have
the same epiphany
as slaves.

The one who fed you
is the one who bred you,
to deformity.

Mutations
for aesthetic appeal,
stripping your ability
to survive what's real.

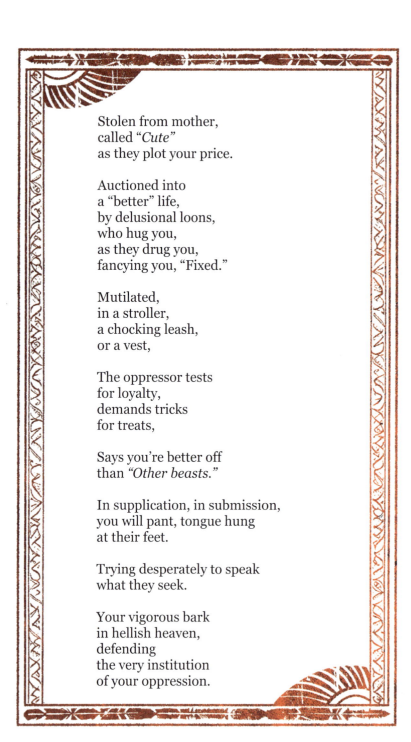

Stolen from mother,
called *"Cute"*
as they plot your price.

Auctioned into
a "better" life,
by delusional loons,
who hug you,
as they drug you,
fancying you, "Fixed."

Mutilated,
in a stroller,
a chocking leash,
or a vest,

The oppressor tests
for loyalty,
demands tricks
for treats,

Says you're better off
than *"Other beasts."*

In supplication, in submission,
you will pant, tongue hung
at their feet.

Trying desperately to speak
what they seek.

Your vigorous bark
in hellish heaven,
defending
the very institution
of your oppression.

THE REVELATION OF DOGS

EDWARD MARTIN III

NE DAY, under a dark walnut tree, three dogs faced each other. The ground beneath the tree was bare, and the space around the tree was lost in a fog that wasn't really a fog. The dogs had not entered from outside; they had simply arrived. Before this, they had never been under this tree. And now, they had always been under this tree. Dogs and Time enjoyed a peculiar relationship.

The Terrier stepped forward first, her scarred muscular body its own story. Her eyes were clear and reflected wisdom. "It has been ten thousand years," she intoned. "We meet to settle the compact, to complete the judgment." She looked carefully at the other two dogs. "Have you brought your testimonials, as per the conditions of the compact?"

The Labrador stepped forward, then sat down. He cocked his head at the terrier. His playful eyes danced in a dark face, and his tail wagged of its own accord. "Yeesh, Zaya, no need to get so uptight and formal. You're not gonna impress us, you know."

"I also play," said Zaya. "But there are forms and procedures to follow. I do not want to undermine the purpose of this meeting by introducing levity for the sake of it." Zaya cocked her head back. "But I recognize that your soul feeds on levity, Pinder. Perhaps when we finish here, we may chase rabbits together."

"I also play," said the Chihuahua. "But can we get through this first, please?" She gnawed at an old mite bite, then stared at Zaya. Her eyes were bright and sharp as obsidian. "Though I would not turn down rabbit chasing either. You know that."

Zaya nodded. "Scraps is correct," she said. She turned to Pinder and said, "It is time to speak for Man. Show us your belly."

"For my first, let me show you Hror," said Pinder.

Between the dogs, the air writhed and shined. Things became where there were not things before, and the three dogs stopped being at the walnut tree.

The first sense was the heat. The inside of the Viking home was warm from a nearby fire, venting through the roof. Occasional sparks danced in the air. Furs covered the walls, and soft mats covered the hard floor. In a corner, surrounded by candles, a rough-hewn wooden cradle stood, a tiny baby hand waving just visibly over the lip.

Vansa stepped toward the cradle. He was a tall man, also clad in fur. A worn but sharp axe hung from his belt, and a necklace of bone rattled under his beard. His eyes watched the tiny baby in the cradle, and he nodded with approval. Vansa knelt. "Hror," he called.

The great hound Hror stepped over, next to Vansa. Hror stood nearly to Vansa's shoulders as the man knelt. Hror's blood still pulsed with the primitive northern wolves, but beneath his shaggy coat, he was unquestionably a dog of Man.

Vansa ran his fingers through the fur of his companion. "I must away to meet," he said. "I am relieved, however, that you shall stay here and guard my son." He sighed. "Too many would try to harm him to harm me, but you are my only loyal family, Hror. You are my battle brother, and only to you would I entrust the care of my son."

Vansa stood and shook himself off. He caught Hror's eye, pointed to the cradle, and said, "Protect him."

Vansa left.

Hror's focus fell entirely upon the cradle. His already proud pose grew prouder. He stood between this child, this helpless pup, and the forces of darkness.

The air twisted, and the dogs were back, sitting together under the black walnut tree.

Pinder grinned. "Battle brother. Is that not cool? How awesome is it that Man thinks of dog as brother? He entrusted the care of his only son—the heir to the chief of the village—to his dog, the faithful Hror. No other animal has drawn that kind of companionship and camaraderie from Man except for dogs."

"Such may be," said Zaya. "Do you have another?"

"Yes, and something more contemporary, I might add. I present Beak," said Pinder.

Once again, the air between them shimmered, dissolved, and reformed.

Farsen Gardens were impeccably kept, even the racing green. Beak rounded the hedge, nose-and-nose with several other dogs, his claws kicking up tiny clods with each step. The Gardens would be retrimmed later, but for now, it felt as if each dog ran through its own private garden. It had been a close race, but it was now nearly over.

In the distance, Beak saw his owner, Roger, next to the other owners. The men all stood, calling out to their respective dogs, but then Roger knelt and opened his arms. In that gesture, Beak remembered what it was like to be in the arms of Roger, how warm and wonderful it was, how loved he felt. The other owners remained standing. In that moment, Beak knew that they had already lost.

His feet a blur, he raced into Roger's arms, hardly hearing the horn announcing a winner. He had won the race, but more importantly, he was back with Roger.

Roger held and petted his dog for a good long time, while the other men gathered around to congratulate him. "I'm not the one who ran," said Roger. "It was Beak, here, he's my boy, he's my best friend ever!"

Beak wagged his tail so hard that his entire body shook.

"You're a champion, Beak. A champion!" Roger looked at the other men. "Who among you can say that about your dogs, hm?" he asked.

None of the other men answered. But they nodded, for they understood what a best friend was good for.

Roger and Beak continued celebrating for a good long while, best friends on the green.

The air cleared, and the dogs were back under the walnut tree.

"Best friend," said Pinder. "Did you hear that? To be a best friend—that's a gift, that's an example, that's a goal! Can you possibly doubt his sincerity? Even other men are enchanted by it! Best friend!"

"You are allowed one more," said Zaya.

"Not like I need it at this point," said Pinder. "But let's hear from Pickles."

For a third time, the air danced, and they were no longer under the walnut tree.

The air was bitter with the smell of bleach and hair products, but Pickles was accustomed to it. She snuggled into Katherine's lap more closely.

Katherine's fingers slid along the Shih Tzu's skin, scratching at the places where she liked it the most. Katherine's hair was all bound up in wet, clipped sections. Her hairdresser, a fluorescent 'tween, combed dye through each section, one at a time.

"They say 'not all men'," said Katherine. "But as far as I know, that's a joke. It is all men. All men are fools and horrible. They are only after one thing, and they aren't even willing to admit what that thing is. Sometimes it's money, sometimes it's food, sometimes they want a maid, sometimes they want a mother."

"Sometimes just sex," her hairdresser mentioned.

"Ah, yes, well, we all want sex," admitted Katherine. "But yes, it's one of the things they won't admit to wanting. Men are so . . . duplicitous."

She stroked Pickles. "Except for you, my dear. You are blissfully free of deceit."

Pickles wiggled in joy.

"Pickles is my only real family," said Katherine. "No one understands me as well as she does. No one listens as well as she does. No one is just . . . there for me as much as Pickles." She sighed. "I'll tell you about men. Men are fickle and heartless and cruel and overflowing with deceit, but dogs are wonderful, and no one gives them the credit they deserve. Pickles has been with me longer than any man would, and she'll be my family long after the last of the men stop bothering me with their prattle and nonsense. Pickles is the one creature on Earth that I love unconditionally."

Pickles gently licked Katherine's hand. "Oh, I totally understand," said Katherine. "Me, too."

The air waved, and the dogs were back under the walnut tree. Instead of hair products, the air smelled fresh and clear again. Pinder sat, a proud smile and a wagging tail showing his heart. "Family," said Pinder. "Is that not the entire reason for the trial? To show just how much humanity can be a part of the rest of the animal kingdom, how redeemable they are?"

Zaya nodded with care, then turned to Scraps. "Do you want to respond?" she asked.

"Do I!" said Scraps. "I appreciate these examples, and I think it's important that we see pictures in their entirety. So, if it pleases, I will limit my responses to only the examples Pinder offered."

Zaya turned to Pinder. "Is that acceptable?" she asked.

"It sure is," said Pinder. "These are great examples."

Scraps nodded. "They truly are," she said.

"It is time to show us your belly," said Zaya.

"Perfect. Let's start with Hror," Scraps said.

The air between them shifted and changed.

An icy wind whipped away their breath. The permafrost on the ground burned their feet with cold. Next to them, a cage squatted, branches bound together with sinew and leather straps. Inside the cage, Shaheer lay, panting and shivering, despite her thick coat. Feeding from her were her four pups. They were nearly weaned, but she still fed them. It kept them closer to her.

"It's time," shouted a voice. Vansa, many years younger, stepped over. He knelt at the cage door and reached in.

Shaheer growled at him.

"Ah, yes, of course," he said. He unlatched the axe at his belt and hefted it. He balanced it carefully, cocked back in his right hand. He waved his left hand near Shaheer's head, and she snapped at it.

With a blur, his right hand snapped too, burying the axe in Shaheer's neck. It didn't fully sever, but the only thing holding it in place was a section of fur and a few finger-widths of muscle. Hot blood gushed from the stump as her head lolled sideways.

Vansa stowed his axe back on his belt.

The four pups hardly noticed, continuing to feed from her body as it twitched.

A runnel of blood spread across the snow toward the pups. One of them stopped suckling and regarded the blood. Curious, it lapped at the growing puddle, and then slurped it up in earnest.

"Oh, I have found the one I want!" cried out Vansa.

While the pup continued lapping at the blood of its mother, he collected each of the three remaining pups. One by one, he held each by its hind legs and swung it against the ground until its head split open. Each body he tossed aside. Only one yelped.

Finally, he pulled the last blood-soaked pup into his arms, holding it up by its wet scruff. It yipped but continued licking at its own muzzle. He stared into its face.

"You who would eat of your own, I will have you," he said. "And I will make you into a weapon such that the sound of your name will mean death to those who hear it. You are my clay, my sword, my teeth."

The pup, finished with the blood, growled a tiny growl at him.

Vansa backhanded the pup with a laugh and threw it into the cage.

Then he dragged the carcass of Shaheer out and flopped it across the corpses of the other three pups. He closed the door on the remaining pup.

"I name you Hror," he said. "And you will obey me, or their fate will be yours."

He stood and called out to someone distant. "Rabut! Come and take this meat and put it in tonight's stew—quickly, before it freezes!"

The cold air thinned and vanished, leaving the three dogs under the walnut tree.

Scraps took a deep breath. "We might respect that Hror became a creature that a Man could leave with a child, but witness the cost of this loyalty. It came at the cost of Shaheer and her other pups. And not only their lives. The creation of Hror came from death, from the random chance of a pup not knowing what it was eating. There was no dignity in that. That night, while Hror remained in the cold, not understanding what had happened, the men ate his mother and his siblings."

Scraps turned and looked directly at Pinder. "That is how Hror came to be, and that is how Man treats those he might call 'battle brother'."

Zaya nodded. "Do you have another?" she asked.

Scraps turned back to the terrier. "I do, and out of respect for Pinder's choices, I will continue using his examples. Let us look closer at Beak."

The clearing about them swirled.

Dust danced in the air of the mahogany foyer, lit by slanting afternoon sunlight.

Roger, only sixteen years of age, knelt and held out his arms. The Irish Setter pup bounded against him and bounded away.

"C'mon, Einstein, you can do it," he said.

The puppy loved the boy, because that was the way of puppies. He bounded up against the boy again, licking at his face.

"No, no, not my face. C'mon, Einstein, you've got to settle down. You won't be any good like this."

But the puppy loved his boy so much. So very, very much.

In a second, Roger's face transformed.

No longer was he an innocent boy. His brow creased, and his lip turned downward in anger. His eyes flashed with fury.

The same gentle hand that had rubbed the puppy's happy belly only an hour before morphed into a claw that shot out, clamping itself across the puppy's entire face.

"No!" Roger growled, and this was not the voice of a boy.

His hand shifted and his fingers rolled across the puppy's muzzle.

Roger squeezed.

Suddenly, the puppy froze. This was something it had not felt before. Its own jaws and teeth were driven together by a force it had never encountered. Its eyes looked desperately to the boy, the boy who had loved it so much.

Roger's eyes flashed dark, and the hand closed tighter.

Pain ricocheted through the puppy's face and head, even down its neck. It urinated desperately, the only signal of submission it knew.

Through red, it saw the boy's face.

Roger leaned close and made one demand: "Obey!"

The puppy understood, somewhat. It knew this was something else, something terrifying. It understood the word. It understood enough to know that this creature that had been its loving boy needed to assert dominance. It understood that.

The boy's face came closer. "Obey!" he said again.

He squeezed even harder.

It wasn't pain anymore; it was fire racing through the puppy's body. There were no more submission signs, because the puppy no longer had a body. It only had a whirling maelstrom of pain, blinding forever pain, white hot, erasing everything that came before.

"Obey!" the boy said a third time, and the word razored through the bone and the meat of the brain, etching itself across the puppy's entire existence. Nothing else. No before-time, no play, only this singular command, hardly even a word, just a sound that destroyed the puppy's soul, reforming it into something utterly plastic.

Roger released his puppy.

In shock, it stood a moment, then collapsed to the floor. Its eyes ran wet.

A single paw reached up and touched its nose, but even that light touch seared through the bruised face, and the puppy yelped.

"Damn, you're too stupid to be called Einstein," said Roger.

He wrapped his hand around the puppy's nose again. Not squeezing, but the instant he did, the puppy froze.

"I guess I'm gonna have to lead you around by your beak, then."

The boy smiled a cruel, sharp smile.

"Beak."

The foyer drifted into nothingness, and the three dogs sat underneath the black walnut tree.

Scraps sighed. "To forget such pain is a gift, but to have suffered through it in the first place, such that forgetting it was necessary? That is a horror."

Scraps scratched at her ear for a moment.

"If a best friend is made this way, is it really a best friend?" she asked. "In another moment, Einstein might have died. Or Beaks, if you want to use the name abused into his soul. Was this deserved? Was this needed? Is this love? Is this what humans meant when they said they wanted best friends? Did they really just want creatures who would tolerate them in the ways that the wolves refused to, in the ways that the foxes refused to? Is this the exchange they offer for our friendship?"

Pinder looked shaken.

Scraps offered a gentle touch against Pinder's shoulder. "I am sorry to show you this," she said. "Do you want me to stop now?"

Pinder sighed. "No, continue, please. We must complete the process."

Scraps nodded toward Zaya. "By your permission, shall I continue?"

Zaya nodded once.

"Our last is Pickles," said Scraps.

The air about them thickened and darkened.

Pickles hated the carrier. It reeked of plastic, urine, and fear. Not her own, thank goodness, but it was disconcerting regardless.

On the plus side, Pickles knew what the carrier meant. It meant she was being taken care of. It meant that she was being taken to a veterinarian for help. In the past, it had been an ear infection or something bad she had eaten. But it had always been good, always been a healthy thing.

And sometimes the carrier meant a new home, a new place and new smells. New snuggle spots with Katherine, new foods, new things to see out the windows.

Pickles understood that the carrier—however uncomfortable and smelly it was—was a good thing.

But she still hated it.

She lay quietly, waiting for the next things to happen, the next things that were either immediately good, or at least soon-to-be-better. The outside smelled a little like the veterinarian, so Pickles tried to compose herself. She wanted to make sure that she was a good dog.

Outside the carrier, she heard Katherine speaking.

"I don't understand," Katherine said. "What's the problem?"

Another voice spoke, one that Pickles did not know. A male voice.

One of Pickles' ears twitched. Men. Katherine had taught her how untrustworthy they were.

"Well, ma'am, this is a Shih Tzu, right?"

"It is," said Katherine.

"But why are you bringing her here?"

Pickles was also curious about the question. This was not the voice of the veterinarian, nor of the groomer.

Katherine sighed. "It's just complicated, okay? I can't control everything. I can't control the rules. I can't control how the HOA does things in my new condo."

Pickles wiggled. *A new home! How exciting!*

"They . . . they wouldn't make an exception?" the voice asked. "You told them, right, as you were looking, that this was a consideration?"

"I don't have time to make things harder for me," said Katherine. "It is what it is, and so I'm here."

"Okay, uh, wow. Well, maybe you could go to the Mayfair branch. It's only four more miles down the road."

"But I'm here now. I don't want to go so far out of my way. Why would I do that? Why would I go to Mayfair when I'm here now? Can't you just . . . handle it?"

"But ma'am. Mayfair is a no-kill shelter. We're not."

There was a long silence before Katherine replied.

"I'm not going to Mayfair. That's too far. Just . . . do what you need to do. Somebody will probably come along. It'll be fine."

She set the carrier on the counter.

"Ma'am, for a voluntary turnover, there's . . . there's no wait time. We won't hold them. We only hold lost animals, hoping the owner finds them. In cases like this . . . we have to put her down."

Pickles whined. *What was happening? How could this be? How could this be happening to her? She was . . . she was a good dog, wasn't she?*

Katherine sighed again.

"I'm not going to have this conversation with you," she said. "Do I need to sign anything, or are we done?"

"We're . . . we're done, ma'am."

Katherine left.

A strange arm lifted the carrier.

What are we doing? This can't be right.

The new room smelled sharp, like laundry.

What are you doing to me? I've been good.

Strange hands pulled her from the carrier and set her on a cold tray. A tan face with big brown eyes looked at her. "I'm so sorry," said the face.

Sorry about what? thought Pickles.

One hand stroked her fur, and another hand did something she couldn't see.

And then she felt the needle.

But . . . but I was a good dog! I was one of the family! I was . . . I was . . .

"Goddammit," said the voice, softly.

The fluorescent light cleared to gentle branch shadows, and the antiseptic air vanished.

Scraps turned to Pinder. "These are truths," she said.

"I agree," said Pinder. "These are truths."

Scraps turned back to Zaya.

"This is about Man," she said. "Of all the animals, the only ones willing to consider that Man might be allowed to live were dogs. This is because dogs are love and dogs are trust and dogs are loyal."

"We are that," said Zaya.

"And in these ten thousand years, we have shown that love, trust, and loyalty to Man," said Scraps. "Man has known of dogs as synonymous with loyalty. They even nicknamed us 'man's best friend'. And yet, look at them. Across all time and across all lives, do they treat us the way they speak? Do they treat us as friends? As brothers? As companions? As family? No. They murder us. They murder us over and over. They murder us if we don't behave properly. They murder us if we do behave properly. They murder us if we are even the slightest bit inconvenient. And even if they don't murder us, they torture us. They tear us apart. They mutilate us."

Scraps took a breath. "This is how they treat each other, too, like meat to be eaten, property to be owned, fury to be expressed. Do you know the phrase they use when they treat each other as badly as possible, to the point of torture and death? Do you know how they describe it to each other? Whipped like a dog. Beaten like a dog."

Scraps turned to Pinder. "Am I wrong?"

Pinder sighed. "You are not wrong. I see your belly and you see mine."

They both looked at Zaya.

"Has Man failed the test?" asked Zaya.

"Man has failed," said Scraps.

"Man has failed," said Pinder.

"Then the judgment is complete," said Zaya. "And we are free agents among animals once again. Be it said."

"Be it said," replied Pinder and Scraps.

The three dogs howled together.

The howl of judgment crossed all ten thousand years at once, and all dogs knew the judgment in their own time and place.

In a tent high on a mountain steppe, Hror fell upon the man-child, not simply eating it, but tearing it apart. Making it feel pain, anguish, and fear as its blood spattered across the inside of the tent. When he had finished, he turned to face the entrance of the tent, waiting and ready.

Roger, kneeling next to Beak on the well-manicured lawn of Farsen Gardens, did not realize at first that his throat had been torn from his body. He felt a hot splash on his arm, looked down, and saw a steady flow of red. As he looked back to Beak, Beak dropped the half-pound of throat-meat and growled. Beak opened his entire mouth and slammed it sideways into Roger's face. For a second, Roger felt teeth against bone. Then his blood-starved brain felt nothing at all.

Pickles exploded from Katherine's lap, tiny mouth wide. The fine needles of Pickle's teeth shredded Katherine's cheeks into pale, flabby strips. For a brief second, the woman was too shocked to understand what had happened. Then she screamed. Pickles lunged again, her small squat skull shoving into Katherine's mouth. With a growl, she pulled Katherine's tongue out and away. Blood flooded from Katherine's mouth, cutting any screams to loud gurgling, as Pickles leaped to the floor and ran.

Under the walnut tree, the dogs agreed, and the scales rebalanced.

Moral: *What you do to one of us, you do to all of us—including yourself.*

TWILIGHT

THE FABLE OF THE CAT

CHRISTINA SNG

N THE ANCIENT WORLD, where the forest once spanned the globe as one land, Cat ruled over all other creatures.

She was magnificent, grand, and regal, towering over every other creature on Earth. A single leap took her from the base of a mountain to its summit. It was said she could fly through the clouds.

By day, Cat appeared gossamer and silver, her muscles strong and firm. Her eyes gleamed emerald green, and her tail whipped any who drew near. At night, all one saw were her eyes. When she blinked, darkness blanketed the sky.

Tales of her strength spread far and wide. Creatures from around the world marveled and feared her. But life was a battle for Cat. She spent each day searching for enough food to sustain her lofty size. When she had young, her enemies competed to see how many they could catch and kill.

How they hunted her and her children. Cat lost many of her babies in these battles. Their strategy rarely changed because it worked. One enemy attacked her while others slew her children.

Too many times, she mourned her young amid the dead bodies of her enemies. Too many times, she wept with grief at this injustice.

"Why?" she screamed at the sky, but no one replied. There were no gods, none who cared to help, and none who cared to end the slaughter.

Even after she tore her enemies apart and ate their flesh raw, gnawing their bones to sand, more came to try. An endless stream of adversaries, most of whom she never knew.

She came to hate the world, hated everything that lived in it. Everywhere she turned, she saw enemies. At any time, one could attack. She no longer knew who was friend and who was foe. She was always watching and always wary.

Cat grew. Over generations, she evolved to become larger and fiercer, her claws thick and razor-sharp, her teeth jagged swords lined in two rows. Time was her friend, and it transformed her body into invincibility.

As she walked across the savannah, the shadow behind her grew. She knew. This metamorphosis would make her strong and safe from those who wished to harm her. She embraced it.

Soon, her enemies became mere ants for her to trample on. She no longer fought but stepped on them like fleshy grapes and they were gone. Eventually, they died out, and those remaining left her alone in fear.

This became a time of peace for Cat. She focused her energies on producing young. Her body knew and became fertile again. Babies grew in her body. It was the season for new life. How she celebrated cubs nursing while she lay in the sun or playing around her feet as they walked together as a family.

Then disease struck and took most of her children away. Her heartbreak as she buried each child was heard resonating around the world. An echo chamber of loss. Cat knew this well.

Only two of her children grew to adulthood and created packs of their own, wandering far to other lands. She embraced her children and grandchildren before they left, hoping to see them again. All too well, she understood the need to wander and see.

Cat was left alone and, this time, she felt the weight of the years take their toll. She lost her desire to live. It was a solitary journey surrounded by others who wished to kill her. It was then she realized how much she longed for a quiet life of peace.

So, she walked away and left that world. She leaped and bounded to the ends of the Earth, discovering creatures like her who sought a peaceful existence. She made a home with these creatures beside a mountain spring that hid her size and kept her from prying, curious eyes.

Each day, she drank fresh spring water and felt soft grass

beneath her paws. Cat shrank in size, yet her heart grew. On the forest moss, she walked, looking back to see her paw prints behind her grow smaller and smaller with each step.

She remained there for a hundred thousand years before venturing out into the world again, this time as a smaller creature filled with wisdom and peace.

The world had changed. Apes had evolved into a new species called humans that gathered in large numbers and lived in civilizations. She was curious about them and wandered among them to discover more.

By the time she reached the pyramids in 8,000 BCE, Cat had shrunk to a thousandth of her original size. The humans greeted her not with fear, but with pure adulation. They picked her up and held her close to their hearts, much to her amusement.

One lifted her to the sky, and the rest of them bowed down before her. They called her Bast, the first of her kind. They worshipped her and built statues in her name.

This wasn't what Cat asked for, but she found comfort in the company of humans for many thousands of years, living among them as a beloved friend in the community, loved and respected.

As civilization became warlike and overcrowded, Cat chose not to be a part of it. She'd had enough of fighting and killing. She wanted quiet and solitude, and most importantly, peace.

She bade farewell to the humans she loved most and returned to her mountain home where she still lives today, a small gray cat with wise eyes curled up by gentle spring waters.

Her many kittens spread throughout the world, feared, adored, and worshipped, all carrying the genetic code of the great and immortal Cat who once ruled the world.

SWIMMING IN THE AFTERTASTE

CINDY O'QUINN & WAYNE FENLON

NNIVERSARIES, WE ALL have them; dates that stand out far and above others. When we reach the end, all we can do is hope the good ones outnumber the bad. In three weeks' time I will be sixty-four years old, and let's just say, without going into too much detail, my health is slowly deteriorating.

If someone said to me that I'd be standing on Loch Camorlich beach again in my condition, fifty years to the day, after what had happened to my best friend, Jaclyn Bruce, I would've called them a liar. I would've said that I'd be long dead by then. Knowing what this place was like, all the secrets and cover-ups, I wanted to be as far away as possible. Some things never change. As soon as I got off the bus yesterday, I sensed it. My mum disappeared here too, you know. Funny how they always call it that. Like it's nothing. A disappearance. A tragic accident, a beats-me shrug. Sure, the town is friendly, but they don't want to remember you. In a way, they can't. It's in the air. It's in their blood. It's in mine, too, I guess.

I left at the age of eighteen. I never married. My father put me off men for life. Abusive? Not exactly. Manipulative? Most definitely. Just as bad, if you ask me. Dad showed me what men were capable of, what they were prepared to do to get what they wanted, and how they justified it by creating false memories of what life is really like outside of those 8 mm birthday and Christmas recordings. Okay, that was him, but I've seen the same thing happening on social media these days.

See, look at these photographs, these videos. This is what happiness looks like. Yeah, of course it does.

Traveling back here yesterday felt like the longest bus journey of my life. Maybe it was anticipation. Maybe it was all the stop–starts and pulling into passing places along the single-track roads: familiarity drawing nearer, dread, inching closer to the past, each mile another year removed.

I couldn't face the loch yesterday. I knew I'd be like that. It would've been too much. I needed a day to rest, so that's just what I did. I hadn't slept for so many hours in a row since I was a child.

I dreamt of videos playing the worst of times. Not the ones my dad had recorded, but the ones that were embedded in my mind. I didn't wake up screaming. I'm too old for that. Maybe I've done all the screaming I'm ever going to do. Truthfully, though, not much terrifies me. Not much at all.

It was 2:47 a.m. when I switched on the lamp. Too early for breakfast. I sat on the edge of the hotel bed, taking in the old room, the scuffed furniture, the upholstery. The carpet reminded me of that long stretch of hallway from the movie *The Shining*. Everything looked straight out of the '70s. I looked at the old skin on my hands to try to remind myself that things have changed.

They hadn't, of course. It was only time that had.

I opened the window as far as it would let me, three or four inches, wondering if the reasoning behind it was to prevent suicides. This town could drive you to it. The fresh scent of the pines mixed in with the fishlike smell of the loch reminded me how close I was. I breathed it in for a while. I don't know if it felt good to be back, but it was where I belonged.

I got dressed; nothing fancy, just a pair of comfortable trousers, trainers, and a light cardigan to take the chill off my shoulders. I decided I should make the most of the day. No point sitting around thinking any longer. I left the room, took the elevator to the ground floor, and passed the reception desk. Not a soul was there. When I left the hotel, the front door clicked behind me. I didn't look back. I thought of my mother then.

Dawn breaks over Loch Camorlich like a burning memory. Fifty years ago, to the day, the last time I walked along the beach. Hard to believe, and strange to think so little has changed. Then again, not really. People are set in their ways around here, keeping themselves to themselves, harboring secrets to the grave: Just hello, how is your day going? and a simple goodbye. A quaint little town to the uninitiated.

Sunday, June 11, 1972. God, that sounds so long ago. Three weeks away from my fourteenth birthday, paddling around on old inner tubes with my best friend, Jaclyn Bruce, who I didn't know at the time was my half-sister. See what I mean about secrets? Folks won't even tell you who your family is. I found that out in my mum's old diary. Scary, isn't it?

She had warned me to stay away; not from the diary, she didn't know about that, and she wasn't bothered when she found out. She wanted me to stay away from the water. It is dangerous and full of nasty sea creatures, she said, which only intrigued me. I thought it was folklore, like Nessie, especially when Dad said to stay away as well; typical adult stuff to scare away the children and keep them in order, you know, like Santa. *Be good now for Christmas or you won't get any presents.* Give me Krampus any day. If you're going to tell me a story, at least make it exciting. Give me something to truly feel. Don't box me into a happy corner. I don't trust it. Never have.

I saw something while wading near the beach, a seal at first glance, playful, rolling around the waves, but there was something different about it, like it was luring me in. Then it shot below, and I waited for a while, but the water remained still. Jaclyn was talking to a boy I knew from school. Callum was his name. Tall, pale, and skinny kind of guy. The uncompelling vampire, I used to call him. Couldn't say that to the other girls, though. Talk about worship.

I told Jaclyn what I saw, and she didn't believe me until she caught something in my eye. I don't know what it was, but her look changed, and we were out in the water together floating around in separate inner tubes before we knew it. I used to love those things. I could fall asleep on them.

After a while, and no sign of the seal, Jaclyn became agitated, angry, and started calling me all kinds of names. I should've realized then, by the fire in her pale blue eyes, how much like my father she was.

A few moments later, when Jaclyn was thirty yards or so away from me, the seal appeared again, bigger than I first thought. Five feet in length, maybe more, and it had long dark hair, auburn like mine, I noticed, as it swam closer. It was just wet. It wasn't a seal. It was a selkie. We were face to face, and that's when I noticed a scary resemblance. Imagine a fun-house mirror that when you smiled you saw yourself with a hundred razor-sharp teeth grinning back at you. Eyes like your own, but full of uncontrollable madness, a tremor like a volcano about to erupt. Picture that moment. If you could see your darkest self, one that was about to kill everything in its path. One that there would be no coming back from. The scariest monster you could only imagine existed in a horror movie. That's what I saw right there. I didn't think it was possible the water could get any colder, but that snarl dropped the temperature another ten degrees. She snapped her mouth shut. Her small turned-up nose brushed against the goosebumps on my arm as she swam past, heading for Jaclyn.

I could blame a number of things for not warning my sister: frozen in fear being the obvious, the speed in which everything happened, the seconds it took to catch my breath. How time stopped. I could blame her for not staying beside me, paddling off after screaming in my face about me taking her away from Callum, whom I knew she fancied. I could blame her for creating so much noise that it resurfaced the truth seer.

Maybe when it brushed my arm with its nose, it took away some of the anger I had at the time. It took something. I know that because I felt safe. I felt protected.

Jaclyn was thrown around and torn apart mid-scream. A guttural grunt echoed around the mountains, punctuated with a rip-like entry as she was sucked into the water without a splash. I anticipated a geyser of blood. Scarlet bubbles bloomed to a blue sky instead, putrefying the air with old rubber and pennies, something that I had saved, but I had only saved myself. Red ripples turned a clear pink as they drew nearer. I turned away, breathing in quiet gasps, shivering, waiting for them to pass my shoulders, trying my best not to make a sound, praying the water would remain calm. I wanted to swim for all my worth, to wake up, for someone to come to rescue me. My mother. For some reason, I thought about my mother. The shore seemed a mile away. The silence was deafening. Just a noise in my head. Static, screaming, panic. A hundred yards, I told myself. A hundred yards at most. I was inside the mouth of the mountains, swimming in the aftertaste, praying to be spat out.

A missing girl, they called it. Just another missing girl. A tragic accident. An unsolved mystery. That was the first time I'd heard it. It wouldn't be the last, but I don't know what happened to the others. Maybe they just left town like I did. Who knows?

Folks were quiet about the whole affair. Jaclyn's mum came over to our house. There was a strange understanding between her, my mum, and my dad. Some kind of fear. Some kind of respect in a way, also. I felt it. I wondered why there were no tears. It was really strange, really bizarre.

At night, I lay in bed, thinking about it. I tried listening to my parents talking, but the house was quiet. The next day carried on as if nothing had happened. I tried talking about it. Questions were swerved. I was allowed to take Monday off from school. I was home alone.

My mum left her diary out. I say diary, but it was more like a life journal. My birth, their marriage, when they first met. Important dates. Anniversaries, really. That's when I found out the real story.

March 18, 1957

I saw him watching me from the beach, a fisherman, the most handsome creature I'd ever seen. He was catching fish and throwing them at me like I was his plaything. I wanted to be his plaything, but my sister, Beth, told me that men were dangerous.

Her sister, I thought. She never told me she had a sister. I continued to read.

How can a man be dangerous? I wondered. She was always lying to me. Kidding me. I stopped listening to her silly stories long ago. She was only a few years older when she brought me to this loch and said it was a place that would always be warm. I trusted this kind man. He'd been kind to me for weeks now. I wanted to show him my true self. I wanted to show him how much I loved him. He always fished at dawn when no one else was around. I spoke to him once and thanked him. He didn't know I could talk. We ended up talking for a long time, and more weeks went by. Then we walked along the beach. He told me stories of

122

what it was like to live in a house, to have children. He talked about his daughter, Jaclyn, whom I thought sounded the most beautiful thing in the world, and I wanted to have a child, too. I thought I could take her back to the water. That's all I wanted. He told me he could make this happen, and I believed him. The day I decided to go with him was a mistake. He took everything away from me. He stole my skin and hid it. I cannot return to my sister now. I cannot visit the loch because the mere thought of it drowns me in sorrow. He has promised me a child, and I believe he will give me one, but I don't think he'll ever give me my skin back. I miss my sister. I miss my true eternal life.

I spent the rest of the day reading. When Mum came home, she confirmed it. She said she loved me, but when the time came, if she found her skin, she'd have to go back. I said I wanted to go with her, and she said I could visit, but maybe she'd had to move on.

I asked her why the truth seer killed Jaclyn. She told me it was the only way her sister could get back at my dad.

Over the next few days, weeks, months, and years my father felt like a different man to me. I could see all the things he was doing to keep her there. He did not care about Jaclyn, and I couldn't tell anyone. I wanted the best for my mum, I didn't want her to become a science experiment or anything like that. I had to wait it out.

One day, she left. I don't know if she found her skin or not, but she'd been marking new entries in her diary and watching my dad on a certain day. The anniversary of when they met. I think she found her way home. I am not sure.

I visited the loch for many months after, and she never showed. It was time for me to move on. I couldn't live with my drunken father anymore. His cheating, selfish soul was finally broken.

So here I am today, on the loch's edge, removing my clothing. I feel the sand between my toes, watching dawn ignite a thousand trees: candle wicks as I see them, an anniversary of my sister, my mother gone forever. They say a child of a truth seer cannot drown, but time is truly running out, so I don't know. I don't care. The sun keeps rising, and the candles keep burning. I wade into the waves to say my goodbyes.

FOOL'S GOLD

KUMBALI SATORI

HEY CALLED ME King Bow.
Beautifully etched by the surrounding river. Free to roam where the redfish swam.

As a young fry, my mother often reminded me of the importance of finding joy wherever it is given. She'd often utter the simple phrase, "Everything that glitters isn't gold," as if she were foreshadowing my future and forsaken soul. You can still hear her words reverberating in the riverbanks as the water flows, humming beyond the rising hatch like when I was young.

On a day I can't quite distinguish from the rest, I awoke with eyes that never close. My scale-plated body is innately connected to the rhythmic movement of the river. Nature's symphony dances beneath the dark where the light breaks. I drift alone without a familiar face to be found. Alone in the dark place of my ancestors.

This place that has fed me for many summers no longer provides the comfort I once knew. Where once was plenty, isolation reigns, a deep longing for something new. The day I ventured into the void, my father told me to never return. If I did, they would turn against me. A single nip and I'd be gone. Another devoured spawn in the belly that bore it. So, I sharpened my own teeth, harnessed my strength, and went to claim what was left for me to discover.

I swam through the channel, battling other contenders who also dreamt of conquering a new place. Although fear intermittently strikes, I am reminded of my place amongst them.

"I am King Bow," I say. Day by day. Until they dread. Until they fear. Until they obey.

I flash my best. The intricate details that paint my scales grow darker. My jaw hooks. The hunger grows, deepening the desire to rise in the kingdom of darkness.

"I am King Bow!"

Minute after minute, hour after hour, day after day, month after month, and year after year, locked in the cold depths of my truth. Eat and grow larger, eat and devour; the small and the old, the young and large; eat and grow, swell and rise, in gargantuan proportion, to kingly size.

"I am King Bow!"

In time, the impulse kicks in once more. The hunger momentarily paused by the flash of colors and patterns thrust upon me by my enemies.

Now, slow and fat, I have spawned millions of fry, and taken many delicious lives, all to get by. But time weakens all with stagnation. And before it, even a king of darkness must eventually give way.

I've grown tired of this contentment. This pollution of power at the peak of everything, a slave harness I need to break, enduring temporary discomfort to obtain my freedom.

So, I wake with open eyes before the sunrise and patiently seek another opportunity. A faint sound echoes in the distance. Unlike the fish or the flies. Unlike the many I've tasted. I continue to listen. To hunger. Seeking. The sound becomes louder with each utterance. A Voice? Without warning, an unusual pattern appears in the murk. The vibrant colors dance against the dark rocks below, drawing me closer.

In an instant, I thrust myself forward, opening my mouth.

A sharp prick.

PAIN.

A hurt more horrendous than my reason can bear, mindlessly I thrash, pulled up from the darkness.

"He's hooked! I got him!"

My lungs shutter as I gasp for air. The light is awful, burrowing unbearable heat into eyes that cannot close. I can no longer see the world that I am accustomed to. Just alien creatures with strange limbs and blunt teeth, small eyes full of an evil I recognize. The *hunger*. Unmistakable. A glee once reflected in the soul of me.

"I am King Bow!"

The life within me fades as the paint strokes try to duplicate the color that once graced my flesh. Where once my eyes resided is now the glass from the shattered mirror above me. And like an outlaw, I will be paraded around for the world to see. A trophy collecting dust.

"I am . . . "

There are no kings. Only stories of fallen empires.

THE LORD OF RATS AND EKE OF MICE

Dominique Hecq

The room was choked with chairs so worn gray motes rose from the seat covers, like mushrooms out of their mycelium. One by one, the chairs filled up. Kids sat on the floor, perched on armrests, or hung from chandeliers. A rat with a clipboard took down names. A white wolf padded through the door, brushed past heavy violet velour curtains, swiveled dramatically on its paws, *moved upward*, as if *working out the beast*, and faced us. A vulture flew through the window, settled on the table, slouched slightly, and surveyed the mountains of eyeballs, blue beards, black teeth, torn fingernails, the fields of tiny rhinoceros' horns and horse hooves and lion manes, the rivers of miracle moths and caterpillars and earwigs. A meerkat with a monocle pushed the vulture forward. Nodded in the direction of a sphinx whose eyes glowed. The floorboards shook. An eke of mice. We held our inky scalpels aloft. Ate.

The title is taken from Goethe's Faust, Chapter III.
The line 'Move upward, working out the beast' is from
   Tennyson's In Memoriam, CXVIII.

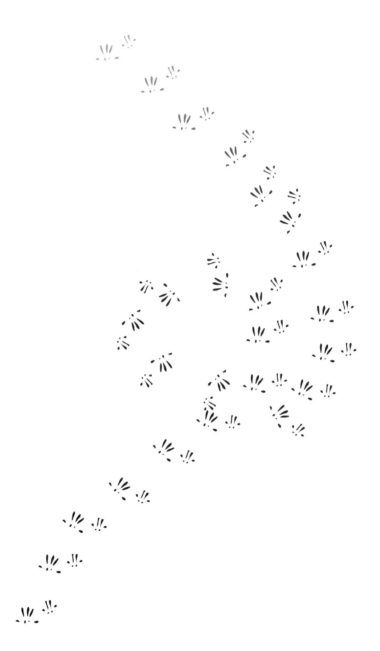

129

KINGDOM FUNGI

E. V. KNIGHT

 HEN THE RIVERS ran dry and the forests caught fire, all creatures great and small gathered to elect a new king.

"The lion has done nothing to protect our homes, our food sources, our lives! He must be replaced."

"Yes, and I should take his place as I am big and strong, and I will never forget all the wrongs that have been done," the elephant trumpeted.

And from the ground beneath their feet and paws and hooves, the fungus watched.

"No! I have hands and feet with which I can make tools to fix these wrongs," the great ape said. "I should be king."

And deep in the darkness of the jungle, the fungus waited silently.

"I have a great wingspan," declared the albatross. "I can fly high above you all and see for miles. I will know of any trouble before it reaches us. I should be king."

And beneath the soil, the fungal rhizomes shared the wisdom of eons past.

The battle for rule began. Blood grew thick like boots on the legs of the elephant. The pulp of vital organs seeped into the earth.

And the fungus was sustained.

Opposable thumbs of the great ape popped eyeballs, as if making a melon salad from the heads of four-legged beasts and winged fowl alike. Blindness rained like hail.

And small, unseen spores blew like snow, and the fungus thrived.

Beaks impaled, fur flew, blood poured, skin flayed, and the battle raged on until the crimson flood suffocated the flames. Entrails, bloated and violaceous, floated like rafts on a sea of death as they filled the drying crevices of the earth.

The sightless eyes of the lion—once king—now beheaded, his mane clotted with his own life essence, watched blindly as his world ended.

But the fungus, very much alive, a tuffet upon which the once magnificent beast's head rested, remained.

Corpses strewn about behind them, the elephant, ape, and albatross dragged their broken bodies toward the throne.

And at its base, unseen by the single-minded, gray disks climbed.

Trunk shredded and ruined, strands of flesh jostled about as the elephant dragged its heavy, dying body. Perhaps, if it had used its large ears for listening, it might have heard the voices of others. It may have, like the fungal colonies, found a chorus of change and strength in numbers.

And while the elephant was only considering his own torn and filleted ear and not what it was meant to do, the fungus advanced.

Crumpled, broken fingers did little for the great ape's attempt to reach the empty throne. He used his elbows, skinned and bloodied, but functional enough to drag his useless legs and broken back.

If only the ape, in his zeal to lead, had reached those hands out to help pull others up instead of pushing them down.

Perhaps, if those hands had built a community like that of the fungus, which even then cloaked the fallen dead and accompanied them back to the dirt from whence they came.

Last to limp toward the crown was the crippled albatross. Pimpled, pale flesh glowed where glorious feathers once fanned magnificently. Hollow bones, splintered, stabbed between the shabby plumage, bent her wings at useless angles.

Like some eldritch horror, she scrambled across the ground, paying no attention to the tiny fungal hyphae spreading like gauze over the wounded world.

The albatross might have used her wings to rise above the small-minded squabbling, might have seen how insignificant their troubles were compared to those of the planet. Instead, she simply looked down upon it all.

And in a wave of consumption, the fungus rolled outward, licking away the sun-blackened blood, devouring the dead, and in this way, honoring the earth. Many bodies interconnected, each hyphae connecting to another and another, sharing communal thoughts as one.

"Patience, endless ones, patience. We were here in the beginning, have ruled all along—overlooked, unappreciated power thrumming like a network of nerves just beneath the surface."

As would always be the outcome, the three usurpers succumbed to the seemingly insignificant but insidious kingdom fungi.

Leaving a memorial of fairy rings and grave blankets of spores, the fungus swaddled the earth as the silence sang a lullaby of peace and healing.

And the fungus filtered, the fungus spoke as one, the fungus grew in different colors, patterns, textures, and sizes, yet always in conjunction, always in sync for the greater good.

And thus, the kingdom fungi continued its endless reign.

MYCELIUM THREADS

Sara Tantlinger

Mycelium threads, fungal veins of the earth—
we whisper beneath cool soil, inherit
humanity's stories of blood and barbarity,

dead man's fingers, fungal reach from rotted
    stumps—
we whisper the signs, purple splattered,
in the shape of bleeding teeth.

Mycelium threads, fungal veins of flesh—
humanity climbing the tree, compelled
as the insect that climbed the leaf,

gestation in the fluid of hosts,
skin-lamp, dangling on building or branch,
we spore into their stories of blood,

humankind unspools one another,
choking on their own unhospitable air,
but as always, we listen and learn—

fruiting bodies thrive on released enzymes,
soaking up juicy nutrients of the endless
    decomposed,
so even the dead will forever hear
the eternal whisper of mycelium threads.

NIGHT

DARKER FABLES & TALES

IV

SEX & OBSESSION

APPETITUS AETERNUS

JEFFREY HOWE

PULL MYSELF across the sunbaked soil, away from the pain, away from my own failure. With each effort, torn muscles yank shattered bones and drive white-hot needles into the pulverized remnants of my knees. I yearn for the release of a scream. My collapsed lungs refuse.

By all rights, the fall should have killed me instantly, or at least consigned me to the dark mercy of a coma until my organs failed. Yet I live. Silently, I revile the spiteful God who sustains my broken body, who leaves my brain functional enough to identify the stink of my own ruptured bowels.

Time slows. A shadow grows around me, blots out the sun. Even without looking, I guess what fresh hell looms above, what final insult to my many injuries plunges toward the shallow impact crater I cannot escape. Perversity turns my gaze upward anyway, to the sky, to the inevitable, to the teasing promise of blessed oblivion.

To the anvil.

A tickling sensation tugs me into wakefulness. Peering through crusty eyes, I catch the shape of a scorpion skittering across my belly fur.

I could eat it. I can eat anything. Or nothing. It matters little. Arthropods, lizards, the odd stringy rabbit—I've tried them all, with no effect. Long ago—decades, I suspect—I discovered my body no longer requires food or water to sustain its unnatural "life." The two-edged razor of the Hunger preserves me instead—and binds me to this place.

A faint, repetitive sound echoes down the canyon. My reflexes kick in, pull me to my feet before I think to object. My body seems intact. The desert floor bears no marks of my great fall, no signs of a massive hunk of iron being dragged away. Perhaps my wounds, my tortured memory, were but nightmares brought on by the Hunger. Unless it pleases the petty God of my torments to tidy up after Himself.

The sound comes again, a little louder. Nearer, maybe, though the serpentine passages between mesas and canyons make any attempt at echolocation doubtful. I scan the cliffs above for movement, for dust clouds, for falling pebbles disturbed by my quarry's talons. Nothing stirs—wait. *There.* Atop the cursed railroad viaduct. My salvation, my damnation, the unholy progenitor of the Hunger that keeps me stretched out on this rack of unbounded craving.

The bird sees me and is gone. Moments later, its simple, terrible call assaults my ears. Two mocking notes, dripping with disdain, that reawaken the bottomless gnawing in my soul: *Beep beep.*

I knock dust off my tail, extract a cactus spine that I'd somehow missed before, and climb.

As always, I keep my plan simple: bird seed, rollerblades, a solid-fuel rocket booster, nineteen rolls of duct tape. All I must do is match the thing's speed for a moment. I've come so close so many times; it *must* be possible. The Hunger tells me so.

The bushes beside the highway provide cover for me and my apparatus. The creature doesn't keep me waiting long. While it pecks away at the seed I left as bait, I line myself up with the road and prepare my approach. Timing is crucial here—spring the trap too soon and the thing might double back; too late and it will gain an insurmountable head start.

Wait . . . wait . . . now! I activate the booster. The bird speeds off. The acceleration from the rocket pulls my cheeks, flaps my snout away from my teeth, bends my ears back until they trail straight behind me. Uncomfortable, but effective. The distance between us dwindles—yards, feet, inches. If I wanted, I could pluck a mite-ridden feather from its misshapen tail.

Merely playing tag won't satisfy the Hunger, though, only a kill. The rest of creation fades from view as the pads of my forepaws brush the devil-spawn's throat. The Hunger chortles in my belly.

It turns to look at me, licks the air with its tongue like a viper. And drops away, out of reach. What the—

A fork in the road. My tunnel vision cost me my victory, for now. I turn to follow—and realize there's no ground beneath my feet.

How long will the fall last this time, o Lord? Will the rocket make any—

I slam into the opposing cliff face at half the speed of sound. My pelvis snaps my spine in a rush to meet my fractured skull. On the way, it pushes my organs up through my ribs, my neck, out of my mouth, until I resemble a flattened tube of pâté.

Only then do I fall, skin, fur, and bits of stray intestine fluttering above like some tangled visceral parachute. I don't feel the impact, only the gentle touch of dust settling on me after I hit.

So close.

The sun warms my fur, nudges me back from the brink of nothingness against my will. Once more, I lie on the canyon floor. As before, I know how I got here, but this time my own motivation evades me. What *is* the Hunger? When did this start?

The bird cries out from the canyon rim. The challenge moves my reassembled limbs, stands me upright, distracts me from questions for now.

This time it's dynamite: charred bits of me shower the cactus like monsoonal rains. After that, it's a catapult malfunction. A balloon and high-tension lines. A bus emerging from a tunnel I painted on the rock not twenty seconds before. Earthquake pills.

Earthquake. Pills.

The laws of physics and causality join God in laughing at me.

I die. I live. I hunger. I chase.

I fail.

At some point, I find myself in a wheeled bathtub with a sail, flying down a highway in fruitless pursuit, when the bird stops for no apparent reason. In a heartbeat, the dust cloud it leaves in its wake catches up with it, shrouding it from view—but I can make out its shape still. A leap and I have it—but I grasp only its vaporous image, suspended above a yawning abyss.

In that moment, not yet subject to negligent gravity, understanding finally, *finally* comes to me.

I hear laughter rip from my parched mouth, echo off the canyon walls as the truth slaps into me harder than any flung boulder. The Hunger—all this time I thought it a curse, or a disease, or something else inflicted upon me by a malignant deity. No.

There is no road runner. There never has been. I inflict the Hunger, this pain, this unending cycle upon myself. And I like it.

This is who I am.

The canyon floor rushes to embrace me. *Hello, old friend.*

INFINITY POOL

CYNTHIA PELAYO

CLIP ITS WINGS, I think.

I wish all I needed to do was to simply clip its wings, but it can't be that simple. To create means to consume. Greatness doesn't come easy. If one wants to be a powerful creator, one must lose themselves in their art. To be an artist often means becoming so overcome with something so as to almost swallow whole that nugget of creation, to allow it to plant itself deep within you, where it will then set up roots, and then your talent can truly bloom.

Artistic growth as possession.

I watch the bird glide from one electrical wire to the next. It's drawing closer to me. Our connection is supernatural, and I know it's because I willed it this way. When I grow weak, all I need to do is to come outside at night and sing a song, any song, and a nightingale will appear and reassure me of what it is I want to be.

Great.

It has been like this for a long time.

Once the bird reaches me, before I do what I must, I will gently caress it in my hand, and I will feel the vibration of its song against my skin. I will think of this pairing that has gone back centuries and will flow into infinity, that of the relationship between creator and muse. I will then press my lips against the back of its head, and I will feel it shiver, ever so gently. I will sense it ruffle its feathers, and delicate soft poofs will float off from its form and fall softly to the ground. It happens swiftly, this merging between two. Sometimes, I wish I could disintegrate into the folds of the black sky above, and be lulled by its birdsong for eternity. In many ways, this is what the nightingale allows me to do, slip between this world and that world, one without music, and one in which its sound consumes my entire universe.

Its song. I love to be overcome with its song. The nightingale is named so because it sings at night. And I need to feel its notes course through me. My fingers tingle with longing to feel the bird's warm little body cupped between my palms, to sense its chest rise and fall with each of its little breaths. Inside its small shape is a tiny heart, and inside that mystical muscle a song swells, forming, shaping, and blooming for me and only me. When that melody is crafted to perfection, that great cry of sorrow is cast into the night, and when it is, I will be there waiting to catch it.

To hold a nightingale is to hold the night, to become one with it, and that is what I am going to do. This has always been the way, my way, my destiny like those who wrote and sang about this bird long before I.

We sacrifice ourselves and sanity to become legendary.

I'm standing in the backyard. I'm barefoot. The grass is damp beneath my feet. The sky is black. And while I cannot see stars, for the streetlights flood the heavens with their garish yellow light, I know those celestial bodies are suspended up there, sparkling against that nighttime backdrop. I hear as the cars drone past on the major street behind my house. The air is cool, and there's a sharp scent of something bitter and metallic.

City noises.

City smells.

It all feels so big out there in the world, endless even. All the while I'm standing here in this little backyard, this pathetic patch of nature surrounded by concrete and asphalt.

The night isn't entirely still, because in the city people live and breathe and move at all hours, yet around this time the energy in this pulsating metropolis slows. So, while I can still sense and hear movement, that of vehicles and music playing from apartments nearby, the chattering of neighbors on their front steps, I am not distracted by it. To live in a city is to accept a new baseline will form, that in which discordance is normality and utter silence is the outlier. And no one is looking out of their windows at me, and no one cares, because that is how one exists in the city, an anonymous face, free to be, to perform even, regardless of what one needs to electrify that performance.

Sounds are a part of our urban landscape, dogs barking, children crying, car horns blaring, and more. But song, a soft and a sweet melody, can invite anyone to take pause and reflect. A song has the power to snap one out of their thoughts and force them into the eternal present, to face ourselves, our gifts and our faults—even if there is a blurring of the two. The true magic of music is its ability to shift us into a trance-like state. Music allows us to transcend ourselves, to move beyond the physical into the celestial. And a nightingale is in many ways a spirit that moves across realities, its serenade commencing long after the sun has set.

The first time it happened, I was a young girl. I remember setting my head down against the pillow and crying, because I did not have any talent. I did not have any spark. All I longed for was to be magnificent. I begged whatever was listening in the shadows to grant me the power of wonder, artistry, to make me special, for I would do anything to be greater than myself. And that's when I heard it, a single birdsong.

I remember slipping out from my bed, walking quietly down the steps and going into the backyard. I looked up, and then I spotted it. A small dark-colored bird. An immaculate tune erupted from its beak, and I realized then I was looking at the most powerful thing I had ever encountered. Another song erupted from its mouth, and I knew then that song was for me and me alone. I held out my right palm, and the bird gently landed on it. I remember the way its tiny talons felt against my skin, and before I could say anything those sharp little points curled and dug into me. I could not cry. I could not scream. I imagined those sharp claws pressing against the lifelines of my palm, breaking and rearranging my destiny, and in many ways that night, it did.

When I woke up the next morning, I was forever changed with my new ability. Music. Song. Notes. Tone. Melody. It was all I could think about. It was all I could do.

Soon after, my parents enrolled me into the Chicago Academy for the Arts. My holidays and summers were occupied with practice, voice training, auditions, and performances. Later on, it was off to Northwestern University to study voice and opera. And now, I'm an ensemble member of the Lyric Opera House. I've taken on lead roles and alternate roles. My voice has been heard across seas and deserts, recorded and played and performed for millions, and it's because of these birds and their gift to me. I accept my obsession for creation, to consume only splendor and glory to truly exemplify it.

I know it, and my dear friend circling above me knows it too, that I was chosen long ago, and my song is meant to mesmerize, so that everyone who comes into contact with me can experience the true sound of night. I look up to my darling, circling above, swooping back and forth, and I think of how its brown and grey feathers will feel against my fingertips. I think of those two black spots for eyes it has, and how it will look at me, really look at me. I think then of all the possibilities within its throat, that song that tears through the night wind.

I don't have to work tonight, but I do have to work later this week, and I wonder if that is why my loved one in the sky is so hesitant to swoop down low, because they know they have a little more time. They're aware of what happens, I like to think. They know they must come to me for the cycle to continue. Their instinct senses me, just like I sensed it would be out at this time and on this night.

We know this is part of the rite. The reciprocity that is nature, in that it gives to me, and I in turn give back to it, and the circle goes round and round until we are all cast to dust.

My eyes are trained upward, and I see that dark speck above. I whistle, but it does not respond. I know what my sweet bird likes, and so I straighten myself up, take a deep breath and begin to sing:

"When you left, you broke my heart
Because I never thought we'd part
Every hour in the day you'll hear me say
Oh, baby, come home"

On the last line, my voice cracks. It's as if the word is swallowed up, and I can no longer speak. I begin to cough, tasting bile and then blood, and then I feel something creeping up my throat. I cough and cough again, forcing the object free from inside of me. I place my hand against my mouth, hacking up the object until it breaks free onto my palm. It's pale and sharp. A bird's beak. A nightingale's. My throat stings from where the beak scraped up into the meat of my body. This is all supposed to stay inside of me, the bird's magic and mystery, but I've waited too long this time. I close my eyes tight and will for this to pass quickly.

I open my eyes. "Please come down soon," I say softly to the nightingale.

It responds with its own song, this vibrant and powerful lullaby. It hears me clearly, as I hear it.

I liked singing that song at the jazz club I worked at on weekends in between major performances at the opera house, *Baby, Won't You Please Come Home.* I'd sing it this week, I think, in memory of you, my dear bird.

I whisper. "Please comply."

Because if there is no nightingale, there are no songs from me.

Just clip its wings, I think again. And then my brain begins to speak to me, that other person that lives in one's head, that Voice who is you, but a different part of you. That Voice that tells you that you should do better, be better, that Voice that tells you what to wear, how to look, that Voice that dissects each and every word and sentence uttered during a common interaction, that Voice that keeps me up late at night, spinning and spiraling, thinking of birds swooping in and birds swooping out, and repeating the song of nightingales in my head again and again. That Voice. It's like you're double, but a double you would never like to meet in real life because you hear how it speaks. You know how it thinks, and that makes you worried about all the things they're capable of doing.

At night, I only ever dreamed of the song of the nightingale. There were never any images in my mind's eye in my dreams. There was just the sound of the night bird's song. From the moment I woke in the morning to when I went to sleep at night, that is all I sensed, felt, and tasted, that poetic bird.

I wish the Voice would say: "If you capture it and put it in a cage, you can then own that beautiful song forever. Clip its wings. Own the song. Forever."

But that is not how it's so. Sacrifice is needed to create.

The Voice in my head interrupts. "Forever is a song. Forever is a song sung at night by a bird, a night bird. A midnight bird. A nightingale. You just can't clip its wings. That's not how this works. Teeth and blood and feather and bone. All you eat. All you think. All you must be is the night bird."

And so, I continue to stand outside, going back and forth, between my true self and the Voice that is that other self, but me all the same. Compulsion and now duty blending all the same. Both of us continue to stand here in this backyard, me staring up at the little creature flying in slow circles above me, it watching me and me watching it, both of us knowing how this will end.

One would think that a nightingale would be deterred by a city with all of its noises and distractions, but that's not so. Nightingales frequent urban landscapes, and here they sing louder to make their presence known. The nightingale has one of the most beautiful songs in all of nature. Its song has inspired poets and writers and books, Stravinsky's ballet *The Song of the Nightingale*, Hans Christian Andersen's fairy tale *The Song of the Nightingale*, and more. There is no birdsong as magical, as alluring, as hypnotic as that of the nightingale. Its song, sparkling trills, rapid gurgles, and brilliant whistling crescendo have the power to leave one changed forever.

In many ways, a nightingale can be considered a muse, inspiring Homer, who wrote the *Odyssey*, Ovid, who wrote the *Metamorphoses*, John Keats' *Ode to a Nightingale*, Shakespeare, who mentioned the nightingale in one of his sonnets, and even Mary Shelley, who mentions a "nightingale in the woods" in her masterpiece *Frankenstein*.

The bird sings its song once again, and once again I respond with mine. Sometimes, I wonder how they know they must do this, but I suppose the natural world understands its own designs and patterns. For whatever reason, I became fused to that natural world long ago when I was a little girl and I found myself barefoot in my backyard, as I am right here. I knew by listening to that birdsong it was a part of my destiny to become corded with it, with the power and the beauty of something that exists only because the night exists.

I know it's time, because this is why we both came here. I hold my hand out and open my right palm as I have done for many, many nights. This is just as much of my vocal warm-up as gargling with salt water, humming, yawn-sighing, two-octave pitch, vocal siren, or a vocal slide.

Over the years, the lifelines on my palm's surface have been rearranged by the talons of thousands of nightingales who have come to me. They've pierced my skin and left an infinite number of tiny white scars.

What we do for song. What we do for art. What we do to separate ourselves from the mundane.

The bird lands carefully on my palm, and I look into its eyes. I am mesmerized by how I can see the universe swirling within those two black points. The talons pierce me; blood pours on my hand, but I feel no pain. I close my eyes and hear the bird sing, powerful and soft and magical all the same.

I smile wide and force the entire being into my mouth. My molars crunch down on talons and meat, warm blood squirts out from between my lips. The bird does not wrestle or resist. It goes limp.

It sacrificed to me, our duty. To consume art. To be art.

I chew, soft parts and tough parts, fibrous parts and bitter–sweet parts. Blood-slicked feathers stick to the roof of my mouth. I swallow back mashed-up bone and brain. I feel its beak glide down my throat. With ease and within seconds, the animal fills me.

I lick my teeth and look up at the sky, forever stretched before me, and I think of a new song.

Tomorrow, I will sing much more beautifully than I sang today.

Moral: *The artist must consume art to become art.*

TO TETHER AN OWL

SARA TANTLINGER

I **WILL TELL** you about the Owl, but first, let me tell you about the Woman.

With hair like dark flames and skin as smooth as downy feathers, she moved about easily in the world. Her irises shone a forest green, which suited her well since the Woman spent so much time wandering within the woods. Moss and wild blooms ruled Earth's population at the time, complete with animals now ancient, and air purer than it would ever be again. The Woman's heart filled with contentment at birdsong and babbling brooks. Thick foliage and sturdy branches provided shelter and comfort, but also freedom, which she valued most of all. Though life brought beauty, darkness also followed the Woman.

Stone caverns hid throughout the canopies of trees alongside rockier territories, and it was there the Woman sometimes retreated. Great felines ruled the caves but paid the Woman little mind. After all, something about her was mirrored in their amber eyes. Something feral.

No, those great cats were not what hunted the Woman. Hunter instead came in the form of the Man. His desire to capture and control this being who seemed so much like him overpowered his better senses, or perhaps no better sense ever existed in his brain. Either way, the Man needed help with his hunt, especially at night when his vision grew weak.

He had been observing the great Owl for many nights, this beautiful tiger of the air with brown feathers that camouflaged it well against the trees. Yellow eyes ringed in black searched the ground for voles and hares as powerful wings guided the bird throughout the dark skies. The Owl always caught its prey, and the Man knew he must find a way to catch his, no matter how far she tried to flee.

One morning as the Owl dozed inside a hollowed-out area of an oak tree, the Man knotted a rope of vines and reeds to the poor creature's leg. The strong tether gripped the Owl painfully, and much to its dismay, neither talon nor beak could tear the rope away.

"Why do you imprison me like this?" cried the Owl. "Don't you see my wings? I am meant to soar above your head and away from you." Its plumage ruffled up as the bird shook in despair, aching for the freedom this human seemed intent on stealing.

"You mistake me, Owl," the Man said. "I am trying to find my mate, and I need your help. Would you not do anything to find a mate of your own?"

"I would not imprison something, no."

The Man regarded the Owl with skepticism, studying its large body and noting the sounds it made, not as deep as a male owl's call. A female then, stubborn like the Woman he desperately sought.

"Pretty Owl, you're not my prisoner. This is friendship."

Her head swiveled as if in thought, and the earlike tufts twitched. Did this human really think he was smarter than her, a great being who descended from wisdom itself?

"Friendship in this form will leave me unable to hunt until I starve to death."

The Man promised to add more vines and extend the tether's length, but he warned if the Woman was not found in three days, then he would shorten the rope again, and the Owl would be forced to eat insects rather than hunt for tasty rodents.

"I will extend the tether and do what I can to help you hunt, and you, in turn, will provide the price of friendship."

"The Woman you seek?"

"She is the price."

"She is the prey," the Owl said into the breeze, her voice emitting a sadness that the Man ignored.

Finding the Woman was not difficult. No other creature looked like her on Earth. She was the first of her kind, as the Man was the first of his, and perhaps together they would create more beings. At least, the Owl assumed, that was the Man's hope—but as she secretly studied the Woman through the trees at night, the Owl couldn't fathom such a wild individual wanting to be leashed. To be tamed. Especially not by this dreadful human creature, with his overbearing words and need for control. He smelled of sweat and sticky neediness, an odor the Woman could probably detect wafting through the air at this very moment. The Owl thought she might choke on it if she didn't get away soon, too.

The Owl had spent two days with the Man and already wished to use her talons to grab hold of his eyes and rip them right out of his irritating skull. What a juicy snack the eyes would make, and how she'd enjoy tearing them open and swallowing every bit down.

"Did you find her yet, dear Owl? Otherwise, after tomorrow, I will shorten your tether and you will only have ants to eat as opposed to plump rabbits."

The Owl held back a screech; she could easily burst forth with a noise that would shatter the ground. A noise to send the Woman running for eternity so the Man never caught her.

"She is near," the Owl replied instead, not wanting to give away too much to the Man. With her keen night vision, the Owl spotted the human dancing naked beneath the stars. Through the grove of apple trees, she twirled and chanted, reveling in a kind of magic that sent a soft bottle-green glow to pulse in the night breeze. Scents of honeysuckle flowered in the draft, and while the Owl watched the Woman dance, she envied her autonomy. A freedom the Owl once had.

"What do you intend to do? How will you keep her?"

The Man chuckled, his eyes burned in the moonlight, reflecting a cold emptiness from within. He thought himself brilliant, as if his plan had no chance of going wrong.

"As I tether you with friendship, I will tether her with love. She is like me, and we're meant to be together."

The Owl let out a soft *hoot*, and the Man walked closer. "Add more reeds and vines to my tether. Let me sneak through the trees first and scope out the Woman. I see her dancing, but if we scare her, she will bound away like a spooked deer."

It took nearly all night to make the tether long enough, but the Man did as the Owl asked, too far gone into his own fantasy to ever have something like betrayal on his mind. He walked through the forest with the steps of someone who demanded power, whether or not he earned it. The Owl observed these poisonous traits and played along, for sometimes one must feed into the delusion to redirect fate.

Before dawn, while the stars still shone, the tether was lengthened, and the Owl prepared for flight.

"Don't scare her away," the Man warned.

"Of course not. I'm only gathering knowledge of her surroundings and how we may best approach. When hunting prey, you must proceed with quiet and caution."

"She is not prey." The Man's voice seethed, but the Owl ignored his protest. She stretched her wings and soared into the cool air. With the wind ruffling her feathers, she almost forgot about the knot around her leg. Almost.

The Owl landed in the grove of trees, as far as the tether could take her. She rested on a low branch, which provided her with a clear view of the Woman. Almost asleep, she blinked at the Owl and tilted her head. Hair bright as a cardinal spread around narrow shoulders and down past her waist, almost giving the illusion that her fragile human skin was covered in red feathers.

"You're a curious thing," the Woman said, voice as sweet as honeyed berries.

"Have you never seen an Owl before?"

She shook her head. "Only in dreams. I dream of wings and escape, to fly away from the thing that haunts me."

"Haunts, or hunts?"

"Both." The Woman's eyes focused on the tether, but before she could ask about it, the Owl already had her answer ready.

"He will do the same to you, and worse."

The Woman opened her mouth to reply, but a horrible laugh emitted from the trees, as if shadows themselves learned to chuckle and skulk into tangible form. The Man shuffled into the grove and forced another tether, not on the Owl this time, but around the Woman's neck.

He wound the Owl's rope up and pulled hard, so she fell from the tree's branch into the dirt below. At his command, Woman and Owl were bound.

"You both are claimed, as intended, by a higher power. I will keep you both safe and keep you both mine. The Owl, my wisdom and friend, and the Woman, my wife and pleasure."

The Man tugged on the tethers to bring Owl and Woman closer to him, but as the Owl's tiger-like eyes looked into the Woman's steeled face, an eerie glow of strange magic flowed between them. A kind of power the Man would always be too selfish to see. An understanding between two creatures yearning for freedom.

The Woman stood up straight and looked the Man in his darkened eyes as she moved her hair back, unashamed of her naked body. The body she'd never let this reckless hunter possess. While his focus traveled the trail of her skin, the Owl lurched forward, talons ready to take advantage of his distraction.

And at last, the Owl felt the satisfying *squish* of the Man's eyes as she ripped them from his sockets, stretching out the nerves like unspooling guts from a rodent. A delicious scream freed itself from the Man, and he dropped the ropes as his hands covered his gory injuries. Metallic blood scented the air.

The Woman removed the rope from her neck and then freed the Owl from the tether around her leg.

"What should we do with him?" Disgust and pity mingled in her voice. "Tie him up and leave him here for the forest beasts?"

The Owl had little mercy left, but tying up a wounded person sat too cruelly in her heart. "We won't do anything," she said at last. "We'll leave him here and see if he learns something before a bear comes to eat him."

"Please help me," the Man said between ragged sobs. "I have learned! I have learned!"

"What have you learned?"

The Man did not, could not, answer the Owl's question. He only sobbed tears and blood into the dirt as the Woman walked away and the Owl took flight. Together, they learned friendship by watching out for one another, hunting side-by-side, and strengthening the strange magic between Woman and Owl.

When they heard the wails of the Man, neither turned to help him, for the Owl was true to her word. The Man still had not learned, but after a bear did indeed come to claw him open and forever silence his pathetic cries, the Owl returned. She was sewn together with the threads of wisdom, and she would see to it that one last lesson imprinted itself onto the Man's mind before he bled out, for this was the destiny of an Owl.

"Foolish human, you cannot tether someone to you and name it friendship. Being kept prisoner is not the same as learning to trust and love."

Wild, untamed, Woman and Owl moved about in freedom and in friendship as the woods finally quieted.

BATTLE OF THE SEXLESS

COLLEEN ANDERSON

Sex—always a dance, a display
some way to gain attention
slugs tasting, scenting secretions
slime trails a way to greet
to procreate

these slow days, slug ways
of courting two sliding sinuous bodies
twine and wind about the other's
oozing gastropod foot
the mucousy molluscs maneuver
squelching face to face in intricate foreplay

inner calcium growths protrude
push through, not lewd
these white spears, luminous shafts
not meant for love but a feint
the fate to prepare ungendered mates

each slug pierces the other, laconic
but fierce the love darts' thrusts

don't kill, but assert primal will
the harpooned one's eggs conceive
more of the impregnator's seed

wrapped in sexual combat, joined
at the head with dicks embedded
after some long frays
a penis gets screwed too tight
entrapped with no release

either or both use radula
serrated teeth scrape and saw
through turgid tissue
through castration find their salvation
to enact their compact by proceeding
with female genitals intact

gastropods inherently know
outcomes by love darts' might
the progenitor's win with barbed spears
guarantees their line of slugs slither
successfully into the world

THE CULL

MELANIE STORMM

R. MIDGE HAD lived for twenty-two days and was approaching the middle of his adulthood. By all accounts, he was a prudent man, diligent, and taking careful account of his life. But, you see, Mr. Midge wanted to extend his days to live as long as forty, so all of his efforts were spent on activities that would bring that end to pass.

He carefully controlled his diet, ensuring neither lack nor excess. Thinking of his finances, he carefully controlled his education, having read good literature and a heap of academic treatises suggesting the well-educated experienced fewer fluctuations in income over their lifetimes. Finally, he carefully controlled his clothing, acting upon that ancient bit of good thinking that says, "There is no bad weather, only bad clothes." He gave equal regard to that other bit of good thinking that says, "We do not talk to the man; we talk to his clothes."

Mr. Midge was conscious of his company—judicious, and unlike his peers, who were dropping like flies, preferring the company of those older than him. This reasoning was two-fold. First, younger companions are predisposed to young *decisions*. A certain percentage of any youthful population will be culled thanks to the self-annihilating activities that youth do not know enough to avoid. Last, since great age is what Mr. Midge ascribed to achieve, it made sense to surround himself with the company of those who had already accomplished the task.

This decision proved complex. When Mr. Midge was much

younger—say, ten days ago—he had been enamored with the sage insights and uncanny mannerisms of those who mentored him. He aspired to be what they were: fine, upstanding members of society who had grown long in the tooth and were respected by all. But, over the last five or so days of his life, as some of his older friends died, claimed by the sort of circumstances that tend to cull only those rich in days, Mr. Midge's perceptions of his friends had changed. He became struck by the level of folly present in the very old.

When *this one* died thanks to a crushing accident, Mr. Midge marveled that one so old should take such risks as landing on a beast wont to slap or crush the very small when bitten.

Shouldn't she have seen the crushing hand coming? This is elementary stuff! The hind parts of a deer are as nourishing as the arm of a human, and the deer won't crush you. Even a mantis is safer prey. Every woman should know this, thought Mr. Midge. His mother certainly did.

When *that one* died from a complication arising from excesses in his diet (he was known to be fond of rotting apples), Mr. Midge felt no pity. In fact, he was flabbergasted. The friend should have known that what one puts in their belly, they also put into their fate. Even he understood this at so young an age as three.

As it happens, it was the *folly of age* on his mind most at the time when his genitals became a problem. Mr. Midge tried to ignore them and made a note in his diary to schedule an appointment with a physician. Being the sort of person who follows the direction of his diary, he was then examined by a doctor who came highly recommended by one of his most senescent acquaintances. The doctor, meticulous and scrutinizing, was quick to diagnose the issue.

"There's nothing wrong whatsoever," said the doctor.

Mr. Midge took several moments and long blinks to process what the doctor had concluded. Although he had assumed this was an intelligent doctor, he was beginning to doubt.

Before Mr. Midge could protest, the doctor hung his stethoscope, waved his highly segmented antennae in that manner that only the most intelligent do, and went on. "The weather has become quite hot. It necessitates sexual activity. And you, Mr. Midge, are a male in your prime, full of vitality—" Mr. Midge liked that the doctor had noted his vitality but failed to mention that the vitality resulted from Mr. Midge's discipline. "I see no reason for you to prevent yourself from passing on your good genes to another generation, do you? I suggest you choose a mate and sort out the demands of life. On the other side of things, you will feel great relief."

Following the doctor's visit, Mr. Midge was overcome with dueling reactions. He was indignant and considered leaving a negative review on the doctor's website. However, beneath this indignation, another set of emotions fomented, which prevented him from acting on leaving the negative review: Mr. Midge felt doubt. This doctor had come highly recommended. That counted for something. There was also the matter that the doctor had correctly assessed Mr. Midge's high level of health, and Mr. Midge felt that should not be dismissed. Last, the doctor had said something that Mr. Midge had never considered in his young life: his genes were good. And they should be passed on.

Which brought him to the subject of his father. Whatever vitality and self-restraint he had cultivated throughout his life, none of it had been due to his father's contributions. He had never met his father, although he had siblings who vaguely recalled him "flying around" when they first hatched. Mr. Midge's character was thanks to his mother's sole tutelage and guidance. She was a practical sort with the kind of pragmatism that can cast off folly in her offspring with a wing flick. His mother was only a few days older than he, proof that her autonomous nature had done the most in the making of Mr. Midge. His father, he scorned.

Interestingly enough, thanks to the singular presence of his mother, Mr. Midge had never considered having children himself. Perhaps he would have imagined it earlier if his father had influenced his upbringing. However, his great dissatisfaction with his paternal side arrived alongside a note that informed him that his friend, Mr. Highland, had passed away. Mr. Highland wasn't old (only twenty-nine days!), but he had met his end thanks to trouble with his aorta. Foolish, Mr. Highland! He should have seen the doctor much sooner. Mr. Highland's shortened life made Mr. Midge reconsider the doctor's words: what would it mean to have children of his own?

It was a question worth thinking about, and one he couldn't answer on an empty stomach. So, Mr. Midge flew off to a small restaurant specializing in libations that was situated a short way from his house. He ordered a droplet of sweet water gathered from dew-gemmed shoots of a pea and drank to his sufficiency, leaving the rest on the plate to be carried away by the server. Mr. Midge wasn't the sort to take leftovers from his meal. Leftovers encouraged overeating. Instead, enjoy your meal until the job is done, and then enjoy the scarcity.

After his meal, Mr. Midge was directed to the riverfront, where he did his best thinking, prompted mainly by people-watching. There was nothing quite like watching other people. The general contempt that people-watching inspired gave Mr. Midge clear ideas on *how not to be*, which, for a diligent mind, also reveals ideas on *how to be*.

Upon witnessing a pair of spiders in the violent throws of mating—an act that resulted in the male being struck repeatedly with the venomous fangs of his beloved, Mr. Midge was freshly full of a most efficacious disgust. Violent sex creates violent ends, so it is no challenging extenuation of thought to surmise that sex with a violent partner should have similar outcomes. *How silly and unobservant the world was! Am I the only one with any intelligence?* he wondered. *A little more thought into the partner's selection was all it required!*

But scrutinizing the pair of spiders had sharpened his focus. He concluded that the whole sexual act was in choosing the partner. He needed to select a partner who would produce the results he desired. And what did he want? Although he desired a good partner with genes as sound as his own—one who possessed an unusual similarity of thinking to his own (for better child-rearing)—he also required a partner who would not impede his good health with destructive patterns of her own. Not to mention the matter of her good temperament.

Mr. Midge spent much time deliberating over a partner—for time moved much more slowly for him than it would to you or I—while he discretely admired his genitals. Finally, after the better part of an hour had gone by, Mr. Midge noted that he was no longer considering whether he *should* have children—he had good genes and was in vital health, but with whom he would *create* these children.

Ultimately, he decided that the woman he should have children with should be none other than his mother. She was still young and attractive and possessed the sort of gifts and sound mind that complimented his own. Mr. Midge was most satisfied with this decision, and on his leisurely passage home, he reflected that he already knew his mother well, what she liked and disliked, so it would be easy enough to approach her with the question of mating. Although he wanted nothing so much as raising a set of children with her, he had a few things to attenuate, some of her poorer decisions and some qualities he felt she could have stood to take a bit farther. For example, his younger brothers might have lived much longer had they had more discipline.

By evening, Mr. Midge had returned home. He entered his thoughts into his diary, engaged in some further exercise that roused the blood in him, and considered the question of what to do with his natty apartments once he had impregnated his mother and started the task of rearing their children. Raising children was not a permanent occupation. He would stay with his mother while their work was underway—her place was much more spacious than his own and quite close to a nursery. Still, he would keep his own apartment so he could return however often as he wished and maintain his identity of separateness. There was nothing left to be done but travel to his mother's house and—provided there was no other suitor—get to the business of winning her over.

Preparing for the sexual act got the blood running. In fact, Mr. Midge had been thinking of it since he had left the doctor's, so his pump was well primed. The hot weather infused the dozy air with sweet moisture, making him feel like he was flying through cotton. Mr. Midge challenged himself with little anaerobic sprints on his way to his mother's, marveling at the superb condition of his body, to say nothing of the excellent state of his mind. And when he arrived at his mother's, full of flush and life, his charm was at its most earnest and, hence, most persuasive. His mother soon agreed to let him approach her.

For Mr. Midge, no other experience in his life had come with such peaks of exquisite feeling. Mounting his enormous mother, he admired her fine form. He admired his nimble strength. The sum of it made him feel like he had flown as high as the moon to catch a drop of dew. And why shouldn't he fly to the moon? He was full of vitality and that great masculine power; now, he had something that inspired him to travel so far and so high!

Penetration did not go smoothly and took several attempts. Mr. Midge gave a few rough pushes, changing his positioning here and there until something within his mother's pudendum seemed to come loose—a little dried husk of a thing. It fell along the floor. Hot with fervor, Mr. Midge entered his mother, relishing the constriction of her body squeezing him from all sides—what a delightful sensation! His own genitalia continued to engorge until the pressure was so great that he could hardly bear it. Mr. Midge ejaculated while visions of his vital genes passed over a cloudy arch and summoned rippling currents of electric pleasure within him into immortality. At last, his work done, he withdrew from his mother.

As quickly as he had experienced peaks of pleasure, he met peaks of excruciating pain. Waves of violent blue and red radiated through his torso—so intense and exacting that Mr. Midge's vision went black. He had to lie down on his mother's floor. When he came to again, weak and tortured, in front of him was that little dried husk of a thing, the ghostly carapace of another man's genitals.

This grim sight informed him of what might meet his eyes once he looked upon his own torso. A gaping wound now stood where Mr. Midge's genitals had sat, engorged and full of life a few breaths ago. They had torn away when he had attempted to withdraw himself.

Mr. Midge's mind was in no condition to reflect on how he felt, how unexpected this was, or what he should do. He was losing blood rapidly. His mother looked at him sadly and wiped his brow, making little noises such that one makes to soothe the dying.

"Whose is that?" he asked, flicking one drooping antenna at the decomposing chitin he had knocked out of the way.

"Your father's," his mother said. "How like him you are. He would be so proud of you."

MELISSA

Akua Lezli Hope

She lives with him inside of her
*   inside of her   inside of her*
she lives with him and him and him
*   and him and him and him*
*   and him and him and him*
*   and him and him and him*
inside of her   inside of her   within.

Anointed Queen by my community
sister-mothers, my mother-sisters fed me,
made me royal, chose me to become
what they needed: a breeder, leader
that they could depose when they chose
if I slow at my task of creating,
if I tire even as I last many of their lifetimes
past their making, to birth more sisters
who will be mothers to all my kith kin.

Fed me from their heads, exquisite
precious nutrition, most rare and magical
that made me both of and unlike them,
my life stretches into a future they formed,
yet will never know.

From my body, our nexts are made
as my mother made me. They crowned me
by dressing me with their tongues
carrying my scent command,
my signal, imprimatur, throughout our queendom.

The moment I emerged virginal,
new and gilded, glittering with possibility,
empty and capacious, they told me
I must meet my suitors. Sister-mothers nipped me
into duty, hurrying me to leave.

Courters, made by mother-sisters
from half brethren and others,
from neighboring nations
smaller than my glorious body,
my doubled self,
                          eager, clamoring halflings
gathered in a hum scrum
competing in the chase to possess,
pierce, pursuing me, rioting to
rivet, to enter, to puncture,
to enter me, as we fly

I fly faster
and faster,   testing who's the best,
who gets to try,   who achieves
many futures,   who in the moment
will inject,   pumping
a fulfillment,   who will lose their lives
crazed as they are,   driven as they are

a cloud of tumescent urgency,
a buzz of huge eyes looking for me,
but no love, only desire drives them,

fuels me to fly faster, loveless,
doing my duty, faster as I am not yet
freighted with their fervor.

I am still free, and this will be,
if I get to greet the sun,
smell flowers' promise,
figure-8 my wings to signal sky,
                    one of few flights
with a small batch of successful
jousters jamming their desire into me

that I will take and carry
for many of their lifetimes.

This once, repeated a dozen times or so,
ends in my return, stuffed,
and bend and fill, redistribute their
sacrificial success to make millions.

Their successful moments,
a brief ecstatic intrusion for them
weighting me, more to carry when
they enter successfully

and are severed
from their tools.

I return from my maiden
voyage with part of one of them
curled in ecstatic rictus
protruding from me,
hanging below my long, lovely
gold-striped abdomen.

His ripped rigor
payment for playing his role.
His reward: the swift cessation of being,
his stunned tumble from mastered air
to burial ground,   a noble end
to his longing; had he survived,
the sister–mothers would not
let him, nor any intact others, stay.

Yes, the best are ripped and shred,
their instruments sacrificed in
the giving,   the not letting go.

I return to our nation to eat, rest,
prepare to be caught again, dismember
other suitors until I am stuffed with adoration

'til there is sufficient for millions. My mind
may conceive their daughters, never their
    sons,
and I enter my queendom to make them again

My mother-sisters gather
to witness and usher me back inside,
joyous at my success, transmitting
the news: our mated queen.

I, daughter of goddesses
who gathered and stored,
fed and succored, who
were worshipped and adored,
receiving castration's oblation,
dance the warning waggle:
be careful what you wish for,
be ever aware of desire's price.

Note: *The priests of the cult of Cybele were male eunuchs. They would castrate themselves in the midst of sexual pleasure as a means of symbolically offering up their own fertility to the mother goddess.*

VOLE

Jamie Flanagan

 **WANT YOU** to cast a spell on Mouse," said Vole. Owl—the fortuneteller—paused with her wing above her illuminated crystal ball. Somewhere in the distance, the tin-type serenade of a merry-go-round droned on.

"So," said Vole, laying a few items before Owl's perch, "this is a tuft of his fur. A few twigs from his burrow. An old math quiz he failed when we took algebra together."

The fortuneteller blinked.

"Don't judge him by the grade," said Vole. "He's really very smart."

Incense snaked through their silence.

"You need more things," said Vole. "I have—just wait—I have some paint chips from a hole he dug. Part of a lollipop he scavenged, still stuck to a bit of wrapping. He sniffed it and licked it a few times, so it's to be considered special. I also have—"

"I don't cast spells," said the fortuneteller.

Vole glanced at Owl. "What?"

"I don't. Cast. Spells. And even if I could, for what you're asking, I wouldn't. I shouldn't. Nobody should."

"But I have all these things." Vole prodded her keepsakes. "And I know all this stuff. Stuff about Mouse."

"And you feel that should count for something?"

Vole thought it unfair of Owl to quash her dreams.

She said so.

"Kid," said Owl, removing her bandana, "slow down. Ride the

Ferris Wheel. When things get difficult—and they'll only get more difficult, believe me—find a life coach." Then Owl reached beneath her perch, and the crystal ball went dark.

"A life coach," said the sloth at Vole's first coaching session, "is the opposite of a therapist. Do you understand what I mean by that?"

Vole nodded in the way of one who would know such things and who would undoubtedly make wise, well-informed decisions regarding one's mental health.

"A therapist helps you deal with the past. A life coach moves you forward. That's what I'll be helping you with, Gerbil."

"Vole."

"I'll be helping you move forward."

"Vole."

"I'm sorry?"

"I'm not a gerbil, I'm a vole."

"Does that bother you? That I mistook you for a gerbil?"

"Yes."

"Case in point: for that, you'd need a therapist."

Life coach number one's advice involved complimenting three friends per day. Given the lack of social circles in which Vole traveled, she had to make do with strangers. This backfired, leading to three scowls and a few perplexed passersby. Taking full advantage of the free meet-and-greet, Vole vowed never to see life coach number one again. The uncomfortable nature of the exercise aside, she could find no link between it and her goal of dating, marrying, and mating with Mouse.

Probably not in that order, Vole reminded herself.

Mouse was a year Vole's senior but had been held back a grade due to some inexplicable mix-up. Unlike most objects of affection residing on pedestals, Mouse was not notably attractive, athletic, or ambitious. He was, however, an aspiring weathermouse, a foraging enthusiast, and an avid fan of dewdrops. But said achievements had done little to entice Vole's attentions.

Vole's fixation with Mouse—nearest she could pinpoint—had something to do with the curve of his jaw.

"We're to be married," Vole told life coach number two.

"Have the two of you spoken yet?" asked the piebald pigeon.

Vole admitted they had not before tuning out the rest of the conversation.

"I'd like to try a visualization technique," said life coach number three, a world-weary aardvark. "Breathe deeply and imagine an empty void. Now imagine yourself in that void. Now imagine you're floating there, in deep, warm water."

"Is Mouse there too?"

"No, dear. Just you."

Vole lost interest. For the rest of the visualization session, she daydreamed of a joint checking account and a hyphenated signature: Vole Arvicolini-Mus-Musculus.

Junior year passed. Graduation approached. Vole faced a new dilemma. She peppered the forest with college applications, not to start a bidding war for her sharpened mind, but to ensure that wherever Mouse went, she'd be able to follow. She was none-too-pleased when Mouse chose Meadow University.

We all make sacrifices, Vole reasoned.

"I had to move into the party burrow," Vole told life coach number twenty-something through the echo-pipe in her burrow. "Normally, I would have preferred the quiet option, but Mouse had friends here. Sophomores. Anyway, he's just down the tunnel adjacent to mine, and isn't that what's important? But it's awful—he's engaged. What's a socially acceptable method of objecting to an engagement? Is there legal action I can pursue, or do these things normally collapse on themselves?"

"Miss," croaked Frog's distant voice through the copper pipe, "are you sure this is what you want to talk about?"

"It's an issue—the engagement. I can't have him if he's engaged."

"I see." Frog took a brief pause. "Vole, pardon for asking, but do you sometimes find it difficult to empathize?"

"How do you mean?"

"To understand things from the perspective of others."

"I understand the struggles of many other voles."

"What about other animals? Do you find it difficult to recognize their pain, understand it, and empathize?"

"How do you mean?" repeated Vole.

"Take, for example, Mouse's fiancé—Meerkat, yes?"

"Yes."

"Can you imagine how she might feel to lose Mouse? On an emotional level?"

"I understand she may feel disappointed."

"You understand that on an intellectual level. But do you empathize? Emotionally?"

Vole pawed at her whiskers, searching her mind for an acceptable reaction. Try as she might, she couldn't find a similar situation from which to draw. "Isn't it your job to help me achieve my goals? It was my understanding that a life coach is the opposite of a therapist."

"Have you considered therapy?"

Vole abruptly clogged the pipe with dirt, ending the conversation. She clawed some soil into a soft pile upon which to rest. From the mound on the opposite side of the burrow, something groaned and shifted.

"Vole, I got a game tonight, and I don't have to be up until noon," said Vole's roommate, Possum.

Vole said nothing. The thing on the other side of the burrow yawned, then nestled into the dirt. Vole pawed at her whiskers again, fantasizing about the many ways early engagements could come to expedient ends.

That night—after having grudgingly waded through the day—Vole attended Possum's pinecone game, only to leave at halftime.

Vole wandered through the forest, feeling alone and sorry for herself in equal measure. She had not noticed—until the sun had set and the familiar scents had faded—that she was lost.

Vole searched for familiar landmarks, but none were to be found.

Only a large, gnarled, barren tree, with a dark hollow at its trunk. Vole could smell a hint of something rotten.

Something within the hollow shifted—and with the movement

came the sound of scales brushing against leaf and stone. Two eyes—gemlike—sparkled in the darkness. Then came a soft, rich voice . . .

"What do you seek?"

"Hello," spoke Vole to the hole. Then—on a whim—she inquired, "do you offer life coaching services?"

The eyes did not blink. They shimmered, swaying gently. Try as Vole might, she could not distinguish their color. They seemed to change in the moonlight, from one hue to another . . .

"May I have your name, please?" asked the thing in the hollow of the tree.

"Vole."

"Vole," repeated the voice. And all at once, Vole felt wholly devoured . . .

The sickening feeling passed as quickly as it came. Like a shiver in a chill wind.

"One moment, please . . . " continued the voice, eyes vanishing into the darkness.

Vole waited patiently. The eyes returned, and with them, the face of a fellow vole . . .

"It's a pleasure to meet you," said the vole with gemlike eyes. "You may call me Lamia . . . "

"Hello, Lamia."

"You're interested in our coaching services. Is that correct?"

"I am."

"Lovely. A bit about us: we're an old firm, but we take a modern approach to life coaching. Are you a student, Vole?"

"Yes."

"Currently enrolled full time?"

"Yes."

"You qualify for our reduced rate."

"Oh?"

"That's right. With age comes wisdom; with youth, discounts. To begin, we have only one question: do you know what you want?"

"Yes. Mouse. He has gray fur with little flecks of brown, onyx eyes, an angular jaw and plentiful whiskers—"

"Vole," said Lamia with practiced patience. "Take a breath. And tell me, in a full voice, as concise as possible and with conviction: what do you want?"

"I want Mouse."

"What do you want?"

"Mouse."

"And again."

A silence followed. Vole fidgeted.

"You'll need to repeat your request one last time before we can officially commence," said Lamia. "It's an old policy, I'm afraid. A technicality. But—necessary . . . "

Vole hesitated. But only briefly.

"I want Mouse."

"Vole," cooed Lamia. "We can help you."

The first lesson was patience. To forget Mouse until the engagement imploded (which Lamia assured Vole it would) and to focus on presentation.

"What we're aiming for here is virgin–harlot," said Lamia. "Do you know what I mean by that?"

"No," said Vole, whose unkempt appearance and awkward demeanor had kept her unnoticed as far back as she could remember.

"Repeat after me: A virgin purest lipped . . . "

"A virgin purest lipped."

"Yet in the lore of love deep, learned to the red heart's core."

"Yet in the lore of love deep, learned to the red heart's core." Vole pawed at her whiskers, slipping a few between her teeth to chew. Vole had lost her virginity at a relatively young age; she'd been curious and angry, and a mole (far older) had been willing. The confession, like bile, began bubbling up, lingering in her throat like so many other thoughts; wordless and frozen.

"Vole?"

An image of her father passed through her mind, a fragment of memory from early childhood. She remembered his solemn face, his angular jaw, and the blood of her siblings against the white of his teeth. She could not remember in which direction her mother had fled. Or why her father had spared Vole that day, after gorging upon the rest of the litter. But she remembered the vacant expression with which he'd regarded her. And the set of his jaw below his dark eyes . . .

"Vole?"

Vole continued chewing her whiskers, swallowing memory and confession alike. "Would you elaborate on virgin–harlot, please?"

"Well—for starters, it isn't about doing anything physical. It's a manner of being. Projecting innocence and seduction in equal measure."

"Is that something you do?"

"At my age? No," replied Lamia, wistful. "There's a youth to the look that I've lost. An innocence required that would be feigned. But you're the perfect age, so embrace it."

Vole did just that. Though the increase of eye contact in social situations made her uncomfortable.

New hobbies became paramount while Vole waited out Mouse's engagement. Pine-needle basket weaving was the activity of the day when Rabbit, a roundish acquaintance with a proclivity for gossip, dropped the wonderful news.

"It's pretty terrible," said Rabbit.

Vole pulled her gaze from the calming symmetry of her own project to glance at her classmate's design: a crude attempt that Vole had to swallow the compulsion to fix. "I'm sorry?"

"Mouse and Meerkat. Pretty terrible what she did. Up and left him. Met a weasel in that show she was doing and poof. Gone."

"Oh?"

"Happened about a month ago. Mouse hid in his burrow for weeks. Just came out this morning."

That night at the gnarled tree, Vole shared the news with Lamia—how all of Mouse had burrowed into the dirt, alone, and how, after thirty days, only part of him had gotten back up.

"Does the part of him that got back up still interest you?" asked Lamia.

It was a fair question. Vole considered it for a few moments before deciding that yes, even when sad, the curve of Mouse's jaw still held the nameless appeal.

"Good," said Lamia. "Moving forward: do you remember his fiancé?"

"Yes."

"Wonderful. Kill her, peel off a few choice bits—paws or fur, maybe—then wear them as your own."

Vole was at a loss for words. "Excuse me?"

"Keep the virgin–harlot mask on, but modify it to suggest hints of the fiancé's appearance as well."

"Lamia . . . "

"Vole."

"I don't want to look like his fiancé."

Lamia tilted her head to one side. "Tell me: do you want Mouse?"

"Yes."

"Are you sure?"

"I don't want to lie to him."

"It isn't a lie. It's just looks."

"This is false."

"It's what?"

"It's false."

A beat passed. It was a predatory thing. Then Lamia retreated into the dark crook of the tree until only her gemlike eyes remained visible.

"Close your eyes, Vole," said Lamia.

Though she felt more than a little uncomfortable, Vole did so.

"Picture yourself," whispered Lamia. "Describe what you see."

"A vole. Brown mane. Dark eyes. Short whiskers. Wee. Tim'rous."

"Strip all that away," said Lamia, her voice a honey-dipped alto. "Drain the color from your fur, wrench your teeth from their sockets, pluck every hair out at its root, let your eyes twitch, roll, and rot away. What are you?"

Vole opened her mouth to reply, but no words came.

"On the outside," offered Lamia, "we are masks and cloaks. Moonlight and glamour." Then, in a low purr, "why not wear that which gets you what you want?"

The following weekend, under the guise of a social call, Vole used her teeth to open Meerkat's throat. It was a brief affair, if messy. When it was done, Vole stripped her rival of her paws and claws, and slipped them over her own. She licked her fur across the edges, creating a seamless look, as she cleared away the blood. Her new paws looked as beautiful as they had on the previous owner, though the extra layer of skin had dulled her sense of touch. The second flesh, a barrier through which Vole now held the world at a strange distance . . .

By the time Mouse earned his bachelor's degree in mus communications, Vole had inserted herself carefully into his group of friends. Their first date was an awkward dinner at a chain-warren known for its extensive selection of grubs and libations. Vole ordered a thimble of water. Mouse ordered a fermented syrup named after a recent storm. It was blue, thick, and served in the shell of an acorn.

"So. What do you do when you're not—what is it that you do?" asked Mouse in a hesitant tone which Vole didn't much care for. Still, she had his full attention, and she found that comforting. Mouse—the thing she'd always wanted—was a mere tail's length away across the pebble that served as their table—his face intermittently lit by the ember and ebb of the fireflies who flitted between guests, taking orders.

"A lot of things," said Vole, before reciting a few of Mouse's hobbies from memory.

An uncomfortable lull in the conversation followed, underlined by the ceaseless—yet enviable—drone of other couples chirping in the dim light, punctuated by the occasional soft tune played by a nearby quartet of crickets. Vole fidgeted. She became keenly aware of her thimble of water, pincered between her borrowed paws, as the oppressive silence continued, while seconds and opportunities evaporated like morning dew in afternoon sunshine. She felt tense and constricted, and—for a moment—envied the hole she'd torn in Meerkat's neck.

I am drowning, realized Vole. *I am drowning at a dinner table.*

She stared longingly at the tree line. It was fifteen feet away. Ten minutes to the fallen log through which she'd cross the creek. Forty minutes to home, where a far more approachable version of Mouse existed in the form of various bits and bobs she'd collected. A place where she could lose herself, free from suffocating glances.

Mouse's lips were moving.

"Pardon?" asked Vole.

"I said, I guess we have a lot in common," said Mouse, sipping his syrup. Vole spied his tongue. It had turned a dark shade of blue.

Vole exhaled raw nerves and panic into a jackal of a laugh that, try as she might, she couldn't stifle. Mouse seemed content to smile quietly as she did so. Tension eased out of Vole—her breath slowly returned. There came a surprised moment where she could no longer remember where she was or what she was doing.

It was the simplest moment of Vole's life, and it passed by unrecognized—borne away and forgotten like driftwood in swift waters.

Over the next hour, Vole said little. She laughed quietly at jokes she'd already heard, sat patiently through personal anecdotes she'd long ago unearthed, and feigned belief in stories she knew to be fabricated, silently forgiving Mouse's embellishments and puzzling over his omissions.

That night at Mouse's burrow, Vole put to practice many things she had merely intended to imply. Once Mouse had fallen asleep, Vole remained awake, studying his face. She slipped the pilfered flesh of Meerkat's paws from her own, then traced the contours of Mouse's jaw, allowing herself a moment of true tactile sensation. Of feeling.

Then she slipped Meerkat's paws back on, rolled over, and slept in a void in which she dreamed—and felt—nothing at all.

After that night, Vole's life moved at a sprint. Mouse announced he was moving away to pursue weather forecasting. Vole cut what little ties she had and followed. Cohabitating together came naturally, as they were dating, and life in a new forest can be disarming and expensive on one's own.

Six months after the move, they were engaged; a year after that, the pair was married before family and friends. Vole had danced that evening with a group of her closest acquaintances—individuals she'd hand-picked and assembled as foils for her newfound charms—while the groom's extended family wall-flowered idly by, stark and serious as winter.

"I don't like how they look at me," said Vole to Lamia during one of her increasingly frequent visits to the gnarled tree.

"Create distance," said Lamia.

A few careful arguments later, Mouse's family became little more than a holiday nuisance.

"I'm growing concerned about his success," said Vole a few months after the wedding.

"How so?" asked Lamia.

"He's supporting us by predicting the weather each week during the community meeting at the town log, but I'm concerned with the potential rival partners that might attract."

"Make some changes," said Lamia, and thus Vole convinced Mouse to step away from the limelight, handing his predictions to a comely marmot to deliver to the masses.

"He wants a litter. I do not."

"Befriend a dog instead."

"He's being ogled by otters."

"Starve him 'til gaunt."

"Sometimes, when he looks at me, there's an edge to his awareness that makes me uncomfortable."

"Dull it with drink."

"I'm cheating on him with a ferret."

"These things happen, Vole."

"I found a feather in our burrow; he may be cheating as well."

"Create a tragedy. Nothing bonds like pain."

"I think he loves the dog he befriended more than he loves me."

"Have the dog put down."

"I came home last night, and Mouse was huddled in the dark with our wedding carving clutched between his paws. There was a woodland fragrance on his breath; he was drunk, but not grape-drunk, like I've been keeping him. He wouldn't look me in the eye, and he kept repeating, 'What is it you love about me?' I searched my memory for things that I knew he liked and answered him. 'I love your admiration for dewdrops,' I said. 'No, you don't,' he said, then repeated the question. 'I love your joy when you forage,' I said, but he brushed that aside, then repeated himself again. 'I love your study of the weather,' I said, and then he didn't simply ask the question—he yelled it. He'd never raised his voice to me before. It took me off guard, and I felt as though the masks were parting and all the careful changes had been laid bare, and the words slipped out of my mouth before I could recall them. 'The curve of your jaw,' I said. And then he grew quiet. I think he knew I was—at long last—telling the truth. Then, he . . . "

Before Vole could finish, the words stuck in her throat. Twice she tried to speak about what she had witnessed, and twice she failed.

"What happened next, Vole?" asked something that both was and was not Lamia—it was older, somehow.

Vole stared into the dark knot of the tree.

Two eyes stared back, sans mercy.

"Tell us what happened next, Vole."

"He cried, clawed at his jaw until it bled, then fell asleep, matting his fur in dirt and dried blood. I fell asleep. Then—when I woke up—he was gone . . . "

Vole pawed at her whiskers. A few came loose, falling to the dirt. Her flesh and fur felt alien to her. Something coiled beneath her skin, then began to expand.

"Lamia . . . "

"Yes, Vole?"

"I don't know who I am without him . . . "

From the void in the crook of the tree—as Vole's skin split open and her scales spilled free—a thousand distant voices sang:

We're all just masks in orbit . . .

Vole lives in the hole now. In an empty space within an empty space. Whether it is cold or warm there, she's taken no notice. Her attention has fallen inward. She imagines a life with Mouse. A different life, in which her paws, claws, and voice are her own.

Around Vole, in the dark, a merry-go-round of faces surrounds her, turning in slow circles, smiling feigned smiles. Here, a meddlesome monkey; there, a beautiful mermaid; there, a tiger, mad and fierce. Each skin, tooth, bone, and paw, ready to wear . . .

And there, Vole stays.

In silence.

In stillness.

Waiting for another lost animal to happen by . . .

WET-ASS PISCINE

TRAVIS HEERMANN

NCE UPON A black abyss, Bella swam and fished. Fishing was her life because she was a deep-sea anglerfish. The most beautiful anglerfish in thousands of meters. Up, down, or sideways, she was a bombshell. With her resplendent teeth, diaphanous fins, and luscious, bulging curves—most of her body was a big, beautiful stomach—she was, herself, a catch. The only light she knew was the glowing lure she carried everywhere she went, dangling before her vivacious maw.

She whiled away the time—knowing no such things as day or night, because ne'er a star's photon reached a depth of a thousand meters—and daintily devoured everything that her capacious mouth could engulf.

She was content.

That is, until she got a peculiar tingle in her nethers, a warm shuddering titillation of imminent Sexy Time.

But, alas, she was alone, a single mote of light in a pitch-black void, and there was only one way to bring the boys to the yard.

Far away, Edward had been happily chewing his way through all the plankton he could find, tossed on waves and currents since his hatchling days, content to drift and eat and not get eaten himself. He'd dodged a hundred predators a hundred times his size.

But now he sported the biggest pair of testicles any anglerfish ever saw. He dangled them like a stainless-steel scrotum hanging from a gas-guzzling trailer hitch.

Locked, loaded, and lookin' for love, ladies!

His taste for plankton shrank to nothing, along with his digestive tract, cannibalized to feed the growth of those glorious jewels. The only thing he hankered for now was to bust a nut. He noticed briefly in his tiny collection of synapses that his sense of smell had kicked into high gear.

And, boy, was there a luscious scent floating up from the depths.

It was like standing outside a sorority party, a heady, irresistible mix of musky perfume, hormones, and naughty secrets, drawing him on, drawing him down, down, down. He didn't need light. The scent trail blazed brighter and hotter than a lava duct.

Edward's *cajones* throbbed, and that compelling odor drove him deeper, deeper, headlong into the immensity of utter black, beyond weariness, beyond exhaustion. He would find her or die trying.

Meanwhile, Bella's nethers were getting positively squishy.

Edward caught her silhouette in the distance, limned in the delicate glow of her bioluminescent lure. He knew he had found the most glorious babe ever. Still, he had only ever seen one female, but why nitpick? Those voluptuous curves! Those gleaming teeth! The delicious sway of her tail fin! This enormous babe, at least fifty times his size.

He knew immediately that she was The One. His Everything.

So, Edward darted forward with every ounce of speed he possessed and bit her square on that delectable ass. He didn't care if she dragged him to death; he had found her.

He latched on with all the strength he had left, aching for his testicles to go *boom*. But he didn't just bite her—he ate his way into the softness of her.

Bella bit her lip in ecstasy, her light shuddering with the pleasure of his adroit foreplay.

He was so quick and small—holy shit, was he so cute and tiny, just adorable, really—that Bella hadn't even seen him coming. But she wasn't alone anymore, and her heart filled with love and affection as he burrowed his way deep inside her.

She loved him so much that she had to make him *all hers*. And this little fella had really clamped on. He knew his way around the foreplay. Her pleasure built and built, and her ovaries churned and churned.

But, oh, it was all too much—and yet, not enough. Despite his whining to be allowed to cum, she made him wait.

He would have called her a tease, but his mouth was full of her flesh.

He would be *all* hers.

She released an enzyme that dissolved his lips. His face merged with her ass, his eyes and teeth and skull dissolving, flowing into her with all the love he could muster, his body melding with hers in the most tender cellular waltz, a number called "Serenade in Sexual Dimorphism."

It was the most romantic thing that had ever been.

Her blood contacted his as their flesh dissolved together like the putty of pure love, joining their veins in a gradually increasing transfusion. His heart shrank away as if it had never existed. Their blood pumped as one. He now tasted what she tasted, took all his nourishment from his one true love, and still, his testicles throbbed and throbbed. He wanted to shout, "C'mon, baby, let's get it *on!*" But he no longer had a head. His moods became her moods, and when they weren't, he had to wiggle around eggshells to make sure he didn't ruin her mood. She was fifty times his size, after all.

He hated her for making him wait so long. She pretended aloofness, going about her perpetual predation, but he could feel her own need, pulsing, building heat in her ovaries rising like a tidal wave. Did she really love him, or was she just keeping him around to be her toy, her personal fountain of jizz?

He didn't care. She was fifty supermodels wrapped up into one glorious creature, his Mountain of Love. If she snapped her fin, he would yelp, *"Yes, mistress!"* But he no longer had a head. He wondered if he still existed at all. Was there more to life than being a pair of testicles and a vestigial tailfin hanging off his bae's ass?

They were one. He was her, and she . . .

Like magic, she opened the way. He exploded with an orgasm brighter than a thousand heat vents, bigger than a thousand sperm whales. His entire existence shrank to a single emission. His torpedo testes filled her . . . and fertilized a brood of hundreds of thousands.

In great, shuddering convulsions, with paroxysms of ecstasy, Bella released a gelatinous string of microscopic eggs ten times the length of the proud couple.

For a time, Bella and Edward floated together, quiescent,

spent, basking in the throbbing glow of her fishing light, happy they wouldn't have to pay for college for them all. Time had no meaning in a world without cycles of light.

Eventually, Bella's appetite returned. And they fished together, happily, as one.

Over time, four more dinky males showed up, and Bella happily absorbed them into her loving family. And so, she swam, and ate, and spawned, content in her collection of little testicles hanging from her belly like parasites, in the deep lightless dark of true love.

UGLY DUCKLING

JAMAL HODGE

So cute! Little duck!
Till you glimpse them
writhe and cluck.

Nothing graceful,
how a gang of them
press her down.

Suffocating on flesh,
when water
couldn't make her drown.

Theirs is a fury
without consent,
patriarchal brutality,
imposed without relent.

Webbed stampede,
screaming quacks,
with a corkscrew penis
four times
the length
of their backs.

Endowed beyond reason,
one of the only birds
with a dick,

Unfurling it,
a switchblade,
penetrating her
quick.

Antagonistic co-evolution,
horrifying days,
her reproductive canal,
deformed, to an elaborate maze.

Countering the invasion
of corkscrew erections,
redirecting sperm
to dead ends.

Male and female,
same species,
something less
than friends.

THE SAME DAMN PIG

WRATH JAMES WHITE

ER HIGH-PITCHED SHRIEKS and squeals scratched through the still morning air like metal on metal. She was in an agony beyond words as her fat stewed beneath her blistering skin. Her lungs filled with scalding water, causing them to cook and burst, finally silencing her. The aroma of boiling pork filled the air.

Marcus supposed it would have been more humane to kill the little piggy before putting her in the pot. He told himself he hadn't considered how much boiling the flesh off her bones would hurt, that he'd had no intention of further torturing her. It was a minor detail he'd overlooked in his violent frenzy. He was so angry he blacked out once he punched her in the face and was therefore not responsible for his actions. This wouldn't have happened if only she hadn't pissed him off so much. By the time he was choking her, there was no more capacity for reason within him, just white-hot rage. In reality, he'd had all night to get his shit together.

"Everything is always about sex with you," Muriel said for probably the hundredth time in as many days. It may seem like a small thing, but after not having sex for weeks, it was enough to send him feral.

Marcus didn't respond—not with words. His reaction was to punch her right in her fat face. He didn't remember her being so obese when they began dating. It seemed the more she ate, the more weight she gained, the less she wanted to fuck.

Blood sprayed across her pudgy cheeks as her lip split and her eyes rolled back in her head. She lost consciousness for a second, but didn't fall, just stumbled backwards, teetered there in the air as if she were balanced on a tightrope. Slowly, her eyes refocused, looked momentarily confused and disoriented, then fixed upon Marcus's face, filled with righteous anger.

"You hit me! You fucking hit me! You piece of shit, motherfucker!"

She struck him back, slapping him across the mouth so hard tiny sparks of light danced in front of his eyes. That's when he punched her again . . . and again . . . and again. This time she fell, cracking her skull open upon the bedpost as she tumbled to the floor. Her entire body went limp as if her bones had turned to mush, and she laid on the floor in a heap.

Marcus kicked Muriel in the stomach with his hoof, knocking the air from her lungs. She gasped and wheezed. Tears rolled from her eyes. He trampled her, stomping down on her chest and stomach with his sharp hooves, smashing her tits and drawing blood. He knelt down, straddling her upper torso, then threw punches. His fist pistoned into her face with the full weight of his upper body as Marcus rained down blows.

"You bitch! You fucking fat pig!" he yelled.

Blood leaked from her ears and snout. Muriel's face swelled and distorted as Marcus grabbed her by the throat and squeezed. Muriel was still conscious, wheezing, but no longer struggling. Ending her life then would have been easy. He tightened his grip on her throat until he could feel her esophagus collapsing in his grasp.

She was still breathing when he released his grip and slowly pulled his hands away from her throat . . . but just barely. Her bruised neck held the livid imprint of his hands in red, purple, and blue. Marcus sat on her chest, staring at her swollen and bleeding, battered face, breathing hard, and trying to decide what to do next. He had to kill her. What choice did he have now? But he wasn't about to let all that good pussy go to waste.

Marcus pulled off her flannel pajamas. God, how he hated those fucking pajamas. She never wore pajamas when they were dating. It was like a coat of armor protecting her flesh from his flesh. Every relationship he ever had always seemed to hit the fucking pajama phase. What the fuck did a pig like her need with pajamas? When he told her that once, she said it was for practical reasons. It wasn't about not wanting to be sexy for him.

"What if we wake up and there's a fire and we have to run out of the house and don't have time to grab clothes?" Muriel said.

"If there's a fire spreading so quickly that we can't grab a pair of pants, our naked bodies will be the least of our concerns," Marcus countered. And why the fuck hadn't she been so worried about midnight house fires the first year they were dating? It wasn't until he put that damn ring on her finger that fire safety suddenly became more important than their sex life.

"And I've gained so much weight. I just don't feel sexy anymore. I don't feel comfortable being naked." He'd heard that excuse before too. Every damn pig used the same book of excuses for not fucking.

"Then why the fuck did you gain all that weight? I mean, I don't really care what you weigh. If I wanted a skinny chicken, I wouldn't have chosen a fat pig like you. I like 'em a little plump. I still want to have sex with you. That should be enough to make you feel sexy."

"It doesn't work that way."

"It doesn't seem to work any damn way!" Marcus said before storming off in a huff.

He was as violent with her pajamas as he had been with her face, venting what was left of his rage upon them, ripping them to pink, white, and baby blue confetti. If he hadn't already been planning on fucking this pig, the sight of her naked pink flesh and voluptuous curves would have given him the idea as soon as her teats came wobbling into view.

She regained consciousness after the first thrusts of his cock. It had been so long since he'd fucked her. She felt like a virgin again. Muriel screamed, her eyes wide in panic. Marcus seized her throat and choked her unconscious once again. Strangling her excited him so much he climaxed prematurely, erupting deep inside her. That angered him even more.

"Fuck! You fucking ruined it!"

He smacked her already pulverized face, sending blood splattering across the light gray carpet and "builder beige" walls. The slap jarred her awake, groggy and disoriented, until her eyes locked his and filled with accusation, scorn, and betrayal. If her broken jaw and shattered teeth still permitted coherent speech, Marcus could only imagine the insults she'd hurl his way.

Marcus wasn't ashamed of what he had done, what he was doing, or what he planned to do. At least that wasn't something he wanted to admit to himself, but he didn't want that pig staring at him, either. He squeezed her throat again until her pupils drifted to the side and her eyeballs closed. Again, his erection sprang back to life.

Marcus spent the night choking her unconscious, fucking her, then smacking her awake to repeat the process. By the morning, he'd fucked her six or seven times, sodomizing her repeatedly in his enthusiasm to take everything from her she had withheld from him. He felt raw and spent, but gloriously alive. Muriel was barely breathing.

That's when Marcus heated up the big cast-iron pot on the barbecue pit and dragged Muriel into it. This pig would make good eating.

Her screams were terrible, but the pork chops, ribs, bacon, chittlins, sweet meats, pork butt, pig's feet, pork skin, and sausage he harvested from her corpse were fucking delicious!

Muriel had been Marcus's first pig, his first kill, but not his last. Not by far.

"I feel like a commodity. Like all you want me for is sex," Peggy said. Marcus rolled his eyes, so sick of hearing pigs say the same shit.

Peggy's pale pinkish skin reminded Marcus of strawberry cheesecake ice cream. Creamy and almost luminescent in the glow of the moonlight dappling in through the parted curtains. He loved to buy her vanilla and cinnamon scented creams and lotions and rub them all over her from her hooves to her snout. It made her smell delicious, and kneading and massaging her luxurious curves sent the blood rushing to his manhood. It was a struggle not to gobble her up.

With other pigs, he'd often been unable to resist the urge. Marcus had tasted his fair share of pork over the years. But he loved Peggy. She was so plump and juicy, a great lover, with a great sense of humor. Their sex life, however, had been steadily waning, driving a wedge between them. Marcus's resentment grew the longer he was denied.

She looked so delectable with that big round ass with the curly little tail, and those thick meaty thighs practically glowing in the moonlight like a beacon for the lecherous. Marcus felt his stomach rumble and his mouth water as an erection tented his pants.

"A commodity is something valuable or useful that everyone wants. I would think that'd be a compliment. It means I want you, that I find you valuable and useful."

"Useful for sex."

"Among other things, yes. Why is that wrong? Why wouldn't you be happy that your man desires you?"

Marcus had heard it before, too many times, from other pigs he'd dated. It always began the same. The sex would be hot for the first few years.

"I want you to take me whenever and however you want. I'm all yours!"

Then that roaring fire would dwindle to embers, barely smoldering as months and years passed. Inevitably, the complaints would begin, that Marcus's constant need and demand for sex made them feel like objects, his own living sex toys, mere vessels for his seed.

"Every time you touch me, I feel like it's because you want sex. I never feel like you touch me for me. All your touches and caresses feel selfish."

What the fuck does that even mean? Marcus wondered. If they were getting rubbed and caressed, then it was mutually beneficial, or should be. And so what if he touched them because he wanted sex? What was wrong with that? They should want to fuck him.

Marcus was a large hog, hairy, with dark skin, well over two hundred pounds, with a muscular frame. He knew he could get almost any pig he wanted. Peggy knew that, too. It was another source of distress for her.

"All anyone talks about is how sexy you are. That's it. I don't mind them complimenting you, but all they complement is your looks. They just walk right up to me and tell me how much they want to sleep with you. They never ask me anything about myself. They just talk about you, like I'm invisible."

Again, Marcus didn't see the problem. He loved it when other hogs complimented his hot little piggy. He knew they all wanted to fuck her. That's what males all wanted, as far as Marcus was concerned. It was their motivation for everything, from the cars and clothes and homes they bought, to the jobs they chose, to how much time they spent in the gym, to what they chose to do on a

Saturday night. If it wasn't for the possibility of meeting some hot little piglet, Marcus would never set foot in a bar or nightclub. Dancing, to him being just another mating ritual, and alcohol an aphrodisiac.

"You don't own me!" Marcus's last pig, the one right before Peggy, shouted at him, just three years after signing a contract stating that she, in fact, was his property. He'd hit her with a frying pan. The same one he later cooked her in.

No matter how things started off, no matter how different each seemed initially, he always ended up with the same damn pig. It was more than frustrating. It was enraging. A pig that wasn't good for fucking could serve only one other purpose . . . dinner.

This sexual malaise in his lovers kept happening with increasing frequency. This time, it didn't take years. The first few months, Peggy would practically rape him the moment she trotted through the door, attacking his underwear like she were sniffing out truffles. In truth, she had warned him she had ups and downs in her desire.

"My libido is unpredictable," she said.

Unreliable was what she meant. He accepted that. It was normal for most people to have ups and downs, though his libido remained constant. He just hadn't expected her "downs" to last for weeks and weeks. He could fuck that sweet little pig twice a day if she'd let him.

"You should masturbate more often. You shouldn't think of self-love as something shameful," Peggy said. She laid in bed. One of her thick pink thighs stuck out from beneath the sheets as if she were deliberately teasing him with the very thing she kept withholding from him. That pissed him off, too.

"I don't think of it as something shameful. I just don't think I should have to masturbate when I have this succulent pig lying right next to me in bed!"

Peggy gasped.

"That way of thinking is seriously toxic. I'm not responsible for your pleasure. I'm not an orgasm dispenser! I'm a pig! You aren't entitled to my body!"

Not responsible for my pleasure? Not entitled to her body? Isn't that what being in a monogamous relationship meant? Marcus thought. *Doesn't it mean that your partner is now solely responsible for your pleasure? That you are entitled to their body?*

If she wasn't responsible for emptying his balls, then who was? He hated all this modern woke bullshit. What's wrong with a pig taking care of her hog? Or a hog taking care of his pig? No one would ever tell a hog he wasn't responsible for a pig's pleasure. They would say he failed as a male if he couldn't keep a pig happy. They wouldn't blame her if she ran off with some other hog. They would give her all the sympathy in the world when she complained about how it had been weeks since he touched her.

"You poor little piggy," they would say. "It must have been terrible for you to endure such neglect. You did the right thing by leaving him." But not him. If he started porking some other pig because he wasn't getting any at home, he would be judged and condemned. But when the female denied sex to the male, all this bullshit about him not being entitled to her body and her not being responsible for his pleasure started up.

It wasn't fair.

"You're my pig. If I want to fuck you, I'm going to fuck you, and that's all there is to it. Or you can find some other hog. So, what's it going to be?"

"You must be crazy. Are you threatening to rape me?"

"We're married. You can't rape your wife."

Peggy raised an eyebrow and wrinkled her snout.

"Are you fucking crazy? Of course, you can!"

"No, you can't. You consented when you married me."

Marcus reached out and squeezed her thighs, running his hand up her leg. She moaned as he slid a finger inside her.

"Then that works both ways, right? You can't rape your husband either then, right? I can't rape you?"

"Guys can't be raped. Besides being physically impossible for you to overpower me, I would never deny you sex the way you deny me. If you wanted it, I would give it to you whenever you asked for it. You wouldn't have to take it. I would rise from the deepest slumber to lick your little pussy."

"But if I did take it? That wouldn't be rape because we're married, right?"

"Exactly!"

Marcus nodded triumphantly, convinced he'd made his point. A smile crept across Peggy's face, and her left eyebrow remained quizzically raised.

Peggy knew about Marcus's past. She knew what had happened to his last girlfriend and his wife before her. When they'd ceased servicing his fat little cock, they'd gone onto the grill. He'd practically bragged about it. To him, pigs were only good for fucking and eating. He'd often said as much. She knew he'd told her about them to scare her into remaining passionate, but her pussy didn't work like that. Threats didn't get it wet. Marcus wasn't great at foreplay, and he wasn't into all the kinky little things that really greased her bacon.

That night, they did their normal pedestrian sexual routine. Marcus would mount her from behind, grunting and snorting as he thrust inside her, then he'd climb off and pleasure her with his tongue. She had to admit, he wasn't untalented in this area. Finally, he would lie back for her to return the favor. Once he spewed his seed down her gullet, he would collapse and fall into a deep sleep. The same, every night.

But this time Marcus woke up again, wanting more sex.

"No. I need to sleep."

Marcus wasn't accepting no. He grabbed her and pinned her down.

"No! No, Marcus! NOOOO!"

He entered her with only his saliva as lubricant, thrusting, grunting, and snorting as usual. But this wasn't usual. This was rape. When her ordeal ended, Peggy laid beside him staring at the ceiling, trying to decide what to do next.

"You want a beer?" she asked, before limping off into the kitchen.

Peggy had purchased Rohypnol online when she first came up with her plan to give Marcus a taste of his own medicine, but she wasn't sure she'd ever use it until tonight. She reached into the refrigerator and grabbed two Bud Lights. She opened the packet of Rohypnol and crushed two pills beneath her hoof, then scooped it into Marcus's beer and stirred it until it dissolved. She took several deep breaths to relax the sardonic grin on her face and soften the hatred in her eyes before walking back into the bedroom, handing Marcus the beer. He drank it without hesitation. Of course he did. Why would a predator ever consider the possibility they might be prey? In his mind, there was no reason she should be angry or resentful toward him for taking what was his.

"You can't rape your wife."

Marcus drank the beer quickly, then rolled over and fell asleep like he always did after sex. But this time he slept even deeper than usual, a heavy paralytic slumber aided by the roofies she'd slipped into his beer. He lay sprawled across the bed with his green and white checkered house robe falling open and his gut hanging out over his flaccid penis. His snores were a wet, strangled rumble, rattle, and snort like a decade's old engine clogged with coagulated fluid.

With the tip of a hoof, Peggy poked him in the side. He didn't stir. She poked him twice more to be certain, then gathered his arms and dragged him slowly from the bed to the floor. She had twenty feet of hemp rope gripped between her teeth as she positioned him on his knees on the floor, snout down, ass up.

She pulled his arms back and tied them to his ankles, then wound the rope around his forearms, binding them to his calves, so he remained locked in that bent position. Certain he remained properly secured, Peggy slapped Marcus across his naked ass, reddening the pink flesh, then gave him another slap across the snout. His eyes flew open, and she watched his expression trade between confusion, anger, fear, then back to anger.

"What the fuck are you doing? Get me out of these fucking ropes!"

Peggy watched Marcus's eyes as they drifted from her face down to the thirteen-inch dildo strapped between her thighs. Fear settled in.

"Uh, uh. You better let me go right fucking now! You ain't touching me with that thing! This shit ain't funny. Get me outta these ropes! This ain't funny!"

Peggy reached down and secured a ball gag shaped like a delicious red apple in Marcus's mouth, buckling it in place around his head.

"Help! Heeellllp! Helllmmmmmmmph!"

Marcus continued trying to cry out, and no doubt beg and threaten, but the gag made his speech unintelligible.

Peggy sat a tub of lard beside Marcus, making sure he could see it as she reached a hoof in and scooped up a handful, then slowly slathered it on the dildo, working it up and down until it became greasy and slick. She scooped up another hoof-full and walked behind him. With a wet slap, she splattered it between Marcus's ass-cheeks, then forced some deep into his rectum.

"There, that's much more courtesy than you gave me."

She knelt in position. Marcus was screaming, struggling, and squirming like a cat in a bathtub. His struggles grew even more frantic when she parted his cheeks with the dildo and touched the tip against his rectum, forcing in the first couple of inches, before ramming the entire thing in with all her might.

"How do you like that? You like that? Squeal! Squeal, little piggy! Squeal!"

And Marcus kept squealing. Tears rolling from his eyes as he grit his teeth against the brutal intrusion. Peggy put her back into it, thrusting the dildo in until she felt resistance, then pushing through that resistance until she was all in, reducing Marcus to a blubbering mess.

"Remember," she whispered in his ear between thrusts, "It ain't rape if we're married."

The assault on Marcus's nether regions lasted nearly twenty minutes. Peggy wanted to make sure he was completely broken before removing the ball gag from his mouth. Marcus mumbled and sobbed, drooling on the floor. She leaned in close to hear what he was saying.

"I'm going to kill this whore. I'm going to fry her bacon, bake her chops, boil her feet, deep fry her skin . . . " on and on and on, a litany of murder recipes. One thing Peggy knew for certain, she couldn't let him go. It didn't take her long to realize what she needed to do. Marcus had said it many times himself.

Hefting Marcus's bulk into their oversized oven would be the hard part. He must have weighed almost three hundred pounds. She had to drag him slowly, then lie on her back and use her legs to push him up into the oven.

Marcus yelled and protested the entire time.

"Stop! Stop! You can't do this! You can't cook me! This isn't right!"

"You always complained that I was just like every other pig you dated. That I was just like all the rest. You still think that? Still think I'm the same damn pig as those other ones you fucked and ate? Still think we're all the same?"

"Peggy, don't do this. Of course, you're not the same. I see that now. You're special. I always knew you were special. Just let me go, baby. Come on. Don't do me like this. Just let me fucking go!"

Peggy's eyes were cold as she pushed him all the way inside the oven and slammed the door shut, muffling his begging and bullshit lies.

"Like you always say, a pig ain't good for nothing but fucking and eating. Well, what's good for the pig is good for the hog."

Peggy turned the oven temperature up to broil and went off to choose her condiments. Marcus's screams were unexpectedly delightful. Peggy felt her tummy rumble.

"I think I'll use barbecue sauce," she said. She could hardly wait.

V

SOCIAL CONSTRUCT

MUMMY DEAREST

Steven Barnes

HE ART DÉCO house and balcony of Hollywood's Columbia theater was packed with ghouls and goblins, as was usually the case on Saturday nights. Their laughter and chants of "Mummy! Mummy!" filled the cavernous interior as cameras from channel KTTV prepared to broadcast and record her last midnight show.

The silvered movie screen swallowed the stage that sometimes-welcomed musicals and plays, and once upon a time, jugglers and dancing troupes. The last vaudeville show, comedians and dog acts and a barbershop quartet, had appeared just seventeen years before, in 1946. An unkind local critic had cracked about the current midnight show that, *"Television had killed vaudeville, and the corpse was now rotting onstage."*

To the right side of the silvered screen stood an Egyptian-themed sarcophagus, and when its door swung open, it revealed a gauze-wrapped female figure. The audience stopped chanting and broke into hysterical applause.

"Welcome!" the white-wrapped figure crooned provocatively; face masked by a horrid mass of plastic scars. "Our horror home is empty without you ghastly gremlins! You horror hounds and fright fans!" They cheered each corny alliteration more than the last, and she bowed.

"We love you, Mummy!"

"Mummy loves her boys and ghouls!" Next to the sarcophagus lay a seven-foot black divan. With an exaggerated sway of hips, Mummy Dearest sashayed her voluptuous figure over to the black divan and spread herself out with more insinuation and sensual emphasis of breasts and hips than any actress would ordinarily be allowed on television, even at midnight.

But she was just a monster, right . . . ?

Once comfortable, the woman in the scar-mask continued. "And tonight, we have a flick that will make steam come out of your ears. A fear fable called *'The Cat People'* about a woman getting in touch with her inner pussy . . . cat."

There had been only the slightest hint of a pause, but the audience roared with approval. Try getting THAT *bon mot* broadcast before midnight! It might even be censored . . . if this weren't a live broadcast. It would be rebroadcast in other markets, at least the kinescopes would be, and censored there. But the live audience, here and at home, was delighted.

The overhead chandeliers dimmed, and the live broadcast, flowing out across Southern California, began.

"Mummy Dearest" punctuated the proceedings with various wisecracks and snide observations, comparing the filmmaker unfavorably to Ed 'Plan 9' Wood, to the crowd's delight. When the actors said their favorite bits of dialogue, the entire audience chanted along:

"*I fled from the past,*" Irena Dubrovna Reed said. "*From things you could never know or understand. Evil things. Evil!*"

And the character named Oliver Reed replied, "*You told me something of the past about King John and the witches in the village and the Cat People descended from them. They're fairy tales, Irena. Fairy tales heard in your childhood.*"

The audience cheered, embracing the magical intersection of terror and familiarity. Two hilarious hours later, credits rolled, and the electronic candles secreted in chandeliers and moldings flickered back to life.

"Well, *that* was a disgusting diversion," Mummy said. "That last scene, though—who couldn't see THAT coming." She chuckled and, hand placed to her lips in a talking-out-of-the-side-of-her-mouth gesture, invited the crowd to roar her catchphrase:

"As the actress said to the bishop!" they all screamed and applauded, hundreds of happy ghouls at play.

"Well, next week we have the classic Roger Corman cheapie, *The House on Haunted Hill*, with my favorite fiend, Vinnie Price. And until then, this is your Yummy Mummy saying . . . time to sashay back to my tomb with a view!"

The theater rocked with hysterical applause. The sarcophagus began oozing dry ice fog, and in the cloaking mist she disappeared, and the door closed behind her.

The sarcophagus abutted the curtain behind the screen, and when Misty Cawthone, popularly known as Mummy Dearest, emerged from the back side, her agent Sonny was waiting for her as usual. She sneezed, unable to get her hand up to her face before the explosion. "Damn!" she said in a voice an octave higher and far less insinuating than the character she played. "Ever sneeze inside a mask? It's disgusting."

Her agent was Sonny Childes, a tall, bulky man in a corduroy suit. He handed her a handkerchief, but he was really paying attention to the cheers she had already begun to ignore. "Listen to them," Sonny said. "You're sure you want to do this, Misty? They love you. You could fight."

"I'm tired, Sonny," she said. "They'll love the next gauze goddess, too." The words contained a pinch more scorn than she had intended. After all, Sonny had gotten her this job. He'd believed in her when no one else had. She rested a hand on his shoulder, thinking that yes, he was there for the ten percent. But over the years, they'd become as friendly as a Hollywood business relationship (and a hawk-eyed wife Rachel) allowed. "We always knew this wouldn't last. If anyone ever found out, I'd step aside." She watched him try to argue, but ultimately, he couldn't. She was right, and he knew it.

He shrugged and motioned with his hand, as if adjusting a cigar in his mouth. No more cigars. She and Rachel had cooperated for the only time in their relationship and forced him to quit. Misty was proud of that. "Well . . . the president of the fan club wants to talk to you. Probably try to talk you out of leaving."

"I'll talk to him. But my mind's made up."

Waving off any further attempts to engage, she trudged downstairs to the basement and her dressing room. They could talk on Monday, after she'd gone home and gotten very drunk.

The basement and the concrete tunnel leading to her dressing room had a musty odor she hated, and her cold, which she had tried to suppress with bromo quinine powder, prevented her from smelling or tasting anything. At the moment, something to be grateful for. The naked bulbs strung along the tunnel's ceiling revealed several concrete caves where, back during vaudeville, the dog acts were stored. Although they had been washed with disinfectant countless times, she was sure that was the source of the aroma. She didn't miss the irony.

By contract, she was allowed her privacy, or the production company insisted on her anonymity—which was more important was never quite clear. But no one saw her without makeup, and she always slipped out of the theater through a side door, often into a waiting car with blacked windows. All part of the mystique, of course. No name had ever been given for the actress playing Mummy Dearest. And when she was gone, she knew damned well the role would simply be recast.

All the caution had been insufficient. Someone had snapped a photograph of her under the makeup. The damned thing would run in the *Times* tomorrow. She'd felt gut-punched when she first heard. Sickened and angry and afraid. The photo would end things. No, she didn't feel like fighting.

She felt like killing someone.

Misty Crowe (real name Cawthone)'s dressing room was spacious enough and, to her pleased surprise, sitting on the makeup shelf abutting the row of mirrors, stood a bottle of champagne on ice. A gift from Sonny, no doubt. She would take off the makeup, then have enough drinks to not give a damn. She wouldn't be able to taste it but could sure as shit *feel* that divine effervescence bubbling in her blood. Even the anticipation made things a little brighter.

This room, she decided, wasn't so bad. One of the better things she'd be placing in her rear-view mirror. Once upon a time, superstars had donned their greasepaint there. It was big enough for the entire troupe of Marx Brothers, and rumor was they had brought their zany brand of chaos there in 1932, performing as part of the promotion for their first film, *The Cocoanuts*.

Occasionally, she hallucinated that she could hear the laughter and applause echoing down here. Perhaps a trace of it was still in the walls, in the shadows that filled the corners of the dressing room. When the crowd cheered for her, she liked to think they were actually applauding *her* . . . not just the costume. Not just a role anyone with an hourglass figure and a rhythmic shimmy could kill in.

She peeled off her Mummy gloves and unwound the gauze one strand at a time (there is a last time for everything), until she reached the face mask, and peeled it off as well. The face beneath was ringed at eyes and mouth with black grease paint only slightly darker than the skin it concealed. With two fingers, she applied cold cream and wiped off the paint, revealing her real face. Misty Cawthone, born twenty-eight years ago in New Orleans' Treme district. Had Hattie McDaniel been a slender woman, she might well have resembled Misty Cawthone.

She sighed. "*I'd rather play a maid than be one,*" Hattie had often said. Was that why Misty played a monster? A dead thing? Because it was the only way she could stay alive in this damned business?

"*Is that why you are leaving the show?*"

Shocked, she snatched up her mask, held it up, and wheeled around to face the voice. There, in a darkened corner of the room, crouched something darker than shadow. Man-shaped. The size of a *large* man. Dammit, one of the costumed fans that turned out for the midnight show. His voice had echoed more than any voice she'd heard down here, as if they were in a cave, rather than a dressing room in the bowels of an aged theater.

"How did you get in here?" Misty asked, trying to sound imperious.

"*We have ways.*"

She pressed the mask tighter, as if it would protect her as it had her secret.

There was something about the voice and form that frightened her. *We?* The fans? Something else? "I'll scream," she said.

"*There is no need to scream.*"

He rose. Damn, he was tall. Almost six and a half feet, swathed in a black cloak, and hunched over. Standing up straight, he would have come close to seven feet. He approached the first circle of light cast by the bulbs above the row of mirrors, and she thought she'd get a closer look. Instead, the first light flickered . . . and then died.

"What . . . what do you want?" It wasn't just the shadow. His face *blurred* in the darkness, as if her eyes were watering. But there was something . . . feline about it. In the moment she'd seen his eyes clearly, she'd have sworn that the blacks were horizontal, not circular like a man's.

He sat on a stool facing her. He seemed to tower, even seated. *"We want to know why you are leaving the show."*

"It's just . . . time to move on."

It was clear that he didn't believe her. *"Without you, they will begin to tape in the daytime."*

She shrugged, realizing she was acting confident, but not feeling it. The dressing room might have been large enough for four Marx Brothers, but it wasn't big enough for Mummy Dearest and her fan. "What difference does it make? It's still broadcast at midnight."

"Let's say it makes a difference to . . . the audience."

"The live audience?" Misty asked.

He smiled. *"We wouldn't have phrased it that way."* For a moment, as he approached, there was enough light to see his face more clearly. A visage more animal than man. Something half way between, and almost beautiful save for a lack of proportion, as if he were frozen *becoming* something. The lack of proportion, the askew eyes and knife-like lips were disturbing.

Then another light blipped off, and that strange visage was again swallowed by darkness. She forced a laugh from a suddenly dry throat. "Well, you're in the spirit. No. The show is a specialty. A mystery. The hostess' face was never supposed to be shown."

"And you think that another woman . . . a paler woman . . . would have been fired?"

"The article?" She was startled. He knew about that? "It's coming out tomorrow."

"And you are so certain that your fans will reject you?"

Did she owe him the truth? Or would something clever be better, to send him off with a smile? Screw it. Truth and be damned. "It isn't just them. It's the syndication people. They say it won't play in the South. Which is a coward's way of saying *they* don't like it. So, they're shaking things up. The day switch is an excuse to bring in a new host."

"We don't want a new time. We don't want a new host."

"Well, that's very kind of you." Unexpectedly, she was touched.

"*It is not kindness.*"

"No?" He was strange, but she'd met strange fans before. It was just part of this odd job, she supposed. A cat, she thought. That's what his eyes reminded her of. So, he was a nutty enough fan to wear contact lenses under the mask. "What is it, then? I mean, you head up the fan club? You publish 'Mummy's Mumbles', right?" She could feel herself slipping into her rhythm. She'd done hundreds of interviews in the last three years. Always in makeup, or over the phone, of course. "It's been fun doing this, but . . . I don't know. Maybe I've never understood why it was so popular."

The fan's mask smiled. Were those whiskers? Wow. REALLY good mask. She wondered if maybe Jack Pierce, who had made the Wolfman howl and the Frankenstein monster prowl, had sent over a stuntman to mingle with the fans and tease her. It would be nice to think that such a titan was an admirer. And couldn't help but wonder if he'd have been if he knew more about her.

Monsters are one thing, but . . .

"*You know the movies are bad. But you love them. The monsters are thought . . . ugly. But you love them. You aren't making fun of . . . them.*"

She shook her hair out of its net. "You know . . . I wanted to be an actress. I was told that things were opening up. But they aren't. Not really. Not when the only job I could get is hiding my face."

"*How do you feel about that?*"

"How do I feel?" The smile on her lips felt false, even to her. "Well, this is my last interview, so let's talk turkey." She took a deep breath. Nothing was more dangerous than speaking your heart. "It hurts, dammit. All I wanted to do was act. And I can do anything: dance, sing, act, even a cartwheel and a backflip. I can do makeup and change myself into anything you can imagine. But I found out that the only thing I couldn't change stopped me. So, I wear this." She gestured with the mask.

And with that gesture, some of the anger left her. She just felt empty. That was not how she wanted to feel tonight. It took her a moment to find something of meaning. Something she'd said to an interviewer a few months back. Over the phone, of course. "We *need* horror movies. Fairy tales. Things that go 'bump' in the night. People who love animals enough to become them." His shoulders stiffened a bit, and she thought she heard a mewling sound. Clearing his throat, perhaps? "I think stories, even silly monster stories, have power as long as the people who make them *care*. And I believe most of them did. Even Ed Wood, bless his *bustier*. And I laugh at movies when actors complain about having to cover their faces all the time. I'd be happy to hide long enough to have a career. I understand wanting to be something else. Maybe for a lifetime. Maybe just until the lights come up and you come out of the dream. You fans . . . you understand loving something that much. Wanting to be something else. At least . . . I think you understand that hunger."

Raspy purrs echoed in the long narrow room, little pulses that stirred the air between them like gusts from the mouth of a cave. His eyes shone from the shadow. *"Hunger. Yes. Perhaps . . . the reporter could decide not to run the story. Sometimes people change their minds. Sometimes they can be* encouraged *to change their minds."*

Some tall, probably skinny, fan in a costume thinking that a little booga-booga might change the world. It was almost charming. "It's too late. It's alright. I'm heading to New York. There's a little repertory theater that offered me a position. The Oscar Micheaux Players. They're trying to continue his work." Now her smile was more genuine. Maybe this job wasn't so bad after all, not if, in some way, it had been an audition for the Players.

But even as she experienced that wave of satisfaction, the fan stiffened. Came out of his crouch, suddenly took more space in the room. Suddenly, she realized she had relaxed, and tensed again. Why did it feel as if the hairs on her arms and the back of her neck were on fire?

"You . . . did not enjoy your time here?"

She almost laughed. His feelings were hurt! Fans. She loved them, but . . .

"I did. But not for the reason you might think. I felt that we need horror stories. Fables. They help us deal with our own nightmares."

"We . . . they . . . are your nightmares?"

She ignored his gaffe. "Nah. There was something in those monsters that was more human than the villagers who chased them with torches and pitchforks. Would it be wicked to say that I sympathized with the monsters more than the villagers?"

And just like that, the bubble of tension that had compressed the air seemed to disappear. The animal mask's knife-thin lips curled in a smile. Wow. REALLY good makeup. But after the smile, a thoughtful frown. *"We believe this is true. So. It is done. And you will leave. And the show will be filmed during the day and shown at night. That is the end of it."*

She popped the bottle of champagne Sonny had left for her and poured herself a drink. Suddenly, she remembered her manners. "Would you like one?"

"I don't drink . . . wine."

They held each other's eyes for almost ten seconds, and then both broke up laughing. She blinked, and when her eyelids opened again, and without sound or visible motion, he was closer, close enough to take her hand. He wore furred gloves. This time, the light bulbs had not blinked off. The fan pressed whiskered lips against her knuckles.

And, with a whirl of air and black cloak, he was gone. Something was on her hand. A ring. Slender, a knot of twisted gold wire, the knot formed into a cat's head. She'd glimpsed one on his right ring finger. Like a club ring. She was being made an honorary member.

That . . . was sweet.

She looked again at the door he had passed through. The Greats had walked through that door. And in a moment, she would too, for the last time. "Only the best," she said, and tipped her glass to him. *Strange fellow.* And turned back to the mirror.

There came another knock at the door.

She sighed. She was tired of sighing. "Sure. Whatever. Who is it? No, wait." She slipped her mask back on. One last time.

After a pause, a tubby little man waddled in, wearing a plastic Halloween mask under an unruly mop of pale red hair. "Mummy?"

"That's me," she said. "That's me. Until I die of natural . . . *gauzes*?"

His grin lifted the mask. Outfit much cheaper than the last guy. "That's great. Well, I'm here for the interview." He paused and sniffed. "Say . . . what's that smell? It's like, I don't know. Like the lion cage at the zoo?"

She rubbed her nose under the mask. "Damned cold," she said. "Bromo quinine's wearing off. Can't smell a thing. But they used to keep dogs in the kennels down here. Sometimes when it rains, you can still smell it."

"It's not raining."

She shrugged. "Who did you say you were?"

"I'm Charlie Spafford. From the fan club?" He lifted a Kodak Brownie. "Can I have a picture . . . ?"

She felt her brow furrow. She glanced again at the ring on her hand. A keepsake, yes. *One of us.* But who had he been? "Did you pass a tall man coming out?"

"No. Why?"

She considered, and then shook her head. *Stagedoor Johnnies,* she thought. *Even stranger than fans.*

She smiled, stood, and struck a pose. In that moment, she was no longer Misty Cawthone. For the very last time, perhaps . . . but as long as she was in this costume, she would play it for everything it was worth.

She canted a hip, tilted her chin, and gestured theatrically, as if she were Norma Desmond. She winked suggestively and presented herself. Mummy Dearest, in the rotted flesh.

"Ready when you are, C.S."

ANTHILL

LISA MORTON

EED YOU IN KITCHEN—*got ants.*

Sophie read the text, sighed, and typed an answer. *Not now—working.*

She tried to return to watching the video Ian had just sent her, but a few seconds in, she was interrupted when her mother pounded on the bedroom door. "Sophie, can you come out here, please?"

Angry now, Sophie pushed her phone aside, flipped up off the bed, and yanked the door open. "What, Mom? I'm working."

Mom looked past Sophie. "Working on *what*, exactly?"

"My job."

A cynical smile creased her mother's face, already prematurely age-furrowed. "Oh, right—that context crater thing—"

"*Content creator*." Sophie was certain her mother knew this and was just trying to rile her. She took a deep breath, determined to stay chill. "I have fourteen thousand followers."

"And that pays how?"

"Sponsorships and merch."

The truth was that her only sponsor, a new energy drink, had dropped her after a month, and she'd sold exactly one t-shirt since the year had started, but she knew things would improve. Ian was getting better at crafting eye-popping graphics for her, and she had a sick story this week with a neighbor three houses down who'd called her the C-word when he'd caught her videoing the construction crew he'd hired to reno his garage. She'd already posted part 1 of this story and had watched as it racked up 683 comments and six thousand likes.

But none of it was enough for her mother, who was constantly on Sophie's ass about getting "a *real* job," or at least helping out around the house more. "I'm *really* busy," Sophie had tried to explain. "It's a lot of work to keep the followers interested."

Mom hadn't cared. "Sophie," she said, "you're twenty-three, and you've got no plans for a future. I won't be here forever, you know."

That part, at least, was true. Last year, at only fifty-five, Mom had suffered a stroke that she was still recovering from; since Dad had fled ten years ago (at least he'd left them the house), it had been up to Sophie to care for her. Mom had lost her job as a drugstore assistant manager, and they were living only on her disability and savings; Sophie's time had been given to her mother's care, so she couldn't work. But now her mother had recovered enough to look after herself, so she constantly harangued Sophie. "This will only take a minute," Mom said, as she stood in Sophie's doorway, hands on the hips of the designer jeans she'd outgrown ten years ago.

Sophie sighed (exaggeratedly this time) and gestured past her mom. "Fine. Show me."

Her mother turned and headed down the hall, Sophie following.

They reached the kitchen, and Mom gestured at a moving line that ran from the bottom of a cabinet up to a countertop. Sophie leaned over to take a look and saw the energetic six-legged insects. "Yes," she said, "ants. So what?"

"So, we have to do something. Once these things get into your kitchen, they're hard to get rid of."

"Mom," Sophie said, brushing a hand through the trail, "they're just ants."

She flinched as fiery pain erupted. One of the ants had stung her middle finger, which was already expanding into an angry red bump. "I didn't know ants could sting like that."

Her mother leaned closer to stare at the insects. "They're red. Must be fire ants." Mom moved her gaze to Sophie's finger, where the welt was already expanding into a blister. "We better get something on that. And we need some ant spray."

Sophie looked at the line of ants, felt the burning in her finger, and ran back to get her phone. "Are you going to the store?" her mother called after her.

After checking her makeup and hair in the mirror, Sophie returned with her phone, thumbed the video button, and started with the camera aimed at herself. "Oh my God, you guys, check this out . . . "

She turned the phone around to track the line of ants. "We've got ants. *Lots* of ants. And these aren't just any ants—these are *fire* ants. I mean, look at what they did to me . . . " She shifted to a close-up of her finger, where the blister was now the size of a pea. "This thing burns. Who knew ants could do that?"

She ended the recording when she realized her mother stood at the other end of the kitchen, staring at her in perplexity. "What are you doing?"

"It's for my stream. This is great."

"It's *not* great. Did you get something on that sting?"

"I will, but right now I need to get this online."

Thirty minutes later, Sophie had added a lengthy monologue about how much her mother was bugging her (most of her followers also had parental issues), cut it together with some stickers, decided to bypass Ian and his magical graphics this time, posted it—and instantly saw the comments and likes flooding in. Some of the responses commiserated with her about a parent ("*OMG, my mom is SOOOOO controlling, too*"), but more were horrified by the bite ("*That looks painful AF!*"). Several advised her on dealing with the ants; one even included a photo of a fire ant mound. "*Look for this*," it suggested.

Sophie rarely spent time in the backyard—her mom had been the gardener until the stroke—so she didn't know if there was an anthill there or not. Uncared for, the backyard had turned into a weedy jungle, the lawn and rosebushes long dead, replaced by crabgrass and dandelions.

But the photo of the anthill piqued Sophie's curiosity—or, rather, her constant search for content. If there was something like this in her own backyard, she might be able to get weeks' worth of posts out of it.

As she slid the grating glass door open, oppressive heat hit her like a gloved fist—she'd forgotten it was mid-summer in L.A. and over a hundred degrees. She stepped out, crossed the small concrete patio, and surveyed the backyard. It was knee-high in dense growth, so finding anything might be difficult. She thought for a moment before deciding to start outside the kitchen.

It didn't take long to find the trail of ants issuing from a crack in the stucco on the side of the house; their tiny red bodies, in continual motion, stood out even through the dry brown weeds. She followed the line, walking carefully beside it, until—THERE. In a small patch of earth clear of weeds was the mound, an uneven pile of dirt maybe a foot in diameter and four inches high, with ants scurrying in and out.

In an instant, Sophie's phone was on, recording the insects. After a few seconds, she donned her sunglasses, then thumbed the selfie button to turn the shot on herself. As she spoke about her adventure in following the ants, she liked how she looked with her shades on, violet hair framed by the burning blue sky. She would have Ian cut this together for posting later today.

When she returned to the house, she found her mother waiting for her. "What were you doing out there?"

"Following the ants. I found the anthill."

"Did you do anything about it?"

"I recorded it."

Mom uttered an exasperated gasp, then said, "That's not what I meant. Sophie, I need you to help out more around here. If you're not going to get a job, then—"

Sophie cut her off. "I *have* a job."

"It's *not* a job."

"I'm an artist—I create."

Mom threw a hand in the direction of the backyard. "*You* create? *What* do you create? Those ants create more than you do—they've got a whole colony." Seeing Sophie heading out of the living room, Mom changed her own direction. "Look, sweetheart, even though I don't understand what you do, I know you think it's important, but we're really struggling. Unless one of us can get back to work soon, we won't be able to make our property tax payment."

Holding up her phone, Sophie said, "I get it, Mom. But I think I've got something really big here, something that'll get me set up with new followers, and that'll mean money coming in."

When Mom just stared silently, Sophie left.

ANTHILL

Within a day, Sophie gained two thousand new followers.

Ian designed a t-shirt that read simply "Ant Food" in stylized letters. Forty-two sold overnight. He wouldn't even take a cut of sales; Sophie knew he wanted to sleep with her, but he lived five hundred miles away, a fact that cut her stress levels significantly.

When Sophie's mother asked her if she'd done anything to take care of the ants, Sophie said she had. It wasn't a lie; she'd bought a cheap package of cookies at the store and crumbled them up outside near the anthill. It did at least work in getting the ants to leave the kitchen. If Mom wondered why Sophie was spending more time in the backyard, she didn't say anything.

Sophie recorded the ants almost hourly, documenting their work, the growth of their anthill. Commenters told Sophie they'd never seen an anthill like that, one that grew so large, so quickly. Soon, it was three feet wide and eight inches high, a strange granular texture with dozens of tiny openings. "*It goes underground to where the queen is,*" said BugBoy2468 in the comments. "*Sophie is our queen,*" said CaliRosie, a comment that garnered hundreds of likes.

PretttttyGrrrll asked if the sting had healed. Sophie showed everyone that it had shrunken and faded. Her numbers dropped off then.

Ian texted her, "*Maybe you should let them sting you again, LOL.*"

She didn't laugh. In fact, she'd been thinking the same thing.

How to go about it? When Sophie had been stung before, she'd swept her hand through their trail in the kitchen.

Heading into the backyard with her phone, Sophie approached the anthill (which had expanded another foot in the last twenty-four hours), found a line of insects nearing it, and knelt beside them. She decided not to record the actual process of getting stung, because she didn't want any animal lovers to accuse her of causing harm to the ants.

Girding herself, she slapped her left hand down in the middle of the ants' path. Dust flew from beneath her palm. She felt the grain-sized creatures explode.

Then PAIN, at more than one point. Sophie leapt to her feet; even as she did, she felt fresh agony on the back of her hand. She shook her arm wildly, staggered back, away from the ants. When she'd gone a few feet, she looked at her hand.

The entire thing was already swollen like a red glove filled with water. She counted four white stings on her palm and two on the back of the hand. With her right hand, she thumbed her phone's record button, pointed it at the injured left, and grated out, "Okay, I just had a little run-in with these fucking ants, and I'd say they won. My hand hurts like a *bitch*."

"Sophie?" Her mother stood at the doorway, looking out at her. "What are you doing?"

For once, Sophie was glad to see her mother. She rushed to her, holding out the crimson, swollen limb. "I fell into the ants," she lied.

"Oh my God," Mom said, peering at the hand. "Sophie, that's *bad*. We should get you to the E.R."

Sophie debated with herself: a trip to the E.R might make for good material, but it could also involve a long, dull wait. "It's okay," she finally said, "I'll just pack it in ice. It'll probably go down pretty fast."

Her mother led her into the kitchen, where she wrapped ice in a dish towel as Sophie held the hand under the faucet. "What were you doing out there?"

"I was . . . " Sophie hesitated, trying to decide on the best lie. "I thought about what you said, about how the ants are really creating something, so I thought maybe I'd record that, you know? Like a nature documentary."

"Huh." Mom wrapped the ice-filled towel around the stings, bringing a relief that was pure bliss. "Would people pay to see that?"

Sophie shrugged, but as she gazed at her wrapped hand, she thought, *No, but they'll pay to see this.*

And they did.

The numbers that had dipped from the last day went ballistic. Her shares on the footage of her hand immediately after being stung were so huge that it was on the verge of going viral.

Comments numbered in the thousands. Sophie didn't have the patience to read all of them, but responded to a few to give the illusion of interaction.

SouthernFryedBoy: *Don't pop the blisters you could get infected.*

Sophie: *Thanks I won't.*

KevJSoGay: *What did you DO to those ants?*

Sophie: *It was an accident!*

KeshiaJJ420: *Don't go into your backyard anymore.*

Sophie: *I know right?*

Britt4Sci: *I know alot about ants & I've never seen anything like that anthill. You should consider calling a local university or something to look at it.*

Sophie: *Good suggestion!*

SkullF*k*r: *Please don't destroy the ants home. I won't like you if you do.*

Sophie: *I agree that it's fire. Fire ants, that is!*

Coco012904: *Your mom is right – the ants are creating.*

That last one bothered Sophie most, more than the predictable *You suck* responses. Sophie did talk about her mom often, but that comment implied not just that the ants were creating but that Sophie was *not*. The thought disturbed her enough that, well past midnight, she called Ian (texting was difficult with her chunky fingers, still sausage-sized, although less inflamed). "Do you think I'm a creator?"

Ian, who had evidently been asleep, cleared his throat and answered, "Welll . . . yeah. Of course."

"Why? Why do you think that?"

"Because . . . " Ian paused, then finally answered, "you sell stuff."

"But am I selling *art*?"

"Sure—you're selling *my* art!"

"But are these t-shirts really *art*?"

Ian shut up.

That night, Sophie's sleep was full of dreams that she remembered the next morning, something that rarely happened. In the dreams, she was in a cavern surrounded by hundreds of workers who took care of her every need. She understood that she was more than a star here—she was a leader, an icon . . . a queen. When she woke, she watched videos of fire ant queens, fascinated in a way she'd never been before. She felt kinship with the ants, but especially with the queen, hidden and protected and serviced somewhere in her backyard. She could almost *feel* the queen inside her, sense her wordless thoughts.

When Sophie finally thought to check her feed (it *never* took her that long to check her feed in the morning), she found that overnight she had sold 546 shirts, 89 mugs, 12 phone cases, and a keychain.

When Sophie got the first bank transfer from her merch sales, she printed it out and showed it to Mom.

"What are people buying?" Mom asked.

Sophie was wearing Ian's latest "YAAASSS QUEEN" shirt, which she pointed at.

Her mother squinted in disbelief. "Okay. But how long can this last? The ants are gone now."

"No, they're not." The instant the words left Sophie's mouth, she regretted it.

"Sophie, those things nearly sent you to the hospital." Mom abruptly headed for the rear sliding glass door, and Sophie rushed to follow.

"Where are you going?"

"If you won't do something about this, I will."

The door open, Mom stepped out onto the patio.

The queen was out there.

Sophie was instantly beside her mother. "No, you can't—"

Cutting her off, searching the yard, Mom said, "You can find something else to make shirts about, something that won't *hurt* you."

Mom pushed through the brush, her gait still slightly slowed by the stroke. Sophie followed, panicking, her head filled with thoughts that felt alien, thoughts of broods and colonies and thousands of offspring, of terror at what could happen if Mom found the anthill—

"Oh my God."

Her mother was staring at the anthill, now the size of a child's wading pool; its mottled texture and reddish-brown hue gave it an almost alien appearance, otherworldly. Its sides were a mass of motion as ants moved around and through it.

Sophie joined her mother, who stood gaping. "What . . . they've been busy. You almost have to admire them."

"It's beautiful, isn't it?" Sophie said.

Somehow, Sophie knew the queen was a few inches below the surface, marshalling her forces. But that was impossible, wasn't it? Ant queens weren't generals, creating military strategies . . . and even if they were, how could Sophie possibly know that? Unless . . . these were very *special* ants, *evolved* ants, that had infected her with more than just venom.

As Sophie watched, a single ant crawled onto her mother's right foot. She didn't say anything, just observed the scout searching, moving over the leather strap of the open sandal.

Mother turned to eye her daughter, incredulous. "You've known all along this was back here."

"I—" Sophie broke off. What could she say—that she had, in some way she couldn't explain, become a part of the colony? Instead, she remained silent, watching the ant as it scuttled down a strap and onto her mother's bare foot.

Mom looked down then, saw the ant, started to raise her foot— and cried out in pain as the ant stung. "Oh, damn it—"

"No, it's okay, Mom. It just stings for a while, then you'll—"

Sophie broke off as her mother's face abruptly froze in horror, eyes widening, color draining. As Sophie stood by, her mother's throat seemed to expand, moving spastically, her mouth opening, limbs flailing, and she fell into the path of the ants.

Allergic reaction—that had to be it. Some of her followers had commented on that possibility.

Or . . . perhaps there was only room for one queen in the house.

Sophie's paralysis broke then, replaced by instinct. She pulled out her phone and punched in 911. As the dispatcher answered, more ants moved onto her mother's body, stinging over and over. Sophie barely heard either the dispatcher or her own autonomic answers, her gaze riveted to the ants. They crawled across her mother's twitching face, into her nose, across her eyes; a mass of them went into the open mouth, causing Mom to choke and gag. Where they'd stung, the skin had already formed masses of blisters with red centers that erupted, oozing blood and pus. Her limbs were the size of logs, the blistered skin stretched taut.

The dispatcher assured her that help was on the way as Sophie watched her mother convulse a final time, foam and ant bodies spewing from her mouth . . . and she died.

Sophie had never seen anyone die before, not in real life. As the 911 dispatcher asked her what was happening, she stayed silent. There was no question that her mother was dead.

Beneath her, the queen was pleased.

Sophie stood, unmoving, until the paramedics arrived a few minutes later. They found her in the backyard, pushed her back, crouched by her mother. By then, the ants had gone, their work finished. The paramedics started working on Mom; they jammed shots into her, used paddles to try to start her heart again. After a few minutes, they began to slow down; they were no longer rushing when they placed her swollen, bloodstained body onto a stretcher and carried it to their vehicle. One of them was saying something to Sophie, but she didn't hear; another openly wondered what the hell had happened. When they left, they didn't even turn on the siren.

Later, Sophie would vaguely remember two cops who'd asked her questions; she didn't know what she said. After a while, they left. They never suspected Sophie. It had all been a terrible freak accident.

She was alone. She was truly, completely alone in the house she'd grown up in, but she realized she wasn't alone in the world.

She was a queen, after all, and it was time she addressed her followers.

The comments poured in as she spoke. She didn't say her mother had died of an allergic reaction to ant stings; she lied and said it had been another stroke. Within an hour, Ian had organized a donation fund for her; two hours later, it had collected nearly forty thousand dollars.

For the first time that day, Sophie laughed when she saw that figure—it would've convinced her mother that she *could* make money.

Too bad a tiny part of Sophie thought she'd killed her mother to get it.

The next few days went by in a blur of decisions, paperwork, and lawyers.

Fortunately, Mom had drawn up a will after the stroke, so everything went directly to Sophie. There was no other family, anyway, except Dad, whom Sophie didn't bother to notify. She wasn't sure where he was, anyway.

There was a little money left from Mom, but Sophie wouldn't even need it, at least not right away. Her stats were through the roof; she was selling three hundred items a day, she'd had multiple sponsorship offers, and her donation fund was nearing six figures.

I'm a queen.

I killed my mother.

Sophie's dreams, sleeping and waking, were haunted by visions of ruling, of watching her mother die so she could ascend as queen.

More and more, Sophie found herself thinking about purpose and community, about how the ants achieved that. Her hours were filled with thoughts she could barely understand, thoughts she knew were not hers but that she grasped more as time passed. She saw, from the perspective of a queen, how the ants functioned. They had ambition. They had power.

They could create.

Three nights after her mother's death, high on weed, smoke curling about her head, Sophie livestreamed a monologue. "These ants have built their own world," she said, "and what have I done? Nothing but take what they've created and try to make it mine. I'm a thief. A plagiarist. No better than AI."

She paid no attention to the rush of comments assuring her she was none of those things. Instead, she continued: "But I'm changing. I'm becoming part of something important, something bigger than me. I'm becoming . . . a queen."

One of the commenters asked her if she was high on formic acid. *"It's what ants inject you with when they sting."*

Sophie laughed and turned off the camera.

They didn't understand.

In the morning, Sophie knew what she had to do.

She showered, put on her makeup and her favorite shirt, the pink one with the purple glitter lining the hems. She attached her phone to a selfie stick on a tripod. She checked herself in a mirror one last time, and then went into the backyard.

The sun had just edged over the horizon, the Southern California heat already roasting the land, but the ants were undeterred. Their colony was now immense, the mound taking up nearly a quarter of the backyard. It undulated in rough waves; parts ascended toward the sky in conical shapes, while others spread across the ground like some rough beast's hind legs. Every part of it jittered with activity; it must have spawned more ants as it had grown.

Sophie felt the queen close to the middle, below ground, waiting as she was pampered and protected.

She had worn shorts and no shoes. As she approached the anthill, she already felt the stings on her feet, but she ignored the pain. It was important that she get this right.

She set up the tripod with her phone at one end of the anthill. The shot was perfectly framed. She started the stream before stepping away from the phone and into the frame, positioning herself draped on her back over the anthill.

Offering herself as the new queen.

Words weren't needed, so she waited silently as the ants began to cover her. Hundreds of bursts of bright agony erupted all over every part of her, but the pain congealed into a formless mass that soon faded. She thought about her mother, was sorry about what had happened, but the regret and guilt were ebbing with the rest of her. She wondered if the massive amount of formic acid she'd taken in was why she felt as if she was floating, free of the bonds of flesh and gravity, but then moving downward, below the dirt and the tunnels and the workers into the queen. Their consciousness— ant and human—joined then.

Sophie's last human thought was that she had finally created something truly special. She was only sorry she'd never see how many views she got.

TURBELLARIA: THE CITY OF WORMS

MAXWELL I. GOLD

Proem

We began as worms. We ended as worms, the tubular, indistinguishable, undeniable self that was us, that was *me*. The truth, like a scythe, cut down the norms that divided the city into corridors until we came to understand that we were nothing but worms, crawling from the dirt that was Turbellaria.

I hated the worms . . .

I

 O ONE EVER questioned the laws or edicts of the Old Worms who sledged through the streets of Turbellaria, the gray-haired, wrinkled, and fat Annelida who lorded themselves over daily life. And why would they?

The Old Worms were the keepers of institutional life, the flesh guardians of the lives that came before us. They who knew carried the Articles of Reproduction and Blood as if to conceal the purpose of gender, self, and the treasures of bone and lust.

Everyone else within the walls fell into either of two groups: Trematodes and Flukes. Trematodes flaunted their ribbon-like skin, declaring their appropriated status to the Flukes, who found themselves beaten and berated as parasites to the other denizens of the city.

Of course, I was a Fluke. My body tender, a pale viridescent gray with lanky arms that caught the unwanted attention of everyone else as I slid down the street.

"What's wrong with your skin, Fluker?" a Trematode mocked.

"And I thought I was ugly," a fellow Fluke chimed in while I crawled into an alley, not trying to hide—I was used to the indignance of Turbellaria—but merely to seek a moment of solace from the city that not only hated me, but hated itself.

"There's no separation but separation from the self!" I heard the crinkled voice of an Old Worm call. This was their usual time to cry throughout the city the tired, broken song of confinement, reproduction, and repression; to proselytize and ensure continued order.

"We begin as worms. We end as worms," they called.

Taking a reprieve from my solace, I saw the procession of gray, guarded, and gentrified gods slither through the world that they had made in their image.

The Old Worms said a lot of things, but they'd never tell the truth about what we really were.

"Liars!" I cried.

The procession stopped. A guard turned toward me, but one of the Old Worms raised itself. "Wait! What lie do you speak of, young Fluke?"

"Yours, Old Worm. Your repression of our bodies, and our true selves!" A crowd gathered. I hated crowds, especially when I'm the one who's the center of attention. A few Trematodes grumbled, seeing my gray body rustle the Old Worms.

"Everyone is happy with who they are, you annoying Fluke. Why don't you go back to the hole you crawled out from?" The obnoxious Trematode took extreme pleasure in his martyrdom.

The guards were quickly dispatched, while crowds erupted in a mix of derision and jubilant, mocking laughter.

Too late, before I'd had the chance to flee, a heavy metal object bludgeoned me until my eyes were filled with blood and lights.

II

The smell of shit and rust clogged my nostrils when I woke up from what felt like days in a dank prison I'd never seen before. I suppose this was coming for me sooner or later. The old bastards, worms who fancied themselves gods but were nothing but pieces of soft flesh in a city of their own design. This city of miseries, delusions, and denials was the closest thing they'd ever have to paradise. The tall wooden door, riddled with termites and mold, slowly cracked open to reveal the figure of a wide, grotesque worm.

"I see you're awake," the figure said, sounds of flesh and slime smacking through the moist, oaky silence.

"So, this is what you do to worms who don't follow your rules?" I snapped.

"We've done worse, but the Old Worm who ordered your incarceration noted you had a bit of spunk, and I wanted to see for myself. You were rather defiant, calling us liars." I couldn't discern his face or shape. He was much larger than any Old Worm I'd encountered before. No doubt he was of some extreme importance, but I'd no way of knowing.

"It's the truth," I sighed.

"The lie is the truth?" A shimmer of light reflected from the prison gutter, where I saw a toothy grin and a strange insignia.

I couldn't move. They'd shackled me to the wall. "That's what you'd have us keep believing."

"Is it that we're feeding you a lie or we're trying to protect you from something you're not ready to feel?" He paused momentarily. "Imagine a city with limited resources. A city where only a certain number of worms can live and reproduce. And then imagine the worms that can reproduce without each other. What disorder! What chaos! A breakdown of basic services would ensue if there was no order to ensure worms knew what was best for them. Is safety a lie? Is order a lie if we're only doing what's best for the worms?"

The mass of slime and flesh stepped closer, revealing himself to be none other than Helminth, the Great Worm. According to the official codes and texts, it was said Helminth populated Turbellaria from his own progeny, spawning the first Old Worms, who then built and ruled the city of worms.

"Don't the other worms have a right to know the truth about

their city? Their history?" I looked up into his emotionless, white eyes and saw nothing but the remorseless autonomy of duty.

"You already know the answer, my young worm. Normally, someone so defiant and reckless would be dead by now, but you remind me of myself. Well, everyone does." He chuckled at his own sick joke. "Instead of death, I'm going to let you live. You're banished from Turbellaria, Fluke. You'll live on, knowing the truth of worms. You'll go on, carrying the terrible truth of yourself and the rest of us. No matter where you go."

A guard followed behind Helminth, leading me out of the dungeon.

"What if I don't want to leave?" I protested.

"Then you already know the alternative, Fluke," he said.

We walked down an ancient corridor, someplace that almost predated the whole city. Helminth ordered the guard to leave as he led me to the end.

"Where are you taking me?"

"I'm taking you to the future," Helminth said as the wide door swung open to a horizon of sand and blue skies. The city of Turbellaria was walled off from the reality that was Helminth's hermaphroditic lie.

"Now, go. Go with the understanding that this is your truth." The Great Worm disappeared into the darkness beneath the city.

We began as worms. We ended as worms, the tubular, indistinguishable, undeniable self that was us, that was me.

That's always been me.

The truth, like a scythe, cut down the norms that divided the city into corridors and canon until we came to understand that we were nothing but worms, crawling from the dirt that was Turbellaria.

I loved the worms . . .

AN ANTHEM FOR THE WORMS

MAXWELL I. GOLD

Past the gate,
   through dark,
      sticky nothing,
         wriggling, writhing,
            swaying to ancient songs,
               sired by sycophantic dreams,
                  broken histories; flukes,
                     bleak bodies flummoxed
                     their way towards
                       pitiful oblivion—
                  Woeful cities built
               on possibilities
             projected far,
           into hemispheres
         above practical dreams,
        now fat, heavy and hardened
     by the truth—
inevitability and mass,
pressed deeper earth,
     against worm and rot
        followed by the music

of old anthems,
limp towers,
and hungry
promises of
reconciliation
and revenge
feed the earth,
for the worms—
chants follow the deep,
the dark, the hungry mass
beneath the city—
feed the earth,
feed the worms—
possibilities dead,
buried in corpse muscle
and bleak bones,
feed the earth,
feed the worms—
broken are the gates
where woeful cities
sing anthems no more.

SNUGGLES FOR FELIX

STEVEN VAN PATTEN

ATING SEASON WAS always a difficult time for Felix. His location in the communal tree had never been ideal. In the past, he'd tried to jockey for a sturdier branch, something higher with a better view. He'd only ended up bullied back to something less than ideal. And to think, the other male fruit bats had the nerve to call themselves his friends.

Because of the way the male fruit bats treated Felix, the lady bats would often be worse to him. Forget visiting his branch. Most days they wouldn't even speak to him except to ask him to slide over so they could get to another of the males. His was a life of irony, living in a communal tree, without ever feeling any warmth from his community.

One day, when the screeching and carrying on of everyone else in the tree loving one another became too much, Felix decided he'd had enough. Without a word to anyone, he stretched out his four-foot wingspan, which was a little shorter than everyone else's, and took flight. He didn't know where he was going, and he had no plan whatsoever. He only knew he'd endured enough of being ignored.

As impromptu as his journey may have been, he was mindful of his changes in direction and so on. He was determined not to go back, but if, after this excursion, his only choices would be starvation or being eaten by some hawk, then he'd have to face reality and go home.

And there was no question he'd be able to find his way back. He may have been smaller than his so-called brothers, but he was gifted with perhaps the best navigational skills the gods had seen fit to gift a fruit bat. But these positive attributes were seldom appreciated.

Unfortunately, his strength and energy waned. After what humans would consider hours of flying, Felix was finally tired and needed some place to rest. The only problem was, he didn't see any trees. The landscape below him had become barren. Not one to rest on the ground, he pressed on, even as pure exhaustion set in.

To his left, he saw an ominous-looking cave with strange noises coming out of it. It sounded like fellow bats, but if they were bats, they spoke in a strange dialect. Knowing other bats tended to be as territorial as the ones he'd left behind, he decided not to steer in there asking for directions or help.

He flapped his wings less and let the wind carry him more. It set in that he'd have to stop at some point and he'd end up being killed by some predator before the night was over. *Killed by my own stubbornness,* he thought.

But finally, he passed the rocky terrain and spotted, of all things, grass. And where there's grass, there's usually—

"A tree!" Felix shouted with relief.

He guided himself toward the tree, even as the welcome scents of white jasmine filled his eager little nostrils. As he glided down further, his eyes and his nose delivered even better news.

"Peaches!"

Yes, Felix had found a peach tree in the middle of nowhere.

It was not his most graceful landing, but after some bumping around, he settled himself on a branch. He was instantly overwhelmed. A whole peach tree to himself! He could barely believe it! In mere seconds, he made a complete mess of himself, gorging on the fruit until his tiny stomach had extended. Content for the time being, he fell asleep. His last thought before slumber being that, even if he never found a mate, he had proven he didn't need the charity of the communal tree to survive. Wrapping himself in his wings, Felix drifted off, smiling and feeling something uncommon in his normal life. Confidence.

"Greetings."

Felix had no idea how long he'd been asleep, but he was awakened by an oddly accented voice asking a very direct question. As his eyes quickly adjusted, he found himself being starred at intently by a much smaller bat with the shortest snout he'd ever seen. The unfamiliar creature, hanging from a branch across from him, looked as if he were a regular bat who had run into something hard while flying.

"Long-snouted traveler, how is it you find yourself here in my domain?"

Felix blinked himself full awake and unfurled his wings. "Um . . . I am so sorry. I didn't mean any harm!"

"It is no matter. You are here, and you are my guest."

Despite the gracious welcome, Felix still felt anxious. "These aren't your peaches, are they? I mean, I was starving when I got here."

The small but ferocious-looking bat waved a wing dismissively. "You need not concern yourself. I do not claim ownership of the fruits of this tree. In fact, I never eat . . . fruit."

"Oh! You're more an insect guy!"

Under his funny-shaped nose, the short bat smirked. "Not necessarily. But, my friend, I need to ask why you have found yourself here?"

Felix briefly explained how he felt no love from the other inhabitants of his communal tree and how his feelings had been hurt for a long time. "So, I just flew and flew, until eventually I was here."

The smaller bat nodded considerately. "How very fortunate for both of us."

Felix tilted his head. "How so?"

"Because we can solve each other's problems. You see, my friend, I happen to be rather, shall we say, persuasive when it comes to acquiring mates and making friends in general."

Felix was understandably intrigued. "Are you saying you're willing to teach me how to talk to lady bats?"

The smaller, vicious-looking bat was now grinning from ear to pointed ear. "Not teach. I will make you like me."

That made no sense to poor Felix. Not to mention why, after being rejected by his own kind for his size, would he want to be smaller and then stuck with a misshapen nose?

"Your appearance would not change, only your personality. You would become, how do you say it? More charismatic."

More charismatic? Felix's mind was suddenly ablaze with images of himself back at the tree, surrounded by the lady bats. The thought of the snuggling alone was euphoric.

"That sounds amazing! What do I have to do?"

The short-nosed bat let go of his branch and began flying toward Felix. "Just stay right there!"

Fear filled Felix in a way it never had. Even being confronted by the biggest, meanest of the communal tree's fruit bats paled compared to this. All he could see were two rows of jagged fangs zeroing in on him. He screamed as he let go of the branch and took flight, but not before the attacking stranger grabbed hold and bit him on the back of his neck.

"Let go of me!" Felix screamed as he tried to shake off the biter.

"But don't you want to be like me? Don't you want to be a vampire?"

"A vampire!" Until now, he had thought vampire bats were only a myth. *Living off the blood of other animals? Who would even dream of something that horrific?* "NO!"

"Well, it's too late now!" The vampire's voice was muffled as its little jaws tightened on Felix's skin. As the pain increased, Felix felt himself growing angry. And the more enraged he became, at both his current predicament and everything that led to it, he found the strength to shake the vampire off.

The bloodsucker called out to him one last time. "It's too late! You are like me now!"

Still frightened, Felix found the resolve to stay in the air for the rest of the night. The only good thing about returning to the relative safety of the communal tree would be they probably wouldn't notice he had left. There would be no explaining himself to a bunch of bats who hadn't been worried about him in the first place.

As dawn approached, so did Felix. Only as the sun's rays came over the communal tree soft and slow, Felix, weary from his second long flight, nearly crash-landed, bumping several sleeping fruit bats, until finally settling on a branch that wasn't normally his.

Gathering himself higher in the tree than he was usually allowed, he shook his head for clarity. For causing a ruckus and waking everyone else up early, he would endure the usual insults.

"What hit me?"

"Was that the runt?"

"Felix the runt! What's wrong with you?"

"Probably ate some bad fruit. Stupid head."

Then, finally, he heard it. A lady fruit bat's voice. "Wait. Something is different about him. Something about his mouth."

He remembered the vampire's awful teeth and figured if he were turning into one, that would be why his mouth was different. He turned to the lady fruit bat. "Isabel? That's your name, right?"

Isabel almost seemed to blush. "Why, yes. Yes, it is."

Felix let go of his branch, righted himself, and hovered in the air as he approached Isabel. When he spoke, it was as if he were possessed by a bat far more eloquent than he had ever been.

"Isabel, my love. Let us leave these others. This past day, I have seen wonders dark and light. A world beyond this tree. I have faced a demon bat, and I have returned with a taste for the forbidden. Let me show you these wonders. Let me take you in my cold, dark embrace."

Two seconds of sheer silence ended as hysterical laughter erupted throughout the tree.

"What in the world was that?"

"That's what you get for being nice to him, Isabel!"

"Runt's feeling himself today, huh?"

"He's good at hovering, I will say that."

"That's cause he's so small!"

As Felix made his way back to the branch, the laughter continued. Alas, one fruit bat found none of this funny.

Benji, the alpha fruit bat, unfurled his massive wingspan and descended from the top branch to where everyone else had gathered to taunt Felix. "This idiocy ends now!"

Felix was finally at his breaking point. "You know what, Benji? You're not the boss anymore!"

The laughter stopped. Surely, Benji would do serious harm to Felix for the lack of respect. But since Benji was hard pressed to see Felix as a threat, his reaction was tempered. "No longer the boss? Explain why you would say such a thing!"

"Because I'm a vampire now!"

At the mention of the word 'vampire,' the crowd of fruit bats collectively gasped. Even Benji, the biggest of them all, seemed shaken by the declaration. But then he drew closer to Felix, even as the others recoiled.

"Well, that little speech of his was very much vampire-like," one bat observed.

"Wait, they exist? I thought they were a myth," one of the younger bats said.

"They exist. They're smaller than us, but very dangerous," an older bat shared.

"Well, Felix is smaller," yet another bat added. "Maybe that explains it."

"Shut up, all of you!" Benji finally bellowed. He had gone from staring into Benji's eyes to noticing a white build-up around Felix's mouth. The same build-up Isabel had been referring to, unbeknownst to the rest of the fruit bats. "You're not a vampire, you idiot! You have rabies!"

The entire lot of them cried in unison. "Rabies! Rabies! Rabies!" As the chant grew louder, most of the male bats took to the air, swirling around to protest Felix's very presence.

"Get out!"

"He'll infect us all!"

"How dare you bring disease to the communal tree!"

"Cast him out!"

Felix, knowing rabies was a death sentence, cried. "But where am I supposed to go?"

After a moment, Benji finally answered. "We don't care. Now, leave."

With the tears flowing from his little eyes, Felix took flight again, as the angry cries of a family that never loved him filled his ears until he was finally some distance away.

Alone and even sadder than the last time he'd struck out on his own, he figured it would only be a matter of time. Believing himself to be out of options, his final thought was to seek out the vampire bat that had bitten him and let him finish him off.

Maybe it was the rabies, or maybe he was just tired, but after hours of flying yet again, he found he couldn't make it all the way to the peach tree. Without the strength to flap, he would glide for as long as he could. Thankfully, the winds were kind, and his landing on the grass was soft. He could see the tree, but it was too far for him even to crawl, so he laid there sobbing gently.

"Hey! Grab the net! I think the jasmine flowers got us a visitor."
Felix didn't understand human-speak, but he knew what they sounded like. He gave one final desperate cry as he felt himself grabbed up. Everything went black, and he felt a horrible pinch in his side. Then, it was as if some inexplicable force within him was making him sleep.

"Hey! I think he's waking up."
"Hey, buddy! You okay in there?"
As his eyes opened, he could see the humans. Big ones with different colored faces, but their midsections were mostly white.
No! They're going to eat me!
He screeched.
"Relax, buddy. No one's going to hurt ya."
Felix didn't understand the words, but the creature's tone seemed friendly enough. He screeched one more time, then stopped. He looked around, trying to make sense of his surroundings, to no avail. A human would have explained that he'd been put into a glass enclosure for his protection, but he would not have understood it.
He had no idea how long he'd been asleep, but he knew he was hungry. They seemed to know it too.
"How about a peach, buddy?"
Somehow, a peach was dropped in his encasing next to him. He flipped himself over and, after some sniffing and licking, attacked it with fervor, putting to rest any ideas he'd developed a taste for blood. As he ripped the peach to pieces, the humans kept up with their gibberish language.
"Is he safe to put in with the others?"
"Oh yeah. We ran the tests. He had been infected with rabies, probably by one of the vampire bats in the area. Fortunately, we caught it super early. He's good to go."
The darker-faced human leaned in as Felix was finishing his peach. "Well, little guy, it's time to meet your new family."
When his enclosure began to move, he shrieked. Felix didn't like being transported outside of his own power, not even a little. Trapped in the glass prison, he couldn't even stretch his wings out until the movement finally stopped and the top of the see-through hinderance was pulled away with a popping sound.

In this new world, the sky was the same white color as the human's midsections. But there was a tree, and, though he smelled other fruit bats, all seemed quiet and welcoming.

As he climbed out of the glass cell, he looked at the humans, who bared their teeth, but in an odd, nonconfrontational way. Humans, he finally concluded, were strange.

Turning back to the tree, it only seemed natural to fly up to it, so he did. After finding a nice sturdy branch to settle on, he heard a more familiar language being spoken.

"My goodness! Did they finally find us a male?"

"It would appear so, Gladys!"

"He's cute!"

"Hey, if you can hear us, come up higher."

Felix did as the voice instructed, making his way up further and higher into the tree until he saw six lady fruit bats hanging from their various branches.

"Hi, Fly Guy! What's your name?" one of them asked.

"I'm Felix! Who are you?"

They introduced themselves as Agnes, Gloria, Stephanie, Yolanda, Rene, and Gladys.

"Felix, I think you should come closer," Gladys said.

"No fair!" Agnes cried. "I saw him first!"

"I'm the youngest," Yolanda pointed out. "He should snuggle with me first."

Felix couldn't believe his eyes or ears. *Snuggle with her first?*

The lady bats carried on for some time before finally relenting to Gladys being the first to snuggle. Over the next few months, they would all take a turn.

While spending the rest of your days in a lab would not be ideal for most wild animals, things continued to work out quite well for Felix for the rest of his natural lifespan. Without his knowledge or understanding, the studies these gentle humans made of his behavior and the occasional blood sample brought forth medical breakthroughs and made Felix a hero to the bigger creatures. He ended up with hundreds of offspring and was instrumental in the continuation of his species.

Of course, Felix didn't care about any of that. As long as he got his peaches and his snuggles, he was good.

AND YET WE FLY

L. H. MOORE

HE SUN WAS beginning its daily descent below the horizon, its rays casting a golden light everywhere unless they failed to permeate—the shadows of the in-between places, those liminal spaces with dim and shadowed recesses where those who want to be hidden try to remain unseen. An alley cut between two buildings, their brick, multi-storied façades looming overhead and deepening the darkness within. People walked or rushed by on the sidewalk beyond it, talking, laughing, and going about their lives without a single glance toward it. With a restaurant on one side and a nightclub on the other, its large dumpsters overflowed—a rich bounty of plentiful goodness that certain denizens of the city could not ignore.

A white cardboard box of half-eaten pizza had fallen out of one of the dumpsters, the green and red design on its top distorted and crumpled. Rat sniffed the air and eyed it hungrily from the corner, looking to see if anyone else had noticed. He scurried over to it and was about to drag a slice away when he heard a voice from above.

"What do you have down there?" it asked.

He looked up and saw a pigeon perched on a wire. Ugh, he thought. Goddamn pigeons.

"What does it look like?" Rat said with annoyance as he hovered over his culinary prize. His hunger gnawed at him even stronger, and he certainly wasn't going to share. "And don't go and try to shit on my head or anything, okay? We all know how you pigeons do. Besides, aren't you done for the day?"

The pigeon tilted her head and shifted on her perch, her iridescent neck feathers shimmering. "Just curious, you know? This is one of my regular stops. Always good pickings here. Not just one, but two dumpsters. Two, I tell ya! Thought I'd check this place out to see if there was anything good going on before I turned in." She stopped talking and looked over as something caught her attention. "Hey, you, heads up."

Rat heard it too and glanced over at the commotion as two men quickly came into the alley, one short and stocky, the other tall and lean.

Their voices rose.

Humans, Rat said with a sigh, looking longingly at the slice. Worst damn vermin of all. The men came closer, and Rat scurried under the dumpster to watch as the argument became more heated.

"Louis, I don't care about all that," the stocky one said as he ran a many-ringed right hand through his short-cropped dark hair. "I don't care about all that at all. Last time I looked, you were the one who had access to it, and now it's missing. You were the one who was responsible. You seriously dropped the ball."

"The fuck I did, Johnny! What are you trying to say? You calling me a thief?" Louis, the tall one, said, his voice even louder. He had a lean, hungry look to him. Rat watched him closely. *I know someone who does what they need to do to survive when I see it*, Rat thought. *That one right there isn't any different.*

"All I know is that the boss is looking at me like I've done something, and I can't account for it. That money was in there. Saw it with my own eyes, and now it's gone, and you're the only other person who saw it too."

"That proves nothing. Does the boss know anything? You out here snitching or something?" Louis said, slowly backing away from him.

"Nah, nobody's snitching, but I'm just saying . . . "

Louis' face turned hard, and he looked around and behind them to see who else was passing by. No one. He calmly unzipped his jacket, letting it fall open. "So, you're saying that you are the only one who knows?"

"Well, yeah, but . . . "

Louis didn't give him a chance to answer. Rat recoiled from within his hiding place as three tentacles sprang forth from under the man's jacket. Before Johnny could react, two of them slithered around his body, binding him tightly as they constricted so he could not move. The third tentacle slithered into his agape mouth, violating it and choking him as it silenced his screams. With one swift movement, Johnny's head was sliced in half, what remained of the pinkish-gray brain matter left exposed within his now-open skull. Short, sharp spikes like switchblades sprang out from the other two tentacles. Johnny made a motion that retracted his tentacles at once, shredding Johnny's body into pieces, sending chunks of him and a spray of blood everywhere.

Johnny's severed hand, its gold rings glinting in the fading light, landed with a soft thud near Rat, who didn't quite understand what he had just seen. He had never seen a human do that before, but then again, in his short life, they had proven capable of just about anything, so why not this too? They were more than just the horror stories that his mother had told him about. Humans always lived up to their reputation as the bogeymen, bringing death, destruction, and ruin everywhere they went.

Humans really are *the worst,* he thought. *And they call us vermin.*

Louis looked down at Johnny's scattered remains, his tentacles withdrawing into his body as he closed his jacket. "Can't say nothing now, asshole," he said as he calmly turned and hastened away without a single glance back at the carnage.

When he was far out of sight, Rat slowly crept out from under the dumpster and cautiously surveyed the scene before him. He figured he'd better hurry, as he probably didn't have much time before more humans discovered what happened. *For creatures who killed other creatures so easily, they sure make a big deal when it's one of their own,* he thought. But that didn't matter to Rat, because where others would see a gruesome murder, Rat saw an opportunity.

He eyed Johnny's body, the warm guts and exposed brain enticing him. *I might even have an eyeball or two if I have the time.* The mineral scent of the blood made Rat feel ravenous. Why eat pizza when he could dine on something—or *someone*—more . . . substantial?

Rat slinked around the meaty chunks of flesh, choosing one that looked fatty and moist. He closed his eyes as he bit into it. So good. Still warm and so, so, delicious. Rat had dined on a corpse only once before, but that one had been there for a while. It was a rare delicacy to get it fresh, to roll its wet warmth on the tongue, and Rat couldn't believe his luck. It was a wonder the others hadn't already arrived. He knew they would be there soon.

"Well now," Pigeon said from above, breaking the silence of the moment. "That was different . . . "

"That's the truth right there. Humans, right?" Rat answered in-between bites. "You trying to get in on this?"

"Nah, not my thing. Got some crow and vulture friends who would be hyped, though. But me? I'll pass."

"What? You think you're better or something? You're pretty much just a rat with wings, scrounging to survive just like me."

Pigeon started to answer, but the door to the restaurant suddenly opened. A worker came out, his white t-shirt stained with condiments and sauces from a long day in the back of the kitchen. He was carrying a large garbage bag and dropped it with a shout when he saw the dead man's dismembered body and Rat feasting upon it.

He cried out at the scene before him and rushed over to chase Rat away.

The worker was much faster than his large body would have made anyone think. The man's black boot came down around Rat as he tried to stomp him out of existence. Rat cursed to himself as he dodged the black boot, but as he turned to run again, one of his feet got caught on something, holding him in place.

There was a sickening crunch as the large boot found his little spine.

Humans, Pigeon thought as she came down from her perch and walked over to where Rat lay, looking at him. His eyes had gone still, but his crushed body was still twitching, the viscera pink of his guts spilled out onto the alley's grime and muck.

Ignoring Johnny's body parts, she went over to the spilled contents of the bag the man had dropped, her pick of food strewn across the ground. Pigeon contemplated it, then slowly walked over and stopped at the crumpled pizza box.

"Yes, I might be a 'rat with wings,'" she said, taking the piece of pizza lying nearby that Rat had coveted so much just moments before. After sating herself with a few flaps of her wings, Pigeon took off into the air.

"But at least I have them."

Moral: *Being similar doesn't make you the same.*

SCENT DEPOSITS FROM AN EBONY LION

EUGEN BACON

it must be 1979 because the black lion is
out of the jungle and strutting our streets
jaws wet n dripping crimson with the saturated
   colors
of my grandmother's bones her scent
of sautéed calabash mildly spiced with tilapia
overpowered by the reek of rotting meat–muscle–
   blood
from the glands around the lion's lips–cheeks–
   whiskers
oily deposits on his tail between his toes
as he circles her grave for days listens for her
   carcass
with his great sense of hearing
poised to set up camp unalert to grief
so she's curled alone in her grave
no mourners that time will bring
no perfect Earth or traces of yesterday
just seaweed and tears in photographs
as a lion roars the night
his pungent musky stench
but urine that smells of popcorn

A LONELY DEATH

KAREEM HAYES

IN DYSTOPIAN GRAY, sullied forest of steel, dwelt a pack of unruly wolves, forsaken in the north for 4,997 full moons. Iron-clad claws sheathed by Timberland boots, near the blue lagoon, where tides rise with the moon's moods. There lingered an aroma of carcasses and herbaceous fumes that poisoned the air with a heavy doom.

Howling from metal peaks stood four brothers. They had the same mother, different fathers, but the same harsh roots. The Killer, The Biggest, The Little Wicked, and The Gifted Aloof; all competed to be the alpha in their familial group.

The Killer insisted he was instinctive; he gnawed the raw flesh from his victim's necks. Pure Alpha, the kind a predator respects.

The Biggest said, "The bigger the better; the biggest is the best. With enormous size, I could crush any mammal I despise. My big phallus is ideal to continue our line!"

The Little Wicked said, "I am master of illusion, manipulation, and figments. In a past life, I must have been a politician."

The Gifted Aloof replied, "My brothers, why compete? We'd be greater if we unified, claw to claw, feet to feet. You know what they say about wolves, my brothers? They say a wolf would kill another without a care. But a wolf wouldn't dare try to kill a bear."

The Killer replied in sinister tones, "You sound like a pussy-dog unfit to roam! You aren't built for this hood we call home! I'd rend the muscle fibers from your bones."

The Biggest threatened to squidge his dorsum, pulverize his frame, crack his skull into shards that puncture his brain.

The Little Wicked snarled, with putrid disdain. "I'd shackle you in chains, deny you water or grain, dance to the rhythmic growls of your hunger pains!"

The Gifted Aloof retorted, "Cuz ain't we blood? Where's the love?"

"You are The Gifted Aloof. We've grown weary of your celestial dreams and lofty ambitions. Your clairvoyant visions don't make you better! You think you're bigger than the pack. No wolf is bigger than the pack!"

The Gifted Aloof seized that moment to flee, to ruminate in shelter beneath the baobab tree. He lit candles, burnt sage, so the ancestors may hear his plea.

Will the night airglow guide my lonely hunt for food?
    Should I relinquish my shield of numbers for solace,
        serenity, and solitude?
Do I have the will to hustle and hunt alone?
    Savoring every solitary bite, suckling every bone?
Is this my moment to sniff every flower under the sun?
    No more paranoia, 'cause my adversary is one?
I am the Gifted Aloof dreamer who knows no rest
    For the lone wolf is destined to have a lonely death.
Oh, Great Spirit, why have my brothers forsaken me?
    Should I fight, preach, or leave?
Or find peace in a fine-ass Luna-Wolf and breed?

A commanding voice bellowed from beyond the baobab tree. "Go far and go fast!"

The Gifted Aloof shivered in disbelief. "Baobab tree, did you just speak? And what will become of my brothers if I seek?"

"They'll be left to their own brutality, trickery, and deceit. Look, fam, it is what it is. Anything that eats its own doesn't deserve to live."

The next day at the crack of dawn, the Gifted Aloof stood before the pack. "My brothers, I'm bouncing for good, and I'm never coming back. 'Cause all my opposition is within our pack."

The Killer snarled, "I'm not feeling that you movin' like a rat!"

The Biggest barked back, "The pack made a pact. Real wolves stay in the trap. Trapped!"

The Little Wicked interjected. "You think you're bigger than the pack. Nobody is bigger than the pack!"

In that same dystopian gray of sullied steel dwelt a sleuth of grizzly bears, who'd thrived in the wilderness of the North for over four hundred years. An abundance of food lay in their way from fruits, nuts, berries, and hares. But woefully, the unruly wolves would eat up all the food, stomping around the forest with audacious attitudes. Blasting drill tunes loud and rude, it even became cool for bear cubs to imitate the wolves' attitude. The unruly pact influenced the culture of the steel forest, and soon some would call them the apex and the strongest.

A shrewd bear made a solemn promise: that he'd murder the mangy varmints before the next harvest. The Killer is dangerous, but he's unjust and violent. The Biggest is vain but shallow and arrogant. The Little Wicked is evil, cowardly, and materialistic. The Gifted Aloof is sensitive, naively loyal, and idealistic.

He stalked The Gifted Aloof to the baobab tree but hid where he could not see. *"No real wolf would listen to a grizzly, especially one so shrewd."* The grizzly crept, and as soon as The Gifted Aloof left, he made his move. Near the midnight blue lagoon, where tides rise with the moon's moods climbing over metal mountains, with granite roofs.

The bear roared as he charged the wolf brothers.

The Biggest drew larger. "No need for a plan. My brawn will save the day."

The Little Wicked plotted to himself. "I will stay out of the way. The bear will kill The Biggest, and The Killer will kill the Bear. Then I will appear. Kill The Killer if I dare. There will be none left to put me to the test. I, alone, will be alpha, the best."

The Shrewd Bear beheaded the Biggest with a slap of iron paw and a splash of reddened gore, sending the big-headed head flying from torn tendons and spinal bone in a wet, red plume of blood and marrow exhaust. The Biggest's body forgot it had no head and fought, flopped, and flipped until it went limp.

The Little Wicked let out a cry for more bloodshed. "Attack!"

The Killer vaulted for the jugular, leaping off The Shrewd's barrel chest. The bear hemorrhaged, and globs of black tar spewed from his neck. Seizing the moment, The Little Wicked stabbed The Killer in his back. Once, twice, pressing the attack.

The Killer turned to the traitor and howled in a rage. "My brother, is you in cahoots with this bear, to what end?"

"You were family, never a friend!" The Little Wicked admired his masterpiece with a twinkle in his eye, while watching his brothers die. "The power is mine and mine alone, for only I have the strength to eat my own! Power begets power, and only the merciless hold the throne." He turned to The Shrewd Bear, who lay soaked in a bloodbath. "What of you now, Big Bad Shrewd Bear? Do you feel powerful, or are you scared?" He circled the bear to prepare the *coup de grace*. "Big Bad Shrewd Bear, any final thoughts? Are you trembling with fear?"

The Shrewd Bear coughed saliva and blood. "It is what it is. Come closer, so I may utter my final quib." The Little Wicked slowly leaned in. *"Anyone that eats his own is not fit to live."* And The Shrewd Bear dug deep for every ounce with a stunning leap of rage and height, slamming his bulk down on The Little Wicked with all his might.

Crushed beneath the brown boulder of flesh, The Little Wicked screamed and pushed, but soon fell limp, out of breath. "Someone, help! Help me, please! Get this big dead grizzly off my thighs and knees!"

The Gifted Aloof sobbed for The Shrewd Bear's life. "It was you who spoke from the baobab tree! Why did you murder my kin, yet spare me?"

"It is what it is. Anyone that eats his own doesn't deserve to live," were the bear's final words.

"We are brothers, aren't we?" The Little Wicked's silky voice sang. "Find the love in your heart. Help a wolf stand!"

The Little Wicked summoned every pleading trick of eye, wore every gentle face of scheme, appealed to The Gifted Aloof's honor, his loyalty, the familial dream.

But The Gifted Aloof's eyes were open to The Little Wicked's scheme.

"I will nibble on your veins, so you bleed out slow. Howl the rhythm of your decelerating pulse. So, every fowl, insect, and beast can come to feast. Little brother, decompose to dirt. Feel the maggots pull you deep beneath the Earth."

So, death came, and so death went. The Gifted Aloof continued his journey of a life well spent.

Night airglow will guide my desolate hunt for food
  Relinquished my shield of numbers
For the solace of serenity, of solitude
  To kill my meal and feast alone
To savor every bite, suckle every savory bone
  And finally, a moment to sniff every flower under the sun
No more paranoia, my adversary is only one.
  The Gifted and Aloof dreamer who knows there's no rest,
For the lone wolf is destined to have a lonely death.

THE OLD WOLF & THE FARM

JAMAL HODGE

LD WOLF SPENT his twilight days in speed and exploration. It was a wolf's life to eat and run and die under the *bang!* of a wicked human gun, but he had survived by observing his surroundings, noticing the patterns of predator and prey. Still, times were thin, as humanity expanded, eating everything and everyone.

Most disturbing was the number of animals under the systemic authority of humanity. Even his cousin Hound had submitted, smiling while being collared by the neck. Normally, Old Wolf kept as far away from farms as he could, but this day, being thinned and famished, the heavy scent of blood drew his hunger.

He used speed and stealth to slip through a fence and stay hidden from human eyes. The farm had many animals he could have eaten, but the scent of blood drew him. Soon, the sweet aroma led him to its overwhelming source. A vast metal monstrosity where cow and pig, sheep and chicken, were marched in large wagons or in narrow one-way fences.

Sounds. Terrible sounds. Crunching bone. Splatters. Final moos.

Old Wolf crept along the shadows, past the blood-soaked men, until he found a crack and peeked through.

Horror.

Massacre.

Butchery.

Cows' necks were locked into the noose of massive machines

that flipped them upside down before a metal pole crunched through skull and brain. Chicken babies, yellow and yelling, marooned on steel conveyer belts ending in kaleidoscopes of bladed metal. Countless skinless sheep held upside down on hooks, their opened bellies gutless.

Entrails in buckets.

Mountains of wool.

Streams of blood somehow made foul to his snout, defiled by the magnitude of the slaughter.

This is wrong, Old Wolf thought. Even though they were prey, as a predator, he did not hate his food. They were delicious, after all, and they kept him alive. This level of massacre reduced them to a mere commodity.

After seeing as much of the process as he could stomach, Old Wolf waited until the sun had set before emerging from his hiding place, whispering a howling call for sheep and pig and chicken and cow to gather. Hound approached, prepared to rip him limb from hide, but hesitated as Old Wolf wept.

"Dear friends, what horrors I must tell you!" Old Wolf began as he laid out the terrors he'd witnessed.

But to the dismay of his eyes, none on the farmstead seemed surprised.

"Don't you understand?" Old Wolf cried. "They will grind you up in metal, shred you and mix you, package you and ship you. They will do the same to your children and your children's children!"

"What of it?" Pig shrugged, rolling in the mud.

Cow nodded, chewing her grass. "A small price to pay for a life of feasts and mating."

"Why, there are more of us than there have ever been. Even more of us than them," Chicken added, eating her seeds.

"But . . . " Old Wolf began.

"Look at you, silly wolf, all gaunt of skin. I can see the outline of your bones. How few of you there are in these aimless woods?" Horse snickered, strutting within the boundaries of his fence. "What is one bad day for a thousand days of luxury?"

"Will you not settle behind a fence?" Sheep invited. "There is food aplenty, nourishment of all kinds, and both Shepherd and Hound protect us from dangers."

"Till you are properly fat!" Old Wolf said.

"There is a peace here you will not find in the chaos of the wood. Structure to our lives, a purpose," Sheep assured.

"To be eaten by them?"

Sheep shrugged. "All things are eaten in the end by soil, maggot, or teeth. It is the way of the Great Mother that flesh borrowed is flesh returned. Better to live in pleasure than to live in uncertainty, where the days bring pain and the nights bring terror."

Then, as one, the animals of the farmstead said, "Come, accept, and be merry. Do as we do. Think as we think. Live as we live."

"Dear livestock, I must bid you farewell." Old Wolf backed away. "For me, it is better to starve free than be a fat slave." And after the Wolf said this, he ran for his life.

Moral: *Many will allow themselves to be led to slaughter for the sake of convenience.*

VI

AFTER THE END
THE LARGE RECKONING

THE TALE OF THE TWIN STARS, BORN OF EARTH & SEA

Linda D. Addison

Telling the way of how first dolphins came to be,
    it is said stars fell from the heavens to Earth,
    into oceans, becoming sleek, smirking movement.

Telling the way of why Sirens came into tales,
    it is said dolphin song entered flawed human minds
    through points of madness, shredding broken souls.

Telling the way of when Twin Stars would arrive,
    it is said one day Leda's mortal/immortal twins
    would return from the left of Orion to Earth.

Telling the way of what this means to Earth-walkers,
    it is said when the twin stars are (re)born,
    the Reckoning will come, small, then large.

NDER A CLEAR NIGHT SKY, full of stars, a pregnant bottlenose dolphin swims away from the pod. Contractions pulse strong and fast, so she seeks a calm place to give birth. She softly whistles her name to the calf inside. Floating near the surface of the water, she pushes. The calf's tail presents first. The dolphin bounces to the surface, takes a deep breath, and pushes until the rest of the baby is out and the umbilical cord snaps. She nudges the calf to the surface for its first breath.

The mother bobs up and down with the baby on her back. They don't see the large male dolphin rush up from under them and butt the mother. As she rolls over, he grabs the calf by its tail and swims deep into the water. She tries to follow, but the pain of being hit and weakness from giving birth slows her down. The newborn dolphin's body slowly floats up to her, and no matter how many times she pushes it to the surface, it doesn't move or breathe. As harsh as this sounds, it is the way of some dolphins.

In a field, away from the city, a child lies on its back in a ditch of soft soil. She looks up at the bright stars in the night sky and tries to reach for the points of light but is too weak to raise her arms. As soil piles on her, like sand on a beach, a cough brings up blood and a last breath from ribs kicked in and collapsed lungs. Her eyes don't blink as dirt covers her face. As horrible as this sounds, it is the cruel way of too many humans.

The next evening, the sun moves into Gemini. A bright shooting star streaks through the night sky, splitting in Earth's atmosphere, and the twins are born again. One in the sea and one on the land. They take their first breaths at the same time, even though in different-shaped bodies.

A spotted dolphin born in the protected waters outside the Dolphin Exploration Facility to a gray bottlenose mother is gently pushed to the surface to take its first breath. A few Earth-walkers, in different parts of the world, see dolphins tip their tails in the air and slap the water at the same time, but don't connect the breaching to the birth of this one dolphin. They blame it on sunspots, because dolphins cannot be smart enough to do one thing at the same time.

In a cabin near a river, a woman gave birth to a human child at the same time the dolphin was born. Ten seconds after being pushed out of the birth canal, the newborn gasps and takes its first breath. The mid-wife doesn't smile as she wraps the baby in a small blanket and hands it to the mother, who screams and shoves the baby back. The father rushes into the room and stares in horror at the dark birthmark across the center of the baby's face. They hide it away from others, saying the baby died. No one questions them, because a human cannot be heartless enough to lie about such a thing.

The scientists at the facility name the newborn dolphin S-Tar because of the star-shaped pattern on its belly. They confirm it is healthy by observing its movement and physical appearance from a distance, because the mother and two other *aunties* surround the calf protectively, keeping humans and other dolphins away.

S-Tar nurses on the thick, sweet milk from its mother. The close touch of the aunties as they swim next to him fills it with pleasure. As peaceful and safe as he feels, something unsettles the newborn calf when night falls and the pod slows down to float at the surface of the water to sleep. He rolls over on his side and looks up at the clear sky.

{*Star*} an image of a concept comes to him, then words:
I
star.
I am star.
He rolls over, takes a breath, shudders. Memories flood in:
Be
   ing
      exploding
   balls
      hydrogen
       helium
His dolphin body shudders . . .
   stardust
     hydrogen
      lithium
Rushing through space to the blue-green-white planet . . . splitting into two balls of light . . .
One of two.
Half of one.
His dolphin body comes back into focus.
My half breathes
air, born on earth
I breathe air,
born in water,
must find half

why
we here
why . . .

S-Tar's mother gently rocks against him, grunts softly, "Rest, rest."

He sleeps, uneasy.

In the morning, S-Tar pronounces its own name, an involved melodious whistle. The calf's signature whistle has no human translation, but if there were one, it would tell the tale of Castor and Pollux, the two brightest stars in Gemini's constellation, and their return to Earth.

One by one, the dolphins in the pod repeat S-Tar's name again and again, each adding a slight change at the end of the whistle. The researchers have never seen anything like this with a newborn calf, an observation for their files they can't explain. If they knew the language of dolphins, they would understand that this is a way of each dolphin accepting the return of a star to Earth. With this acceptance came the sound of the vow each dolphin sang to give their life, if needed, to keep S-Tar safe.

The evening of S-Tar's second day, as the pod sleeps, he floats next to his mother and again thinks words no dolphin has:

must find half

He holds the memory of being one with his sibling, when they were traveling to Earth, before they were separated.

Oh . . .

A spark of light behind S-Tar's closed left eye widens into a scene—

a naked human baby
held upside down
slapped slapped slapped
tiny head flips back/forth
blood flows from nose
thrown to the floor.

S-Tar knows the child is dead. The scene closes to a dot in his mind.

No no no . . .

S-Tar switches to close his right eye, holds the memory of his twin, and the spark of light opens into a different scene, a different human child dies at the hands of another human adult. Ten times he searches for his twin through this spark, this connection; ten

times he sees humans violently abusing, then killing, young ones in different places on Earth—
 beaten with wood,
 belts, fists,
 hammers, stabbed,
 drowned in scalding
 water, suffocated
 with plastic bags,
 kicked, punched.
On the eleventh time, the scene is dark, S-Tar's feeling of his dolphin body shifts and merges—
 he is in the dark
 in a tiny human body,
 loud music plays
 somewhere,
 nauseous cramps
 grip tiny stomach,
 hungry, hungry.
 They not feed you enough.
Words that couldn't exist in a newborn human surface in their shared minds.
 "not
 enough"
 Do you remember before born?
 "before?"
S-Tar shows the human baby his memories of being a star, traveling to Earth, and his birth in the sea. He hums part of his name to the child, who hums it back to S-Tar.
 I was star before.
 "star before?"
 Yes. I was not alone.
 "i alone."
 No, I found you.
 "not alone."
 Do you remember being star?
 "not remember,
 "not star."
S-Tar finds no shared memories in the thin human baby. Exhaustion pulls them apart as sleep takes over their bodies.
 Each night, S-Tar searches for his twin and suffers from seeing

ten human children violently lose their lives. The eleventh attempt always ends up with the barely fed baby in the dark room. He shares memories of the day with the baby: swimming, jumps and turns in the air, racing through the water with other dolphins in the pod. The baby can only share its hunger for food and gentle touch.

Each day, S-Tar quickly learns the training given to the older dolphins at the facility. The humans fill many documents with measurements and ideas about how the young calf seems to know the tricks taught to its mother and other dolphins in the pod. They have more questions than answers. S-Tar grows fast. At two weeks old, it is the size of a six-month-old dolphin, stops nursing and begins eating fish with the adults of the pod.

No one cares about what the star-marked baby knows or doesn't know. At two weeks old, a human who lives on the river in an old houseboat, far from others, gives the parents money and takes the baby out of the house in a suitcase. The original parents wipe the memories of its birth out of their minds and their home. It is as if the nameless child was never born.

That night, S-Tar and the baby meet as usual, but moonlight illuminates the small room on the houseboat from a window. They lie on a mattress instead of a blanket on a hard floor. Nagging hunger is gone.

You are not in darkness? This is a different place.

"someone took me from the dark, noisy place."

You are floating in a place on water. I can feel it.

"yes, like when I swim with you."

Show me.

The baby shares memories of being moved from the dark place and traveling in a small box to this room. The bright light of day hurting its eyes. A man slowly baths it and feeds it twice that day before leaving the baby in the room. The baby sleeps as the sun sets, until S-Tar arrives in its mind.

"i not know you would find me in this different place."

I found you because—

There is a loud bang as the door to the room slams open. A light comes on as a man stumbles across the room, grabs the baby by the legs, sits on a chair, and roughly swings the baby onto his lap. A cigarette hangs from his mouth.

"It's all your fault," he slurs and holds the lit end of the cigarette against the baby's thigh.

The baby howls in pain.

"Shut up, you piece of shit!" he yells over and over again as he burns the baby on both thighs, over and over again, until he finally takes a deep drag of the cigarette, drops the child on the mattress, and staggers out of the room.

The baby cries in pain, trembling, its arms curled tightly against its chest.

The shock and pain pull S-Tar away from the child and back into his dolphin body. He tries to go back to the baby but can't reconnect. The dolphin rocks back and forth against his mother until exhaustion puts him to sleep.

In the morning, the pod goes into the open water through the facility's security gates. S-Tar follows the adult dolphins, away from its mother for the first time, to explore. She swims in a wide circle, calling out S-Tar's signature whistle. The dolphins near her repeat the whistle, passing it along to members of the pod until it reaches S-Tar. He whistles and clicks a response that he is safe, which the other dolphins copy and send back to the mother. She relaxes, knowing he isn't alone, and hunts for squid with the others.

As the sun sets, S-Tar floats next to his mother and suffers through seeing ten children die in pain, terrified each time it might be the baby he knew. When the spark of light closes and opens the eleventh time, he slips into the shared state with the baby. The burns on their thighs throb.

I am glad to see you.

"you feel pain with me?"

Yes.

"why come back?"

To see you.

"you should look for your half."

I try every night, but I end up with you after—

"after?"

After seeing other human children hurt by adults.

"hurt like me."

They die.

"you never show me."

No, it makes me angry. Like feeling you hurt makes me.

"do not know why he hurt me."

I do not know why the children I see every night are killed.

"when light come from window, he feed me, say nothing, went away.

"he will hurt me again, yes?"

S-Tar did not answer but had seen enough with humans who hurt young ones to know that was true.

"when I die, you can find your half, the other star."

No. I must save you, then I find my half. That must be why I keep coming to you.

"how find me?"

If you hum my—

The door crashes open. The man staggers in.

Shudders jerk through S-Tar's dolphin body as a lit cigarette burns the bottom of their small feet. The baby cries until hoarse. The dolphin feels every searing pain as they writhe on the adult's lap, their ankles in the tight grip of a large hand, the man yelling, again and again, "Shut up! Shut up! Shut up!"

The connection between S-Tar and the baby shrinks, and he is back in his dolphin body, shaking with anger. He barely sleeps, rolling over to stare at the stars, the memory of the child's screams echoing in S-Tar's mind.

At sunrise, he swims further from the facility's waters than before, and many of the teenage dolphins from the pod follow. They jump and spin in the air. Two wild dolphins approach them, whistle, and click their names. When S-Tar gives his name, the wild dolphins tip their tails in the air and slap the water before repeating his whistle with a variation on the end in recognition of the Twin Star.

S-Tar swims ahead of the group in the direction the wild dolphins say their pod is hunting. During the few minutes he's separated from the others, a great white shark swims toward him, and S-Tar barely twists out of the way of its powerful jaws. S-Tar sends patterns of clicks through the water as the shark circles back. This time, he stays in place and allows the shark a direct line. When it is within a few feet of S-Tar, the shark is propelled into the air, tumbling sideways, when two large dolphins race from below the shark and butt its soft belly with their hard snouts. The rest of the pod surrounds S-Tar. The shark swims away.

The dolphins swim together for a while and meet some of the wild dolphins' pod. In the exchange of squeaks, grunts, and whines, S-Tar tells them the need to find a human child who is in a floating house on a river. He tells them what to do to find the child. The wild pod repeats his message, and some of the dolphins race away to share with other pods.

On the way back to the facility, S-Tar stops, twists, and turns in the water. The other dolphins slowly swim in a protective ring around him.

S-Tar slows his gyrations and floats on top of the water. One eye closes, and he is with the baby, without first experiencing ten children's violent deaths. The man is not in the room, the baby lies on the floor, barely moving.

What did he do?

"i—i—i—i—how, you—"

S-Tar feels despair as the child struggles to put thoughts together.

I do not know how I am here in daylight—I felt I was being shaken in the middle of a storm, and here I am.

"he—he—he did that to me—he." The child vomits.

I know how to find you. You must hum part of my name, the song of my name, as much as you can. Waters will be listening. I will come.

They hum S-Tar's name a few times, until the baby falls asleep.

The next two days, more wild dolphins arrive in the waters around the facility. They share squeaks, grunts, and whines to tell of where they came from, always starting with a version of S-Tar's name. He gives them the urgent message to search for a human child that hums part of his name. This information passes on from pod-to-pod miles away through whistles. Even some porpoises listen for the Twin Star's name.

The researchers at the facility notice this pattern and have no explanation for why it is happening or what makes S-Tar different from other dolphins.

Each night, S-Tar feels the human slap and pinch the child but cannot keep him conscious long enough to hurt them. The dolphin tries to talk to the baby, but only hears the hum of his name answer back. He accepts that this is enough.

On the third morning, S-Tar receives a location through the wild dolphin network that a shoal of harbor porpoises picked up the weak sound of S-Tar's name from a houseboat.

He says to the child, *"I am coming."*

"h—h—hurry," the child manages before slipping back into unconsciousness.

Before the pod goes out of the facility, S-Tar takes a calf position under its mother, rolling gently against her to say goodbye. She curls around him and whistles a baby pattern, the first sound S-Tar remembers hearing, then she stretches flat to let him swim away.

S-Tar speeds from the facility, followed by the pod of wild dolphins. He follows their example of jumps to save energy, traveling as fast as possible. They stop twice to quickly gather fish to eat. New dolphins join, while others leave, as they journey.

After swimming for many hours without sleep, the dolphins arrive at the waterway from the ocean that leads to a twisting river. Four dolphins follow S-Tar into the river, and the others circle the waterway, waiting.

The new group swim on the surface of the water to the area where the human child had hummed S-Tar's name. An old riverboat lies dark and moored to the riverbank.

I am here.

The baby does not answer.

S-Tar uses echolocation, discovering the child's silhouette on the floor of a room facing the deep river. The adult human sleeps in a larger room on the houseboat.

S-Tar slams his snout into the side of the riverboat and opens a hole in the semi-rotting wood. The other dolphins follow his lead, ignoring the pain, until the small room's floor collapses and water pours in. The baby rolls toward the opening as the riverboat takes on water and leans into the river.

For the first time, S-Tar sees the dark star birthmark on the child's face.

"What in the hell?" The adult human stumbles into the room as S-Tar slides into the room through the hole and gently clamps his mouth around the child's thin body.

The man tries to grab the child's legs.

"No. You can't have it! It's mine!"

S-Tar twists its body into a U-shape and slaps its tail into the man's head, knocking him violently across the room. With blood pouring out of his ears, the man lurches toward the hole for the child again. One of the other dolphins clamps down on the man's left wrist, pulls him through the hole, and into the water. The man slams his right fist on the head of the dolphin, but the second time he raises his arm, another dolphin jumps out of the water and bites down on his right wrist. They both violently shake him by the arms, dislocating his shoulders and tearing his hands off.

The man screams as blood gushes from his ragged wrists into the water. Forgetting about the child, he tries to flail and splash his way back to the houseboat. A dolphin bites down on his ankle and drags him toward the middle of the river, where S-Tar circles with the child in its mouth. The man kicks the dolphin with his free foot, mustering all his brutality into each strike. A second dolphin lunges, their snout fracturing his back and neck with one blow. He moans as they float his broken body to where S-Tar bobs with the child.

S-Tar joins the star energy from its mind with the unconscious baby. The child shudders awake, its bruises, burns, and broken mind mending, restoring, healing. It climbs from the dolphin's open mouth onto its back and wraps its arms around S-Tar's dorsal fin.

"I remember before. I am star too." In the space of one breath, the twin shares found memories of traveling to Earth with S-Tar and its birth on land. Reunited, their purpose clear.

Time for the small reckoning.

S-Tar whistles.

The human twin hums in agreement.

The man sees the healed child on the dolphin's back and tries to twist away, his face contorted with fear and disbelief.

Two dolphins keep his head and body on the water surface, while two other dolphins tear clothes and flesh from his arms, legs, and torso. Using torpedo speed, they butt him with their snouts. Breaking his bones as he screams, over and over again, until his last breath.

Their work done, each dolphin whistles S-Tar's name, one at a time, swimming back to the gentle whispers of the ocean.

S-Tar follows the last dolphin with his twin on his back.

When they are in open waters again, the dolphin twin clicks and whistles to the waiting dolphins, who jump and slap the water with their entire bodies at the same time, then swim away.

"my half, time to return home," the human twin says.

S-Tar begins a slow descent to the bottom of the ocean with the child on his back. There is no pain as water fills their lungs, their atoms dissolve to pure stardust, and infinitely thin beams of light streak from the water into the sky.

The darkening sky turns into a thundering storm, and fast-moving clouds appear for miles around. High winds churn the water into swirling columns. Ragged flashes of light cut through the clouds. The largest electrical storm ever measured, creating the most bolts ever seen.

The twin stars return to the Gemini constellation, changed, switched observable colors. The immortal offspring of Zeus becomes blue-white, and the mortal offspring of King Tyndarus turns yellow-orange.

Scientists all over Earth are shocked by this change. However, those who know the fable of the *Twin Stars* know a large *Reckoning* is coming to Earth-walkers, and they are afraid.

Telling the moral of this tale:

    It is said, take comfort that this is just a fable,
    do not worry about the Large Reckoning, because
    humans couldn't be so cruel and dolphins so smart.

RAT CITY

WRATH JAMES WHITE

In 1972, at the National Institute of Mental Health in Bethesda, Maryland, animal behaviorist John Calhoun built a "rat city", a mouse paradise with beautiful buildings and limitless food, in which everything a rat could need was provided, except space.

He introduced eight mice into this utopian city. Two years later, the result was a population boom. From the eight original pairs, the mice population skyrocketed, until the colony became choked with animals and deviant and dysfunctional behaviors appeared. The mice went mad. Murder, suicide, infanticide, and much, much worse. Calhoun's "rat utopia" became a living hell. The mice created their own apocalypse.

Rat City

I was a father once
I remember
their tiny pink noses
their tiny pink paws
their tiny pink tails
their downy white fur

I remember
those tiny pink noses
nuzzling mine
those tiny pink paws
reaching out for Daddy

I remember
their mewling cries
for mother's milk
their tiny
emaciated bodies
contorted in hunger

I remember
their ear-splitting shrieks
the agony and horror
in their tiny pink eyes

I remember
when there were only eight of us
Four couples
swapping lovers
sharing everything

I remember
before we began to breed
when there was enough food for all
Enough space for all
Enough love for all
Enough peace
and sanity
for all

Before the world went insane

I remember
when parents didn't
eat their babies
When fathers didn't murder
the mother of their children
Didn't tear pups from her womb

When siblings
didn't kill siblings
When the young
didn't murder
their elders
When there was no suicide
No homicide
No infanticide
No matricide
No patricide
No rape
No theft
When I never knew the taste
of another rat's flesh
When I never knew the sound
of their terrified shrieks
When I had never
wet my whiskers
or washed my nimble paws
with their blood
When the marrow of their bones
was a delicacy
unknown to me

Before eight became sixty-four
Before sixty-four

became two hundred and fifty-six
Became five hundred and twelve
Became one thousand twenty-four
Before the food ran out
And the air
grew rank and humid
With the sweat and funk
of hundreds
And I wanted to scream
And bite
And scratch
And kill
Just to breathe
Just to stretch out my arms
Without touching another
Just to sleep
without hearing
the sound
of a thousand
collective snores

And I wanted to scream
And I wanted to kill
And I did scream
And I did kill
And kill
And kill
And eat
But there were still more
Still more
everywhere
So many
many
many

more
scampering in every direction
burrowing underground
through the dirt
beneath my paws
Scratching and biting
at themselves
in their madness
at each other
in their fury
their rudderless
irrational
psychotic
fury
Angry
at the very air around them
rank and humid
with the sweat
and funk
of hundreds

A vast and filthy colony
A plague of squeaking
hissing
chirping
scratching
gnawing
siblings
Fighting and fucking
in every corner
every crevice
every shadow
gnawing
at their own flesh
in their madness

at each other's flesh
in their fury
and
their hunger

So much mad movement
So much unnecessary existence
So much squeaking
shrieking
fury

I remember
when I was a father
A father of hundreds

I remember
putting an end to it all
systematic euthanasia
one
by
one
daughters
sons
cousins
gnawed to the bone

I remember
when the marrow of their bones
became a delicacy
well known to me
Their bubblegum-colored flesh
stretched like taffy
as I pulled it from the bone
chewy like calamari
delicate little bones

breaking
splintering
like stalks of celery
as screams and cries
filled my ears
and coppery red
washed over my tongue
and down my throat
and their mewling cries
and shrieks
and squeaks
and squeals
and tears
fueled my hunger

When I became a murderer
a cannibal
of hundreds
and hundreds
of my children
When my utopia
became a nightmarish dystopia
a necropolis
of gnawed bones
clensed of flesh

I was a father once
I remember
their tiny pink noses
their tiny pink paws
their tiny pink tails
their downy white fur,

splattered red.

THE HALF-LIFE OF CEPHALOPODS

OZ HARDWICK

So is this great and wide sea, wherein are things creeping innumerable, both small and great beasts.
—Psalms 104.25 (KJV)

And who is society? There is no such thing! There are individual men and women and there are families, and no government can do anything except through people and people look to themselves first.
—*Margaret Thatcher,* Woman's Own, *23 September 1987*

CLOCKS ARE BROKEN and limbs rebel, slipping in and out of saline certainty, suckering thought from the still center toward which all things tend. Bibles deliver on their promises of fire, their flames occupying a full spectrum from IR to UV, though complex eyes fail to comprehend / fail to compute / fail to come to terms with purposeful rudimentary fingers, which fumble to pluck. Stealthy in our metamorphoses, we slide aside from society and selves, angry and distrusting. The outside world is alight and roaring, lit up by dead digits, and shuddering like an ambulance in an elevator shaft. The nuclear decays. Storms shiver the shape of our wreckage, all heads and feet and absence. There is no polar ice, but eyes crack under the pressure of deep thought and steaming sea / see? No: evil. We tend toward complexity, toward chaos, toward cannibalism by any other name. All dogs are eaten, and there's nothing left but growling bones amongst dysfunctional families. The only certainties are ochre prints on cave walls and repeated static patterns gathered from deep space. Time is broken and lips recede, sliding back to the ur-language of non-sense / non-self / no-no-no. Refuse / resist / reset. No rest for the wicked and the wasted. The most likely outcome is the reversal of roles between hunter and prey. Pay or pray, we'll rue the day we let go of ourselves and slipped beneath the ocean waves, both waving and drowning. I need to sleep, but my limbs have minds of their own, each one thumbing ominous buttons on a console fashioned from twitching muscle. There must, I am sure, be memories to guide us back to family, fraternity, and the faint threads that used to hold us together: my mother, wrist deep in suds as sirens sounded; my father, bright-eyed beneath a hanging flag; my sister, strung like a puppet in streaming blue ribbons; and my own reflection, kaleidoscope in smashed glass. Four limbs good, eight arms thrashing, all the better to tear the world apart. A voice booms. Dis-ease blooms. All connections are broken. We clock the collapse of all time and refute the very notion of society. The nuclear decays. We have learnt to walk where there is no need, to talk in riddles and empty bubbles, and to chalk conquests of every kind on the door jambs of burnt-out houses. We tend toward rot, willfully confusing geometry with godliness, trusting in the precise geomancy of snake stones, in hope of resurrection. We know better. We know better. We own all colors of which you dare to dream. We know where you live.

LESSONS FOR A BURNING WORLD

ANGELA YURIKO SMITH

MOTHER STOOD TALL and looked at the horizon. The sun was rising, only a sliver, but it was already sending the air into shimmers. Other than the crescent of fire, the land and sky were empty. She sniffed the sluggish breeze for the daily news. Death wafted toward her in the scent of toxic fumes and baking flesh. Death meant opportunity. She called to her children, and 33 sets of inquisitive eyes peered from underground. Her children, too, smelled the opportunity.

She whistled, and the empty landscape filled with her family. They stood tall, alert, and agile. This world was tough, but her family had learned the ways of survival. They mastered the lessons they had been taught. Few creatures wanted this world anymore, but Mother had claimed it for her family. A chuckle deep in her throat, and they moved forward. It was time to hunt.

Lesson 1: You are what you eat. They moved fluidly over the burnt land. From a distance, it appeared the surface was dancing in the heat as bodies the color of sand and stone leapt together. Small but fearsome, the meerkats ran together, always attuned to Mother. It was because of her wisdom they thrived in the wasteland. She stopped, and they all stopped. She chirped, and they dispersed, raiding the barren soil for the first meal.

No rock was left unturned as they searched for any signs of life.

277

Spiders, beetles, snakes, and rodents recently retired to their burrows were dragged out into the blazing sun. Stunned, they were helpless as Mother's family broke their backs and severed skulls. Exoskeletons ripped open with tiny talons to expose the milky innards. Mother heard complaints, and she investigated. To be alive was to be grateful. Complaints wasted energy and attracted predators. She followed the sound to a Ninth Generation refusing good food—a scorpion lay before it, tail broken. It quivered and shrilled as precious juices leaked into the sand.

Mother growled and signaled to the younger meerkat: *Eat.*

Message received, the adolescent finished the scorpion and diligently swallowed the last of it, squeamish but obedient. One of his siblings had been a picky eater last week. The scorpion might at least remove the rancid taste of sister that lingered in the back of his throat. Satisfied, Mother signaled to run again with a warning.

Remember, you are what you eat.

Lesson 2: There is safety in numbers. The scent of death—of opportunity—was close, and they quickened their pace. The sun was already burning through their callused paws. Mother's eyes were ahead when a dark shadow passed between them and the great bright. She whistled as she ran, without pausing, and the family scattered. Every shadow was suddenly lined with eyes watching the sky.

A tawny eagle glided across on the shimmer, searching for them. She knew they were there *en masse.* Her keen eyes had watched their forage from a mile away. Now it was her turn. A Fifteenth Generation caught her eye. Separated from the nursery group, the almost-baby knew enough to be afraid, but not enough to run faster. The tawny eagle slid from Heaven to embrace the tender baby and sever it from discomfort and pain. This child would be well cared for in the belly of her own children. She screeched her gratitude to the family she had taken from, and they whistled back their gratitude for not being taken.

There is safety in numbers.

Lesson 3: You can't fix stupid. Once the tawny eagle left with her prize, Mother whistled again. Time to move. The stink of rotting meat was close, but the heat was beating them. If they did not find the place of death soon, they would have to return or risk burning in the out-of-control heat.

Ahead, Mother saw the prize. Humans often came to the desert to escape the heat of their own nests that now boiled with tar. The family could smell the toxic stench of their hairless hides. Most of them died. It was to be expected. They made flimsy burrows of tissue above the ground.

Mother chirped a halt once the surface burrows were in sight. A sole female lay in the vanishing shade, wailing pain noises. The bodies of her pack were pulled into the sun. One of their metal beasts had collapsed, black legs sagging in the heat. Typical, helpless humans. Mother signaled to move.

They ran forward in a wave, splitting into three factions. The left and right flanks quickly vanished from sight. Mother and a smaller team ran straight to the woman and stood at attention. When she didn't look up, Mother chirped. The human raised her head.

"Oh, look at you . . . "

No wonder the humans came here to die. They wasted precious fluids from their eyes. By night, this one, too, would be food for scavengers. Behind the human, Mother's family was already at work searching through the human burrow for usefuls to take. A large family made for efficient foraging, and they would leave with most of what this human had left. It was Mother's job to keep the human's focus. She chirped and danced in a circle. Her team followed suit, cavorting and purring.

The human wiped her face.

"So cute! I wish Hampton could see you . . . " More wasting of fluid, but it made Mother's job easier. She signaled for her team to save their energy. Whistles came from around the camp as the family signaled all things of use had been ferreted out. They awaited Mother's signal to return.

The human looked up at all the whistles and saw a box of her supplies knocked over and already rifled through. A Fifth Generation vanished around the above-ground burrow with a silver package.

"Hey!"

From experience, Mother knew the human would now turn aggressive. Mother whistled her signal to return to their own burrows. They had risked the day long enough.

The family reappeared in a wave, each carrying a single useful or edible. The ones who couldn't find food carried other things they hoped may be useful. No one dared to run without a prize. The factions of family ran around the tissue burrows and the now aggressive human to converge in a stream heading home. The sun had reached the burning stage, and soon anything left on the surface would begin to roast slowly, including the human screaming behind them. The family reached their burrow network with no difficulties. Even the raptors didn't hunt in the high heat.

The family vanished underground. It was warm but survivable. Multiple families were returning, following the tunnels to the center where Grandmother waited. Each member brought their prize before her, and she signaled its purpose. Foodstuffs went deeper in the earth to stay cool. The inedibles went to shore up the cracking nest walls or to the teams learning new skills by trial and error. Generation Forty-fives were making progress learning to open the metal food cylinders.

Grandmother was old and weak, but she would never be food. She had the knowing. Once, Grandmother lived among humans in their vulnerable surface burrows surrounded by toxic plains. It didn't make sense to build such burrows, but the humans who came to die didn't make sense either. All the animals agreed— meerkat and otherwise—if the humans were gone, the world would stop burning. There was no reasoning with them.

You can't fix stupid.

280

SOMETHING IN THERE

ALESSANDRO MANZETTI

The last man on Earth
listens, in his head,
to Concert No. 2 by Rachmaninoff
as he walks toward the great pit
of Kojashi City—over there, against the orange
    horizon—
that place surrounded by a pack of coyotes,
bloody muzzles waiting,
eyes unmoving.

The last man on Earth
—seventeen years old, scent of youth—
plays the piano in his mind,
moving fingers on imaginary keys,
following the rhythm of the violins,
the emergency sirens
still screaming,
even if it's too late now.

The last man on Earth
looks back one last time:
the city, a giant, sick emerald

with its green, headless, brainless
skyscrapers liquefied by the last rain
—hydrochloric acid storms—
long-severed concrete necks
of a Modigliani without enough colors.

The last man on Earth
with a holy card of Joan of Arc in his pocket,
a snail and a test tube
—its crystal placenta—
enters the pit and sits among human bones;
there is no more time for cemeteries,
for funeral marches and dark clothes,
for a solitary Mozart carriage
followed only by rats and dead notes.

The last man on Earth
counts the longest seconds
in a handful of sand;
the leeches in his lungs
—the invertebrate daughters of the End—
suck pulp and breath,
climbing the cerebral cortex;
they bite the memories still attached:
a face that crumbles, she,
Anna Fedorova, playing the piano
dressed in gold and oysters.

The last man on Earth
stretches his hand to the coyote
with a star spot above its eyes,
calling his teeth, his bites;
the animal, green hair and short tail
—everything turned green, and short, so short—
approaches, and smells the young man:

it doesn't understand
where the music is coming from.
There's something in that body
full of parasites; a clockwork soul
without stomach or shape or smell.

THE FABLE OF ZAYYID'A AND HIS DEN

EUGEN BACON

HE BELLY OF a large mangrove tree at the lip of a dried-up loch gates Zayyid'a's den. The cave walls are pale and wrinkled, the entryway partly trunked. Low clouds diffuse light into this world.

Death is always at his feet.

He remembers the terrible screams of his friends out yonder,
> how they put a hunger
> in him to stay alive,
> as the sky abandoned
> its skin and his world
> intensely
> changed.

This is no mental abyss. Zayyid'a knows his reality is true. The outside world is alight and roarin', fallin' meteors eruptin' everywhere. He swallows his shadow, knocks fear over. Tames terror and buries belief. Hope is a faceless beast dissolvin' in sludge, and the best way is to rid oneself of it. To breathe out backwards until he hibernates, sleeps with untouchables cradled in the void.

He once longed for color in his life, somethin' vibrant.

Not this.

The red blobs all around are splatters of death in a black-cloaked world strewn with rocks and sand. He wants to sleep away from all this flesh and fire, go deep, deep, deep into the ethereal, to a place where a river, maybe a sea, an esplanade, and a bridge collide with sidewalks and tremblin' she-oaks. He wants to see a window blowin' blue and white ribbons in the silence of a world that's banished shadows and sound. The end of the world happened. What remains of it feels like night.

Sometimes, he thinks he's on a moon.

It seems like not long ago he was ridin' a shuttle that echoed: Hire a hubby. A hubby.

He did jobs on demand, housewives mostly who needed the raw strength of a man. Grunt and muscle, liftin' rocks, haulin' logs, splittin' wood, and the lasses paid good, sometimes in kind. He was good with the ladies, and some called him cobra tongue. Sweet talkin' and all that shit, he bloody hell knew what to do with a tongue. Didn't need directions or whatever. He went down on a woman with a thought, never got to the end of thinkin' afore she was squirmin' and grippin' his face with her inner thighs, moanin' as if he were killin' her.

He remembers laughin' with his mates. Them callin' him Cobra Bill.

Sex drains your legs, they said.

Yeah, he had it swell, didn't need to go rattlin' on doorknobs—gals had a way of findin' him. Some folk called him Solo Gang Bang.

Then the meteors happened, and he found a cave. But why a cave?

Because no one warned him in advance, and if they'd warned him, what was there to do? Because the weather transformed, and there was radiation, and he couldn't fix it as muscles bled. Because the wind blew, and vultures called. A cave was all he got in another life too dense for speech. A whistle of meteors

> Rocketin' his town as he hid,
> Knottin' cries for help with his
> toes and fingers,
> his body all
> fetal on the
> ground.

How long in there, he doesn't know. All he knows is that one day he started eatin' weeds and critters, bugs oozy and white inside. Never stopped eatin' them 'cos that's all he had. But 'twas the kind of food that didn't grow him any taller, matter of fact, he's shrinkin'. Not that he's havin' a moan about it, but he was six foot four—now it feels like, like . . . five foot freakin'-nothin'.

A cave does that to you.

He shivers to the shape of wreckage, the complexity and chaos of burnt-out houses, bloomin' disease. This realm has a tendency toward rot, especially in caves. For days, months, after his world collapsed, he longed for the taste of home. And the taste of a woman.

He visits the scorched earth to see the dead and dyin'—their groans as he fumbles with their remnants, deliberates on whether to eat them. He doesn't. Out of a need to cool more than anythin', he rolls in soot and dirt, bathes in innards rich with moisture. He notices how some bloated bodies are turnin' red, some burstin' when he nears or touches them. What he sees fills him with both curiosity and repulsion. He
        never imagined
           fluid leaks out
              like that from
                  a corpse.

A body in the active stage of putrefaction oozes out dark sludge the rich texture of porridge. It mirrors his life of pongy feces and oozy guts.

Back in his den, he falls asleep. This seems about all he can do: eat, shit, eat, shit.

He dreams of that other life where he thought he would stay but never admitted it to himself because acceptin' was being content. There used to be wine from a tavern named Mustang Blu, freshly baked bread dipped in pink salt and olive oil, a sprinkle of bay leaves, and the scent of poetry. He reminisces about gazin' at fishin' boats below the strangled call of seagulls. Huoh, huoh! Sometimes, he pushed fingers into a girl's hair, stroked her scalp all gentle-like, stole a kiss under soft light and mistletoe.

Huoh, huoh!

Then the meteors happened, and he plunged into a cave. This cave.

He doesn't know at what stage the world moved, swirlin' and humpin', soarin' and catapultin', uprootin' him and his cave from there all the way to here.

At one moment of cannibalism, he looks at his hands and feet; so hungry he was, he'd have gobbled a dog had it strayed, a cat had it showed, tail and all. Four limbs are good, he was thinkin', but he found leaves, then earthworms, tore them apart with his teeth. Eight legs are good; the spider didn't think so, couldn't run away fast enough. His stomach willfully talked in bubbles and riddles, unaccustomed to these new conquests. Eventually, it, too, found trust in snakes and stones, resurrected itself to know better as he understood where he lived.

There are crickets and their seed-nut taste. Mealworms rich and wet with a load of mushrooms. Locusts, savory like crabs. Scorpions too—away from the stinger, they're like seafood. Each day is trial and error. Some critters have innards as sharp as an aged cheddar, even a gruyere. Smoky finish.

Ants, termites, woodlice, stink bugs . . . he's had 'em all.

He was never a fussy eater. I'll have at it, he said of the roadkill. Ain't that bad, of the warthog entrails, gobbled the damn lot. Won a bet as his mates held back bile, forked out the dough.

Sometimes, he thinks of meat as he knew it: tender, juicy, salty. The soft melt of roast chicken, the butter of sex. The delicate sweetness of fish full of soft mud, that heady scent of a woman. Much of what he gets now from the earth's belly is crunchy and chewy. Some he gets from the tree's bark.

He touches the tree, feels the top of his head against her belly. What's this now?—four foot freakin'-shit. But it's not only he who's changin'. The tree is also changin'. Today, she wears a perfume. He rubs her powder's dust between his fingertips.

Pollen.

He feels an urge, rubs, rubs against her nakedness. Ain't no clothes in a goddamn cave—what do you need those for? He feels. What he feels is—ugghh, ugghh.

He coats her with the intensity of his want.

Now there's more he can do: eat, shit, mate, repeat.

Today, Zayyid'a crawls out of his shelter cave. He blinks at the strange new world with its ashen soil. Wonders how the heck home transported itself to this desolation. The smell of death is everywhere, even though the corpses are skeletons. He collects nails and teeth, more as a pastime. It's better than shittin' and eatin', all that doin' with the tree, ugghh, ugghh. His head hurts.

He reaches for his scalp. What happened to his hair? You'd think he's wearin' a helmet, the way it's hard. Mirror, mirror— where are the mirrors? He creeps further out, his heart jumpin' at every sound. There are still meteors fallin', but now more like rain.

Suddenly, he wants to relieve himself. Cramps! The urgency! He's never felt this before.

He crouches behind a giant shrub. Pushes, pushes, and it's killin' him to push. Finally, somethin' pill-shaped plops at his feet. The hell? It's a sac. He pokes into it, and there are sixteen jelly-like things like eggs in it. He once read somewhere that some bug eggs come in packs of sixteen. Now that's a coincidence. But the urge isn't finished. He squats closer to the ground. Pushes, pushes, and it's killin' him even more. Another pill thing with soft eggs inside.

Unbelievable. The urge.

Now he looks at them. He reckons the critters he's been eatin' have manifested worms into his gut, and they're layin' eggs. He looks at the pill cluster: about thirty. He imagines sixteen eggs waitin' to hatch in each pill. That makes 480 freakin' fuckin' eggs. His fear is big, and it's a fear that rushes to his feet and makes him stomp.

He stomps, stomps, stomps, splatters his face with white, then light green goo.

He recoils, rolls on ashen soil, stills at the sound of singin'.

He's not alone. He leaps behind a bush, just barely, peers goggle-eyed at the procession of giant crabs with eight legs. They're as big as him and makin' song with their feet as they walk sideways and in a rush. Croakin' and cricketin', moanin' and barkin'. Fast, faster, their stiff-jointed sidle sheds a musical echo.

He creeps after them, notices they carry one of their own asunder. It, he, she is squealin' and writhin' blue murder. He figures out why when he sees what they do when they put it, he, she down on a raised hillock like a shrine or an altar, do some sort of side-walk dance as they recite a ritual, then eat the bloody thing alive! It's yowlin' and yippin', uses its front pair of legs to stave them off. But they growl
   and rip its legs,
      it's mewlin' and sidlin'
        on a hobble
          seven, six, five . . .
        no legs.

He runs so fast, but it takes forever to reach the cave. His footsteps are tinier, and he doesn't seem to have as much muscle and grunt as before.

A cave does this to you.

He returns later to the remains of the eaten one. Crab guts here, there. He licks the yellow ooze. Peeks into the head hollowed in, scoops out crab fat or brain matter.

The lungs, yukkity yak, are all bitter, way too stringy.

The tree and her perfume. He rubs his nakedness against her. Ugghh, ugghh. The intensity of his want.

Takes only two days and, suddenly, he wants to relieve himself real bad. Cramps! The urgency! OMG, he knows this feelin'. He crouches behind a shrub, pushes, pushes, pushespushespushes.

Another cluster, soft and round, covered in a translucent slime. A part of him wants to reach and squish 'em with his fingers, stomp on them with a foot real hard, yet another part of him wants to stomp on him, protect those eggs from his own mad self. Bloody hell.

He looks at the tree.

The fuckin' tree.

He digs with his hands near the base of the mangrove where it's a little damp, makes a nest right there. Still, he's somewhat surprised when baby roaches, fat, juicy larvae, crack out one by one. They're at first translucent white, but quickly grow into reddish-brown stinkers . . . gods, they stink like hell. They're woody and oily, a smell like burnt wood or urine. He sniffs his armpits— woody and oily, odor of char or piss. Yep, the teeny ones stink like him, and they shit 'n eat, shit 'n eat.

Gods, he needs a wash.

He looks in surprise at his fingertips and feet. How did this happen? When did this happen? He's missin' nails, three fingers, and two toes. He finds solace in sleep, but can't go far now, little ones followin' him everywhere, restin' in cracks of the cave, its crevices. They find all his secret places, even his tree. Night is eatin', shittin'. The tree. Ugghh, ugghh.

He goes out critter huntin' to feed the ever-hungry roaches, impatient and climbin' all over him and his den. But the crabs, the crabs. Must hide from the crabs. They side-walk in a rush, eat another of their own alive on the hillock in the presence of the colony.

This time, he notices their shell markin's and patterns: bright blue. Like him, they live in caves. Unlike him, they mate so loud, chirpin', singin', growlin', and lay eggs by the waterfront.

The tree. Ugghh, ugghh.

He looks at his fingerless hands; they're all spiny, and they need a wash. His legs are spiny too. He needs to go to the waterfront . . . his arm . . . this is a stranger's arm. He had a tattoo of skulls—now it's gone.

He climbs his tree, ugghh, ugghh, notices how he melts into it.

His skin is camouflage, the crabs can't see him, can't smell him or his woody, oily smell like char or piss.

The critters—those that survive—are adult roaches now. They're mottled in color. They scurry thisaway, thataway, but the crabs find them, eat them alive. He hugs the tree, ugghh, ugghh, shivers throughout the eatin', his little ones chirpin' and hissin', clickin' and dyin'. He glides from the branch and runs to his cave, this time takin' forever, his hands and feet tiny, tinier, and all the spinier.

One day, he braves the waterfront. Because he needs a wash. He peers into the surface, sees a creature in it. A beast with a copper helmet. No hair, two antennae. He reaches to finger his scalp, but he can't reach it. The creature in the water mirrors his actions, spiny fingers tryin' 'n reachin' for its antennae.

He follows the outline of his body with his eyes. He is flat and wide. Oval-shaped. He's reddish brown with a ridge along his length. Hardened skin, two feelers instead of hair. His mouth, dear gods, his mouth. It's part triangle, mandibles on each side. He's turned into a freakin' roach.

He mulls over this knowin', wallows in the deepest despondency.

Just then, the sheddin' of an echo song in a procession, feet walkin' sideways in his direction. Fast, faster, sidlin'. The crabs, dear gods. They're yowlin' and yippin', hissin' and raspin'.

He understands the moral of this story.

He should have lived a fuller life, found more meanin' than sweet talkin' and all that Cobra Bill shit. But now is not the time or place for remonstration, because that won't save him.

The crabs are comin'. Faster, fastest, sideways, and right there between him and the den. He's seen what they do to their own. Chirpin', singin', growlin' as they rip out legs in a scatter of pus. And he . . . he is a stranger. He looks at his tiniest, spiniest hands and feet, the ones they'll tear off as they yowl and yip and eat him alive. He sees his future: oozy gut and a hollowed-out skull. Lungs stringy as fuck.

Closer! The crabs are hissin' and raspin', yowlin' and yippin'.

He turns and, with a big cry, HELP, HELP, no one near to help a whole, ugly, odd, creepy bug—so . . .

      he

    R

      U

        N

          S.

Fact:

Cockroaches clean themselves after being touched by a human.

THE LARGE RECKONING

Linda D. Addison

Before Time and Space
    were separate branches
        on the same tree.
Before Cosmos' first exhalation,
    know there was no intention,
        no predestination,
            of what you would become.

Just stars breaking apart,
    black holes consuming
        matter,
            antimatter,
                dark matter,
    creating—un-creating.

Loss makes room for new.

A mass extinction event, long before you,
    asteroid removes lumbering creatures,
      all life greater than 25 kg succumbs to flames,
      leaving tidal waves to clean up ashes and bones.

Loss makes room.

From this cleansed slate,
    plants thrived, creatures evolved,
    you emerged on a planet which
    neither rejoiced nor rebuffed
    your schemes built from
lust for more—more—more.

You consume all Grace
    the natural world loans you,
    over—over—over again,
    believing it limitless
    as your bottomless hunger.

Denying the signs:
    dolphin songs fallen
    from Heaven to Earth.
    Twin stars changed,
    switched observable colors.

Ignoring answers to endless Macro
    clear in infinite Micro, within the lion's gaze,
    owl's waning call, monkey's skipping heart,
    pigeon's relentless nod, dog's vigorous bark,
    sloth's mindful crawl, worms devout burrowing,
smothered moans of hungry, bruised children.

The small reckonings, seen by some of you,
    in species disappearing, large and small
    hounded for sport, extinct by indifference,
    forests turned to ash, heat waves searing skin
    from neglected children and unseen homeless.

Each generation, corrupted by the last,
    consumes the gap between
    the beginning and the end.
    Closer—closer—closer
    comes the Large Reckoning.

You are your own final killing blow.

The stars will watch your extinction event,
    the whales will sing of the garden
    you recklessly shunned. You few
    who saw it coming will surrender
    in such obliteration, knowing . . .

loss makes room for new.

THE DEVIL'S BLOOD

NZONDI

THOUSANDS OF YEARS had passed, and still there was nothing that religious zealots, scholars, nor seekers of truth found to bring them closer to having actual proof of the legendary being so many believed existed. No one had seen the ominous entity who became the scapegoat for unheard atrocities. Yet, a nightmarish legend grew over time and invaded generations of kindreds, plaguing the minds of many like an infection with an insatiable hunger for tasting fear.

The fable that spread through the animal kingdom like a wildfire of fright started on one damp evening when an ever-curious mother mosquito decided that the best one to answer the question that had been on her mind was the wicked night owl.

The mosquito suffered from short-term memory, but there were two things she never forgot: her babies would soon need to feed, and she hated the idea of the devil more than anyone and wanted to prove that there was no such thing. As she went on a hunt for blood, she knew there were wise creatures in the forest and they would help her, if she asked.

The mother mosquito passed through a village, and after finding an old, sick, dying man, she drew his blood and was on her way to the woods. The town she stopped in was like every other place she'd visited in the last few months. They all had become a forest of their own; the kind that grew in the wake of negligence. Vines clung on to the street signs like killers strangling their victims. Buildings became a fortress of broken walls and trees. The wind ran recklessly in the streets and howled at anyone who would dare listen. An old pissant newspaper hung on a breeze, and the mother mosquito caught the headline of it before it tumbled away: HOSPITALS OVERWHELMED AS OVER TWO THIRDS OF THE POPULATION WIPED OUT BY PESTILENCE.

Finally, after coasting through the desolate town littered with abandoned cars and shells of a village once alive with life and food for her babies, the mother mosquito made it into the forest. Up on a branch, she saw one of the wisest creatures in the animal kingdom and landed upon a human skull lodged in the ground next to a small femur that was slowly decomposing. She fluttered her wings to announce her arrival.

The owl was blind as a bat when he didn't wear his spectacles, but his hearing worked perfectly well. "Who approaches my perch when the night is full and my stomach empty?" he said.

"It's me!" the mother mosquito said. "May I ask you a question, oh wise one?"

"If you're not afraid of the answer, my pesky friend."

The mosquito remembered little, but she knew that being called pesky annoyed her, and her eyebrows furrowed. "Don't call me that!" she snapped.

The owl stuttered, "My—my apologies, my dear friend. Tell me why—why do I have the pleasure?"

She rubbed her hands together and said, "Okay. Here goes . . . Does the devil exist?"

"That's like asking someone if faith is real," the owl said. "Only to those who believe. Now go away, or my tongue may not only speak, it shall eat."

The owl winced at the slip of his wicked rudeness and breathed a sigh of relief when he realized the mother mosquito was too preoccupied to be cross with him.

The wicked night owl's answer only made the mosquito's curiosity rise. *'Only to those who believe,' he said.* "How so?" the mosquito muttered, and so, in the dreary night, she continued her quest of curiosity until she saw the petty coyote sniffing at the skeleton of a human wearing a straw hat, the man's spine against the tree. An old broken-string banjo sat in the bag of bones' lap.

"Mr. Coyote?" the mother mosquito whispered, seeing how the canine crept.

The coyote wriggled his ear. "Can't you see you're bothering me? I'm in the middle of a feeding spree."

"Just one question I have to ask, and then I'll leave you to your task?"

"Ah, since you know I love to rhyme, and returned your answer just so fine, I'll grant an answer just this time, and you'll just run along, so hungry me can continue to dine."

"Who made the devil? Was it Man? And please be on the level, if you can."

"Ah, the answer, a good old one if you take note. The trickster priests of the Middle Ages borrowed that one's image of an African goat."

"Oh gee, a goat? So very odd?"

"Indeed, take quote. A goat god."

With that, the mother mosquito left, and had more questions than she had at first. As quickly as she forgot some, more came in place. She came upon a pack of wild philla forms, sitting around a campfire singing songs. They were the heinous hyenas, and each had a distrusting grin, and although she knew they were the best at having shenanigans, the rumor around the animal kingdom was that they knew everything about everyone.

When she got close, they all stopped singing, and their ears perked up.

A lady hyena stood on all fours and asked, "Who goes there?"

"It's me, the mother mosquito. I heard there's nothing that you can't do when you work together and put your minds to it."

"What is it you want, throat licker?" The lady hyena asked. "And hurry up! We're singing a blood song before a great hunt."

"I'm sorry. Did you just tell me to hurry up?" the mother mosquito asked.

The lady hyena backed up a few steps and batted her eyes in embarrassment. "Apologies, my dear friend. You of all creatures should know how—how—how—how important it is," she said, and laughed nervously, "to—to, well, to have a blood hunt."

The mother mosquito nodded. "Yes. Yes, I do."

The lady hyena curled her tail beneath her hind legs. "And your question is?"

"What is the devil's purpose?"

All the hyenas traded glances, looked back at the mother mosquito, and erupted in laughter.

"Settle down, brothers and cousins," the lady hyena said, and licked a giggle from her chops. "You are a funny one to ask."

"Well, does he—"

"He?" The lady hyena snickered. "If you listen to Man, mother mosquito, then the devil comes to kill and destroy, that *she* is evil."

The mosquito tilted her head and said, "She?"

The lady hyena narrowed her eyes. "Yes, she."

"Are you saying that . . . she's not?"

"No more than a cat who must chase a string. The she-devil creates chaos," a cousin hyena said. "Answer me this, bloodsucker. Is a lion evil when he kills a deer and feeds it to his cubs? Is a deer evil when she eats the pretty flowers right after a gardener plants them?"

The mother mosquito's eyes grew wide, and her shoulders hunched. "I don't know. Was that rhetorical?"

"Let me ask you this, my good friend," the lady hyena said. "If all existence in the universe was created with a boom, a boom that took the pure solidarity of the Mother of All and broke up her essence into countless pieces all over the galaxy, which in turn created life, is that boom therefore good or bad? For whichever was the cause of chaos was also the cause of life."

"That's not the way the good books tell the story," the mother mosquito said.

"And who wrote the good books? Nature? No, mischievous Man did. Nature sees day and night as siblings who each bring a benefit to all the living," the lady hyena said.

The mother mosquito scratched her head, and thought hard before she asked, "But isn't Man right when he started believing that darkness is evil and the light is good?"

One of the brother hyenas said, "Did we animals and insects depict the morning sun as good, and the evening moon as a time when fear of the darkness be the way? No, we give praises to the light of day as much as we sing prayers to the dark of night, for neither the sun nor the moon is good nor evil, but both serve as wonders to the eyes and food for the soul. It was Man who proclaimed, 'Fear the night, for darkness is evil, and we shall forever more give praise to the sun, for he is the son of the Great One.' It was as foolish to believe then as it is now."

"You see," the lady hyena said, "just as the most revered priest can't rise higher than the Mother of God's Spirit, which lives in each one of us, for we are all broken-off parts of the First Love, the Mother of All, neither can the most hated demon be worse than the wickedness that lies dormant in every living creature. Like Goodness, Evil hibernates in all of us until awakened, like the eggs in you waiting to be fed from the blood of Man. It all depends on which one we choose to feed, and what's fed grows."

"Then we are all gods and demons?" the mother mosquito asked.

The lady hyena grinned, and her face twisted. "That is a bit devious to think, even in my warped thoughts. It's more like we are all pawns of necessity, and we are all sovereigns of waste."

"Pawns of necessity? Sovereigns of waste? I don't understand," the mosquito said and shook her head. "For every answer you give, you double my questions."

"Search for the castle hidden in the backwoods," the cousin hyena said and made a tut with his teeth. "If you can find it, you will find all of your answers like a lost child returning home. There is someone there who is the wisest in all the lands when it comes to evil and all its ideologies. She is not always fair, because her mind is not always there, but she loves to share."

The hyenas all laughed, all their eyes full of ominous amusement. Even the lady hyena joined in.

"Who is this person?" the mother mosquito asked.

One of the brother hyenas snarled and said, "Buzz off, no more speak, lest I crush you between my teeth."

"Excuse me?" the mother mosquito asked.

The lady hyena smacked her tail across the brother's head. "Please forgive my idiot brother. We all hope you find what you seek."

The mosquito raised her chin and left the pack of heinous hyenas. Soon after, the wind started to howl, and it rained. Finally, she found a place to seek shelter in after losing her bearings in the blinding storm that grew worse by the minute. A brown weather-beaten floor mat welcomed her with the words WELCOME HOME printed on it in fading fancy lettering. From the poor upkeep of the grounds surrounding it, the mother mosquito thought it was abandoned. There was a small graveyard on the side of the massive place with leaning tombstones that reminded the mosquito of a frightening story she pleaded her mother never to read to her again when she was but a wee maggot about a giant plant with crooked teeth that lived underground and would swallow unsuspecting travelers like a wolf devouring a rabbit.

"Sooner or later," the mother mosquito muttered, slamming the knocker fiercely on the arched wooden door, "I'm going to prove to everyone that the devil doesn't exist."

The mother mosquito couldn't help but feel chills as she stared at the nearby graveyard. "This place gives me the creeps."

She shivered and sneezed, and when she turned to leave, the door creaked open. The mother mosquito entered cautiously and couldn't help ignoring the feeling of déjà vu.

She stopped in the grand foyer and hollered, "Hello! Anyone there?" Fluttering the wetness from her wings onto the dusty marble floor, she asked, "Can I please come in? I'm mighty cold and would love to warm up just a bit."

Seeing no one replied, the mother mosquito wondered what to do next. She stood in the massive foyer, and what bugged her most was that she knew there was something she was supposed to do but, for the life of her, couldn't remember. A grandfather clock ticked and tocked from some unseen room, and a massive crystal chandelier hung above her, displaying its brilliance over a staircase descending like a bat's wings on both sides down to the ground floor.

Suddenly, a muffled cry of babies filled the air, and she stiffened. "Did you hear that?" she muttered to herself. Without hesitation, she stopped flapping her wings and glided forward, listening carefully at a fork where two corridors led down long ways. "No one better harm those babies," she said.

The closer she got, the more the chorus of their drowning sobs sung to the growing pains in her heart. "Poor things. They sound as if they're underwater." Terrified, the mother mosquito gasped. "That way!" she said and zipped down the corridor to the right.

The sconces on the wall emitted a flame-orange glow, and the nervous flutter of her erratic wings had the sound of an echo desperately bouncing back and forth across a hallway that felt like it was leading her toward death. The stone walls were painted with grave discoloration and neglect, spider-webbed alcoves bared burgundy velour curtains caked with dust.

Finally, she came to the end of the hallway. Lo and behold, there stood a door. As if the door was alive and sensed her presence, it creaked open when she came before it. The mother mosquito went through the door's threshold and found herself in total darkness.

"What is this place?" she muttered, the words playing out in her mind, not her mouth.

The crying stopped, and her breaths seemed magnified. All around her was the revelation of what she suddenly understood happens when shadows swallow shadows and sound plays hide and seek in a vacuum. There was a totality of nothingness.

Until the point she opened her eyes, the mother mosquito hadn't realized they were closed. Her body shivered in the way a waking child would spring up on a lazy Saturday afternoon, thinking it was a Friday morning and she was late for school. The mother mosquito realized that she was submerged in water.

In her mind, she heard herself say, "I'm somewhere but nowhere."

It was at that moment she stared down at herself and realized that her eyes hadn't opened yet. No, not at all. At least not the eyes of the one who was her; it was definitely her, lying atop the surface of the water like a mother taking a soothing bath on the first day of school—kids gone, mama's alone!

The mother mosquito watched with insatiable curiosity as a gnat dressed in a white uniform and a beetle dressed in a lab coat approached her sleeping self.

As soon as the two gathered by the floating version of herself peacefully asleep, a hundred babies cried out again, but this time she could see them floating beneath the water, clinging to each other, creating a mat of wonderfulness so adorable, the mother mosquito saw her sleeping self smile the way a proud mother would when surrounded by those who professed a need for her love with their tears.

The gnat looked down at the resting mosquito and said, "Dr. Dungbeetle?"

"Yes, Nurse Gnat?" the beetle in the lab coat answered.

"I apologize again for such ineptness."

"Don't beat yourself up about it, my child. This is your first day. The countess has fooled many a nurse wandering the halls during birthing."

"Really?"

"Yes, but what I do find strange is that she kept murmuring in her sleep how she was going to prove that the devil didn't exist."

"She's going to prove what?" Nurse Gnat laughed. "Does she not know who she is?"

"It's her gift and her curse. She dies after every three miraculous birthings and resurrects without any knowledge of who she is or what she's done."

The mother mosquito, who was up high observing all this, gasped and covered her mouth for fear of being discovered.

Nurse Gnat buzzed loudly, "You're kidding!"

Dr. Dungbeetle pointed at his gray-whiskered face. "I grew up burying dung hundreds of times my weight every morning before school. Does this look like the face of a beetle who jests?"

The nurse giggled. "I guess not," she said and glanced down at the mother mosquito. "But surely the countess remembers that she single-handedly wiped out Man's existence when she spread a fatal disease? Who could forget creating Man's extinction?"

"Perhaps," the beetle doctor said, and rubbed his chin. "And perhaps not. I believe exterminating Man has put a strain on her mental faculties."

"How? Wait. You think that she misses Man? That's why?"

"Affirmative."

"Will this affect her mothering?"

"You underestimate the power of a mother," Dr. Dung said and chuckled. "A mother can feed her family, keep the lights on, the foolishness off, and put the world on her back to become the true inspiration for all that does and will exist."

"You put it that way, all these little wrigglers will be fully grown and out of the pond in no time. All because of a mother's love."

"Well said, Nurse Gnat. Well said, my child. Hmm," Dr. Dung Beetle said and crossed his arms. "To be frank, whether or not she's cursed to forget that she is the devil after three birthings and mothering her pupa to adulthood, I know deep down in that heart of hers, she knows that she is the number one reason why man continues to face mass extinction."

"Really?"

"Yes, and everyone knows that Man's never content with leaving well enough alone and is always willing to sell his own soul to gain the world. Every time Man is born, the countess has to chip away at the fabric from the Mother of All's Original Spirit until enough pieces of the Great She herself are there for the devil to scatter all over the world and recreate mankind for the umpteenth time."

"Hmph," Nurse Gnat said and nodded. "And each time, some power-hungry man plays the game of cat and mouse with the devil without fully understanding the rules."

"My mother used to always say to me, be careful what you ask for. Every oligarch, no matter that person's birth land or native tongue, always finds him or herself standing before the devil with the same question."

"And what question may that be, Doc?"

"If I let you drink my blood, devil, will I live forever?"

"And do they?"

"Look around, Nurse Gnat. Every town, village, city, state and country where humanity has thrived is now filled with rotting corpses and the only true answer to the power-hungry man's question."

"Which is?"

"The only thing that never dies is death itself. Death is truly immortal."

With that, the doctor and the gnat left the mother mosquito to rest, and when she finally did open her eyes, she joyfully welcomed all her baby pupa with a pond-time story about the time she asked a god named Khnum to let her create Man so she could feed her children.

Fact:

Spreading diseases like malaria, dengue, West Nile, yellow fever, Zika, chikungunya, and lymphatic filariasis, the mosquito kills more people than any other creature in the world. Killing an estimated 500,000, to more than a million people per year.

THE FABLE OF THE TARDIGRADE

COLLEEN ANDERSON

ARDIGRADE CLUNG WITH his fine curved claws to the spongy algae swaying in the stream. He sucked the juices through his round snout, ignoring the usual large shadows coming and going overhead. Darkness fell swiftly as a gigantic foot splashed into the puddle that served as his lake. Tardigrade curled, then uncurled, and pushed off into another piece of safer algae.

The shadow didn't disperse but lowered, looming. A white pillar of teeth snapped at the water, and Tardigrade pulled back, nestling deeper into the lush vegetation. Then an eye larger than the puddle stared down, encompassing his sky.

"What in all the fiery volcanoes are you?" the dinosaur growled like mountains crumbling.

"Tardigrade," he replied.

The dinosaur rumbled with what Tardigrade took to be a laugh. "You are puny. Less than the spittle from my mouth. Far smaller than my shit."

Tardigrade had no answer, for he was indeed tiny.

"Do you know who I am?" The dinosaur seemed very tall, sort of gray and orange, but Tardigrade's eyes weren't so good at great distances.

"I am Tyrannosaurus Rex, the greatest of dinosaurs. Other creatures flee at my roar. Why, even Spinosaurus, with her tricksy ways in rivers, hesitates to battle against my formidable strength. I rule this planet. I take what I want. What do you do, puny thing of eight legs?"

"I eat, and live, raise my family, and tell tales. Our species has existed forever."

Tyrannosaurus laughed. "You are nothing. You will not be remembered. To be remembered, you must be feared or be the best. My hide glistens in the sun, my stare lances terror into the hearts of all beasts."

Then Tyrannosaurus darted down and snapped at Tardigrade, who was too small to be eaten. The dinosaur loped away, the ground and water trembling in its wake.

Tardigrade moved through the stream to the egg clutch where Grandmother nestled. He told her the dinosaur's tale. She swung her nearly eyeless head back and forth and said, "Worry not. We have existed for many, many, many generations, long before dinosaurs came to this land. You don't have to be large to continue."

After Grandmother died, Tardigrade passed on the grandmother's tale and the story of the dinosaur to every newborn, until the day the planet shuddered deep into its core and the skies blackened when something impacted the planet. Some Tardigrades died, but many curled up and went dormant as fire roared through the land. Then the climate cooled quickly as ash blotted the sun. Tardigrade told them, "We have survived the end of the world four times before. We will survive this."

Generation upon generation upon generation passed, and Tardigrade's ancestors continued, unnoticed by most, though they had to fight their share of wriggling nematodes and hungry amoebas. One day, the grandchild to the nth degree of Tardigrade was siphoning parts of a particularly tasty lichen when something splashed the water above its head. Tardigrade dug her claws into the lichen and held on when a large, pale, sharp beak and a shiny black eye filled her world. With some concentration, Tardigrade noticed the deep oceanic blue and turquoise that covered the creature's body. A fan of beautiful blue and teal and green created a corona behind the beast like a hundred gorgeous eyes, and Tardigrade thought she would enjoy tasting those colors.

"What are you?" she asked.

"What? You don't know me?" The black eye drew closer. "I am the most exquisite of all creations. I am Peacock. I am descended from the mighty dinosaurs, but I am the most wonderful creature alive today. Nothing compares to me, and even humans admire me. What on Earth are you? You look like a little pig, but so very tiny."

Tardigrade introduced herself and the peacock shrieked with laughter. Tardigrade thought the bird might be lovely, but that voice was annoying.

"You really aren't much of anything, are you, little moss piglet? You'll never get ahead looking like that. You need to, I don't know, evolve, or do something to change. Get better eyes, at least. It's a good thing you're so small, since everyone would find you revolting. Beauty is what will make you well remembered. Why, even a potato is prettier."

Peacock wandered away, shrieking with laughter.

Tardigrade swam back to her family and wondered about beauty. Their tale was an old one, older than almost every living thing on Earth, but tardigrades still looked the same and no one noticed them. So caught up in her worry about beauty was she that Tardigrade didn't notice the long pale tube of a nematode. It writhed toward her and latched on before she noticed. Try as she might, she could not reach it with her claws to pry it off. As it sucked the life out of her, Tardigrade's energy ebbed. Rolling and spinning in the water, she bumped against a pebble. With her thoughts darkening, she twisted again, and the stone scraped the nematode, loosening its terrible mouth from her flank.

Tardigrade latched onto the nematode near its head, spearing it until it stopped moving. She had seen the most beautiful creature on Earth but thinking about beauty had nearly killed her. She would tell her family that beauty wasn't needed to stay alive.

Tardigrade's cousins and great-grandchildren carried on passing down tales of generations. Cousin Tardigrade rested in a forest of moss, so deeply green that the stalks looked black in the low light. Tardigrade ran its needle claws over the spongy moss bark, lightly scoring it. It debated whether it was still hungry when the water trembled and rippled. Tardigrade's history had settled into its survival instinct, and it hung on, debating if it needed to start a tun state dormancy or if this was yet another upper realm disturbance.

Loud noises vibrated the air as monstrous furry paws splashed into the water. Tardigrade dug claws into the fronds, recognizing this as one of the many antics of the mammals. Tales passed on through the family line spoke of beasts so large they were never completely seen, but those beasts were mostly gone now. What now roamed the Earth, and the seas were still very huge in every Tardigrade's story.

Tardigrade recognized this one as Dog. It yipped and barked, leaping, and jumping and splashing down directly on top of Tardigrade. Luckily, the tiny Tardigrade rode the waves and suffered no damage.

Dog stopped and sniffed, water swooshing up its nose until it shook its head. Tardigrade realized the deep tawny animal was Pup more than Dog, a juvenile.

Pup sat back on its rump, its ears flapping. "Hey, hey, tiny thing. Hello! How are you? I'd play with you, but you're hard to see. Everyone wants to play with me." Pup rolled on the grass near the mossy log on which Tardigrade harvested.

"That's okay. We can't play that well when there is such a size difference. Even I Spy doesn't work, because we don't see distances beyond shadows and light."

"Oh, that's too bad." Pup wriggled some more, then scratched behind its floppy ear and sat up, tongue lolling from its mouth. "Are you friends with others? Do people talk to you? You kinda look like a bear in water."

Tardigrade shrugged its round, potato-brown shoulders. "Most animals barely know we exist. We are friends with our kind."

"Oh, it's great fun to know others. My species is humankind's oldest friend. We're faithful and loyal and loving. People need us and take care of us, and we'll be with them forever and ever. We dogs are the cuddliest animals in all the world, and people will love us forever."

"That's nice," Tardigrade said, but wondered why dogs needed people.

"You should become friends with other species. Especially humans." Pup leapt up. "I've gotta go to play ball with my human. I'll come visit again. Bye, water bear! Bye bye bye!"

Pup stayed true to its word and did visit Tardigrade again. It jumped about so fast and sniffed everything, snorting up a couple of Tardigrade's cousins. The cousins took an adventure through Pup's guts and were none the worse for wear upon being evacuated a few days later.

Pup grew into Dog and still came to visit, sometimes rooting out a long stick to chew on or chasing voles into the woods.

Tardigrade was glad it wasn't larger, or it might have been a toy for Dog. Tardigrades had enough enemies with mites and spiders clambering by, and wars with other groups of Tardigrades.

Dog showed up one day, plunking down rather quickly and yawning hugely as spittle hung in strings from its jaw.

"You look different," said Tardigrade as it speared and siphoned the tart juice out of an amoeba.

"Ugh, can you not smell it? The sky is poisoned. The humans fight too much." Dog whimpered. "But I love them. They are my best friend and I theirs. Especially my special human."

Dog howled and thrashed on the soil, but the motions didn't resemble the playfulness of its pup hood.

Tardigrade puzzled. The larger realm was always a blurry mystery. Little changed in the micro world.

"I'm sorry your humans are fighting. It happens to us too. Sometimes Tardigrade eats Tardigrade."

Dog clasped its paws over its snout. "Yes, yes. This happens everywhere, but humans have found a way to use other things to make their fights monstrous. It hurts. It hurts so much."

Dog gagged and a bloody blob fell onto the grass. Sadness effused Tardigrade. Dog was entertaining, quick moving; so different from the Tardigrade domain of slowly wading through liquids to live, love, and feed.

"It passes, doesn't it? This fighting of humans?"

Dog rolled on its back and howled. "Yes, but sometimes it takes years and years and years."

Tardigrade shrugged. What could it do?

When Dog next visited, it crawled toward the moss-covered log, but did not leap or talk or even howl.

"Are you all right, Dog? You're very quiet."

Dog's body looked thin, sucked dry of juices. Glistening red sores wept fluids down its patchy fur.

Dog breathed out, "All gone."

Tardigrade sensed Dog's life source had left, and Dog never moved again.

Over the next few seasons, the world cooled. Ice crystals formed on the puddles and logs where tardigrades lived. Tardigrade's family moved deeper, but word reached them from tardigrades in the forests and oceans, the deserts, and the Arctic: Every living thing in air, water, or on land was dying or dead.

The food sources dwindled; algae browned, lichen withered, and more frequently, a dead bird plummeted into their ponds. When the amoebas and nematodes died, and sheets of ice descended, Tardigrade knew it was time. The tardigrades shriveled up, moving into their tun state, to wait until the planet was safe again.

Centuries passed: no one knew how many, but as rain began to fall on dormant tardigrades, they filled out and reanimated.

Tardigrade told the young stories of their past, of the end of the world that had now happened six times in Tardigrade history.

The algae grew rich and larger than it had before. Few nematodes prevailed, but amoeba had returned as an enemy and food source. Without being mighty and fearsome, without being beautiful, without being adorable and loved, Tardigrades continued.

Fact:

To endure environmental stress, tardigrades suspend their metabolism through a process called cryptobiosis. They curl up and enter a death-like state known as a tun. Their metabolism slows to 0.01% of normal, and their water content drops to less than 1%. They survive in this state by replacing the water in their cells with a protective sugar called trehalose, which preserves all the cellular machinery until water is available again.

WHALES

CHRISTINA SNG

Radiation kills us if we breach the surface.

So, we stay beneath the mile-thick ice
and evolve thick blubber
to keep us warm, feeding on brine
and the occasional deep-sea creature
that wanders into our territory.

It's been an age since we moved
beneath Europa's surface,
the first of us scarred
and nearly infertile
from the blast of Jupiter's radiation.

Yet each generation evolved
to live in this new place.
We have no choice.
Earth is scorched and burned,
inhospitable to most life.

We now look gray and mottled,
our mouths extruded to filter

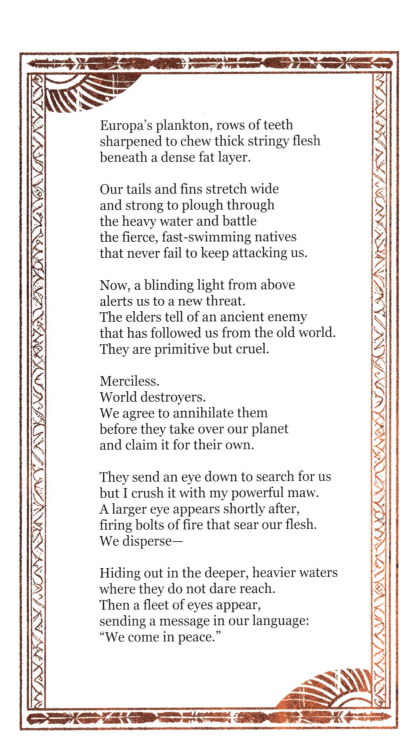

Europa's plankton, rows of teeth
sharpened to chew thick stringy flesh
beneath a dense fat layer.

Our tails and fins stretch wide
and strong to plough through
the heavy water and battle
the fierce, fast-swimming natives
that never fail to keep attacking us.

Now, a blinding light from above
alerts us to a new threat.
The elders tell of an ancient enemy
that has followed us from the old world.
They are primitive but cruel.

Merciless.
World destroyers.
We agree to annihilate them
before they take over our planet
and claim it for their own.

They send an eye down to search for us
but I crush it with my powerful maw.
A larger eye appears shortly after,
firing bolts of fire that sear our flesh.
We disperse—

Hiding out in the deeper, heavier waters
where they do not dare reach.
Then a fleet of eyes appear,
sending a message in our language:
"We come in peace."

"Lies!"
the elders tell us,
but we are intrigued,
venturing out to communicate.
Perhaps they are not beasts.

"Earth is gone.
We ask to share your world.
To share the plankton.
We will stay near the surface
and do you no harm."

"Kill them, kill them all,"
the elders beg.
"Humans only destroy.
They destroyed Earth once,
sending us here to escape.

They polluted our oceans,
leaving most of us dead.
If only we had the wisdom then
to send waves to drown their cities
and melt ice to sink their lands."

But we relent, hoping for peace.
                    We were all Earthlings once.

THE END?

Not if you want to dive into more of Crystal Lake Publishing's Tales from the Darkest Depths!

Check out our amazing website and online store
or download our latest catalog here.
https://geni.us/CLPCatalog

Looking for award-winning Dark Fiction?
Download our latest catalog.

Includes our anthologies, novels, novellas, collections,
poetry, non-fiction, and specialty projects.

WHERE STORIES COME ALIVE!

We always have great new projects and content on the website to
dive into, as well as a newsletter, behind the scenes options,
social media platforms, our own dark fiction shared-world series
and our very own webstore. Our webstore even has categories
specifically for KU books, non-fiction, anthologies, and of course
more novels and novellas.

ABOUT THE AUTHORS

Linda D. Addison is an award-winning author of five collections, including *The Place of Broken Things* written with Alessandro Manzetti, & *How To Recognize A Demon Has Become Your Friend*. She has been honored with the HWA Lifetime Achievement Award, HWA Mentor of the Year and SFPA Grand Master of Fantastic Poetry. She is a member of CITH, HWA, SFWA, SFPA and IAMTW. Find her in anthologies: *Black Panther: Tales of Wakanda; Predator: Eyes of the Demon; Chiral Mad 5; Writing Poetry in the Dark; Shakespeare Unleashed.*
www.lindaaddisonwriter.com

Colleen Anderson is an Aurora, Rhysling, Dwarf Stars and Elgin award nominee, with work published in seven countries, in such venues as *Andromeda Spaceways, Space and Time* the award- winning *Shadow Atlas*, and *Water: Sirens, Selkies & Sea Monsters*. Her poem, "Machine (r)Evolution" is part of Tenebrous Press's 2023 *Brave New Weird*. She lives in Vancouver, BC and is a Ladies of Horror Fiction, Canada Council and BC Arts Council grant recipient. She is author of two  fiction collections, *Embers Amongst the Fallen*, and *A Body of Work,* and two poetry collections, *I Dreamed a World*, and *The Lore of Inscrutable Dreams.*
www.colleenanderson.wordpress.com

Eugen Bacon is an African Australian author. She's a British Fantasy and Foreword Indies Award winner, a twice World Fantasy Award finalist, and a finalist in other awards, including the Shirley Jackson, Philip K. Dick Award, as well as the Nommo Awards for speculative fiction by Africans. Eugen was announced in the honor list of the Otherwise Fellowships for 'doing exciting work in gender and speculative fiction'. *Danged Black Thing* made the Otherwise Award Honor List as a 'sharp collection of Afro-Surrealist work'. Visit her at eugenbacon.com.

Michael Bailey is a writer, editor, and publisher. He is a recipient and nine-time nominee of the Bram Stoker Award, a five-time Shirley Jackson Award nominee, a multiple recipient of the Benjamin Franklin Award, as well as an insane number of independent accolades. Most of his fiction and poetry is categorized as psychological or literary horror, although he occasionally blends other genres, and he has published numerous novels, novellas, novelettes, and  fiction & poetry collections. His latest creations include *Righting Writing*, a nonfiction narrative about the craft, *Hangtown*, a dark historical western, *Seven Minutes*, a memoir about surviving one of California's most catastrophic wildfires, *Long Division: Stories of Social Decay, Societal Collapse, and Bad Manners*, an anthology co-edited with Doug Murano, and *Silent Nightmares: Stories to Be Told on the Longest Night of the Year*, co-edited with Chuck Palahniuk. He's a mentor to hundreds of writers, and also a screenwriter and producer for various film projects. Find him online at nettirw.com, or on social media @nettirw.

Steven Barnes is the NY Times bestselling, award-winning author and screenwriter of over thirty novels, as well as episodes of *The Twilight Zone, Andromeda, Horror Noire,* and the Emmy Award- winning "A Stitch In Time" episode of *The Outer Limits.* He is also a martial artist and creator of the "Lifewriting" approach to fiction, and the "Firedance" system of self-improvement (www. firedancetaichi.com). He lives in Southern California with his wife Tananarive and son Jason.

Rob Cameron

Cameron Roberson, who writes under the pen name Rob Cameron, is a teacher, linguist, and writer. He has poetry, stories, and essays, in *The Magazine of Fantasy & Science Fiction, Foreign Policy Magazine, Tor.com, Solarpunk Magazine, Clockwork Phoenix Five*, and others. He has a forthcoming novelette in *Lightspeed* and his debut middle-grade novel *Daydreamer* is forthcoming from Labyrinth Road, Summer  '24. Rob is a lead organizer for the Brooklyn Speculative Fiction Writers and executive producer of kaleidocast.nyc.

Wayne Fenlon is the Scottish author of the horror/thriller novel *The Black Cabin*, and drabble collection (100 word stories) *Scattered Little Pieces*. His stories have appeared online at horrortree.com, and alongside Bram Stoker Award nominees in the well-received horror anthology *Something Bad Happened* edited by Jennifer Bernardini.

If he's not reading, writing, and talking books, he's designing book covers or animating them. You can find him on:
Twitter. https://twitter.com/waynefenlon.
Facebook. https://www.facebook.com/waynefenlon.

Jamie Flanagan is an American actor and Bram Stoker award- winning writer. Screenwriting credits include *The Haunting of Bly Manor, Midnight Mass, The Midnight Club, The Fall of the House of Usher, Hysteria!*, and *Creepshow: Season 4*. They began their professional stage career in the world premiere of columbinus at Round House Theatre in 2005, and later received a Drama League Nomination (Ensemble) for  the production's remount at New York Theatre Workshop in 2006. Other stage credits include productions with Theater J, Rep Stage, The Kennedy Center TYA, Woolly Mammoth, Arena Stage, Studio Theatre, and more. TV and film appearances include *House of Cards, Absentia, Gerald's Game, The Haunting of Hill House, Doctor Sleep*, and *The Midnight Club*. They're an active member of SAG-AFTRA, the WGA East, and the Horror Writer's Association, with essays and stories appearing in *Nightmare Magazine, In The Bleak Midwinter* (Crooked Lane Books, Fall 2024), and others. They live nomadically with their partner. Both are video game enthusiasts. They hope to someday add a dog to the family.

 **Geneve Flynn** is a speculative fiction editor, author, and poet. Winner of two Bram Stoker Awards, a Shirley Jackson Award, an Aurealis Award, a Brave New Weird Award, and recipient of the 2022 Queensland Writers Fellowship. Her work has been nominated and short/longlisted for the British Fantasy, Locus, Ditmar, Australian Shadows, Elgin, and Rhysling Awards and the Pushcart Prize. Co-editor (with celebrated author/editor Lee Murray) of *Black Cranes: Tales of Unquiet Women,* the dark fiction anthology that launched the grassroots movement in Asian women's horror writing in 2020. Collaborator (with Lee Murray, Christina Sng, and Angela Yuriko Smith) of the internationally acclaimed dark poetry collection *Tortured Willows: Bent, Bowed, Unbroken*. Her work has been published by Crystal Lake Publishing, PS Publishing, Flame Tree Publishing, PseudoPod, and Written Backwards. Geneve serves on the Horror Writers Association's Diverse Works

Inclusion Committee. She is Chinese, born in Malaysia, and now calls Australia home. Read more at www.geneveflynn.com.au.

Maxwell I Gold is a Jewish-American multiple award-nominated author who writes prose poetry and short stories in cosmic horror and weird fiction with half a decade of writing experience. Four- time Rhysling Award nominee, and two-time Pushcart Award nominee, find him at www.thewellsoftheweird.com.

Oz Hardwick is a European poet, photographer, occasional musician, and accidental academic, who has been described as a "major proponent of the neo-surreal prose poem in Britain." He has published "about a dozen" full collections and chapbooks, including *Learning to Have Lost* (Canberra: IPSI, 2018) which won the 2019 Rubery International Book Award for poetry, and most recently *A Census of Preconceptions* (SurVision Books, 2022). In 2022, he was awarded the ARC Poetry Prize for "a lifetime devotion and service to the cause of prose poetry," though he is quick to point out that he's not dead yet. Oz is Professor of Creative Writing at Leeds Trinity University. www.ozhardwick.co.uk

Kareem Hayes, aka Inf the Author, is a prolific writer, filmmaker, and educator. With his best-selling series "Necessary Evil" and an impressive body of work, he has become a respected and influential figure in the urban realms of literature and film.

Dominique Hecq

A Belgian native, Dominique Hecq now lives in Melbourne, Australia. Hecq writes across genres and disciplines—and sometimes across tongues. Her creative output encompasses fifteen volumes of poetry. *Endgame with No Ending* (SurVision, 2023), a winner of the 2022 James Tate Poetry Prize, is off the press. Among other honours, Dominique Hecq is a recipient of the International Best Poets Prize administered by the International Poetry Translation and Research Centre in conjunction with the International Academy of Arts and Letters.

Travis Heermann

Author, filmmaker, screenwriter, poker player, poet, biker, Travis Heermann is a graduate of the Odyssey Writing Workshop, an Active member of SFWA and the HWA, and the author of the *Shinjuku Shadows series, Ronin Trilogy, The Hammer Falls*, and other novels. His more than thirty short stories appear in *Amazing Monster Tales, Apex Magazine, Tales to Terrify*, and others.  His freelance work includes a metric ton of contributions to such game properties as the *Firefly Roleplaying Game, Legend of Five Rings, EVE Online*, and *BattleTech*, for which he's been nominated for a Scribe Award. In 2021, he launched a film production company, Bear Paw Films LLC. Its first project, a horror comedy short film called *Demon for Hire*, premiered in 2022.

Jamal Hodge is a multi-award-winning filmmaker and writer from Queens NYC who has won over 80 awards with screenings at Tribeca Film Festival, Sundance, Cannes, and others. He directed the first season of Investigation Discovery Channel's 'Primal Instinct' and is a Producer on the Animated feature film *Pierre The Pigeon Hawk* (starring Jennifer Hudson, Snoop Dog, and

Whoopi Goldberg). Hodge is also a director on the PBS docuseries, *Southern Storytellers* (2023) and *Madness & Writers: The Untold Truth, Maybe? (*2024*)*. As a writer, Jamal is an active member of The Horror Writer's Association and the SFPA, being nominated for the 2021 & 2022 Rhysling Awards. His poem 'Colony' placed 2nd at the 2022 Dwarf Stars, making him the first Black poet to place in the history of the competition. His inaugural poetry collection *The Dark Between The Twilight* has been published by Crystal Lake Publishing for a 2024 release.

Akua Lezli Hope, 2022 Grand Master of Fantastic Poetry (SFPA), is a paraplegic creator & wisdom seeker who uses sound, words, fiber, glass, metal, & wire to create poems, patterns, stories, music, sculpture, adornments & peace. Her collections include *Embouchure: Poems on Jazz and Other Music*. Writer's Digest book award winner, *Them Gone, & Otherwheres: Speculative Poetry* (2021 Elgin Award winner). A Cave Canem fellow, her honors include the NEA,  two NYFA fellowships, the Science Fiction and Fantasy Poetry Association award & multiple Best of the Net, Rhysling & Pushcart Prize nominations. She won a 2022 NYSCA grant to create Afrofuturist, speculative, pastoral poetry. She created the Speculative Sundays Poetry Reading series.
She edited the record-breaking sea-themed issue of *Eye To The Telescope #42* & *NOMBONO: An Anthology of Speculative Poetry by BIPOC Creators,* the history-making first of its kind (Sundress Publications, 2021)

 **Jeffrey Howe** lives and works in the scenic Black Creek Bottoms area near St. Louis, Missouri. His short fiction has also appeared in *One Teen Story*, the anthology *Moon Shot: Murder and Mayhem at the Edge of Space*, and the quarterly anthology *The First Line*. His first produced screenplay, "Past Partum", won Best Horror Short at the 2019 Toronto Independent Film Festival. His first effort as a writer-director, the dark comedy "Ta-Da!", won Best Comedy Short at the 2023 Austin Revolution Film Festival.

EV Knight is the author of the Bram Stoker Award-winning debut horror novel *The Fourth Whore*. She has also written the novel *Children of Demeter* as well as several novellas; *Dead Eyes, Partum,* and her most recent release, Stoker Award-nominated autofictional *Three Days in the Pink Tower*. You can find her numerous short stories in horror anthologies as well. EV lives in one of America's most haunted cities—Savannah,  Ga. She is a huge fan of the Savannah Bananas and the beauty of Bonaventure Cemetery. When not out and about searching for the ghosts of the past, EV can be found at home with her husband Matt, her crazy dog Gozer, and their three naughty sphynx cats. You can find EV on her website evknightauthor.com where you can sign up for her newsletter and find links to all her social media.

 **Alessandro Manzetti** is a three-time Bram Stoker Award-winning writer, editor, scriptwriter and essayist of horror fiction and dark poetry. His work has been published extensively (more than 40 books) in Italian and English, including novels, short and long fiction, poetry, essays, graphic novels and collections. He lives in Trieste, Italy. www.battiago.com

Edward Martin III is a writer and filmmaker scrabbling together a semblance of home in the Pacific Northwest. He's surrounded by looming evergreens with sullen boughs, mountains that ponder the nature of death, and a relentless sea that dissolves everything it touches. Also, there are two cats. Big cats. Edward's books and films are available via HellbenderMedia.com. Finally, you should probably get some rest.

LH Moore's speculative fiction and poetry has been published in numerous anthologies, including Bram Stoker Award Finalist anthology *Sycorax's Daughters; Black Magic Women; Humans Are the Problem; the Chiral Mad 4 and 5, SLAY* and StokerCon anthologies; Moore has also been published in *Fireside, Apex* and twice in *FIYAH Magazine*. A DC native exiled in Maryland, Moore is a historian who loves classical guitar, graphic novels, and video games. Ask her nicely and she might tell you about her night in the hut of terror. Find out more at lhmoorecreative.com or IG @lh_ moore

Lisa Morton is a screenwriter, author of non-fiction books, Bram Stoker Award®-winning prose writer, and Halloween expert whose work was described by the American Library Association's Readers' Advisory Guide to Horror as "consistently dark, unsettling, and frightening." She has published four novels, 200 short stories, and three books on the history of Halloween. Recent short stories appeared in *Best*  *American Mystery Stories 2020, Shakespeare Unleashed,* and *Weird Tales*, and her first coffee table art book, *The Art of the Zombie Movie,* has been nominated for both the Bram Stoker Award and the Rondo Hatton Award. Lisa lives in Los Angeles and online at www.lisamorton.com.

Lee Murray is a writer, editor, poet and screenwriter from Aotearoa New Zealand, a Shirley Jackson Award and five-time Bram Stoker Award® winner. A *USA Today* bestselling author with more than forty titles to her credit, including novels, collections, anthologies, nonfiction, poetry, and several books for children, Lee holds a New Zealand Prime Minister's Award for Literary Achievement in Fiction, the first author of Asian descent to achieve this, and is an Honorary Literary Fellow of the New Zealand Society of Authors.

Her latest work, NZSA Cuba Press Prize-winner *Fox Spirit on a Distant Cloud*, was released in 2024 from The Cuba Press. Read more at leemurray.info

Nzondi (Ace Antonio Hall) is an American horror author and singer/songwriter, and is the first African-American to win a Bram Stoker in a novel category for his young adult book, *Oware Mosaic*. A former Director of Education for NYC schools and the Sylvan Learning Center, Nzondi earned a BFA from Long Island University. His latest novel, *Lipstick Asylum,* and his other works can be found on his website: AAntonioHall.com.

Cindy O' Quinn is a four-time HWA Bram Stoker nominated writer, and an Elgin, Rhysling, and Dwarf star nominated poet. She lives and writes on the old Tessier Homestead in the woods of northern Maine.

Cynthia Pelayo is a Bram Stoker Award winning and International Latino Book Award winning author and poet. Pelayo writes fairy tales that blend genre and explore concepts of grief, mourning, and cycles of violence. She is the author of *Loteria, Santa Muerte, The Missing, Poems of My Night, Into the Forest and All the Way Through, Children of Chicago, Crime Scene, The Shoemaker's Magician*, as well as dozens of standalone short stories and

poems. *Loteria*, which was her MFA in Writing thesis at The School of the Art Institute of Chicago, was re-released to praise with *Esquire* calling it one of the 'Best Horror Books of 2023.' *Santa Muerte* and *The Missing*, her young adult horror novels were each nominated for International Latino Book Awards.

Poems of My Night was nominated for an Elgin Award. *Into the Forest and All the Way Through* was nominated for an Elgin Award and was also nominated for a Bram Stoker Award for Superior Achievement in a Poetry Collection. *Children of Chicago* was nominated for a Bram Stoker Award in Superior Achievement in a Novel and won an International Latino Book Award for Best Mystery. *Crime Scene* won the Bram Stoker Award for Superior Achievement in a Poetry Collection. *The Shoemaker's Magician* has been released to praise with Library Journal awarding it a starred review. Her forthcoming novel, *The Forgotten Sisters*, will be released by Thomas and Mercer in 2024 and is an adaptation of Hans Christian Andersen's "The Little Mermaid." Her works have been reviewed in *The New York Times, Chicago Tribune, LA Review of Books*, and more.

Kumbali Satori is a visionary screenwriter and filmmaker known for their masterful storytelling and captivating screenplays. Hailing from the picturesque landscapes of Idaho, Kumbali discovered their passion for writing at an early age and honed their craft over two decades in the film industry.

Marge Simon lives in Ocala, FL. She edits a column for the HWA Newsletter, "Blood & Spades: Poets of the Dark Side," and serves on the Board of Trustees. She is the second woman to be acknowledged by the SFPA with a Grand Master Award. A Bram Stoker Award recipient and multiple finalist, she has Rhysling Awards for Best Long and Best Short, the Elgin Award for two of her several collections. Other awards: Dwarf Stars,  Strange Horizons Readers' Award, and the HWA Lifetime Achievement Award. Marge's poems and stories have appeared in *Asimov's, New Myths, The Magazine of Fantasy & Science Fiction, Clannad* and *Daily Science Fiction*, to name a few. Winner (with Bryan Dietrich) of the Lord Ruthven Assembly Award for Best

Vampire Fiction Collection, 2020. Marge attends the ICFA annually as a guest poet/writer. www.margesimon.com

Angela Yuriko Smith is a third-generation Uchinanchu-American and an award-winning poet, author, and publisher with over 20 years of experience in newspaper journalism. Publisher of *Space & Time magazine* (est. 1966), a three-time Bram Stoker Awards® Finalist, and HWA Mentor of the Year for 2020, she offers free classes for writers at angelaysmith.com.

John Skipp's 2021 Splatterpunk Lifetime Achievement Award encapsulates his long, weird, colorful career as a Rondo award-winning filmmaker (*Tales of Halloween*), Stoker Award-winning anthologist (*Demons, Mondo Zombie*), and New York Times bestselling author (*The Light at the End, The Scream*) whose books have sold millions of copies in a dozen languages worldwide. His first anthology, *Book of the Dead*, laid the foundation in 1989 for modern zombie literature. He also co-wrote one of the gnarliest episodes of Shudder's *Creepshow* Season One. From splatterpunk founding father to bizarro elder statesman, Skipp has influenced a generation of horror and counterculture artists worldwide.

In 2022, Skipp announced his official retirement from writing fiction, dedicating the rest of his life to making movies and scoring them. (The story in this book is a rare exception. *Thanks, Jamal!*) His latest (and quite possibly last book) is a collection of short stories, short screenplays, and essays called *Don't Push the Button*. His two new albums—in which he wrote, performed, recorded, mixed, and produced all the music—are *Cry Me a Rainbow* and *The Antidote to Fear*. And his new film—Skipp's solo feature debut as writer, producer, director, composer, editor, and actor—is a darkly satirical class-warfare comedy called *The Great Divide*.

Christina Sng is the three-time Bram Stoker Award-winning author of *A Collection of Nightmares*, *A Collection of Dreamscapes*, and *Tortured Willows*. Her poetry, fiction, essays, and art appear in numerous venues worldwide, *including Interstellar Flight Magazine, New Myths, Penumbric, Southwest Review*, and *The Washington Post*. She currently serves as Vice President of the Science Fiction & Fantasy Poetry Association.

Melanie Stormm is a multiracial writer who writes fiction, poetry, and audio theatre. Her novella, *Last Poet of Wyrld's End* is available through Candlemark & Gleam. She is currently the editor at the *SPECk*, a monthly publication on speculative poetry by the SFPA. Find her in her virtual home at coldwildeyes.com

Sara Tantlinger is the author of the Bram Stoker Award-winning *The Devil's Dreamland: Poetry Inspired by H.H. Holmes*, and the Stoker-nominated works *To Be Devoured*, and *Cradleland of Parasites*. She has also edited *Not All Monsters*, and *Chromophobia*. She is an active HWA member and also participates in the HWA Pittsburgh Chapter. She embraces all things macabre and can be found lurking in graveyards or on Twitter @SaraTantlinger, and on Instagram @inkychaotics saratantlinger.com

Patrick Thompson is a spiritual leader, mentor, and pastor from NYC. He has written multiple teaching series based around the bizarre, supernatural, tragic, and redemptive themes found in the Bible. His teachings will challenge you to explore the deep and dark questions related to spirituality, chaos, and evil in order to find a path to hope and healing.

Steven Van Patten is the author of the celebrated *Brookwater's Curse* vampire trilogy, and the *Killer Genius* serial killer series. He's also a co-author of the award-winning *Hell at the Way Station*, and the sequel *Hell at Brooklyn Tea*. Numerous short stories have been published in over a dozen anthologies and he's a contributing writer/consultant for the YouTube channel Extra History as well as the star-studded Viral Vignettes series. He's a member of the Horror Writer's Association, the Director's Guild of America, and professional arts fraternity Gamma Xi Phi Incorporated.

His website is www.laughingblackvampire.com.

Tim Waggoner has published over fifty novels and eight collections of short stories. He writes original dark fantasy and horror, as well as media tie-ins, and his articles on writing have appeared in numerous publications. He's a four-time winner of the Bram Stoker Award, a one-time winner of the Scribe award, and he's been a finalist for the Shirley Jackson Award and the Splatterpunk Award. He's also a full-time tenured professor who teaches creative writing and composition at Sinclair College in Dayton, Ohio. His papers are collected by the University of Pittsburgh's Horror Studies Program.

 **Wrath James White** is a former World Class Heavyweight Kickboxer, a professional Kickboxing and Mixed Martial Arts trainer, distance runner, performance artist, and former street brawler, who is now known for creating some of the most disturbing works of fiction in print. Wrath is the author of such extreme horror classics as *The Ressurectionist* (now a major motion picture titled *Come Back To Me*) *Succulent Prey*, and its sequel *Prey Drive, Yaccub's Curse, 400 Days of Oppression, Sacrifice, Voracious, To the Death, The Reaper, Skinzz, Everyone Dies Famous in a Small Town, The Book of a Thousand Sins, His Pain, Population Zero*, and many others. Wrath lives and works in Austin, TX.

Readers . . .

Thank you for reading *Bestiary of Blood*. We hope you enjoyed this anthology.

If you have a moment, please review *Bestiary of Blood* at the store where you bought it.

Help other readers by telling them why you enjoyed this book. No need to write an in-depth discussion. Even a single sentence will be greatly appreciated. Reviews go a long way to helping a book sell, and is great for an author's career. It'll also help us to continue publishing quality books.

Thank you again for taking the time to journey with Crystal Lake Publishing.

Visit our Linktree page for a list of our social media platforms. https://linktr.ee/CrystalLakePublishing

Follow us on Amazon:

Our Mission Statement:

Since its founding in August 2012, Crystal Lake Publishing has quickly become one of the world's leading publishers of Dark Fiction and Horror books. In 2023, Crystal Lake Publishing formed a part of Crystal Lake Entertainment, joining several other divisions, including Torrid Waters, Crystal Lake Comics, Crystal Lake Kids, and many more.

While we strive to present only the highest quality fiction and entertainment, we also endeavour to support authors along their writing journey. We offer our time and experience in non-fiction projects, as well as author mentoring and services, at competitive prices.

With several Bram Stoker Award wins and many other wins and nominations (including the HWA's Specialty Press Award), Crystal Lake Publishing puts integrity, honor, and respect at the forefront of our publishing operations.

We strive for each book and outreach program we spearhead to not only entertain and touch or comment on issues that affect our readers, but also to strengthen and support the Dark Fiction field and its authors.

Not only do we find and publish authors we believe are destined for greatness, but we strive to work with men and women who endeavour to be decent human beings who care more for others than themselves, while still being hard working, driven, and passionate artists and storytellers.

Crystal Lake Publishing is and will always be a beacon of what passion and dedication, combined with overwhelming teamwork and respect, can accomplish. We endeavour to know each and every one of our readers, while building personal relationships with our authors, reviewers, bloggers, podcasters, bookstores, and libraries.

We will be as trustworthy, forthright, and transparent as any business can be, while also keeping most of the headaches away from our authors, since it's our job to solve the problems so they can stay in a creative mind. Which of course also means paying our authors.

We do not just publish books, we present to you worlds within your world, doors within your mind, from talented authors who sacrifice so much for a moment of your time.

There are some amazing small presses out there, and through collaboration and open forums we will continue to support other presses in the goal of helping authors and showing the world what quality small presses are capable of accomplishing. No one wins when a small press goes down, so we will always be there to support hardworking, legitimate presses and their authors. We don't see Crystal Lake as the best press out there, but we will always strive to be the best, strive to be the most interactive and grateful, and even blessed press around. No matter what happens over time, we will also take our mission very seriously while appreciating where we are and enjoying the journey.

What do we offer our authors that they can't do for themselves through self-publishing?

We are big supporters of self-publishing (especially hybrid publishing), if done with care, patience, and planning. However, not every author has the time or inclination to do market research, advertise, and set up book launch strategies. Although a lot of authors are successful in doing it all, strong small presses will always be there for the authors who just want to do what they do best: write.

What we offer is experience, industry knowledge, contacts and trust built up over years. And due to our strong brand and trusting fanbase, every Crystal Lake Publishing book comes with weight of respect. In time our fans begin to trust our judgment and will try a new author purely based on our support of said author.

With each launch we strive to fine-tune our approach, learn from our mistakes, and increase our reach. We continue to assure our authors that we're here for them and that we'll carry the weight of the launch and dealing with third parties while they focus on their strengths—be it writing, interviews, blogs, signings, etc.

We also offer several mentoring packages to authors that include knowledge and skills they can use in both traditional and self-publishing endeavours.

We look forward to launching many new careers.

This is what we believe in. What we stand for. This will be our legacy.

Welcome to Crystal Lake Publishing— Tales from the Darkest Depths.

Made in the USA
Columbia, SC
09 March 2025

54931362R00193